MW00462832

JUDITH

JUDITH

ZACK BUDRYK

Quill

Published by Quill, an imprint of Inkshares, Inc., San Francisco, California

www.inkshares.com
Cover design by Katie Dvorak

ISBN: 9781942645412
e-ISBN: 9781942645429
Library of Congress Control Number: 2016941825

First edition

Printed in the United States of America

This book is for all the strong women it has been my privilege to know and love, including but not limited to Alysha Newton, Katie Dvorak, Leslie Small, Meredith McGlynn, Kate McDonald, Alyssa Huntley, and my amazing, beautiful wife, Raychel.

And for Caroline Wall, 1991–2016.

"If I die in Raleigh, at least I will die free."

Nemesis is lame; but she is of colossal stature, like the gods, and sometimes, while her sword is not yet unsheathed, she stretches out her huge left arm and grasps her victim. The mighty hand is invisible, but the victim totters under the dire clutch.

—George Eliot, "Janet's Repentance"

Taking the law into your own hands, fuck, what's wrong with that?

—Joyce Carol Oates, *Rape: A Love Story*

PROLOGUE

He awoke, looked around, and realized he was not in his bedroom.

That, in and of itself, wasn't necessarily cause for alarm. Anyone who's stayed overnight in a hotel or a house not their own knows that little jolt. In just a moment, you remember how you got there, and the jolt fades.

Unless, of course, you then realize you're handcuffed, gagged, and on your knees.

He sputtered through the gag. He wasn't really even trying to say anything so much as refusing to acquiesce to it. His vision adjusted to the lighting just in time to see the back of a black-gloved hand swing toward his head. The pain seemed too intense for a backhand before he realized that the blow had landed on an open gash in his scalp, most likely the one that directly preceded his being dragged here.

"You make another noise, you lose a finger," a woman's—a woman's!—voice hissed.

Between the force of the blow and the tone of her voice, he had no problem believing her. He focused on what lay in front of him and made out a camera on a tripod. Next to it stood a woman who might have been unusually tall, but it was hard to tell given his vantage point. She was wearing black jeans, a red hoodie, dark glasses, and a red scarf over the bottom of her face, which made him wonder why he was so sure she was a woman at all.

Then she confirmed it by turning to the woman who had hit him. "We're ready."

The woman next to him raised a finger and then roughly jerked the gag out of his mouth. She held a revolver a few inches from his face and cocked the hammer.

"You are only to speak in response to my questions. If you say anything that is not a response to my questions, I fucking shoot you. Do you understand?"

He nodded.

The camera's light flickered on.

"What's your name?" the woman asked.

His voice tasted strange in his mouth after the gag and the enforced silence. "Martin Vickner."

"What do you do for a living, Martin Vickner?"

"I own a bar."

"Who is Octavia Tuck?"

He forgot himself. "Hold on, what the fuck is—"

She grabbed his right hand by the wrist, yanking the cuffs' chain taut, and blew his index finger completely off.

She let him scream for a while before she made him continue, which was generous of her, considering.

When he had quieted down, she put the gun against his earlobe. "Who is Octavia Tuck, Martin?"

"NRRRRRRRR . . . she was a fucking waitress at my— GAHHHH—bar. RGGGGGGGGHHHHHH!"

"There's more to it than that, isn't there?"

"Yes, there's more to it than that, but you just shot off my fucking finger!"

She seemed like she was getting impatient. "Please continue, Martin, and remember that you only get nine more chances to fuck this up."

"She . . . she accused me of raping her."

"And?"

"And the charges were dismissed."

"Why?"

"Because the DA knew there was a drug dealer who sold out of my place and I rolled over on him in exchange for the dismissal."

"And did you rape her?"

He was about to say, "Fuck you," but he thought better of it. He exhaled slowly. "Yes."

"I'm glad you're being honest with us, Martin. That's going to make things go quicker." She put the gun in her waistband. "You see, we've been investigating you for months. God knows we don't want to do anything without making sure it's necessary."

She turned back toward the camera. "This man, Martin Vickner, is an admitted rapist, but he will never serve a day in prison. Is that justice?" Her voice sounded more frenzied. It was frightening, even after you adjusted for having been kidnapped and mutilated. She derailed his train of thought when she yanked his head upward by a handful of his hair. "We are Judith"—it sounded like "Judith," anyway—"and her name was Octavia."

He saw the knife in her hand just as it bit into his throat. The pain was unbearable, but only for a moment.

KATHERINE KINNEAVY

The dead don't look like people. I don't think so, anyway.

People ask me how I do what I do—homicide detective, not undertaker, in case you were confused—and stay sane, and the answer is really that simple. Maybe it makes me a latent sociopath, but when I see something so devoid of warmth or breath or movement, I just can't fathom the idea of it ever having had any.

That might change at some point, of course. Maybe in five, ten, twenty years, an avalanche of realization will reduce me to a twitchy clump of neuroses suitable only for desk work. But I think more likely it's just a small-scale version of what we feel when we're in mourning. When you're told someone you love is dead, whether you wail and rend your clothes or just put your hand over your mouth and sit down, you don't really understand in that moment that the person is never coming back, and all that that implies. Not really. Why, then, should I feel that way when I see the body of a stranger?

The guy in Seward Park with the slit throat was far from the worst I'd seen, but he caught my attention because he was positioned in a way that made it look like he was staring right at me. I know I just made with the big song and dance about how the dead don't bother me, but this is less to do with their being dead than it is to do with the feeling of being watched.

It was 7:00 a.m. It was far too cold and too early to be without coffee, but the coffee we had was too hot to chug. Frustrating, but we were having a better morning than the vic, at least. I dug his license out of his wallet.

"Hey, Donnie," I called to my partner. "Get this. Martin *Vick*ner."

Donnie bark-laughed. "Maybe we should find Jimmy Perpington and haul him in."

Donnie Klein is a skinny Jewish guy from Flatbush Avenue who's tough in the way you can only get from a lifetime of people assuming you're weak. He's on edge a lot, which can be a problem in our line of work. He's not dumb by any stretch of the imagination, but he moves too quickly to consider all the angles. That said, he's great for banter.

I leaned in over the body. "Cause of death appears to be severed jugular. Shape and cleanness of the cut strongly suggests it was done with a knife. Head wound, blunt force trauma. Wound is scabbed over everywhere but the bottom. Vic was likely dealt a softer subsequent blow in the same general area." I slowly lifted the body's arm by the sleeve of its jacket. "Bruising on wrists is consistent with handcuffs. Right index finger has been forcibly removed. Powder burns indicate by firearm."

Donnie broke into my trance, even though he fucking *knows* I hate that. "We looking for a bullet?" he asked.

I shook my head and pulled my scarf tighter around my neck. "None of this was done here. To cut his throat this thoroughly without putting him on his knees, you'd have to be about seven feet tall, but there's no dirt or grass stains on his pants."

I stepped back and took a deep breath. This is the part I call BTO—Besides the Obvious. I used to always explain that it didn't stand for Bachman-Turner Overdrive, until I realized that nobody under fifty got the reference. I feel old enough at thirty-two already, so I dropped it. "Okay, so the finger thing, first off. I'm not sure what the purpose was, but I'm pretty sure it wasn't torture."

"Why not?" said Donnie.

"We know they had a knife, right? If you're gonna take somebody's finger just to inflict pain, you go with the knife. Much more intimate, takes longer, shows you're not squeamish, way more so than shooting off a finger."

"Gang thing? Kill a stranger, bring back his finger to prove it?"

"But why blow it off if you need it intact and you've got a knife with you? Especially if it's just some guy off the street. Gunshot is going to bring the cops. And beyond that, if they're not out simply to inflict pain, why not shoot him rather than cut his throat? But on the other hand, if they're out to inflict pain, why not cut the finger off rather than shoot it off?" I stood there with my eyes closed for a second. "So I'd say what we've got here is, the killing was personal—hence the knife—but their time was limited, so whatever purpose the thing with the finger served, it had to be done with the gun." I cautiously tilted my coffee toward the tip of my tongue. Finally suitable for drinking. "Let's head back, see what we've got on the guy. Let's hope there's something on the books that jibes with a slit throat, because otherwise, we're starting from scratch."

Any police department, particularly a big-city police department, is still very much a boys' club, whatever they might tell you. I'm good at what I do—I'm not going to pretend otherwise—but these aren't circumstances one person alone is going to change. I'm sure it would be worse if I were some skinny blonde with huge tits. As it is, I'm about five eight, black hair, blue eyes, with an ass and a belly. When you see a woman cop on TV, she doesn't look like me. The boys are much more subtle these days—I'm not getting my ass grabbed or porn stuck in my desk, but I've felt their gaze every time I've allowed myself to get angry or passionate about anything on the job. I can just hear the shared mental groan go up among all the lads—*Bitches be emotionally compromised, am I right?* That's why I would never be able to work Domestic or Sex Crimes— hell yes, I'm emotionally compromised when it comes to that.

So I shuddered when I put Vickner's name into the system and found the forcible rape and sexual battery charges from 2005. I'm not the kind of person who thinks every man accused of rape should be presumed to be guilty, but the evidence and facts of the case were very much against Vickner. Well, except for the fact that he was willing to snitch for them. Loath as I was to admit it, Vickner's priors meant I was going to have to talk to Octavia Tuck. You ask a cop why they became a cop, and you'll get all sorts of answers of various levels of sincerity, but I doubt a lot of them will say, "To shake down rape victims." Some of them might think it, though.

Forensics had determined that Vickner's time of death was around three in the morning, indicating that he was either dropped in the park by someone who had to travel at least an hour to get there or who wanted to wait until the rain stopped. Unfortunately, this also meant Octavia's alibi would likely be that she was at home in bed, with no one to corroborate. I put it off for as long as I could, looking around for known associates of Rashard Powell, the dealer Vickner had rolled over on, but none of them were credible enough as killers to bear further investigation. The ugly truth was, Powell had been a small-timer who was mostly just selling nickel bags to his friends and didn't even appear to own a gun, but as far as the cops could tell, he was a threat to the community (and black), which automatically made him a bigger fish than a rapist. I drove to Octavia's apartment in Bed-Stuy around eleven in the morning, girding myself to feel like shit.

Octavia answered on the second knock. She was a gorgeous woman in her late twenties with huge liquid eyes who wore her hair short and natural. She looked tired, but she was fully dressed. I tugged the bottom of my jacket aside to show her my shield.

"Hi, are you Octavia? I'm Detective Kinneavy, Homicide. Can I come in?"

She looked genuinely surprised, which was good news for my conscience. "Yeah, yes, of course. Come on in."

I crossed her threshold. Her apartment was small but well decorated and felt like somebody's home. She'd done a lot with a little. I looked around with the sincerest nice-place-ya-got-hyurr face I could manage and tried to make what I had to say sound conversational.

"When's the last time you spoke to Martin Vickner?"

She gave a small start at the mention of his name. That's something most survivors do, in my experience. It doesn't matter how young or old, how recent or distant the experience, how they're dealing with it. There's always something about hearing that one name that shakes you on a primal level. Some women—some people, I should say—have learned to suppress it, but her reaction was impossible to miss. If I had to guess (and I'm a cop, so of course I have to guess), I'd say she hadn't thought about him in a while before I brought him up. The not-feeling-like-shit train had left without me.

Octavia fixed her eyes on the wall opposite her. "I haven't spoken to him since he raped me, Detective. Why, is he dead?"

Bullshit time was over, apparently. "Yeah, he is, Ms. Tuck."

"He suffer?"

"That's not something I can go into."

She closed her eyes for a second, then opened them. "Wow," she said. "I don't feel any better at all."

"Did you think you would?"

"I don't know. I never seriously thought it'd happen anytime soon. He likes to feel stronger than people. Someone like that, I figured he'd steer clear of anyone who might hit back."

"Lot of people have brothers or fathers."

She shrugged. "I wouldn't know nothing about that. I do know he waited until he was sure I didn't have anybody before he went for me. But let's just cut the bullshit and you ask me where I was when it happened, and I tell you I was on a plane."

This I hadn't seen coming. Bad detective, no donut. "A plane? From where?"

"North Dakota. Just got back about a couple hours ago, matter of fact."

I tried not to let my relief show. "Who's in North Dakota?"

"My cousin Jessica." I must have looked confused, because she said, "There are black girls in North Dakota" kind of defensively. She got up and picked up her purse from the counter, fishing out a boarding pass. Red-eye from Bismarck Airport, ETA 9:50 a.m. She was clean, thank God.

"Guess my work here is done," I said, getting to my feet. "Sorry to bother you, Ms. Tuck."

"Detective," she asked, "you gonna find whoever killed him?"

"That's what they pay me for."

She stared at me a little too long. "I hope it wasn't one of the girls he hurt that did it." She shook her head. "I don't like the idea of him driving someone to kill on top of everything else."

I truly had no answer for that, so it was a relief when I felt the purr of a text against my thigh. It was from the captain, a link to a video, with the added message, *The fuck is this?* I headed for the door and turned to Octavia.

"Thanks for your time, ma'am. Have a nice day."

WENDELL ROANE

I'm not a crime reporter. I'm a political reporter.

Ha-ha, you just repeated yourself, you say, because you think you're the first person to come up with that even though you're not. Jay-Leno-level canned bullshit aside, the main difference between the two (and the reason I thank God I'm the latter) is that political reporters mostly have to talk to politicians, whereas crime reporters mostly have to talk to cops. I don't know why journalists and cops hate each other so much, but I think it's to do with what Freud called "the narcissism of small differences." We're both—in theory—out for answers, and we both have to get those answers by talking to official sources and, oftentimes, by hitting the streets, where the people we need to talk to might be suspicious or openly hostile toward us. We both have to live with the reputation our institution has gotten due to the presence of some real pieces of shit in the ranks. Hell, we even both have bars that cater to our profession.

As to where the hostility comes from, that's where you get to the key differences. Cops are looking for answers, but once they find them, they're not to be shared; they're to be acted upon and then tucked away. I imagine it must frustrate them that there are people out to do something similar, only after they're done, they let the public know about it. By the same token, I can tell you it can be frustrating as shit that when cops find the bad guys, they grab them and shove them in cages, whereas when we dapper ladies and gents of the Fourth Estate do the same, we write about how they're mean and then hope somebody cares enough to write their congressperson.

I've covered city council and the mayor's office since I started at the *Septima* eight years ago. We're a small but bothersome alternative weekly that operates out of Midtown on a floor that's not high enough for a majestic view of the skyline but probably high enough to kill yourself. If you think that's a morbid way of looking at things, you don't have enough newsroom experience.

Our name derives from the Latin for a period of seven days, which doesn't quite mean "week" because the Romans didn't have weeks, but it sounds smart. The cops and, from what I hear, the mayor call us "The Septic Tank," which whoever came up with the name probably should have seen coming. I've had at least one article a week in here for the past seven years, with particular emphasis on women's rights and governmental transparency. One of the only fully apolitical bits of reporting I've done was a multipart series on the day-to-day life of a sex worker in the city, with particular emphasis on how the mayor's crackdowns on the industry were doing way more to increase the pimps' leverage and keep the women from reporting abuse than they were to keep anyone from hooking. It won several local awards and came close to being nominated for a Pulitzer, rumor has it. Just to almost be nominated is an honor, et cetera (more Latin).

All of this is a roundabout way of saying I have no idea why whoever it was chose to send the envelope to my desk on Tuesday morning. Like a lot of industries, pretty much all of our communication is done through email nowadays, so whenever I get actual mail, I figure it's an old person, a crazy person, or some combination of the two. In December 2001, back when I was doing briefs for the *Chief*, the NYPD confiscated a lumpy envelope from an unfamiliar address that was sent to me before it turned out to just be a rambling letter by an elderly fireman's widow telling me how much she appreciated my profiles on first responders. It was kind of heartwarming until the part about how inspiring it was that a "good-looking mulatto boy" had done so well for himself.

The envelope today contained a folded, typed letter, and a CD-R. I shoved the disc into my laptop. After three minutes, my antivirus software, which is so overenthusiastic that to this day it insists ecards from my aunt are malware, pronounced it clean. The only thing on the disc was a WAV file. The footage was pretty grainy. I couldn't tell if their issue was lighting quality or camera quality. I could distinctly see a tall guy on his knees, with someone wearing what looked like black jeans, a red jacket, and combat boots standing slightly to his right. The overall effect reminded me of things like the murder of Daniel Pearl, and I'm pretty sure that was the effect whoever had filmed it was going for as well. Combat Boots was making hand motions, so I was guessing he (?) was saying something (I keep my computer on mute at work as a rule), which was seemingly confirmed when the man on his knees opened his mouth as well. After a few more wordless pronouncements, I saw a muzzle flash behind his back, unmistakable even in the shitty lighting, and his face contorted with pain. I could make out blood behind his back as well. I lurched forward, paused the video, and decided maybe I should check out the letter first.

Mr. Roane,

Many of us have read your writing, and the publication you represent, over the years. It is for that reason that we have decided you—and it—are the best option to spread our message. Please print this letter in full. The man in this video is Martin Vickner, age 54. He is guilty of the rape and battery of a woman he previously employed as a waitress. Mr. Vickner made a deal with the district attorney, which resulted in all charges being dropped despite his factual guilt being acknowledged by the police, the prosecution, and the defense. Mr. Vickner is the first such person to come under our scrutiny, but he will not be the last. Our decisions will not be made lightly. Our eyes are well placed and diverse within the court system, the police, and on the streets, and if someone is targeted by us, it will be with good reason and ample justification. We have a substantial backlog to work through, but any cases which occur from this point on will be prioritized. Neither men in general nor society as a whole should fear us, but if the police and the courts wish us to stop our work, they can do so by getting to these people before we do. Rest assured, they will not have much luck stopping us any other way. They have never caught us and they never will.
JUDITH

Tony, my editor, didn't want to run it. Tony's a skinny guy in his late forties with a face that's got far more nose than chin, and there's nothing he fears more than being perceived as sensationalist. He didn't even advertise my sex worker story on the cover, not because he didn't think it was a good story, but because a cover tease about hookers is *"Daily News* shit." I liked working for him and I admired him a lot, but at the same time, I always thought it was easier to decide you're not going to be sensationalist when you already have a reputation to sell. It's a principled stand with all the inherent risk of a rich guy's kid deciding to "live off the grid for a while."

"Tony, come on," I said. "They want us to run it, *Septima* specifically."

"Oh, we negotiate with terrorists now?" he snapped back. "Buncha fuckin' psychos climb to the housetops, it's not our job to be their megaphone."

(That dichotomy with cops I was talking about also makes a lot of editors feel compelled to talk like police captains.)

"It's news, Ton," I said. "It's news, and we're the only ones in a position to publish it."

"Oh, you think so? You believe everything crazy people tell you? How do you know they didn't send this to the *Times* and the *Post* and every other fuckin' paper?"

The more frustrated I get, the more condescending my voice sounds, so I knew I was walking a razor's edge. "Tony, if the *Post* got a snuff film in the mail, do you really think it wouldn't be all over the Internet by now?"

He put the tips of his fingers to what was probably his hairline at some point.

"Wendell, you get that if we run this, your job gets a lot harder, right?"

"How do you figure?"

"We get the exclusive on a serial killer or whatever the fuck, we're not just the paper for the cool kids out of Williamsburg or the poor people who just take three copies of everything that's free. We are in for some major scrutiny."

"All eyes on us," I responded, doing my best not to get that goddamn Britney Spears song stuck in my head.

"Exactly. You ready for that?"

I popped two pieces of gum into my mouth (I take them two at a time—with just one, I feel like there's too much unused mouth space). "I've been in this business since I was striking out with hot broadcast majors in J-school. I don't think it'll be a problem."

If this were a movie, this would be followed by a cut to something that proved I was completely wrong. It's not, so I'll just tell you: I was completely wrong. I wrote up my preface to the letter for the new issue of the weekly, which was hitting stands in two days, but I uploaded the video and an Instagram photo of the letter immediately. Within the hour, I got an email from someone claiming the killers were obviously Jews, a second saying they were obviously Muslims (they both used the word "obviously," with different incorrect spellings), and a third claiming credit for the murder but maintaining that he had only done it because Governor Cuomo had his bichon frise, and to please let him know so that he could give it back.

It was at this point that I received a call from one Detective Kinneavy, who had apparently been introduced to my writing very recently. She immediately proved that point I was making earlier about the Sharks-Jets thing we in the press have going on with New York's finest.

"What the merciful fuck is the matter with you?" she screamed, loudly enough that I nearly dropped my phone, swept it into a dustpan, and humanely took it outside rather than stomping on it. "You have video of a goddamn murder and your immediate response is to fucking post it online?"

"Detective, calm down—"

"Fuck you, 'calm down.' I am about to calm down my sensible flats so far up your ass you'll be coughing up arch supports."

"What? Look, there's also a letter—"

"You got a letter from them and your fucking hands got all over it?"

"Oh, come on, how the hell was I supposed to know it was evidence without reading it?"

Either I had her there, or she was pausing to think of more shoe-related threats.

"Mr. Roane," she said, "I want that letter as soon as humanly possible if you want to write anything besides cover letters to 7-Eleven's corporate headquarters ever again."

"Are you threatening me, Detective?"

"You bet your ass I am."

"And what if I say I'll tell your superior officer what you said?"

That got a laugh. "My superior officer is a six-foot-four ginger who wears a necklace made from her ex-husbands' tongues, you little shit. You'll be begging for me back if you talk to her."

The more I thought about it, the more I thought an obviously insane cop having my literal and figurative number wasn't a great way for things to be. "Detective, maybe we can make a deal of some kind."

"I just told you the deal, motherfucker. You give me the evidence you're withholding and I generously don't book your ass for withholding it."

"Look, there is a real story here. Please try to understand this from my perspective." I tried to sound as sincere as I write, which is harder than you might think. "I know you think I'm just some vulture who's gonna fuck everything up for you, but please, listen to me. It's really important to me that this be written about. I can't explain it, I just feel . . . I feel called. I know that's stupid. But do you . . . have you read any Joseph Campbell?" If your big gambit is asking a cop if she's read Joseph Campbell, it's probably not going to turn out great.

There was a pause that dragged long enough that I thought she might have hung up, and then she said, in a softer, much less ass-threatening voice, "Can't refuse the call, can you?"

I tried to mask my surprise that she knew what I was talking about and apparently did a shitty job of it.

"Don't act so shocked," she replied. "I just looked him up on my phone. Why do you think I paused for so long?"

I wasn't sure how to respond to that, so I plunged ahead with my proposition now that she'd stopped yelling. "Detective Kinneavy, here's what I'd like to make happen: I give you this letter and, not in return but just so we can make up for having gotten off on the wrong foot, you're my source as this case unfolds. I know our publication has a reputation for not giving the department's side of things, so here's your chance. I'm your ride along on this case, and no matter how many anti-stop-and-frisk editorials we run, you get your say."

She was either considering it or Googling more curse words. "And anything else you get, you'll bring straight to the police?"

"I'll bring it straight to the police *after* I've taken pictures and submitted them to my editor."

I heard her sigh, and I figured she was doing the same thing Tony had, only with more hair, probably. "You sure you want this arrangement, Mr. Roane? It's gonna be way worse for you if you can't keep to it than for me if I can't."

I leaned back in the swivel chair. "I had a relationship like that with another source too," I said. "By which I mean, every reporter-source relationship I've ever had. I managed."

That got a chuckle. "I'll see you and that infinitely more interesting letter at McSorley's at seven, Mr. Roane." She hung up and I punched the air a couple times.

Tony stuck his head into my cubicle and said, "Wendell, if you get me sued by the NYPD, I promise you, I'm going to find some way to register you as a sex offender," before going back to his office.

Around six o'clock that evening, I noticed I had a new email. It was from Will D'Annunzio, one of my sources. We don't really live in an age where the mob regularly makes the news, but it was nice to have a source inside regardless. Will was a gofer for Joe Cataldo's crew on the Lower East Side, which has never been particularly violent but moves a hell of a lot of cocaine. Will isn't going to help me break any major exposés, but he was a gold mine in terms of water-cooler buzz about who was getting made, who was getting promoted, or who was getting frozen out. His email read as follows:

Hey W—

Somebody did Russell Milazzo. Cops trying to keep it quiet but our guy in the departmint said his throte was cut. Call me on burner tonight.

—WD

JOE CATALDO

I'm getting too old for this shit.

I wish that movie hadn't used that line, because it's something I need to express all the time, but now it just sounds like I'm referencing that fuckin' movie.

I'm forty-five. That's old enough to be getting too old for this shit but not old enough to have been around for the glory days, or what the old-timers call the glory days, before Gotti ruined the nice suits and the pinkie rings and all the cartoony shit for everyone. I still wear a pretty nice fuckin' suit, but if it weren't double-breasted you could mistake me for a Wall Street type with a tan. Pretty much my entire career has been in this more muted, nondescript era. That's how I know there's nothing noble about Our Thing.

I'm not saying that's a bad thing; it's not. I don't think there's anything noble about laying bricks or selling bicycles or doing consultancy neither. It's just work. And this thing of ours, this thing that was supposedly what kept us together when we stepped off the boat, kept all the thugs out of our faces and our pockets, connected us to the homeland while it helped make a better life for us here—that's bullshit now, and I'm not sure if it was ever anything else.

One of the good things about this is it keeps down the violence. We haven't had anything like a war in about a decade. Violence gets you noticed by the wrong people, and in a worst-case scenario, it makes the cops and prosecutors decide that the best way to cover their asses is to convince people that the kinds of gangsters they've seen in movies still exist and then hang a bunch of them out to dry. I've only killed seven people, which is probably more than you but would put me way the fuck below average in the '70s and '80s. Again, it's a business. Love it or hate it, this is the way it's supposed to be.

So when I went down to the docks to make a collection early one evening and happened to run across my captain with his throat opened from ear to ear, I really hoped it could be resolved with a minimum of fuss.

Russell Milazzo wasn't someone I was sorry to see go; he enjoyed using his position to be an asshole, which is really, really bad for business. I'd also been hearing stories about him trying to move into running girls, illegals from Asia and Eastern Europe, which was strictly the territory of the Russians in Brighton Beach, who were crazy fucks that I didn't feel like offending. The Russkies are big into knives, so when I saw the wound, I figured it was them or, if not them, one of the kids in the *moulinyan* or spic gangs. Someone who didn't know or care how we do things. The cop on scene was a guy named Mikey Kolchak; I didn't own him, but we were friendly. He gave me a nod.

"The fuck is this?" I said as I strode over to the crime scene.

"Not sure yet," Kolchak replied. "I'm just keeping him warm 'til Homicide gets here."

A green Corolla rolled up, and a pale dark-haired broad in Heineken-green sunglasses got out and made her way over to the body. Nice ass on her. She shook Kolchak's hand.

"Kinneavy, Homicide. Pretty sure this guy's connected to my case. Thanks for saving a spot while I got here." She turned as if she was just noticing me. "You need something, sir?" she asked.

"Yeah, I'm his employer." I tried not to sound threatening.

She tilted her coffee and poured a bit of it on the dock. "Sorry for your loss. Run along now."

Bitch.

I had several calls to make, and I really wanted the Russians to be the last one. They are not pleasant people.

First I texted Flaco, the rep from the Latin Kings. (Yes, everybody has reps now. I told you it's a business.) I explained the situation and asked him to make sure none of his people were involved in it. I hoped he understood I didn't mean "his people" like *that*, because that's hard to convey over a text.

Next, I called the boss, which you're pretty much only supposed to do if someone's dead. Anything else can, in theory, wait long enough to set up an appointment. "Contain this, Giuseppe," was all he said. My Christian name is not actually Giuseppe, but I've never corrected him, because (a) if I ever get caught on a wiretap, it'll be helpful to be able to say, "Who, me? That's not me. He's talkin' to some fuckin' guy named 'Giuseppe,'" and (b) the only people who would ever think to correct an elderly Italian man are people who have never tried.

Then I called Brickman, my guy in Homicide, and asked if he knew anything. He said Detective Kinneavy—I assumed that was the chubby cunt from the docks whose name I'd forgotten—was being cagey about the whole thing, but had told the captain that she thought it was connected to a rape-o who'd been done the same way the night before. He promised to keep me posted, and I gave him the name of the guy he'd be dialoguing with in place of Russell.

Then I called said guy and offered him Russell's territory, and then it was time for a fuckin' drink.

In hindsight, I was kind of asking for trouble going all the way to Brooklyn for a drink, but I was cranky and worn out, and I didn't want to run into anyone I knew who could ask me for a favor. I found a place that the younger members of my organization tell me is for "hipsters." I'm not entirely clear on what a hipster is, but as far as I can tell, they're really concerned about appearances at the expense of every other fuckin' thing, and I know from experience that people like that aren't worth the trouble. I sat down and asked for a fifth of Jack, not because I'm particularly fond of Jack but because this didn't look like the kind of place that would have what I like. A few minutes after I got my drink, a guy got up from a table in the corner and sat down next to me. He was a skinny little guy with sandy hair fading into silver wearing a fuckin' beautiful charcoal Armani pinstripe and a lavender tie. He looked familiar, but I was pretty sure we'd never spoken extensively; I might have been introduced to him at some christening or something, but you meet a lot of people that way.

"You are Mr. Cataldo," he said. He made it sound more like an announcement than a question. He sounded like Boris Badenov.

"Yeah," I said, trying not to sound rattled. I wasn't in my own territory and a name means way less than it used to.

"My name is Valery Degtiarenko, and we have business to discuss. You will come to our table, please?"

I followed him, probably against my better judgment, and sat down at his table. Degtiarenko was the only one there in a suit and the only one under six feet. All the other guys were Hagrid-looking motherfuckers in three-quarter length leather jackets or tracksuits. There were four of them, which seemed like a bit much.

"Mr. Cataldo," Degtiarenko said. "Your friend—someone just recently kill him, yeah?"

I took a small sip of my Jack. If the only way I could fuck with him was to make him wait a few seconds for an answer, that was what I was gonna do. "Who wants to know?"

"He want to know, that's why he fucking ask you," rumbled one of the giants, leaning forward slightly and rattling everyone's glass. Degtiarenko held up a hand. "You not been down to Brooklyn in a while, has you, Mr. Cataldo?" he said. "I Ron Burgundy here these days. Kind of big deal, you know?"

I wasn't particularly intimidated, and I didn't see any reason to pretend to be. "So I guess you called me over to tell me you did it?"

Degtiarenko's expression darkened. "No, Mr. Cataldo. So I take it you don't know neither?"

"Nope."

"Well, this is problem. You know how your guy had been make his money lately?"

"You referring to the hookers?"

"Yes, the girls. This was very big problem. That is my business. Your man, he has connections in shipping and Coast Guard and Port Authority I don't, so he bring them in with much less hassle than I does, make bigger profit, even though I was doing it first. This is fair?"

I shrugged. "It's capitalism, Mr. D. Thought youse guys were into that now."

That got me a pretty nasty look from his guys. He ignored me and kept talking. "Matter of fact, plan was to take care of your friend tomorrow before this third party take care of it for us."

Now he had my attention. "I gotta tell you, that's not how it works here. You remember what you were saying about having more connections? Nobody gets killed unless everyone's okay with it, and definitely none of mine get killed."

He wasn't smiling anymore. "Well, someone didn't get memorandum, yes?"

"Obviously. That's why I need to find out who it was."

He leaned in. "Here is what I think, my friend. I think, your man, only thing that set him apart from your other men is that he got into whores. So I think anyone else who want to kill him, they don't appreciate him stepping on that business neither. And that mean I still have a problem with threats to my business."

"And what's this got to do with me?"

"What it got to do with you is, here is how you can make it up to me for not taking care of this problem. Whoever did this, they're trying to move on my territory, just like Mr. Russell, and that's why you find him and kill him for me."

I was not a fan of the direction this conversation had taken. "Listen, Drago," I said, pointing with my empty glass, "I feel like you been off the boat or out of the shipping container or whatever the fuck long enough to know this isn't how it works. Okay? You don't fuckin' tell me what to do. I tell you what to do. You don't fuckin' threaten me or my people, unless you want a war, and believe me, you don't. Because if the gloves come off, you might think you're hard because you got a bunch of big hairy retards who can't get any work now that they can't break fingers for the KGB no more, but I have you in firepower, politics, numbers . . . if shit gets real, I'm Superman and you're the dumb fuck who tries to stick him with a knife. So think real hard about where you go next with this."

He just smiled at me for a second. Then he grabbed my wrist and dug his nails into it. "I tell you what I think, you soft guinea faggot," he hissed. "I think you been practicing that speech for years and you think if it sounds good enough, you never have to back it up. I think you think everyone so scared to hit you, you don't need to learn how to hit back. But especially I think that you want to keep things quiet more than you want to look like a tough guy. I think you want everyone to get along because you know if things get ugly, we do things much, *much* nastier than you do. And if I'm wrong, why do I even have you in this position in first place? How have I laid hands on you?" He let go of my wrist. "Mr. Cataldo, I want this business rival by the end of the month. I don't want anything else from you; you can go about all your other business. But if you don't bring me someone"—he pulled a butterfly knife out of his sock—"you going to see, in detail, what I did for KGB. You fucking *wish* I broke their fingers."

I met his eyes. "You all done, Mr. D.?"

He nodded.

I stood up and smoothed my tie. "I'll do what I can. I don't need this fuck running around any more than you do." I gave him my card. "And just so you know, Boris, if you come to my neighborhood with this shit, I'm not gonna invite you over to my table."

I left and made for the Williamsburg Bridge, trying not to be obvious about how often I was looking over my shoulder.

KINNEAVY

I got back to the station with about an hour to go until my meeting with the reporter. While I was typing up my notes about the dead wiseguy from the docks, Donnie told me the captain wanted to see me.

Captain Meghan Neville bore an eerie resemblance to a middle-aged Florence Welch and was covertly known as "Scarlet Witch" among the detectives. She would not have gotten either of those references. I was pretty sure she had heard of Marlene Dietrich, though, because her style ran in the direction of men's suits and Brooks Brothers ties. About ten years ago, back when she made captain and got her first taste of media scrutiny, a handful of moral guardians, led by Marvin Devaney of the Decency League, threw a shitfit about the "message this sends to young girls," who I guess look up to police captains or something. Eventually, the chief of detectives was ambush-interviewed about Neville's wardrobe and said (this is an exact quote), "She's the most qualified for the job. What do I give a shit if she likes to dyke it up?" Various gay-rights groups puzzled over that one for a while before deciding that even if the chief's wording was problematic, the sentiment was admirable. The next week, *Avenue Q* opened on Broadway and a high school in Queens made *The Color Purple* required reading, so Devaney abruptly lost interest in Captain Neville.

All bullshit aside, Neville really was ideal for her job: nobody better if you needed leadership, nobody scarier if you were out of line. I hoped to God I wasn't out of line.

"Door. Sit," was all she said when I walked in. I closed the office door behind me and took a seat in front of her. She was wearing a double-breasted sharkskin with a black silk tie and pocket square. Her desk and the wall behind it were unadorned except for an ashtray shaped like a skull and a "Hang in There" cat poster that instead read, "Go fuck yourself."

"Heard the stiff from this afternoon was connected," she said.

"Uh, yeah," I replied. I checked my notes. "Russell Milazzo, made member of the Cataldo crew. Priors include aggravated assault, two different unlicensed firearms, DUI, resisting arrest—that was the same occasion—and Lieutenant Ciorra in Organized Crime says they were trying to build a case on pimping."

"And what's the connection to the guy in Seward Park this morning?"

I cleared my throat. "Well, I personally believe them to have been committed by the same person."

"Why's that? Just because both their throats were cut?"

"Well, no, because both their throats are cut with what appears to be a blade of similar width, with a single, more-or-less unbroken stroke, the, for lack of a better word, confidence of which indicates familiarity with such matters, because of the bruising indicative of handcuffs on both bodies, because of both men's history of accusations of violence with little or no actual legal penalties as a result."

"I was thinking the same thing, if we're being honest."

"It's possible. I'm not willing to stake everything on it being the same perp, though. I just think the motivation has something to do with their priors." I paused for a second. "Captain, Martin Vickner was a rapist. I believe the targeting of these two men may have had to do with their history of violence against and exploitation of women."

"Aw, fuck me," Neville said. Somewhere, Marvin Devaney's head exploded. She thought about it for a second. "Listen, Kinneavy, I don't know if this is going to end up being big news. It might not be, and it might just be on you to find two different people with big fuckin' knives. But if you're right about a connection, any connection, the official line is this is gang related, got me?"

I was confused. "Why gang related?"

"Because the more adamant we are about that, the less likely someone will decide it's terrorism or a serial killer, and any whiff of either of those is going to send the feebs stampeding in here with their dicks in their hands, and I want to share an office with them about as much as I want to share a cab with a Scientologist. Someone like me in a job like this, how much room do you think I have to fuck up?"

Her features relaxed. "They'll never get it, will they?" She inclined her head toward the blinds separating her office from the bullpen. "How it is for us. They just get to do this job whichever way comes naturally. You and me, though, we're the trailblazers." She lit a cigarette, putting a finger to her lips. "And what that really means is, anything we do, right or wrong, proves some broader point about women and their fitness for the job." She gestured to her tie. "You think I fuckin' like wearing ties every day? They're a huge pain in the ass. But I can't stop now." She turned away and blew smoke over her shoulder. Her voice still sounded like the narrator of a Mickey Spillane audiobook, but her eyes were shot through with fear. "Because when everybody assumes they can fuck with you, you never give them an inch. Doesn't matter how inconsequential it is. 'Just wear a skirt' turns into 'give me a blowjob' turns into 'retire early for half a pension so one of the boys from the club can have the office he's earned.'" She took a drag. "Here's the short version: If someone is killing men who hurt women, and you and I can't bring them down, do you really believe anyone will think it wasn't for lack of trying? I mean, really?" There was another one of those pauses that had been so commonplace. "I'm asking, Detective."

"No, Captain, I don't believe that."

"Then please, please don't fuck this up. Right now, my balls are in a vise. Please don't tighten it." She nodded toward the door.

I stood up. "I don't plan to, Captain."

She stabbed her cigarette into the skull. "Nobody plans to, kid."

McSorley's Old Ale House is the oldest Irish pub in New York, and it's kind of hard to tell what's actually been here the entire time and what's modern affectation that nobody notices because it fits with the image we have of places like this. The floors are covered in sawdust, the beer comes to you in pitchers as big as your thigh, and your server's hair and face will probably be a white and red, respectively, not found in nature. Oh, and they also had to be sued back in 1970 to allow women inside, but to their credit, they seemed just as hostile toward everyone else in there as they did to me.

"Snug and evil," Wendell Roane said, nursing his drink. "That's what E. E. Cummings called this place."

"Yeah? What does Wendell Roane call it?"

He looked around, dragging his eyes over the smoky air and the kitsch on the walls. "It's all right. I feel way safer with a woman. Folks in here probably don't know who to attack."

I rolled my eyes. I liked him a lot more than I thought I would, but even if you find someone charming, make him feel like he's got to work for your goodwill. Just one of those things you learn growing up Irish.

I had the letter in a plastic evidence bag inside my coat. I hadn't told Roane that it had pretty much confirmed my suspicions about the motivations for the murders—or for Vickner's at least. I had, however, explained Captain Neville's insistence that Judith was a gang and given him a (brief) look at the photo of Milazzo's body, just to confirm that he'd been killed in the same manner. I figured it wouldn't do any harm now that he apparently already knew Milazzo had been killed.

"Why are they called Judith?" I asked. "Do you know?"

He took a folder out of his messenger bag and laid a print-out on the table. It was a reproduction of an oil painting. It showed two women holding a big bearded guy down in a bed while the one at the front hacked off his head. The one doing the hacking was a brunette in blue with a frighteningly intent expression.

"In the book of Judith, which appears in the Catholic Bible and the Septuagint but isn't acknowledged by Jews or Protestants, Judith was a Hebrew widow who walked into the tent of the Assyrian general Holofernes when he was about to lay waste to her hometown and got him drunk. When she had his attention, she and her handmaid beheaded him. She's developed some resonance among feminists because, even though she's a character in a religious text, she uses her sexuality to achieve her aims and that's presented as okay."

I couldn't take my eyes off that picture. "But they kill rapists, yeah? Holofernes doesn't rape her."

"Ah, but there's a bit of a story behind this particular depiction of it." He pulled out another reproduction of a painting. This one was a fair-skinned, plump woman with dark hair painting with a brush and palette. She bore a distinct resemblance to the painting of Judith and also, weirdly enough, to me.

"Artemisia Gentileschi," Roane explained. "Baroque-era painter. Judith was one of her specialties, but she also did a lot with Esther and Jael."

"All the badass women."

"Pretty much. And a lot of people think the reason for her preoccupation with Judith is that she was sexually assaulted by her colleague, Agostino Tassi. Artemisia's father had him charged and convicted, after which he served a staggering sentence of one year. Artemisia confided that in this particular painting, she deliberately made Holofernes look like Tassi."

I slid the two pictures around so that they were side-by-side. "So it sounds like they've got more in common with Artemisia than with Judith."

He shrugged. "Well, I think maybe that's deliberate. Judith's story isn't about sexual assault, but Artemisia makes it about that because she needs to sublimate her rage at what was done to her, and Judith, an independent woman who can go toe-to-toe with a man, is the ideal vessel for it. Judith the organization is appropriating Judith the person—and Artemisia's appropriation of Judith the person—in much the same way. It's meta, as the kids say."

I killed my beer. "Is that what the kids say? When I was a kid, we just cursed a lot." I looked around. "Back then, I couldn't wait until I was old enough to go in here. That was the one thing I thought would finally make me a big girl."

"Planning ahead for the rebellious phase?"

I laughed a little. "Yep. Dated a black guy at Gotham U too, thought I'd piss off my dad a little. No offense." I sighed. "I wonder how old Barack's doing these days." His eyes went wide. I flicked my fingers off his shoulder. "I'm just fucking with you, Sarah Jane."

He smiled. "Don't touch me unannounced, okay? I still think of you as a threatening voice over the phone. It makes me instinctively look for something to defend myself with." He checked his phone and put it back in his pocket.

"You got somewhere to be?" I asked him.

"Got another source to call once we're done here is all."

"I'd better let you run along, then." I slid the pictures back to him. "Got one more thing to say, though. And you can quote me on this."

"Sweet." He took a silver voice recorder out of his coat pocket.

I hesitated. "I . . . I meant as an anonymous source within the Homicide department."

"I knew what you meant."

I leaned in. "However we may feel about this organization's aims, its violent methods make it a criminal organization, and it will be treated as such. You want to know why I think they don't follow the story of Judith exactly? Because I think they want a symbol, but they also don't want to be predictable enough to get caught, as is the case with most murderers. But you can bet your ass we're going to catch them. All of them."

I laid a ten on the table and got up and left, wishing I'd had a mic to drop. I was Little Katie Soundbite now, apparently. God help us all.

ROANE

I called Will on his burner as soon as I got back to my apartment.

"This is D-Nunz. What up?" was how he answered the phone, which made me worry he was dumb enough to be taking calls from his friends on this phone.

"It's Roane. What you got for me?"

His voice dropped. "Hey, man, so look, somebody cut Russell Milazzo's throat and dumped him on Pier 17 this afternoon."

Milazzo and I had met very briefly once a couple years ago when I tried to get a quote from him on a recent longshoremen's union agreement. He responded by calling me a nigger and slapping me a couple times before Joe Cataldo, to his credit, did that "Hooooooooooo!" thing Italian guys do and pulled him off of me. I hoped this had been Judith too, because otherwise, I was worried I'd been sleepwalking.

"So what's Cataldo's play? Do you know yet?"

Joe Cataldo was stretched pretty thin even on his best day, even though he was nominally only a regional underboss for the Dellaponte family; Old Man Dellaponte had gotten out of prison eight years ago and had pretty much been telecommuting from his lodge in Ithaca ever since, so Cataldo was left with all the legwork associated with being the boss on top of his own duties as a capo.

"Well, Mr. C. figured it was the Russians out in Brighton Beach, but I heard they say no."

"Why would it be the Russians?"

"'Cause Russell was running pussy. Foreign girls."

I was pretty sure I'd spotted the thread. "Why foreign?"

"Why do you think? Because there are sick fucks that'll pay through the nose for a girl they can hit or cut up or whatever else, especially when she can't go to the cops."

"And the Russians don't like that?"

"The Russians fuckin' *love* that, and they don't want anyone else stepping on it. Especially since all of us are citizens, so Milazzo and his crew are taking way less of a risk bringing the girls in. Or were."

"You know anyone with the Russians who might talk to me?"

"No-o-o. No. Get that idea outta your head before it can grow. Nothing good will come of trying to talk to them, I promise you."

"Okay. Jesus."

"Hey, I'm lookin' out for you, man. And I'm not picking on the Russkies either. My people would fuckin' . . . *liquidize* me if they found out I was talking to a reporter, 'specially a colored guy. No disrespect."

"Do they know my mama was Italian?"

He snorted. "That makes it *worse*, dumbass. Look, I gotta go. I'm ditching this phone as soon as I'm done. I'll text you the number for the new one." The call ended.

So now I understood why Judith wanted Milazzo dead, but I was a little confused as to their methodology for targeting people. Milazzo was an abusive piece of shit, but there was no indication he was a rapist per se. I wasn't defending him; I was just curious as to what met their criteria.

I opened my laptop and launched Firefox, Office, and iTunes. When I'm working at home, I need the right kind of music to do it properly. In my case, that's bouncy pop by female solo artists. Make as much fun of me as you want. The beat focuses me.

I logged on to my Twitter account. I've had one since 2009, but I don't use it too often. My thoughts tend to run pretty long-winded (maybe you've noticed), so a character limit doesn't suit me too well. I mostly use the account to post links to my latest, although once, Paul Krugman wished me a happy birthday on here, which was pretty cool. I typed the following: "Attn: Judith—Russell M. not rapist, just pimp/abuser. Targeting all abusers? Email or call and tell me detail proving you're really judith." I posted it and then something else occurred to me: "RM also hadn't been acquitted. Thought you didnt target anyone pretrial." Hey, I just met you, and this is crazy, but here's my number, so prove you killed a guy, and we'll go from there.

About an hour later, I was halfway through my piece on the most recent developments in the Judith case when I heard the buzz of a new text. It was (naturally) from a restricted number. It read, *RM was in navy tracksuit, gray sleeves, St. Anthony medal around neck. Wait for email.* I turned back to my laptop. An email from a Hotmail address appeared in my inbox. I opened it and read.

Mr. Roane.

Thank you for your prompt response. To answer your question, we are not an assembly line; although our primary focus is rapists, we target anyone who facilitates violence against women; in Mr. Milazzo's case, especially, as his trafficking activity directly facilitated several acts of rape. As to your question regarding his acquittal (or lack thereof): again, we have to be practical. Mr. Milazzo's position in his organization was such that he would likely have direct knowledge of his superiors' criminal activity, making it a near-certainty that any attempt to pursue charges against him would lead to a deal. In addition, when was the last time you heard of a gangster serving time for pimping or sexual battery? Attached is some photographic evidence of Mr. Milazzo and his clients' handiwork; we're sure that, after looking at them, you'll agree he needed to go.

Don't try to reach us again; we will be in touch with you. Look for the video in the mailroom tomorrow; we would send it to your apartment but that seems vaguely threatening and we don't want to give you the wrong idea.

JUDITH

I opened the attachment and immediately wished I hadn't. The black eyes, scar tissue, and badly healed broken bones on the women in the pictures were high-octane nightmare fuel, but what was worse were the expressions of utter hopelessness in all of their eyes. This had been happening long enough that they were resigned to the idea that this was as good as it got. I looked at the pictures, and I fully understood the instinct to kill a man who made that happen. It was pointless to just be angry at Milazzo, of course. He was only half of the problem. The other half were the people whose money and sick desires created a market for this kind of thing . . .

Holy shit.

A cartoon lightbulb went on over my head as I realized what Judith's next play would be. I lunged for my phone and dialed Detective Kinneavy. She answered on the third ring.

"This is Katherine."

"Detective, it's Wendell."

"What's up? Did you forget something?"

"You need to get Milazzo's client list. They're gonna go after his johns. Maybe not next, but eventually."

"Well, how the shit am I supposed to get it?"

"I know a guy inside. Let me make some calls."

She paused. "The list itself won't prove anything. We'll need to find the women too."

"I'll find the women. They're prostitutes, they're not gonna trust you."

"I kinda doubt they're gonna want to trust much of anyone."

"Yeah, but they've probably been threatened with the cops or INS the entire time they've been put to work. You focus on the list, trust me. And that reminds me, they emailed me from a Hotmail account. I don't know if it's the same person who wrote the letter, but I'll forward it to you. Maybe you can figure something out about whoever wrote it from the phrasing or whatever."

"Will do. Keep in touch." She hung up.

I stared at the almost-certainly abandoned Hotmail address on my screen. I finished the article and submitted it to Tony. Then I did research for a while, mostly relating to the biblical Judith and to resources available to undocumented immigrants in the city. I must have nodded off at my desk. Just a little while later, I was woken up by my ringtone.

"Hello?" I said, trying my best not to sound like someone who had been out like a light at nine fifteen on a weeknight.

"Yeah, is this Wendell Roane?" The voice on the other end was a harsh, cab-driver-risen-above-his-station bray. It sounded familiar, but I was pretty sure I'd heard it on TV or the radio rather than one-on-one.

"Yeah, it is. May I ask who's calling?"

"This is Marvin Devaney with the New York Decency League."

Oh Jesus. "I see. What can I help you with, Mr. Devaney?"

"Well, I was sent a link to the story you posted today, and I just wanted to ask why a journalist with as prestigious a history as yours would agree to become a mouthpiece for a bunch of militant lesbians."

"Mr. Devaney, do you know something about these women I don't?"

"I know they're killers and your magazine's website is giving them space to justify their criminality."

"Oh, for God's sake." I had had too long a day to humor this dipshit. "We're not 'justifying' anyone. We're reporting. Do you think Jimmy Breslin is pro-serial killers?"

"You reprinted an entire letter from them and posted that grotesque video. That's glorification."

This had to be a nightmare. "Mr. Devaney, if I wanted to glorify somebody, it'd be kind of counterproductive to publish video evidence that they were murderers. If my sympathies were with these people, I wouldn't be publicizing their activities."

"But that's what they *want* you to do!"

"Yeah, a lot of people want to be noticed. Sometimes, that helps people catch them." I took a turn for the ill-advised. "Maybe you'd better go. I think I hear a gay guy getting an abortion."

"Oh, is this a joke now? All this is funny to you?"

"Mr. Devaney, neither rape nor murder is a laughing matter. But yeah, the fact that you called me at home at nine in the evening to yell about lesbians is pretty funny."

He sounded faintly apoplectic. "You know, Mr. Roane, considering you write for a publication that owes literally the entirety of its revenue to advertising, I would think twice before you offend an organization with our track record when it comes to organizing advertiser boycotts."

I had a headache. "Suck my ambiguously brown dick, you fat fuck." I hung up and turned the phone off. For reasons I couldn't fully articulate, I was more disturbed that Marvin Devaney had my cell number than I was that a terrorist organization knew where I lived. At least they were being polite about the whole thing.

CATALDO

*S*hit. I knew I forgot something.

The windowless concrete basement was beneath a warehouse on Orchard Street. The room was lined with ratty, awful-smelling sleeping bags. At the very back was a discolored tile section with a shower head about six feet up the wall. Huddled against the wall on both sides of the room were about fifteen women, pretty much all of who looked like drowned rats that whoever drowned them had also hit with a hammer a few times. Most of them were white, but there were three or four Chinks.

"Wait a minute," I said. "If they got a shower, what the fuck is that smell?"

"Aw, Jesus!" yelled Paulie from the far-left corner of the basement. I walked over to where he was standing. A few feet of the floor appeared to have been caved in with a shovel; inside the hole were the bodies of three more women.

If I wanted a business that never got ugly, I could have gone into dry cleaning. But this was just fucked up.

Paulie followed me back over to the door. "So what do we do with, you know, the ones who are still here?"

I wasn't sure, honestly. Nicky Brunaldi, Russell's replacement, definitely wasn't cut out to continue where his predecessor left off. Killing them wasn't an option either. There was no way we could make fifteen bodies disappear at the same time unless we took them to different parts of town one at a time, and I had day-to-day shit I had to attend to. It occurred to me that maybe I could turn them over to Degtiarenko as a peace offering and avert a war without making him feel like he had me by the balls.

I knelt down in front of one of the white girls. She was blond with green eyes, and I could tell she wasn't any older than twenty-seven, but she managed to look older and wearier than my mother. "You speak any English, sweetie?"

She just stared at me, then said, in an accent thicker and harder to place than Degtiarenko's, "Hey, daddy. Four hundred straight, five-fifty up the ass. Sounds good?"

Her eyes looked so dead as she said it that I recoiled a little. I hadn't felt that kind of shame since I told Father Philip I'd been spanking it when I was ten. I sighed and pulled out my phone and dialed somebody.

"Charlie, any way you can get me a school bus? With tinted windows? And a piece of cardboard and a marker."

About an hour later, Charlie came through. The bus was Nassau County Public Schools, but beggars can't be choosers. Paulie and I got the girls on their feet. All of them seemed like they were able to walk, at least. I couldn't communicate with them much, but they all understood that I wanted them to follow me. I filed them onto the bus, got in the driver's seat, and headed northwest toward the Williamsburg Bridge. Once I was in Brooklyn, I headed north until I reached Twelfth Street, right around where Williamsburg starts to fade into Greenpoint. I pulled up at the Cathedral of the Transfiguration of Our Lord. I turned around toward the girls.

"Everyone sit tight for a second, okay?" I said. I tried to mime the concept as best I could. I uncapped the marker and wrote on the cardboard, "WE HAVE BEEN SEXULLY AND FYSICALLY ABUSED. WE DO NOT SPEAK ENGLISH BUT SOME OF US MAY SPEAK RUSSIAN. PLEASE DO NOT CALL THE POLICE OR WE WILL BE DEPORTED."

Paulie and I herded the girls off the bus and to the front of the building. I pushed open the door and hustled the girls inside, making sure not to enter the building myself. The blond girl I'd tried to talk to was the last in. I stopped her and gave her the cardboard.

"Hold this," I said. I made two fists and held them parallel at chest level. "Understand? Hold this, make sure the priest can see you." I pointed to my eyes. I lightly pushed her in the door, then closed it.

Paulie and I darted across the street, leaving the bus behind. We ran until we got to Bedford Avenue and took the train the rest of the way back to Manhattan. By the time we got back to the Lower East Side, it was about eleven in the morning. My phone rang and it was a number from the 607 area code I didn't recognize.

"Hello?"

"Giuseppe."

"Mr. Dellaponte! Good morning."

"How are we doing on the Milazzo situation, 'Seppe?"

"Uh, pretty good. I've made some calls, I have Nicholas—you remember Nicholas, Pleasant Avenue Nicky?—taking over for him. He's a good earner."

"That's not what I'm talking about and I'm pretty sure you know that. What's this I hear about him getting clipped for running girls?"

"I told you he got clipped. I called you right away."

"You didn't tell me about the girls."

"Well, I didn't think it was of major importance."

The boss had one of those voices that sounds like a roar when it's raised even slightly. "Your job is not to decide what's of major importance, you fuck, and if you didn't already know that, you would have been dumped in a hole with your face blown off before your twentieth birthday. Now, you might think it's a pain in the ass making an appointment with me to tell me about something like that, Giuseppe, but I have earned the right to be a pain in the ass. Now, if you were completely uninvolved in this particular business venture, that means Russell wasn't kicking up to you, which means you weren't kicking up to me. Now, if you—or he—want to do business without giving me my cut, you can make sparkly barrettes and sell 'em over the fucking Internet. Starting this weekend, you're coming up here every Saturday to give me an in-person update, and that goes for after this Milazzo situation is resolved too. If you ever blow me off, you die by Sunday morning, and I'm going to make sure that fucking pussy Nicky is the one who does it. You understand me?"

"Yes, sir."

"Have a nice day." He hung up.

Jesus. No good deed.

I headed to Rao's for some lunch. I generally work out when I'm stressed, but sometimes a bit of the Old Country is the only thing for it.

I was just finishing up my *panzanella* when Paulie and Nicky came in and approached my table. "Sit!" I said. When they didn't, I knew something was up.

Paulie spoke first. "That kid," he said. "D'Annunzio. He's a bagman, right?"

"William? Yeah, good kid."

"So you vouch for him?" Nicky asked.

"What, like, to get made? Little early, don't you think?"

"That's not what I mean. You trust him?"

"Well, yeah. What's this about?"

Paulie took a plastic baggie out of his jacket pocket. There was a small black phone inside.

I tilted my head. "The fuck is that?"

"William was seen chucking that in a storm drain last night. He threw the battery in separately and it went all the way down, but the phone itself lodged between the floor and ceiling of the drain."

I stared at the bag. "So we got no way of telling what he was using it for?"

Paulie sighed. "No, but really, Joe, how many things could it be?"

Entirely too much shit was happening at once. "Well, what the fuck does he know? I mean, it's not like he's sitting in on meetings. He's way low-level."

"Joey, that's not the point and you know it," Paulie said. "I know you like the kid. I'll take care of it if you want."

I shook my head. "I'll take care of it. Thanks for letting me know."

Will was shooting pool in Nolita when I found him. Poor kid wanted so badly to be a tough guy, but everything he knew about it, he learned from the movies. I caught him just as he was leaving.

"Hey, Will, how long you been with me?" I asked him as he was about to speed past me.

He looked confused. "Uh, three and a half years, Mr. Cataldo, sir."

"That long? Goddamn," I said. "Listen, what do you think about, uh, opportunity for advancement?"

He looked surprised and I hated myself even more. "I'd feel great about it, sir."

"Well, listen, I got a package to run out to Staten Island tonight. Feel like driving?"

"Wow, yeah, definitely. When do you need me?"

"You got a car of your own?"

"Uh, no, not yet."

"I'll bring mine by your place around eight. See you then."

Will didn't talk much as we took I-78 toward the Mid-Island area. As he flicked my high-beams on, I found myself thinking how out of place this whole area always looked. Willowbrook was heavily wooded. Back when I was a kid, there had been a home for retarded kids out here, and sometimes we'd sneak out on Halloween on dares, half hoping and half fearing some deformed, crazy ghost boy would grab us and drag us down to hell. There was a big-ass exposé on the local news in the mid-'80s, a little while after I got too old for those kinds of stories, and I remember thinking, when I saw the footage of the kids drooling and crowded together in corners, wearing rags, and sitting in their own piss, that this was much, much worse than the stories we told each other. I suddenly realized part of why the sight of the basement room shook me up so bad—it reminded me of the pictures of Willowbrook State School.

The main road started to dwindle.

"Stop here," I told Will. He parked, and we walked a little way into the woods. "My guy's gonna pick it up as soon as he sees us leave. He's paranoid like that."

"Okay," Will said, and I could tell he was getting a little nervous.

We walked a little further until the moon and the stars were all we had to go on.

"Will," I said. "You want to tell me why you dumped that phone in the sewer last night?"

"Huh?" he said. "Mr. Cataldo, I didn't dump no phone. Who the fuck said I did?"

"Kid, come on," I said. "There was a voice mail on it. They used your name."

"Hey, that's bullshit!" he yelled, and the panic and anger in his voice rang through the trees. "There was no fuckin' battery in . . ." I could see his face fall, even in the darkness. "Oh fuck. Listen, Mr. C., it ain't what you think. It's . . ."

I sighed. "Just turn around for a second, Will."

He shuddered. "Gimme just a second. Okay? Just a second."

I did, and he rubbed his index fingers against his temples for a second, nodded, and turned his head. I pulled the .22 from my waistband and double-tapped him at the base of the skull. Then I walked back to the car and took the shovel out of the trunk. Before I began digging, I fished out my phone. Reception was shit out here, unfortunately. I looked up the number for the hipster bar in Brooklyn and asked for Valery. A little while later, I heard that cartoony fucking accent on the other end.

"Joey Cataldo, my great friend. How you doing?"

"I found him."

"Who you found?"

"Guy who killed Russell Milazzo, like you told me to."

"Really? Excellent. What his name?"

"Will D'Annunzio. He ran errands for me. I guess he got a little too big."

Degtiarenko laughed. "I guess so, yes. Tell him come to see me."

Aw, shit. "He's . . . he's already out of the picture, Mr. Degtiarenko."

"Tsk-tsk. I think this might be what you do, Mr. Cataldo. He is on plane to California, I bet."

"Hey, are you fuckin' calling me a liar?"

"Calm down, Mr. Cataldo. All you have to do is prove to me, yes? Bring me hand."

I looked down at the body. "Excuse me?"

"Bring hand. Right or left. I take your word for it. Even if it not your Mr. D'Annunzio, you care enough to go find somebody's hand, I give you credit for trying so hard. Meet me tomorrow night and give it to me." Click.

I stared down at the body as I felt a few drops of rain. I found a more-or-less flat rock, laid Will's wrist across it, and lifted the shovel back behind my head.

KINNEAVY

Jalisa Thorpe's been my best friend since the first day of sixth grade, when I sat with her at lunch because I thought none of the other girls would sit with a black girl. (Really, it was that she was voluntarily avoiding the other girls because she thought they were "too loud," but just one white girl would be okay, she guessed.) We spent lunch (and a good bit of our next class, the hell with Sister Margaret) chatting. I didn't think of it as a sacred bond or anything, but then the next Saturday, a little after I'd finished my lunch, Jalisa took a bus all the way from Harlem to Inwood and came shuffling down a street lined with Irish death glares to see if I wanted to hang out. The Crown Heights riots were less than a month in the past, and particularly in blue-collar white neighborhoods, you could almost see the tension piled up like the first snowfall.

Jalisa, being an eleven-year-old girl, probably didn't understand all of this at the time—I know I didn't. But somehow I knew that even if she had understood, she wouldn't have cared. I still don't know what I did to inspire that kind of loyalty, but I did my best to be worthy of it. When I look back at the next twenty years—cheering on our shitty football team, getting drunk for the first time one summer night when we were seventeen and my dad yelling at me, not for the drinking but for bearing his name and being such a lightweight—I thank God that there was no Facebook back then, because we would've gotten obnoxious as shit.

After college, I tried to find something to do with my lit major before drifting over to the NYPD, whereas Jalisa ended up in the DA's office. We still kept in touch, of course, and for a time we collectively referred to ourselves as Law & Order before deciding that was stupid. Where she was, Jalisa was an excellent resource for my work, but she was also fiercely professional enough that I knew I'd never put her in a position where I was exploiting our friendship.

As we sat in her office, I explained the situation with the late lamented Russell Milazzo and his client list. She thought about it for a second. "It'll be tricky," she said. "Twenty years ago, it'd have been easier, but I doubt there's a hard copy of that list anywhere. From what I hear, Joe Cataldo's obsessed with running things like an actual business, so it's probably in an Excel doc somewhere, a doc we'd have to go through Cataldo to get."

"Yeah, but you're assuming Cataldo was intimately involved with the human trafficking."

"You don't think he was?" Jalisa asked. "Dude's a control freak from what I hear."

"Well, my friend in Org Crime seems to think this was entirely Milazzo's thing. And if we move quickly enough, we may be able to seize his laptop before Cataldo can cover his ass even if he was involved."

She leaned forward and laced her fingers together. "*Or*, if we don't move quick enough, we let him know we're going after him."

"Well, (a) we're not going after him, we're going after the people who killed Milazzo, and (b) he already knows I'm looking into this because he saw me doing it."

She shrugged. "I mean, let's say I can get you a warrant for Milazzo's laptop. Let's say it has his client list on there. What do you want me to do from there?"

"I want you to help me send a canary into the coal mine. We're gonna dangle all these perverts and rape-os in front of the perps, and when they take the bait, we grab them too."

Jalisa rolled her eyes. "I've seen that look before, K. Don't go all cowgirl, now."

"Wait, when have you seen that look before?"

She thought about it for a second. "It was a while ago— oh! You know what it was? It was that time freshman year when that drunk guy catcalled me. Remember, you chased him through Times Square and when you caught him you just started slapping the shit out of him?"

I tried to remember. "Wasn't that, like, right under the *Mamma Mia* sign?"

"Yes! And you only stopped when that cop pulled you off!"

I snorted. "I know that cop. He's still a patrolman too."

She sidestepped over to her computer and fired off an email. "So who's that light-skinned fella you're drinking with these days?"

"Wait, how do you know about that?" I asked.

Her expression turned serious. "Neville has our office tailing you."

"Wait, what the fuck, J? First, why? Second, why your office?"

She held up her hands. "It's entirely ceremonial, K. Neville says she told you how nervous she is about this particular case, and she wants people from outside so no one can call bias."

"Why am I under investigation at all?"

Jalisa sighed. "You're *not*. At the captain's request, the DA's office had a trial observatory period for this particular case. You've passed. Okay?"

I was still pissed off. "He's a journalist, if you must know."

She narrowed her eyes. "What are you telling him?"

"Boilerplate shit. Don't tell the captain, though."

She gave a little cluck of mock offense. "Now, would I be me if you had to tell me that? The tail was DA Suarez's call. I had nothing to do with the decision, I just thought I'd let you know. It was a *favor*, sweetie."

Steady, Katherine. "Okay. Sorry. And thanks." I got up. "I really appreciate this, J. You understand that, yeah?"

She gave me a hug. "Of course. Just relax, okay? Or try to." She pulled away for a second and met my eyes. "You sure you got this, K? You know why I'm asking."

"Oh my God, *yes*. Why would you ask me that?"

"You *know* why I'd ask."

"Well, yes. My God. I've got my big-girl pants on and there's a Glock in them. Jesus."

She shook her head again. "I swear, you practice those lines, girl. Don't argue 'cause it wasn't a question."

"You're just jealous 'cause I'm hot."

"Bitch, please, I'm the one with the tasteful pantsuits."

We exchanged another tertiary hug, and I left the office. This was really not a turn I wanted things to take. I knew exactly why I'd gotten the news I was being followed from Jalisa, of course: Neville had almost certainly fed Jalisa false information about the extent to which I was being tailed, knowing I would trust anything I heard from her. (A little misanthrope on my shoulder reminded me that Jalisa could very well be in on it too, but I liked to think she wouldn't have brought it up if that were the case.) Until given reason to think otherwise, I decided to just assume I was still being followed. That might seem like a paranoid conclusion to draw, but like the man said, just because you're paranoid doesn't mean they're not out to get you.

Once I got to the car, Donnie let me know that Judge Howard Mendez had texted us that he had signed a warrant authorizing the seizure of Russell Milazzo's personal effects. After we picked that up from him, we headed for the storage unit that was registered as Milazzo's business address.

The Senegalese guy who owned the place repeated, "Show me the fucking warrant" several times even after we produced it. I guess cop shows don't really give you a clear idea of what they look like.

After about ten minutes of that, Donnie just said, "Shithead, if you don't open that door for us, you're gonna have to rent out that place with a big fuckin' hole in the door, and that's if anyone wants to rent from you at all after they hear the cops making noise around here, which they won't," and the guy muttered something and unlocked unit 501 for us.

Milazzo's office had all the organization of a seventeen-year-old boy's bedroom, and for some reason, just about as much pornography. Maybe he had to work nights.

Donnie squatted and began sifting through the debris. "This is my favorite suit too," he said, in a way that made it sound more like a Shakespearean aside than a complaint.

"So take off your jacket."

"And put it where? Everything in here looks like a giant used it to scratch his ass." He gingerly hefted a repulsive-looking beanbag chair to one side before his grip slipped. "Agh, fuck, Katie, it's gonna fall over on me, catch it catch it catch it."

I caught it and flipped it backward. The laptop—or a laptop, at any rate—was underneath. On the one hand, under the biggest single thing in the unit was a pretty obvious hiding place; on the other, Milazzo was probably pretty smart to think no one would ever want to touch it.

We didn't look at the laptop's contents until we got back to the station, per Neville's orders. She snatched it from me as soon as I was inside her office.

"Why the hell weren't either of you wearing gloves?"

Donnie offered, "Because there's nothing on our fingers that'll keep us from reading a spreadsheet?"

She gave Donnie the same look my mother gave me when I was thirteen and decided I was "mature enough" to start calling her by her first name.

Captain Neville set the laptop on the corner of her desk and cracked it open as Donnie and I huddled behind her. As luck would have it, the laptop wasn't password protected. This kind of made sense to me. For all his obsession with legitimacy, Cataldo's employees were not IT guys, and it followed that one of them figured a lock and himself (unless something really weird happened like a bunch of militant antirapists killed him) was all the security he'd need. Neville opened Milazzo's documents folder. All it contained were seven Word documents which appeared to be expense reports, but nothing was clearly labeled. All of it was about as helpful as a hot bath to a burn victim.

Neville brought the heel of her hand down on the desk. "Cunt!" She opened several more folders. Nothing. A few red strands fell across her forehead. She didn't seem to notice.

"Hold on," said Donnie from the back. "Lemme look."

He took his place next to Neville and opened "My Music," then "iTunes." The folders contained therein were mostly Springsteen and Stones, which kind of upset me because I didn't want to have anything in common with this guy. At least there wasn't any Pogues. Donnie scrolled until he got to "Unknown

Artist." He opened that and then "Unknown Album." Inside the folder was a single Excel doc. Donnie double-clicked.

"Come. To. Daddy," he said.

The spreadsheet was four pages long and alphabetized. It had addresses, phone numbers, and even a separate column for johns who'd started a tab.

Neville grabbed Donnie by the shoulder and kissed him hard on the cheek. "How the hell did you know to look in there?"

"It's how I used to hide my porn in high school," Donnie replied, too flush with having figured things out to be embarrassed. Or at least I assume that's what it was.

Neville's eyes returned to the screen. She scrolled down a bit and then placed a hand over her mouth. "Ho-ly shit," she said. "Judson Crowning is on here."

"Who?"

"The mayor's chief of staff. The fuckin' . . . iron fist in the silk purse or whatever the term is."

"Seriously?" I tilted the laptop my way. There he was. Crowning, Judson, 212-555-8223. I doubted there was an overabundance of Judsons in the boroughs, and the address was in a Long Island neighborhood that seemed just about right for an upper-level city hall salary. Donnie broke into my fugue state yet again, but considering it would take me five seconds to confirm it one way or the other, I wouldn't fault him this time.

"Son of a *bitch*," Donnie said. "Marvin fuckin' Devaney's on here!"

I followed his finger. "You're *shitting* me."

"Hey, kids, calm down," Neville said. "Could be a different guy."

"Call the number," Donnie said.

"I'm not calling, you call it."

"I'll do it," I said. I put my phone on speaker and dialed the number given for Devaney in the spreadsheet. It rang a few times, and then we heard a voice that sounded like it should be telling a teenage girl she looked like a whore.

"Yeah, hello?"

All three of us instinctively burst out laughing, mostly out of shock, I think. I fumbled for the phone and turned it off just as I heard Devaney angrily ask who this was.

Neville was, naturally, the first of us to calm down. "So now what?" she said. "There's, like, sixty names on here. I sure as hell don't have the resources to tail them all." She laced her fingers together and pointed at me. "What's the next stage in your master plan, you magnificent bitch, you?"

As was often the case with Neville, I wasn't entirely sure what in there was sincere praise, but I plunged ahead anyway. "Well, you'll notice—and I figured this would be the case—the names on here tend, with a few outliers, to fall into three distinct categories: organized crime figures, people associated with municipal politics, and your wealthier private citizens. Which makes sense, because Milazzo was running a specialist enterprise and it wasn't gonna be cheap. So rather than shadowing everyone on here, I suggest we shadow two johns from each category. If a week passes without incident, we move on to the next two, keeping any initial surveillance in place to the best of our ability. I know we run the risk of leaving a significant percentage of the list exposed—"

Neville waved her hand. "Kinneavy, I don't give a happy assfuck if any of these people die. They all have it coming. You and me and Klein all know that. I just want this case closed, ideally without the media turning you into Johnny Depp in *From Hell and Back*."

I nodded, but I was confused. Did Neville know I had talked to Roane? Was the media reference a subtle threat of some kind? Subtlety in general isn't really the captain's style, particularly with regard to threats.

Donnie coughed. "It's, uh, it's just called *From Hell*, actually."

Neville turned toward him. "Klein, if you ever interrupt me again, I swear to God I will come to your house and put a naked mole rat in your mouth while you sleep."

Like I said.

For the first phase of the operation, Donnie and I were assigned the organized crime figures. There were only about ten of them on the list, which I guessed was to protect Milazzo's exclusivity. You don't invite the other chefs to your dinner party. I was assigned to follow Frankie O'Halloran, which I only agreed to after Neville promised me body armor and guaranteed backup if I ever had to get out of the car.

O'Halloran, if you believed the word on the street, had done the kinds of things you normally heard descriptions of in UN war-crimes trials. Territorially, he had always been satisfied with a small chunk of what they used to call Hell's Kitchen, but he didn't take kindly to incursions from outside. About seven years ago, the Dellapontes sent a mook over to O'Halloran's territory to demand a cut. The guy was sent back with no legs, hands, ears, or nose and to this day is unable to say anything other than "Don't." Word is that over the years, O'Halloran's fine-tuned his strategy a bit: anyone fucks with him, the first thing he does (where applicable) is kill their kid. The implication, of course, being, *If I start out by killing a child, what do you imagine I'll do if things escalate?* I used to see him in the neighborhood occasionally when I was a girl—a huge, broad guy in a black scally cap and a long black leather coat, the lapels of the coat and his aviator shades making it all but impossible to see any of his face but his big drooping burnt-orange mustache. He had this way of rolling his head on his neck when he walked that I found terrifying as a kid, and this was before I heard half the stories; something about it just made me think, "That's not how people are supposed to move."

I envied Donnie, who was tailing Daniel Legenza, a Greenpoint coke dealer known to his associates as Danny the Polack, because, as far as I could tell, that was the only semino-table thing about him. I tailed O'Halloran from right around the ass crack of dawn, gulping those vile little energy-shot things that they sell at the pharmacy on the rack above the pregnancy tests, which is a funny juxtaposition because I'm pretty sure they're an abortifacient. The Pogues' *Rum Sodomy & the Lash* was the only thing keeping me lucid when O'Halloran lum-bered out the door. I hadn't actually seen him since I was a kid, and until we found his name in the spreadsheet, I hadn't even been entirely sure he was still alive, so I was kind of surprised to see he had exactly the same aura, for lack of a better word, as he had twenty years ago. Inanimate objects somehow seemed like they were scrambling to get out of his path. (The same couldn't be said of people, because they were never anywhere near his path in the first place.)

That said, if this was a normal day for O'Halloran, his rou-tine was pretty mundane. Most of his day was just making pickups. Maybe movies have given you a different idea, but without "Gimme Shelter" playing in the background, watch-ing gangsters make pickups is really fucking boring. I mean, it's a guy handing money to another guy. The only variation in O'Halloran's case was how terrified everyone else looked through the whole thing. At about eleven in the morning, O'Halloran went into an auto parts shop on Dyckman and stayed in there awhile. With an eye still on the door of the shop, I took advantage of the lull and turned up "A Pistol for Paddy Garcia." Right as I was getting embarrassingly close to air-drumming in the car, I heard a knock at the window. I gave a small shriek that I hoped was muffled by the window. Outside, a skinny black kid of around twelve was standing at the window with a brown paper bag. I cracked the window.

"What do you need?"

The kid cleared his throat. "Mr. O'Halloran said you looked kinda hungry, and it was getting on for lunchtime, and to bring you this." He dropped the bag into my lap and darted back across the street. Against my better judgment, I opened the bag. It was what looked like a normal cheeseburger. I didn't worry about poison or anything; this was a guy who chopped off people's testicles with a meat cleaver, not a Borgia. Goddammit, either way.

I elected to keep tailing O'Halloran. He might have made me, but then, he wasn't the only one I was staking out. If he was modifying his routine for my presence, he made no indication. By five, the sun was setting and he was heading home.

I sat in the car across the street and finished the Pogues CD. I opened my coffee cup, pulled a flask from inside my coat, and Irished up the coffee. A light, cold rain started plinking my car as I switched the CD out for Springsteen's *Nebraska*. I grabbed my binoculars and looked through the illuminated window of O'Halloran's place; he was sitting on a ratty couch and reading. I turned back to the dash as "Atlantic City" queued up.

> *Now, our luck may have died and our love may be cold,*
> *But with you forever I'll stay;*
> *We're going out where the sand's turnin' to gold;*
> *Put on your stockings, baby, 'cause the night's gettin' cold.*

As Bruce's harmonica sliced through the cold stillness of the car, I noticed a large dark shape moving across the street. I clutched my piece and stared through the windshield. The rain had picked up a bit, but I could tell he was standing right in front of the car.

He circled around to the driver's side window. "Detective," he said, his ground-glass voice raised slightly to be heard through the window and over the rain, "would you like to come in and warm up?"

I didn't say anything. He wove around my car to the passenger side. "May I sit for a second?" he said. He held open his coat. "I'm not packing. Take your gun out if it makes you feel better. I just want to discuss some things with you."

After a little while, I reached over and unlocked the door, knowing I shouldn't all the way. He bent nearly double to fit in, pulling his coat around him so he wouldn't shut it in the door. I angled the gun in my lap toward him, keeping my grip tight. He nodded a bit to the music. "This was really where he started to stretch, I think," he said. "To challenge himself. I think if he'd gone any darker with this album it would've come off kind of ridiculous, but he walked that tightrope and we got some great fuckin' music out of it. Excuse my language." He wiped some rain off his sunglasses and turned toward me. "So am I really the best Commissioner Clarkson can do at this point, Detective?"

"You're not the target of our surveillance, Mr. O'Halloran. It's our belief that you're the target of a criminal enterprise and we decided that if we let you know we were following you, it'd make it harder for all involved to do what we do."

He nodded. "Judith, you mean?" Goddammit, did everybody know more than me? He turned his head back toward the front of the car. "Is this because I showed up on that dumb fuck Milazzo's list?"

"How do you know that?"

He laughed, which sounded even worse than him talking. "Can you name anyone who works for me, Detective? You'd have to look it up, right?" My silence apparently answered the question to his liking, and he kept going. "But most everyone's heard of me. I got this dumb little cooze hound works for me, Mickey Heffernan, he wants a better deal on one of Milazzo's fillies, so he gives him my name and contact information because he thinks it'll get him a discount. Now I'm on that wop prick's radar, God rest him." He crossed himself. "Nah, but I'm afraid you're out of luck if you expect Judith to come after me, Detective. We've had some contact, believe it or not. We disapprove of the same things, I've found."

I had just wasted an entire day surveilling this psycho. No way was I going to listen to him sell himself as a folk hero on top of everything else. "You kill *kids*, Mr. O'Halloran."

He didn't seem angry, but then, I had the gun. "That's a business strategy. And I know that's not going to make it any more palatable to you, but when that happens, there is no malice toward those kids. The men Judith kills . . . what they do, Detective, is an act of war against all of you. And there's no percentage either. Even in a business like mine, someone who'll do harm just because it makes them feel good is just not on."

I stared at him as the rain picked up. "You mean to tell me you don't enjoy inflicting pain, Mr. O'Halloran?"

"Oh, quite the contrary. But I enjoy it precisely because I know they've earned it."

"You know, Mr. O'Halloran, I wasted an entire fucking day shadowing you. If you're trying to impress me, it doesn't really endear me to you that you just let me do that even though you knew it was pointless."

He spread his hands. "I apologize for the inconvenience, Detective." He tipped his cap and leaned toward the door handle. "By the way, the rest of the client list is pretty much accurate. Devaney's not going to give you much. He's into getting spanked, shit like that. I'll allow it's hilarious, but he's on the low end, degeneracy-wise. Crowning, though . . . Crowning scares *me*, Detective. My advice? Follow Crowning. Sure as you're born, they'll be getting around to him sooner or later. You want to feel like you really did a public service, make sure he gets got by one or the other of you." With surprising speed, he opened the door, slammed it behind him, and then he was gone.

I gave Donnie a call and explained the situation to him before driving over to Legenza's apartment to back Donnie up. Donnie had slightly more to show than I did, but only in that Legenza definitely seemed like enough of a creep to belong on the client list. Donnie admitted he was mostly basing that on the way Legenza spoke to his employees, wife, and mistress on the phone. The rest of his notes was just a single question, written on the first page of his notepad: "How many times can a guy jack off in one day?"

I tossed the pad back to him. "The answer, my friends, is blowing in the wind."

Donnie raised his index finger. "Hold on, shut up for a sec." He tuned the car radio and the dispatcher's voice faded in. "All units in Brighton Beach area, multiple reports of shots fired at the Zhar-Ptitsa restaurant—"

My phone rang. I snatched it up. It was Neville. "This is bad," she said. "This is fucked, Kinneavy. This was a goddamn massacre. I need you both over there right-the-fuck now."

She was loud enough that Donnie had heard her too. He peeled out toward the Lower East Side. "Was it Judith, Captain?"

"What the fuck do you think? Yes, it was Judith. We have a roomful of bodies and I need—"

I heard her shriek on the other end. "Captain?"

Her voice was calm, but *wrong* calm, like my dad when he told us he had lung cancer. "There are two dead cops in my office, Detective Kinneavy. In my office."

"Shit—Donnie, turn around, we're going back to the station."

"*No.* You're not my only fuckin' detectives. Don't you dare turn around."

I ended the call. Donnie's knuckles on the steering wheel were sickly white.

"Jesus Christ," I said. "How many of them are there?"

ROANE

I do my very best never to be late for the Monday morning staff meeting, and the next Monday I came too close for comfort. I darted into the conference room just a few minutes ahead of Tony, largely due to my cunning strategy of screaming, "Holy shit, what's that?" in the lobby and making him miss the elevator. I am the Brer Rabbit of my generation.

When I came to a stop in my seat, I'd built up just enough momentum that I nearly elbowed Rosalind Garwood, the small, eminently snarky brunette with a smoker's voice who's our financial correspondent, in the face.

"Awww, Tony's gonna make you beat erasers," she said as I moved my chair back to the edge of the table. (I'd knocked it halfway to the window when I sat down.)

"Have you been saving that one, Ms. Garwood?" I asked as I slapped my notebook down on the table.

She made a fake sad face. "Be nice to me, you dick. I spend every day getting quotes from Wall Street bros and I'm never allowed to snap at them. You have no idea how that backs up inside a person."

I gave her my best "bitch, please" look. (I'm allowed to say it, but I waive my right to catch a cab no matter how nicely I'm dressed.) "Really, Roz? You wanna cry to the guy who has to talk to City Council about this?"

Tony sauntered into the room. "Turns out it was a dragon, Wendell," he said to me. "Too bad you ran off. Story of the century."

He took a seat as the rest of the staff made their customary confused faces and then their customary "okay, I guess we don't get any context for that one" faces.

"Happy Monday, you bastards," Tony continued as he took his seat at the head of the table. He pointed at Rosalind. "Rosalind, what have you got for us?"

"I'm maybe seventy-five percent done with the piece on the Worldlink sell-off," Rosalind said. "Give me until the end of the day to bug the NYSE guy, and if I can't get him I'll just 'could not be reached for comment' him and then I'm good."

"Magic," said Tony. He pointed to Dewayne Broward, our music critic. "Where we at with the 'Music of the Revolution' spread?"

Dewayne had been working on a multipart story in which he talked to veterans of the Black Power, feminist, and gay-rights movements in New York about the use of music to further their causes. I was kind of jealous.

Dewayne looked excited. "Guess who I scored an interview with?" He went on when he realized no one was going to guess. "Dhoruba bin Wahad."

Rosalind whistled. "*Nice.*" Even Tony looked starry-eyed. Dhoruba was a major figure in the New York Black Panthers before he was convicted of the attempted murder of two cops. He was released when it turned out evidence that favored him had been withheld. After that, he'd done community organizing in Ghana for a while before returning to the city. Needless to say, an interview with him was a hell of a coup.

Tony did a slow clap for Dewayne, which was eventually joined by the rest of us. Then he turned to me. "And Wendell, listen, I may have given you my share of crap about publishing the Judith letters—"

"And the accompanying story."

"And the accompanying story . . . but credit where it's due, because circulation is up five hundred percent this week. And that's not page views, that's circulation of the physical magazine. People are so into your story they wanted to read the whole goddamn magazine. We are getting this town back into serious journalism, and all it took was a bunch of crazy rapist hunters. It's all so simple, in hindsight." He raised his arms. "*L'chaim*, motherfuckers."

He dismissed us but stopped me at the door after everyone else had headed back to their desks.

"So, Wendell," he said, in the worst fake casual voice I've ever heard (and I've heard my share). "Can you think of any reason I might be getting angry emails from the Decency League?"

I shrugged. "Because you're Jewish?"

"Well, I doubt that helps, but this seemed to have more to do with you."

"Yeah?"

"Wendell, did you tell Marvin Devaney to suck your dick?"

I looked at my shoes. "I *asked* him, more like. Didn't put any pressure on him or anything."

"Jesus, Wendell."

"I know my maturity is kind of on probation at this point, Tony, but he started it."

"I'm sure he did, Wendell, but he's talking about an advertiser boycott."

"Oh heavens, you mean he might cut into our conservative Catholic readership? The monster."

"*Hey!*" Tony snapped, which is not a thing he does, generally. "I don't care whether he can actually deliver or not. That's not what this is about. What this is about is my people don't get in fucking rap beefs while they're representing my publication."

"Oh, why's it gotta be a *rap* beef?"

Tony rolled his eyes. "I know for a fact your iPod is full of fucking Ke$ha, so don't start with me, Wendell, okay?"

"It's not full of her. She only has two albums," I mumbled.

"Look, Wendell, did this all start because you're covering the Judith thing?"

"More or less."

"Okay. I want you to work on something else on top of that. You're doing great work with it, but maybe Marvin the Martian will back off if it's not the only thing you're associated with."

"Sounds fine. What you got for me?"

He pulled a business card out of his breast pocket. "So you know Judson Crowning, the mayor's chief of staff?"

"I know *of* him."

"Not many people know much of anything about him. I think it'd be interesting to do a profile. Just a neutral thing. I talked to the press secretary. She says he's interested, just call this number."

"Why you want me covering the mayor's office?"

Tony gave a crooked grin. "'Cause he says he'll kick my ass next time he sees me and I believe him."

I called the number on the card as soon as I got back. He answered on the first ring.

"Judson Crowning, Mayor Peters's office, how may I help you?" His voice had the nasal, reedy twang of a transplanted Virginian or Carolinian, but none of the pronunciation. It was made even harder to place by his weird staccato delivery. He sounded like an old recording I'd heard of J. Edgar Hoover.

"Hi, Mr. Crowning, this is Wendell Roane at the *Septima*—"

"Ah, yes, the reporter. I can meet you outside Castle Clinton in an hour. Have some questions ready for me, please." He hung up.

I got to Battery Park in just about forty-five minutes, but Crowning was already there. He was about fifty, a little over six feet, with a square jaw, neatly combed dark hair, and a high forehead. His eyes were a strange dark blue that made the iris seem to subsume the pupil. He leaned forward and shook my hand when I approached him, which struck me as odd, for no other reason than the fact that he struck me as someone who wouldn't shake hands with anyone.

"Let's walk," he said. I asked him my questions as we circled the walls of the fort. He was from DC, as it turned out, and his father had been an aide to H. R. Haldeman.

"I'd known for a while that my daddy worked for the president," Crowning said—the word "daddy" sounded bizarre in his voice—"but when I went to watch him at work, I saw this one man—this skinny gentleman with a brush cut, getting everything done, everyone jumping at the snap of his fingers, just generally coming off like he owned the place. I said, 'Daddy, that man's in charge, he must be the president.' My daddy said no, that was the chief of staff. I met the man himself shortly afterward. All sweaty and hunched over and wild-eyed and, 'Ah, you must be Caleb's boy, happy to have you here.'" Crowning did a passable Nixon impression. "I could tell, even then, he was a striver. I have no patience for such people. If you have to make that much effort to seem like the man in charge, Mr. Roane, you are not the man in charge."

The rest of the walk was a run-through of his routine and a couple choice anecdotes about county commissioners who he said would "remain nameless," which as far as I knew was generally what county commissioners did anyway. And then about an hour after we started, he turned around and asked, apropos of nothing, "So how's Detective Kinneavy?"

His voice hadn't changed at all, but something about it scared me regardless. He was smiling, for some reason, but it looked more like a grimace turned slightly up at the ends.

I didn't see any point in bullshitting him. "What's Detective Kinneavy got to do with this?"

He got a little bit closer to me. "I want to know what she's got to do with it, Mr. Roane. See, that's how you play to win, Mr. Roane. You make everything your business."

I wiped my glasses on my tie. "What do you want from me, Mr. Crowning?"

"At present? Nothing major. But that might change at any minute, particularly given your involvement in this whole Judith imbroglio."

"And why do you care about Judith?"

"The mayor is my nominal superior. Some vague sense of loyalty compels me to nip anything that makes him look bad in the bud."

"And you think trying to intimidate reporters is the best way to do that?"

"You're not listening to me, Mr. Roane, which I feel like you should, as a journalist. Detective Kinneavy, your source, is one of the primary investigators of the Judith case. I'm concerned that her interest in the case goes beyond simply finding the perpetrators. You're to let her know at your earliest convenience that she's not doing a goddamn sociological study on these people, she's putting them in jail."

I looked at him for a second. "You said 'I.'"

"Pardon?"

"You said, '*I'm* concerned,' even though you were talking about how Judith was making the mayor look bad. Is this personal for you in some way, Mr. Crowning?"

His smile flatlined, and then he made a valiant attempt at forcing it back into shape. "Do you know why I said 'I,' Mr. Roane? Because I'm the only one you need to worry about right now. And I would strongly advise against antagonizing me, Mr. Roane, because, to paraphrase Tolstoy, I have as many hands as there are balls to twist." He was only inches away from my face now. "Do you want it to get out what your new friend, Detective Kinneavy, got up to in college? Or how about I cook up some evidence Ms. Garwood is fucking her sources? She seems like the type, doesn't she? Or maybe your editor, Mr. Mendelsohn, wakes up one day and finds himself arrested for possession of drugs. I'm not just some guy who schedules meetings, Mr. Roane. I can bury you and anyone connected to you so deep, Australians can see the tops of your heads. And I can do it all without firing a shot or throwing a punch. Although I'm happy to do either of the above if we reach that point. Do you want us to reach that point, Mr. Roane? Because I'd hate for anything to interrupt your mother while she's watching her favorite show from seven-thirty to eight, or while she's sitting up reading for the next hour, both directly in front of the south-facing panel window."

I didn't give him the satisfaction of looking scared. At least, I hoped I didn't. "Mr. Crowning, I'm getting kind of used to people threatening me this week. So tell you what: next time I see Kinneavy, I'm gonna talk to her about whatever the fuck I feel like, and whatever little heartwarming street urchins you're paying a nickel to spy on us can tell you how that goes, okay? And for now, keep your old-timey-radio-announcer ass the *hell* out of my personal space."

He stepped back. "I apologize for the leaning in," he said. "I often forget myself. I don't believe we'll need to take any drastic measures at this point, Mr. Roane, but consider yourself on notice."

I rolled my eyes. "Can I go back to my office now?"

He walked backward toward the north end of the park a bit. "A few years ago, there was a union rep giving us trouble," he said. "So in the interest of him giving us less trouble, this gentleman's wife met with an unfortunate accident. Now, when he still wouldn't play ball, it somehow got into the rumor mill, after a little while—*somehow*—that this man had poisoned his wife. And further investigation unearthed an online receipt for several grains of cyanide as well as a Google search for 'how much cyanide to kill instantly.' Now, this man protested his innocence, obviously, and could afford an excellent lawyer, but it was all for nothing. He was convicted, and sentenced to life in prison. Now, wait for it, Mr. Roane."

"Okay, I'm waiting."

"The gentleman's wife? She died in a car accident. I mean, that was common knowledge. The coroner's report was on the kitchen table when they arrested him. Isn't that the damnedest thing?" He quickened his pace and strode out of sight into the financial district.

A guy like that, you never know how much of his power is actual capability and how much is his ability to fuck with your head. Crowning was clearly more of a legitimate threat than Devaney, but that song and dance was probably usually deployed against city employees—the kinds of people who, at the end of the day, could be fired if you stepped out of line. He might have been a good bully, but the whole point of being a good bully is that you never have to back up any threats you make.

All the same, I gave Kinneavy a call on my way back to the office. It went to voice mail. "Hey, Detective," I said after I heard the beep. "This is Roane at the *Septima*. Listen, Judson Crowning just talked to me and I don't know what his deal is, but he seems like he's gunning for you on a personal level. It wouldn't surprise me if he got in touch with you sometime soon, so tread carefully if he does."

I hung up, perfectly aware of the hypocrisy of advising anyone else to tread carefully, thank you very much. I got back to the office and started typing up my notes from my pre-ugliness conversation with Crowning. Judge me as a person if you like, but I feel like being able to write a balanced profile of a guy who implied he'd murder my mother speaks well for my journalistic objectivity.

The office phone rang. It wasn't a recognized number. "Wendell Roane, the *Septima*."

"Don't react in any way to this call. Don't say anything that makes sense out of context." The voice was modulated, and I was pretty sure I knew who it was. "You need to go to the Cathedral of the Transfiguration of Our Lord, in Brooklyn, and you need to do it now."

"Um, okay. Why now?"

"We have something planned for tonight in that area. There'll be police in the area, and the women will be too scared to talk to you."

"Women?"

"Go and you'll understand. Now."

"But it's only one o'clock."

"Crowning pulled his people off of you for the interview. He's on his way back to his office and once he gets there, he's going to put them back on. You need to be out of the borough before he has a chance to follow you."

The call ended. I put my notes in the drawer and walked around to Tony's office. "Hey, Ton'? I gotta head out early. Got someone to talk to in Brooklyn."

"Hey, great," he said. "Try not to tell anyone to suck your dick."

"No promises."

I had the whole subway ride to ponder my newfound moral crisis. I had been forewarned of illegal activity—shit, murder, let's call a spade a spade—and I had a cop's name in my phone, and I was doing nothing with that information. I told myself "tonight" and "that area" wouldn't be any help; I told myself Kinneavy wasn't answering her phone, but I couldn't sell myself on the idea that it was anything other than conscious refusal, because that would be bullshit. Why, though? Did the story mean that much to me? Or was I starting to sympathize with these people? Or did I just want to see what would happen? I was pretty sure it was a combination of the three, and I wasn't sure I liked what that said about me. In the absence of anything else, I just repeated, like a prayer, that whoever they were hitting tonight had it coming. I repeated that until it drowned out the other voice telling me that that was Dillinger's excuse too.

It was a pretty wild-looking church. It was the biggest building on the block, and it had those big-ass onion-looking domes you always see in tracking shots of Moscow. I tried the door. The inside was just as impressive, all marble and mosaic and icons. As far as I could tell, the main church was empty. I wandered down the aisle and for the first time noticed a young priest lighting candles. From where he'd been standing, he'd been out of my field of vision until I got to the altar.

"If you're police, you must leave," he said without looking at me, his accent a mélange of Russian and Jackie-Gleason Brooklyn. "I know the law."

"I'm not a cop, Father, I'm a journalist."

"Ah yes, one of these horrible little men who runs around trying to take pictures of famous people and write about their sex lives. Well, we have no famous people here and our sex lives are better than our friends in Rome but still pretty dry."

I walked past the altar and moved closer to him. It's hard to argue your case when you're not making eye contact. "Listen, man," I said. "I think there's someone in here I might need to talk to. My name's Wendell Roane, maybe you've heard it over the past week."

It sounded way cockier than I'd meant it to, but he didn't seem to take it that way. He tentatively offered his hand. "Chris Mirzoyev," he said. "You wrote about those murders, didn't you?"

"Yes, I did. And that means a big chunk of the city's watching right now, and I don't want to waste that. I want to give a voice to someone no one would ordinarily be listening to, and I promise I can do it without using the girls' real names or exposing them in any way."

He looked me over. "You're assuming they're even here. That seems like it could be very embarrassing for you if you're wrong."

I shrugged. "Can't be a good a journalist if you're afraid to embarrass yourself."

His eyes twinkled. "Same could be said of the priesthood. Maybe you missed your calling, Mr. Roane." He led me past a column and down a longish hallway. We stopped at the fourth door on the left. "They speak hardly any English," he said. "I'll interpret as best I can. Keep in mind that they also have hardly any education, and if they feel you're trying to intimidate them, they won't talk to you. Do you understand?"

"Yeah, definitely."

He opened the door. The layout and décor of the room indicated it was ordinarily used as a classroom. There were several tables folded against the wall, presumably to make room for the multiple cots toward the middle of the room. There were about fifteen women, some sitting on cots, a few sitting around an Asian woman sitting upright in a chair with a Bible in her hands.

"The bilingual edition," Father Mirzoyev explained. "For the ones who want to pick up some English. Oksana!" He beckoned to a blonde sitting at the edge of the circle. She put her palm against her chest and he nodded. She walked slowly over to us. She had a painful looking bruise down one side of her face and some distinctly finger-shaped ones on her throat. She pointed to me and said something to Father Mirzoyev. Obviously, I don't know any Russian, but her inflection made it sound like a question. Father Mirzoyev responded in kind and she looked relieved.

"Oksana, I'm a journalist," I said. "I write for a magazine that wants to tell people about the kinds of things that were done to you and maybe get some changes made as a result. I'm not gonna tell anyone your real name or where you are. Will you help me, please?"

Father Mirzoyev translated for her. She looked confused and said something to him.

"She wants to know, will the people who hurt her and the other girls know that she talked to you?"

"No, ma'am. In fact, the man who did most of the hurting is dead. And if you talk to me, it may help stop the other men who hurt you from hurting anyone else."

She looked back at the priest, as though seeking his approval. Finally, she looked back at me and nodded.

"Let's sit in this corner, shall we?" said Father Mirzoyev, pulling up a couple chairs. We sat down, and I got out my note-pad and voice recorder.

"So how did you come to this country, Oksana?"

"Her mother was very sick, and she needed a way to make money. There was a man in her town who said they needed secretaries in America, that it would pay good money. She went with this man, he took her to the hold of a boat, and she spent the next two weeks in the hold. When she got to New

York, they put her in the back of a truck. She doesn't know how much time passed in the back of the truck, but when she got out, she was in a basement with all the other girls. There was a man who she thinks was in charge, he kept yelling at them, but they didn't understand. Finally, they brought in a man who knew a little Russian, and he said that they were all going to fuck any man who came in there, and if they didn't, they'd be deported. If they objected to anything the men did to them, they'd be deported. If they tried to leave, they'd be deported."

"Was it only the first man who hurt you, or did all the men who came in hurt you?"

She shook her head violently. "There . . . there were many men who hurt her, one in particular. But almost all of them hurt her. Some of them didn't start out that way, but they couldn't . . . you know, do it properly, and they got angry and hit her."

"How often were you fed?"

"Once a day. Usually . . . I think she's trying to say McDonald's. She's not quite sure, but it tasted like McDonald's. It was usually only two or three sandwiches to go around."

"Was there competition at all among the women? For food, clients, anything?"

"No, not at all. She says she'd be crazy if she didn't have the other girls around. It helped her feel like she was staying alive for someone other than herself. She's worried they'll have to be separated eventually."

"The one man who hurt her . . . tell me about him, if you can."

"He was a big man but not fat. He wore a suit and seemed important. He had a razor . . . an old razor, the kind that unfolds . . . and sometimes he would cut her on her thigh or her shoulder blade while he went inside her. When she screamed, he would hit her very hard, and seemed to really start enjoying it at that point. He would grab her hair and force her to meet his eyes. His eyes are . . ." Father Mirzoyev looked back at me. "I'm sorry, Mr. Roane, I must be rustier than I thought. She says his eyes were the navy. I have no idea what that means." He looked back at Oksana, whose eyes were shining. "I think perhaps we've talked enough, yes?"

"Wait. Navy. I think she means . . ." I opened Google Image Search on my phone and prayed there wasn't a country singer or anything with the same name. Jackpot. There he was. I held the phone out to Oksana. "Is that him?"

She recoiled a bit when she saw Judson Crowning's face. She must not have needed a translator for that, because she nodded and handed the phone right back to me. She was full-on sobbing by now. Father Mirzoyev asked her something, and when she weakly nodded again, he placed a hand lightly on her shoulder and began rotating it.

I got to my feet. "Thank you, Father. Can I reach you later on if there's anything I need to ask?"

"Of course," he said. He dug into his cassock and took out a business card for the cathedral. "Mr. Roane?"

"Yeah?"

He gestured toward Oksana. "Don't have put her through this for nothing, yeah?"

"Father, I'm generally not in the promises business, but tell her I promise it won't have been for nothing."

I went straight home, but I kept working after I got there. I was done with the Crowning profile by seven. I hated reading it back, remembering the look on Oksana's face; reading my own descriptions of Crowning's "efficiency" and "reputation for turning around struggling local campaigns" and "running a tight ship" were starting to make me physically ill. This was the life I'd chosen. Sometimes, to report the news is to rattle off a man's career highlights even when you know something awful and venal and only tenuously human is scuttling around beneath the surface of things.

The picture we were using for the profile's opening splash had been taken by the staff photographer once Crowning got back to city hall and then emailed to me. It showed Crowning in profile, standing on the steps of city hall and staring across the street, his hands in his pockets. His eyes were half closed. It made him look hypercompetent and emotionally uninvolved. His eyes had opened far wider when he'd spoken to me candidly, and I was willing to bet they'd been even more so when he was holding a fistful of Oksana's hair and holding a straight razor to her throat. I looked at the picture and decided I was going to be the one who gave this man what was coming to him, not Kinneavy or Judith or anyone else. And I was going to do it my way, no matter how badly I wanted to Moe-Greene-special him right in one of those creepy fucking eyes.

My increasingly Kafkaesque vigilante fantasies were interrupted by the phone, which I was this close to just turning off at home. It was Tony, who usually restricted himself to email. "Turn on the news," was all he said. I grabbed for the remote and flicked to the NBC affiliate. "BREAKING: BRIGHTON BEACH BLOODBATH," screamed the chyron. I rolled my eyes involuntarily. Broadcast journalists.

". . . reputed to include key organized crime figures. Although the organization known as Judith has yet to claim credit in the media, detectives on the scene say they believe it was responsible. Captain Meghan Neville has scheduled a press conference for tomorrow morning."

They were taking it up a notch. If they knew about Crowning, he was right to be scared. I turned off the TV and navigated to my email, hoping against hope that another video wasn't forthcoming, because this time, I would know its content was only possible because of me.

CATALDO

A t some point on Monday, before my evening meeting with Degtiarenko, I realized I was eventually going to have to kill him. I considered having my crew take the long way to Brooklyn and kill Degtiarenko's guys as soon as he left the meet, but I had no guarantees his entire crew would be around, and besides which, shootouts in the street were exactly the kind of thing I didn't need. (That didn't mean I was driving without insurance. There was going to be a sniper on the roof watching to make sure that when the Russians left the restaurant, so did I.)

Because as much as it pained me to admit it, the weaselly little commie fuck was right: I'd lost my edge. We all had. All the individual revenue streams and business models aside, our only real job was to keep people from fucking with us. No, scratch that—to keep people from ever thinking that fucking with us was something they could do in the first place. I wasn't Superman; I was Old Man Giannini from when I was a kid.

Old Man Giannini had lost a foot—just the foot, not the leg—in World War II, where he'd also gotten a bad head injury that made him trail off on consonants. He had a little strip of grass between his front stoop and the curb, and he called it his "lawn" and got super fuckin' pissed at any kid who cut across it. But nobody ever took him seriously, because even though he was only a stone's throw away from us, he never did anything other than shake his crutch at us and yell, "You keeppppp yourrrrr goddamnnnnn assessssss offa my lawnnnnnnnn." Then one day, Old Man Giannini's brother Carlo visited him for a weekend. Carlo was nearly as old as his brother and didn't look much tougher. But the first afternoon he was there, Paulie (we go back) cut through Old Man Giannini's yard on the way home from school, and Carlo shuffled over, looked down at Paulie, and said, "Kid, you step on my brother's lawn again, I'll beat your little fuckin' ass so red they'll make you live on a reservation." Carlo was gone Monday afternoon, but none of us ever cut across Old Man Giannini's yard again. That's power.

I'd been discussing this with Paulie as we drove to Brighton Beach for the meet. Paulie couldn't come in, but he was gonna wait at the curb with several guns of varying sizes in case things went sideways and Mark Nobile, the guy on the parallel roof, missed any Russians. Paulie's immediate reaction to my thoughts was to insist that it had been me, not him, who got yelled at by Carlo.

"Goddammit, Paulie, you know that ain't the point."

"No, yeah, I know, I'm just sayin'."

"Well, don't. Don't 'just say.' I'm talkin' about goin' to war and you're 'just sayin'."

"So you're having this meet to get out of goin' to war so we can do it later?"

"It's strategic. It's like how Joshua Chamberlain gave Hitler Yugoslavia so the English could have peace on time and kick his ass later."

"Don't you mean Stalin? I mean, these pricks are Russian, right?"

"Yes! They're Russians, Paulie. It's a fuckin' analogy."

Paulie turned down a side street toward the restaurant. "I don't think there's been real war in our lifetime," he said. "Least, not since we got made. You think we're ready?"

I shrugged. "We're gonna have to be." I turned to look at him. "Paulie, you know they're gonna come at us eventually if we make them think they can. That's how it works. There is no peaceful option at this point." I pointed to a neon sign shaped like an orange bird with its wings spread. "This is it."

Paulie pulled to a stop in front of it. "It's funny," he said. "You know, it's not like it used to be. Shit was tough when we were growing up, but there was a ton of stuff we coulda done when we grew up. I mean, this ain't the Depression, it's not like Our Thing was the only option."

"What are you saying?"

"I'm sayin' the only reason I decided to do this was 'cause I wanted life to be like a movie. And all this time, it really hasn't been, and I'm realizing I'm okay with that, and the idea of it being like a movie is what scares me."

I felt bad for the guy. This was exactly the kind of vulnerability we grew up being taught to shun. But fuck that. All the rules had been jumping out the window lately. Why the hell couldn't a man admit he was scared? I placed a hand on Paulie's shoulder.

"Paulie," I said. "I know. It scares me too. But we are the big dogs, *paisan*, and they are not gonna yank our chains. And they're gonna die knowing it was the meanest fuckin' wops in America that killed 'em."

Paulie sucked his breath in a little and put his hand over mine. "Thanks, Joe," he said a moment later. He pushed my hand off his shoulder in mock disgust. "Now get outta here with that queer shit."

I laughed in spite of myself. I reached into the glove box and drew out the paper bag. We'd cleaned it as best we could and evened out the cut with a steak knife, but I still felt filthy holding it in my hand. I clutched it to my chest, nodded to Paulie, and stepped out of the car.

The place was called the Zhar-Ptitsa; it was a classy Russian restaurant, which was apparently a thing. I'd been told to knock rather than just enter. When I did, a guy in a pin-striped suit over a V-neck and a gold chain let me in.

"What you want, man? You the Italian?"

"No, I'm the fuckin' Jamaican."

He looked confused and then raised his eyebrows. "Joke! Yes!"

"Yes, joke. Tell Mr. Degtiarenko I'm here."

He nodded. He patted me down and then pulled out a phone and sent a text. "They are upstairs," he explained. "Private party."

The restaurant was empty. Ordinarily it would have been open for a couple hours longer, but the doors had been locked tonight.

The man's phone buzzed and he turned to me. "They ready for you in just a minute," he explained. "Please, take the seat."

I sat down on the velvet bench in the restaurant's waiting area.

Ten minutes later, they still hadn't called for me. The doorman smiled apologetically when a loud noise upstairs made us both jump. There was a crash, and what came next were unmistakably gunshots. The doorman jogged to the bar and pulled an Uzi from behind it.

He held up one hand. "You stay there," he said to me. He checked the magazine and jogged up the stairs.

About a minute later, I heard another gunshot. I really wasn't sure what to do. I didn't hear any footsteps on the stairs, but I got up and ran to the curb anyway.

"I need one of your guns," I said to Paulie when I opened the door of the car.

"Whoa, what the fuck's going on, Joe?"

"I don't know, I think somebody else showed up."

"Well then, what the fuck are we staying here for?"

"Just gimme something, huh, Paulie? You and Mark keep me covered and if I'm not back down in five minutes, get the fuck out of here, huh?"

He sighed and handed me a Beretta Stampede from under the seat. He snapped his fingers next to his eye. "Look at me. Be fuckin' careful, got me?"

"Always."

I walked back into the restaurant and up the stairs, gun at the ready. When I was at the top of the stairs, I heard several thumps that sounded like boots. I could tell they were below me, but they sounded like they were hitting pavement, and the lobby of the restaurant was all carpeted. At the top of the stairs was a single closed door slightly ajar. I eased it open with the gun.

Well, at least there was no one waiting inside.

There was so much blood, it took me a minute to realize there were even bodies in there. I jumped back when I realized the doorman, his chest in bloody shreds, was lying at my feet. He hadn't even gotten off a shot. The rest of the room seemed mostly to be Degtiarenko's entourage. It was hard to tell anything about the bodies, they'd been so worked over, but a few of them looked as though they'd been smaller and better dressed, so I was guessing they'd been bosses like Degtiarenko.

Speaking of Degtiarenko, he was sitting at the head of the table, slumped slightly forward. There were no wounds I could see on his body, but his throat was cut from ear to ear and the half of his face that didn't look extremely puzzled was completely caved in. Shotgun, from the looks of it. A window at the far end of the room was wide open; I ran over and looked down. Short drop and a fire escape. No wonder I hadn't seen anyone leave. I stuck the Stampede in my waistband and jogged down the stairs.

I jumped into the car and I screamed, "Drive!" to Paulie. I realized, in spite of myself, that him and me, driving for our lives . . . this was just like a fuckin' movie. And it made me laugh a little.

Of course, I stopped laughing when I realized halfway back that I'd left Will's hand in the restaurant.

We had good lawyers, and I was pretty sure no one could put me at the restaurant that night, but all the same, I feared the worst when there was a knock at my door the next day. The man who answered was carrying a black combination brief-case. He was better dressed than me or anyone I worked for, so I knew he wasn't a cop, but I could tell he wasn't there to have a beer and watch the ball game either.

"Mr. Cataldo," he said. I couldn't tell if he was asking or telling. "My name's Judson Crowning. I'm with the mayor's office and we have business to discuss. Can I come in?"

"Uh, yeah, sure." I stepped back to give him room.

My place isn't flashy, but it's nice enough that most people, upon coming in, look around without meaning to. Crowning didn't do that. He just turned to face me as soon as he was over the threshold.

"Mr. Cataldo, I've got a problem," he said. "You ever read an alternative weekly newspaper they call the *Septima*?"

"Can't say I do. I've heard of it."

"I find it smug and overly moralistic. Objectively, their reporting is excellent, but I despise reporters as a rule. They lack the will to shape history and they lack the patience to be historians. 'So then because thou art lukewarm, and neither cold nor hot, I will spew thee out of my mouth.'"

"Spew *me*?"

"No, not you, Mr. Cataldo, it's Revelations."

"Ah, okay."

He just stared at me for a while after that, and then he said, "Mr. Cataldo, there's a gentleman employed by this particular publication—one Wendell Roane—who's causing me quite a bit of trouble. I've had him under surveillance for a few days, but yesterday he bucked his handlers and they have yet to pick the thread back up."

"Well, I mean, he's got an office, doesn't he? How hard can he be to find?"

"It's not a question of finding him. It's my own fault for showing my hand. People who know they're being followed find all sorts of annoying little ways to give you the slip. Even if it's only for a little while, it can throw a wrench into things."

"And what's that got to do with me, all due respect?"

"Well, Mr. Cataldo, I fear my relationship with Mr. Roane has reached a crescendo, so to speak. Mr. Roane, you see, has been covering the Judith affair."

"Who?"

"They're a criminal organization, Mr. Cataldo. They killed Mr. Milazzo and they were responsible for the scene you stumbled upon in Brighton Beach last night." I opened my mouth and he held up a hand. "*Please* don't waste our time with pointless denials, Mr. Cataldo. If you were the last to be seen with a missing person, it would behoove you not to misplace his hand, don't you think?"

Shit. Shit shit shit.

He kept talking. "Now, here's my issue with Mr. Roane—much like his counterpart in the police department, he's not keeping his eye on the prize as far as the Judith case. He's digging into the people they target as well, and that could potentially lead him to information that I cannot abide him obtaining."

"Cut the bullshit. Are you asking me to kill him?"

He looked shocked and shook his head. "Oh no, absolutely not. I'm *telling* you to kill him."

Fuck this. I wasn't going through this again. "Mr. . . . Crowning? You wanna get the fuck out of my house right about now. I'm done being told *anything* by people other than my boss, and I don't give a good goddamn if you want to blackmail me or whatever. I am not the man to fuck with and I'm making sure everyone knows that."

I thought he'd get angry, but he didn't sound it when he spoke. "You're missing the forest for the trees, Mr. Cataldo," he said. "You think *I'm* trying to fuck with you? Judith—and you really should read up on them, you're going to have a hard time following along otherwise—not only have they killed one of your captains, I have it on good authority that they're going after people who pay tribute to you. You think the Russians didn't show the proper respect? The Russians were a bunch of new-school punks. These women are mad dogs. You want to reassert your authority? Start with them."

"You say 'start with them,' but you want me to kill a reporter."

He opened the briefcase; it was crammed full of banded stacks of hundreds. "Five million dollars, Mr. Cataldo," he said. "Five million dollars and a guarantee you will never face any criminal charges in this city so long as you shall live. You should help me undermine Judith for the reasons I've already expounded upon, but you should resolve the question of Mr. Roane because, again, five million fucking dollars. Are you going to take it or are you going to pass it up because you'd rather find fault with my logic?"

I sighed. "I'll take it."

There was nothing about this that wasn't a red flag. Hits for outside operators were a huge no-go, Crowning was clearly a psycho, and a hit on a civilian, especially a journalist, would be an even dumber move from a PR standpoint than the whole shootout-on-a-sidewalk bit. But God help me, I had been so ready to go to war with the Russkies that I needed an outlet for that momentum. Crowning and I shook on it, we hammered out some details, and he left the money with me, and the whole time, I wondered what the fuck was wrong with me that the money was the least intriguing part of the whole deal.

KINNEAVY

Captain Neville was wearing a black chalk-striped Kenneth Cole three-piece; her long red hair was pulled into a telegenic (if precarious) bun. She placed a red carnation in her lapel as she approached the lectern set up in the main lobby of the station. Donnie and I followed close behind like bodyguards, an effect somewhat undercut by the good six inches she had on both of us.

Neville had called the press conference shortly after the restaurant incident, determined to keep the narrative from slipping any further out of her control. The victims in Brighton Beach had essentially been the backbone of the Russian mob in Brooklyn. According to the FBI liaison, all of them were connected to human trafficking, but none more so than the little blond man at the head of the table. His name, according to the file, was Valery Degtiarenko, but he'd gone by at least five others. From what little they could piece together of his history before the fall of the Berlin Wall, he'd been a low-level KGB operative who'd operated a rape room. After the dissolution of the USSR, families of his victims chased him through Georgia, Bulgaria, and the United Kingdom before they lost track of him in the United States.

I didn't personally know either of the two cops whose bodies had been left in Neville's office, but I recognized them from news reports. Darius Gill had been charged with sodomizing a teacher in Manhattan two years ago but had been acquitted because the DA had charged him with rape, which New York state law at the time defined as requiring vaginal penetration. Back in 1999, Brett Augustine had been the ringleader of a group of cops who brought a Haitian immigrant in on a disorderly conduct. Once they got to the station, they beat him with their nightsticks and the butts of their guns for about twenty minutes, after which Augustine sodomized him with a plunger.

Augustine, who'd had ten years, had been allowed to leave the force with half of his pension. Gill had still been a cop.

The two cops had been bound, back to back, in a sitting position on Neville's desk. Stapled to Gill's chest was a note bearing three words: CLEAN YOUR HOUSE. Both their throats had been cut, but the blood was mostly dry, and there was no pooling on the desk. I had, however, followed up on a hunch regarding a small section in the middle of the back room at the restaurant; it had caught my eye because it had clearly fallen and pooled at a slight downward arc as opposed to looking like gunshot spatter. The autopsy also found slugs in both cops' legs that matched up with the last-man-to-die's gun. It looked like they'd shot up the room, either cut the two cops' throats or had been preparing to, been surprised by the last Russian, and used the cops as shields.

Degtiarenko had been killed (or shot, rather—his throat had already been cut) by a suppressed 12-gauge to the face, which was what had resulted in the first 911 call—whatever the movies may tell you, a silencer makes a shotgun silent like China is a People's Republic. Everybody else in the room had been killed with a handgun. The only victim who had gotten off a shot was the last man to die, who had clearly just stepped into the room when they shot him. So however many there were (and the fact that they'd deliberately obfuscated where and when the two cops had died made me think they didn't want us to know the answer to that), there were enough to overwhelm a room full of guys with semiautomatics.

I scanned the midsize crowd. Besides the reporters, I saw Commissioner Clarkson at the back of the room, along with Jalisa and DA Suarez. There was also a guy leaning against the back wall that I was pretty sure was the mayor's chief of staff. There was a little brunette with freckles in the second row back that I felt like I'd seen on the *Septima*'s staff page too. Neville advanced to the lectern as a couple of flashes went off.

"Ladies and gentlemen, thank you for coming out at short notice. I'm Captain Meghan Neville of the New York Police Department's Homicide division. Yesterday evening, in Brighton Beach, twelve people, all believed to be involved with Russian organized crime syndicates, were murdered. Two former members of this department were murdered in the same location, and their bodies left in my office afterward." She flipped the page over. "Analysis has confirmed that these murders were the work of a criminal organization styling itself 'Judith,' which has also claimed credit for the recent murders of reputed Mafia figure Russell Milazzo and local business owner Martin Vickner. According to dispatches from the organization, Judith's mission is to extrajudicially kill rapists and abusers of women who have evaded, or are likely to evade, justice. But ladies and gentlemen, however lofty their stated goals, their methods are those of a murderous gang, and they will be addressed as such by this division. Due to the excellent work of Detectives Kinneavy and Klein, we have amassed valuable intelligence on the group, but it would appear that Judith is escalating their campaign, as demonstrated by last night's incident. To that end, I have convened a task force within the

Homicide department to focus on apprehending them. Their work begins as soon as this press conference concludes. Thank you very much for your time, ladies and gentlemen. I will now take questions."

The little brunette raised her hand. "Rosalind Garwood, the *Septima*. Will the detectives currently assigned to the case remain on the task force?"

"Yes, as I said, Detectives Kinneavy and Klein have been exemplary on this case, and they'll be spearheading the task force."

"So your solution is to put the same people who haven't caught them yet in charge of the task force? How do you justify that?" said some asshole from the *Daily News*.

"Detectives Kinneavy and Klein are the reasons for any and all progress that has been made on this case thus far; in particular, it was due to Kinneavy's detective work that we even know that all of last night's victims were killed in the same location. That they have not single-, or rather, double-handedly shut down a completely anonymous criminal organization in five days can hardly be considered a poor reflection on their skills as police. And incidentally, Ed, if the *Daily News* thinks progress on this case is so long overdue, I would think they would have covered at least one of the homicides."

Oh damn. Don't ride the subway without a surgical mask, because someone has a *sick burn*.

"Why is what sounds like a terrorist organization being dealt with in Homicide?"

Shit. There it was. Make it count, Scarlet Witch.

"Well, I think it's a bit of a loaded question to presuppose anything 'sounds like' a terrorist organization, first of all, but as things stand, these people are not hijacking planes or trains, wiring bombs, or assassinating diplomats. They kill with knives and guns, and while they may publicize their crimes, they seem far more concerned with killing the people they target than with spreading fear. As such, we're not going to give them the dignity of treating them like threats to national security. And if you'd rather think of them as terrorists, I'll just say that terrorists have a history of wishing they'd chosen a different city."

Red meat. Well-played. A few more hands flew up, but Neville was determined to finish strong.

"That's all we have time for today, ladies and gentlemen. If you'll excuse us, we have to go walk the walk."

She stepped back from the lectern and headed down the hall, with Donnie and me following close behind. Midway down the hall I became aware of footsteps clacking behind us and whirled around to tell whomever it was to fuck off before I realized they weren't press. It was Jalisa, DA Suarez, and Commissioner Clarkson.

Tom Suarez was a barrel-chested, hard-eyed man with close-cropped silvering black hair who looked a lot more like the typical image of a police captain than Neville did. My experience with him was minimal, but he wasn't a favorite among cops. This was half because of his lack of enthusiasm toward prosecuting nonviolent drug offenses (i.e., the kinds of arrests for which the department was counting on convictions and the resultant good-looking closure stats) and his considerable enthusiasm toward violating the unwritten rules and going after cops if he had evidence of substantial wrongdoing. I, on the other hand, was a fan, in part because Jalisa swore by him and in part because, since taking office in 2010, he'd gone after sex offenses with a ferocity I wish my fellow cops had matched.

Commissioner Liam Clarkson, meanwhile, had a reputation as a father to his men, if your father was a paranoid careerist. A rail-thin bald gent with right angles for cheekbones, he looked like a disgruntled undertaker who had just about had it with you pricks implying you knew more about embalming than he

did. Post-9/11, he'd militarized the department to an unprece-
dented degree and conducted a large-scale, several-years-long
surveillance program on Muslim organizations in New York
and north Jersey. None of this had unearthed any actionable
terrorism-related intelligence, although Clarkson continued to
insist that this was only because the press reporting on it had
put the subjects on their guard. I genuinely don't think he was
a bad person or a racist; he was just one of those people who
went through life believing war had already been declared on
him. Regardless of intent, it was exactly the kind of mind-set
that made regular people hate cops.

Neville turned around a second after I did. If she was surprised to see them, she made no indication.

"One at a time, folks," she said.

"Yeah, we have a few things to discuss, Captain," said DA
Suarez.

"What few things?"

Commissioner Clarkson stepped in front of Suarez. "Cut
the bullshit, Tom. Captain, why the hell is your lead detective
on this case talking to reporters?"

Neville's eyes flashed fire. "What?"

"These are courtesy of the mayor's office." Clarkson pulled
an envelope from inside his coat and pulled a few pictures out.
They were of me and Wendell in McSorley's. Oh, fuck on rye
with light mayo.

Neville turned back to me. "Kinneavy, you have one minute to explain. Go."

"Captain, the only thing I told him was a variation on
what you just told them. I gave him the tough-girl line and he
printed it anonymously. He doesn't know anything classified.
He's been giving me everything they've mailed him. That's the
only reason we've been meeting."

"And why should we believe that?" asked the commissioner.

"Because nothing he's written for the *Septima* came from me except 'Blah blah, make my day, punkettes.' Have you even read what he's written?"

"Nobody fucking *reads* the *Septima*," Clarkson snapped, as though I'd just asked a castaway dying of thirst why he couldn't just drink from the ocean. "And you know, missy, you can say you haven't given him anything that undermines the investigation, but the fact remains that you have produced a resounding fuck-all on this case even after they walked into a restaurant and shot a man in the face. So I don't think you have to be leaking evidence for me to wonder why the hell you're still on the case."

Donnie stepped forward slightly. "All due respect, Commissioner," he said, "I've been on this case from the beginning too, and I'm kind of wondering why you're singling out—"

"Do I work for Clearasil's marketing department, son?" Clarkson asked.

"Uh, no, sir."

"Then why would I give a good goddamn what you're wondering?" He turned back to me. "Kinneavy, you don't have to convince Captain Neville. You have to convince me. So fucking do it."

I met his eyes. "Will you please follow me for just a minute?" I asked.

He didn't say no, conciliatory type that he was. I led him and the others into the bull pen and over to my desk. I gestured to the crap piled up on it.

"I have a running profile of the person likely to have written the letters based on word choice, font, paper quality, and the fact that they're hand-delivering letters in the first place. I have three bullets in the wall of the restaurant that whoever gathered up the casings must have missed, I have typed specs on the guns used, I have people looking for those guns right this minute, and I have the ballpark height of the person who killed Vickner and the one who killed Degtiarenko. So I hope that's enough for now, five days in, Commissioner, but if you're still not satisfied, I'll see if I can do something about this troublesome uterus."

Nobody spoke for a minute, even though I distinctly saw Jalisa make the face she makes when she tries to stifle a laugh.

Finally, Commissioner Clarkson spoke. "Detective Kinneavy," he said, "I'm not going to lie, I'm impressed. And you better be glad I am, because anyone who talked to me like that without impressing me would be directing traffic by the time I finished this sentence." He turned to Neville. "Don't fuckin' make me come down here again." He did a very theatrical turn on his heel and clacked back down the hallway.

Neville turned back to Suarez and Jalisa.

"So help me decide," she said. "What do I do first, see what you two want"—she turned and pointed at me—"or yell at you for mouthing off to our petty, capricious god-king?"

"You could yell about what they want," I volunteered.

"Ah, Captain," Suarez said. "Are you familiar with Martine Rivette?"

"Sounds familiar."

"He's France's minister of finance," said Jalisa. "He was in town addressing the UN, and a maid in his hotel accused him of sexually assaulting her."

"Oh Jesus. Did he?"

"Well, we decided to prosecute, obviously. They just finished jury selection," Suarez said. "That said, she's not the kind of victim juries take to."

"How's that relevant?" Donnie said, Brooklyn rage dancing around the edge of his tone.

"It's not, in terms of guilt or innocence," Suarez said. "But it could still make all the difference in terms of how the jury finds."

Jalisa looked at me. "Canary in the coalmine, K."

"What does that even mean?" Neville said. Between the press corps and Clarkson, I could tell having to spend so much of her day being diplomatic was starting to wear on her. She looked back at Suarez. "Make your point."

Suarez held up his hands apologetically. "I believe Mr. Rivette to be guilty, Captain. I believe I have what I need to convict him. But if I could predict the future, I'd quit my job and play the horses. So if we don't win this, he's high-profile enough that it's not unrealistic to think Judith may target him. So to our mind, it's win-win. If I get a conviction, he's put away. If I don't, you wait for Judith to go after him."

"Uh, there's a third possibility," I said. "They say they research everyone before deciding to target them. What if he's found not guilty, and he really isn't guilty?"

"Well, thank God for the task force," Jalisa said. "You have the resources to continue the investigation all through the trial, and if Rivette is convicted, you can tail him without completely taking your eye off the ball."

"Tom," Neville said. "You realize if it comes out you deliberately botched a case, you could get disbarred, right?"

"That's not what I'm proposing, Captain. Like I've told plenty of police personnel before you, my office is not an extension of the NYPD. But I'm a big fan of scenarios that can be turned to our advantage whichever way they go. I can't tell you when charges will be brought, but we'll be in touch." He offered Neville his hand. "Always a pleasure, Captain."

She shook it. "Sometimes a diversion, Tom."

I was not at all a fan of the task force idea, and I would have told Neville that if I didn't feel like I was already kind of on her shit list. Donnie I trusted to be discreet and not get mansplainy, but the rest of the task force was another story. I'd done a little work with all of them before, on separate occasions, and pretty much all of them were entirely wrong for the job. Brickman and Lyndstrom were the kind of bullying douchebags who called black eyes on a woman "Irish sunglasses." Wysocki, Torrio, and Lauder were good police and fairly nice guys, but they had still come up in a culture that couldn't process a woman knowing more about the case than any man in the room.

Once we were all assembled in the station's conference room, I stood up at the head of the table. I had a vague idea of how to get started without making them feel like they were prisoners of Queen Uppity Bitch, Thief of Balls, but I wasn't sure.

"Let's start at the beginning," I said. "You've all been given my report on Judith. What do we know about them? Think. Think about everything."

They stared at me for a minute before Torrio tentatively raised his hand.

"You can just talk, Dominic," I said.

"Okay, well, maybe not all of them, but they probably have to have at least one person who's police or military."

"Interesting. Why do you say that?"

"Well, first off, the way they've handled guns so far. If you can hold a piece steady enough to blow a guy's finger off, clean, it's probably not your first time."

"And several of the Russians were ex-military," Donnie threw in. "Takes more than the element of surprise to do them like that."

"The people they've targeted indicates they're probably predominantly white," Lauder said. "Only nonwhite victim so far is Gill, and they probably know him from the news."

"Have we found any of the guns, incidentally?" asked Wysocki. "I mean, they weren't just chucking them in storm drains and dumpsters as they ran."

"There's this thing called water," Brickman said. "Sometimes you can find it in places with 'Beach' in the name."

"Chucking a shotgun off a beachfront is hardly gonna get rid of it," I said. "Besides which, we have a witness who reports a white panel van tearing ass down Oceanview one minute after the call came in. The Zhar-Ptitsa is three minutes' drive from the beach, and that's with far less traffic than there was in the area last night."

"Do you have a point, or do you just think you have a pretty voice?" asked Brickman, in what I figured was the same voice he used to tell hookers that, well, there was *one* way they could avoid getting booked.

"Well, first of all, Howard, I have a fucking *gorgeous* voice. They don't let just any twelve-year-old play Lady Larken. Second, given the level of planning Judith has put into everything they've done thus far, I'm operating under the assumption that they have a standing plan for their guns as well. They could very well be destroying them, but if they're not, I think we should seriously consider the idea that they use a launderer."

"Do we have any compelling reason to think they do?" Lauder asked.

"Beyond what I just said? No. But the whole point of this task force is to give us the resources to go at this thing from every angle. Now, if they've got someone cleaning murder guns for them, who's more likely to be the key? A bunch of true believers, or some fence who's only in it for the money and will give us everyone he's ever sold to if we threaten him with jail?" I turned from Lauder back to the room at large. "Wysocki and Brickman will be responsible for looking for the guns and/or the cleaner."

Brickman sat forward. "Are you shitting me? I've got five years on you, Kinneavy. You're not sticking me with that."

"Actually, Brickman," I said, "I'm in charge of this menagerie, so I kind of have the last word on this."

"I got ears. You *and* Klein are in charge. He hasn't said shit."

"I'm with Detective Kinneavy," Donnie chimed in.

Weirdly enough, this didn't improve Brickman's mood. "Oh yeah, naturally. Make sure you hang the whip up when she's done with it, you little fuckin' faggot."

I pushed back from the conference table and walked around to where Brickman was sitting. I stopped about an inch from him.

"Don't you ever talk to him, or anyone else here, like that again," I whispered.

He leaned back slightly, trying to avoid making it obvious. "Or what? You gonna tell Internal Affairs I said a no-no word?"

"No, sweetie, I'm gonna jam your balls so far up your nostrils you asphyxiate. But you can tell Internal Affairs about that if you want." I circled around the table and back to my place at the head. "And you know, none of you have to take me seriously, as police or as a person. If you want something to call me, over drinks later on, I recommend Detective Cuntneavy or Shertwat Holmes, but don't feel like you have to limit yourselves to those. But in this room, working this case, Klein and I are your superiors, and you will treat us as such. If you don't, this whole endeavor is going to go badly. And take it to the fuckin' bank, you do not want it to go badly."

I turned back to the corkboard. "Lauder, everyone I've talked to in organized crime has known Russell Milazzo was involved in trafficking, but no one I've talked to outside of the life appears to have known. That tells me Judith has some kind of connection to the mob. You and I are looking into the Dellapontes to see what we can find out about that." I knew the odds were long on the mob giving a black cop or a lady cop the time of day, but we were the only ones who would work. I was pretty sure Lyndstrom was dirty, they'd eat Donnie alive, and Torrio was one of those Italian guys who grew up with wise-guys, went another way, and was now obsessed with making a distinction between them and himself.

I pointed at Lyndstrom and Torrio. "You two and Klein are gonna make like a high-priced dominatrix and stay on top of Martine Rivette from now until his trial concludes. And on top of what you've been assigned, all of us will continue working the existing witnesses and sources, with particular empha-sis on the Brighton Beach incident. Everybody clear on your respective duties?"

There were nods and shrugs around the room. Yay, leader-ship. I needed a drink as soon as humanly possible.

ROANE

Normally, when someone tries to kill you, your week can only improve. My week wasn't normal.

I don't think I'd ever actually heard real gunshots before, so it took me a minute to recognize them as such. I'd just left my apartment and I was heading down Eighth when I saw two little puffs of dust emerge from the outer wall of the brownstone adjacent to me. I probably would have kept staring until I got a chunk taken out of my head if the next one hadn't taken out a window. I finally got the picture and ducked into an alley so fast, I practically left a smoke outline of myself. That's another difference between me and a cop: guns terrify me.

I waited for a few minutes, and when I didn't hear any more shots, I tentatively stepped out of the alley and called 911. The dispatcher told me to stay where I was, even though that would make me late for the staff meeting and Rosalind would have one over on me. (He didn't mention Rosalind specifically, but it is a scientific fact that all white people know each other.)

The cop on the scene, a big Ultimate-Fighter-looking Latino guy, asked me if anyone had any reason to want me dead, which I get is a reasonable thing for a cop to ask but seemed weirdly accusatory, like he was trying to make up his mind whether to side with me or Johnny Sniper. I told him no, which was accurate. I'd pissed off Crowning, but this didn't seem like him. Far too imprecise and not enough of a statement.

"Yeah, I doubt this was a pro," the cop said. "Whoever he was, he couldn't handle a rifle worth a fuck." He jerked his thumb at the holes in the wall. "You just never know, man. Not after that crazy shit with the Russians over the weekend."

Oh shit.

I left the cop on the sidewalk and sprinted the rest of the way to the office, not bothering with the train. Fuck fuck fuck fuck. Of course.

I don't have a lot of experience with actual violence, but I know the history of crime in this city, and I can tell you there's nothing more volatile than a criminal power vacuum. However thoroughly the guys in Brighton Beach had been taken out (i.e., very), I guarantee someone else had already stepped in to take their place. I don't know why they'd target me, but my immediate thought was that their next priority would be to go after the girls in the church. I might have needed the tip-off to find them, but for someone who was part of that community, I'm sure it seemed like a much more obvious hiding place. Maybe I was leaping to conclusions, but I needed to be sure.

I breezed through the newsroom and over to my desk. I looked up the number for the church and dialed it on my desk phone. I was nearly hyperventilating by the time I heard Father Mirzoyev's voice on the other end.

"Hello?"

"Father! It's Wendell Roane, from the *Septima*."

"Ah, Mr. Roane. I read your article. Excellent stuff. Thank you so much."

"Father, is everyone okay?"

"Yes, why wouldn't we be?"

"All the girls are still okay?"

"Yes, Mr. Roane, the women are fine." His voice started to sound a bit suspicious. "Why? What's going on?"

"Nothing's going on, Father, I just wanted to make sure all of you were okay."

"Well, thank you, we appreciate it. God bless."

I hung up. Good to have that out of the way, at least.

I was messing around on Facebook and getting paid for it when Rosalind stuck her head around the side of the cubicle.

"Hey, look who showed up," she said. "Thomas Tardy's *Far from the Meeting Crowd*."

"That is contrived as hell, Ms. Garwood."

"Cut the 'Ms. Garwood' shit, I'm not your secretary."

"Of course you're not. I'm yours."

She rested her elbows on the top of the wall, dangling her upper arms like a cat. "So, hey, reason I came by is, Tony offered me the Rivette trial."

"The French guy?"

"No, the Congolese guy named Martine Rivette. Anyway, the Worldlink thing has me swamped as hell, so I wanted to ask if you wanted the trial. Seems like your cup of tea, and you know the usual suspects are gonna be victim-blaming out the yin-yang. Figured someone should provide balance."

I thought about it for a second. "Sure," I said. "Thanks."

"No problem," she said. "See you around, late-monger."

"That's a slight improvement," I called after her, which is really not a snappy enough comeback to yell after someone.

I did background on the Rivette case for the next two hours when my desk phone rang. The incoming number was that of the Cathedral of the Transfiguration of Our Lord. I answered.

"Hello?"

"What did you do?" Father Mirzoyev sounded close to tears. "What did you do, damn you?"

"Father, what are you saying? What's going on?"

"An hour after you called me, ICE shows up, says they have probable cause to search the church. I try to stop them, but I'm the only one here at this hour. They took all the girls. What did you tell them?"

"Father, I promise you, I didn't tell anyone anything."

"Oh, this is all a coincidence, then? You promised me, Mr. Roane. You promised me and you promised them that they'd be safe."

"Father, I don't know what's going on, but I did everything in my power to keep them safe—"

"You didn't promise that you'd do everything in your power. You promised they'd be safe. It's not the same thing and you know that." Now he was audibly crying. "None of those women is older than twenty-five, Mr. Roane. They will pass from this earth without ever having experienced lasting security or comfort or pleasure. I could have bought them a little time. Just a little."

"Listen to me, Father," I said. "Whoever did this, they're going to get what's coming to them. And that I can definitely promise you."

"Give me something other than talk. Give *them* something other than talk."

I didn't know of a nonawkward way to respond to that, so I hung up the phone. Phone etiquette is not really my thing.

As I hung up the phone, I noticed a thin green wire trailing from the end of the receiver and clinging tightly to the back all the way up to the top of it. I slid open the back of the receiver; there was a green plate studded with wires.

Oh, fuck me gently.

I yanked the phone's cord out of the wall and then pried the bug out of the receiver. I strode over to Tony's office.

"Bad time, Ton'?"

"If I say yes, will you care?"

"Answer hazy, try again later." I dumped the bug on his desk. "Someone bugged my phone."

Tony grabbed the coil of wire and plastic off the desk. "The hell did you get that?"

"My phone, where do you think?"

"Who the hell would be bugging your phone?"

"The illustrious Mr. Crowning, possibly."

"Aw Jesus, Wendell, what did you say to him?"

"Nothing. But he's crazy and paranoid."

He raised an eyebrow. "*He's* crazy and paranoid."

"Tony, the church where I interviewed those prostitutes just got raided by immigration, and I think they were able to find them because of me."

"Okay. And?" He held out his arms. "What are we supposed to do about that?"

"I have to keep them from falling through the cracks, Tony. This is my fault."

"Wendell, that's not what we're about. We're a newspaper."

"I'm not talking about the newspaper, Tony. I'm talking about me."

"Oh, imagine that."

I looked him in the eye. "Tony. Please. I know I'm too close to this, I know I never should have let it get me like this, but please. If there's anybody you know . . . you've been doing this way longer than I have . . ."

"You know, Wendell, you're the only guy I know who'd call someone an old fart while you were asking them for a favor."

"Yeah, well, you're the only guy I know who'd be more inclined to help me if I did it."

That got a smile out of him. He fished his cell phone out of his jacket. "Look, Wendell," he said. "My boyfriend works in the Justice Department and he knows a guy at INS. He's not a bigwig, he's not gonna pull any strings, but he knows all the loopholes and shit. No promises, and I can't give you any more help after I make the call. And you owe me more drinks than you will ever be able to afford at one time. Capisce?"

"Don't say 'capisce,' that's very offensive to my people."

He turned back to his phone. "I'll take that as a yes. Get back to the Rivette story while I do this, wiseass."

A few minutes later, Tony came around to my desk. "So, the good news is, my guy says there may be something they can do. If they've been subjected to abuse, they may be eligible for visas through VAWA. If that doesn't work, they may be able to testify against members of Milazzo's crew in return for protection. They're on route to the detention center in Buffalo now, which is a five-hour drive, so we won't know for sure until tomorrow morning."

I pumped his hand. "I really, really appreciate it, Tony. Really."

"Yeah, yeah, yeah. I get a drink on you whenever I say so for the next year, unless you'd rather I take it out of your direct deposit."

As luck would have it, the drama over the prostitutes had completely sidetracked me from what I was supposed to be working on that day, a midlength obituary about the death of a beloved stevedores' union organizer. As a result, night was falling by the time I filed. As I put my shit away and headed for the door, Tony emerged from his office.

"Wendell," he said. "I've got some bad news."

"What?"

"I have a snitch in the state police. He said an ICE bus was run off I-80 about an hour ago."

"Wait, was run off? How do they know it was run off? It couldn't have, like, skidded or anything? I mean, it's raining—"

He stopped me. "They know it was run off the road because whoever did it also took the time to shoot each of the women and the driver in the head."

Something horrible and cold grew in my chest and spread toward the pit of my stomach. My vision felt like it was blurring. I turned around and ran down the hall, and I didn't stop until I got to Lower Manhattan.

The Ear Inn isn't my favorite place, but I wasn't in any mood for my favorite anything. I bellied up to the bar and ordered a Jameson's. I couldn't get Oksana's expression when I showed her the picture of Crowning out of my head. Her face had been a perfect storm of terror and weariness, the union of all the unspeakable things that had been done to her and the fear that, no matter how safe she seemed to be now, they would find her again. And they had because I was an idiot and didn't believe a powerful, dangerous man when he told me I was being watched.

I finished my drink and bought another one. I was about to reach for it when Tony sat down next to me and grabbed it. "Thanks," he said.

I didn't respond. Tony looked over my shoulder and took a gulp of the whiskey. "How old are you, Wendell?"

"Thirty-two."

"Ah, so you wouldn't remember El Mozote."

"I've read about it, but it was before my time. I'm half in the bag, so refresh me."

"Well, back in eighty-one, the Salvadoran army was shitting their pants over their problems with the Marxist rebels, and America being America, we were wiping their asses for them, financially. A unit of the army arrived at the village of El Mozote after a firefight with the guerillas, and they ordered all the villagers outside and into the square. First they separated the men, the women, and the children. They tortured most of the men first, then they killed them. Then they started in on the women."

He killed his drink. "Raped pretty much all of them, even the girls. Machine-gunned 'em afterward. Decided the people they'd just committed an atrocity looking for weren't there, set fire to the houses, moved on. I was doing photography for the *Times* back then. When we got there, this was all over a month past. Bodies piled up as far as the eye could see, so many of them it was like they were part of the ground. You ever imagine you hear a sound, even if it's not actually there, just because it makes sense that you'd hear that sound? Screams. That's what I heard. Nothing but screams. This little girl told me how she'd been raped in front of her parents, and when her mother tried to stop it, one soldier was about to shoot her, but his commanding officer said they'd need bullets for men. So the soldier bayonetted her instead. And while this little girl was telling me all this, I must have looked pretty horrified, because she looked at me with this face like, 'What the fuck gives *you* the right to be appalled by this? You, you fuckin' middle-class white man from Howard Beach who came here of your own volition, you haven't earned the right to turn away. It happened to *me*, and this experience will be with me for the rest of my life, and I'm telling you all this without even a change in my expression. Who the *hell* do you think you are, thinking you get to turn away?'"

He set the glass down on the bar. "She was right. Without having to say anything, she was right. You and I, we'll never understand what it's like to live with the possibility—the likelihood—that there are people out there who will hurt us this way, given the chance, and they'll have help at an institutional level. Women, young and old, rich and poor, black, white, brown, yellow, that's the possibility they live with. But they just keep going. They don't get to turn away when it seems like too much. You can't turn away when you're surrounded."

I slid my glass down the bar. "Did you come here to tell me I'm lucky to be a man, Tony? 'Cause I knew that. I'm not drinking because I'm a man. I'm drinking because I got twelve women killed."

"Here's what I came here to tell you, Wendell: it's easy to be idealistic when you're still a virgin. You want to really make a difference? Keep trying after you've seen what people can do to each other. If you can't do that, it doesn't really count for anything, does it?"

"Are we the good guys, Tony?" I asked. I don't know why I asked such a stupid, infantile question, but in my defense I do not hold my liquor well.

"Shit no," Tony said. "We do what we do because we can't help ourselves. We have a compulsion disguised as a calling. Whether you turn that to a good end is entirely up to you."

A text buzzed in his pocket, and he leaned back to check. His eyes went wide as he looked at the screen.

"What's up?" I asked. "Who is it?"

"My guy in the staties," he said, still looking at the phone. "One of the women's still alive."

CATALDO

Nothing about the arrangement with Crowning felt right in hindsight, but what especially felt wrong were all the specific instructions he gave me. First the creepy asshole gave me a rifle to do the deed even though I told him I was no good with a rifle. Then he told me to leave it there after I was done, even though that was insane. ("I will take care of it" is not an explanation, guy.) Then after I fucked up the hit (because *I am no good with a rifle,* you dick), he told me not to worry, that the deal had been called off, and that I could keep the *five million fucking dollars* as a courtesy.

It's an awful feeling, knowing you're getting played but having no idea how.

Five days later, I was sitting on the outdoor patio at the boss's lodge upstate with the boss and two other guys. It was late November and cold, and it looked vaguely like snow, but the Old Man insisted we sit outside. One of the other guys, I knew. He was a big guy in his sixties with the face of a boxer who quit too late to be pretty but still early enough that his face didn't scare kids. Everyone called him "Soldato." I have no idea if that was a name or a description, but it worked either way.

Soldato was the only one standing; the other guy was someone whose face I'd seen, but I couldn't remember his name. He was about my age and was doing a bad job of concealing how scared he was.

Old Man Dellaponte took a drag on his cigarette and looked out past the table over his backyard. He turned to look at the other seated guy. "Giuseppe, you know Carmine Sandrelli, right?"

"Sure," I said. I nodded to Carmine.

"You drink tea, Carmine?" the Old Man asked. Carmine looked like he wasn't sure if this was a trick. Dellaponte got sick of waiting for him to answer and said, "Soldato. Go make us some tea. Warm us right up."

Soldato nodded and walked toward the sliding glass door. Dellaponte raised a finger as Soldato put his hand on the door handle. "Leave the bags in, yeah?"

The boss turned back to me and Sandrelli. "Carmine is a smart guy," he said, talking to me but looking at Sandrelli. "Got a lot of respect for a smart guy like him. But the thing about a smart guy is, sometimes, he thinks that because he's smart, everyone else is stupid. Which is really not the same thing at all. Like Carmine, he makes pickups for me. Various people and entities. Comes out to twenty thousand a month he brings me. Always cash, always on the last of the month. Like fuckin' clockwork. So I'm going over the books the other day, when what do I find but, for the last seven months, I been getting fifteen thousand a month from Carmine. Now, what's that come out to that I ain't got for seven months?"

"Thirty-five thousand," Sandrelli mumbled.

"You hear how quick he did that?" Dellaponte said. "Told you he's smart. Now, I talk to the various people Carmine's responsible for making pickups from, and every single one of them insists they paid in full. Strangest fuckin' thing. Ah! Here we go!"

Soldato came back out with the tea on a tray. As tense as the atmosphere was, a guy like him carrying a tea tray gave me a really unhealthy urge to laugh out loud. Soldato set the cups down on the table. Dellaponte took his and nodded for us to do the same. I took a sip of mine. It would have been unbearably hot if it hadn't been so cold out.

"No, not you, Carmine," Dellaponte said. "Not yet." He sighed and looked across the table. "I mean, I understand why you did what you did, Carmine. Money makes us stupid. Nothing—not a fine pair of tits, not drugs, not family—nothing makes a smart man stupid quite like money. Because like I say, Carm, I know you're a smart guy. You think on your feet, which is very important. That's why I'm gonna let you make this right." He jerked his head toward a wastebasket in the corner of the patio. "Soldato. Bring that over here."

Soldato set the wastebasket next to Sandrelli's chair and stood behind him. Dellaponte leaned forward. "Now, Carmine, here's the deal," he said. "You lift the bag out of that mug and drop it in the trash without a drop falling in the meantime, all is forgiven. You understand?"

Sandrelli didn't say anything. He looked like he was trying to figure out if the Old Man was serious. "While we're young, Carmine," Dellaponte said.

Finally, Sandrelli raised a hand toward the cup of tea. He began closing his fingers before they even reached the string, holding it for a second without lifting it, as though he liked the way it felt between his fingers. Then he inhaled and lifted the bag out, slowly. He took his time pulling it over the table, toward him and the wastebasket. It was hovering over the edge of the table when, suddenly, his hand gave a violent spasm and a big fat drop landed on the table where the metal rim met the glass.

Sandrelli slowly looked up and opened his mouth like he was about to say something when blood exploded from where his right eye had been. Soldato stuck his gun back in his overcoat and lifted Sandrelli's chair from under him.

Dellaponte turned back toward me as though nothing had happened. "Thank you for your punctuality, Giuseppe," he said. "Sorry I made you wait."

"No problem at all, Mr. Dellaponte," I said. "So, ah, first off, I guess you heard about the Russians."

"I did, I did," he said, rolling a cigarette between his fingers. "That's . . . that's troubling to hear. And these are the same people that clipped Russell?"

"They say they are."

"Giuseppe, when Russell's ticket got cancelled, I seem to recall I told you to contain this. This doesn't sound like it's contained."

"All due respect, Mr. D., the cops got to it the same time I did. Everyone's watching it now and it's hard to contain it as a result."

"Fair enough. I hear the cops are all in on this after what happened to the Russians."

"That's what Brickman says. He's on this task force they assembled, so I'll be able to update you."

"Is he in charge of the task force?"

"Nah, it's not one of yours. Little Irish *puttana*." Nothing gets on his good side like gratuitous Italian. "Connelly or something. Real hard-ass, from what Brickman says."

Dellaponte curled his lip back. "I know the type. Busts your balls until you put her in charge, cries and makes you look like the asshole if you ever second-guess any of her shitty decisions." He stubbed out his cigarette. "Nobody plays their part anymore. The world is going to hell. These bitches who killed Russell? They never could have existed without women like her."

"Well, I also wanted to let you know, it sounds like she's a cowgirl. She may try to talk to you."

Dellaponte glowered over his tea. "This is starting to sound like a person we don't want in the picture."

"Mr. Dellaponte, that really is not the way we want to go with this. Now, you want me to contain this? Well, I can't do that if I got cop-killer heat on me. This is not a thing it's safe to even think about."

"Okay, point taken, Giuseppe. Make sure eyes are kept on her, yeah?"

"Yeah, of course."

Soldato walked me to my car and thanked me for coming out, like it was something nice I did as opposed to a response to a death threat.

The sun was going down as I turned onto I-81. It was a long drive to make every week, but I didn't mind. I rarely get to drive alone, so this would be pretty much the only time I could listen to my music without feeling self-conscious.

The best genre in American history, hands down, is the colored girl groups from the early '60s. The Crystals, the Blossoms, the Supremes . . . all of that is some of the greatest shit ever recorded. No one can do what they did anymore. The artists nowadays who get the closest all seem to be limeys for some reason, like that chick with the beehive who flamed out or that little chubby broad who won all those awards, the one who talks like Audrey Hepburn in *My Fair Lady*. They're okay, but they still can't touch the girl groups at their peak. Something about listening to them just takes me back to a time I wasn't even around for; this brief, shining moment in the early '60s where we were gonna be okay and everything was going to work out class-wise and race-wise, before Lee Harvey Oswald slapped us awake.

As "Little Boy" cued up, I wondered about the boss. What I'd seen scared me. He was never a choir boy—none of us are—but he never used to like to fuck with people before either. That shit with the tea bag—what was the point? To send a message? Killing him sent the message. Nobody would ever know the details beyond that. The only reason to kill a man like that was that you enjoyed inflicting pain. That's a bad way for the person who calls the shots to think.

I was worried that killing a cop had even occurred to him as well. That was the oldest rule in the book. Hell, it was older than the book. We had that rule even back in the wild old days—back in the '30s, Dutch Schultz got it in his head he was gonna clip Thomas Dewey, the big-shot prosecutor who was getting to be a pain in the ass. The commission found out and they killed Schultz while he was taking a piss.

I got back to the city around eight. I sat down on a bench overlooking the East River and waited for Brickman to show up.

I've talked about how this line of work means tolerating unpleasant people, and Howard Brickman was the best possible example of that. He was the kind of cop the NYPD desperately wanted you to believe they'd completely purged in the '70s. When he spoke, you could just see him walking the beat and grabbing an apple out of some poor schmuck's cart, taking a bite, and smiling like he dared him to say something.

He showed up about ten minutes later, wearing a cashmere topcoat over a dark blue Hugo Boss.

"Jesus," I said. "Is that new?"

"Newish."

"Did you just come from the station?"

"Yeah."

"What the fuck are you doing wearing shit I paid for around the station, Howie? What the hell purpose does that serve? Are you doing some deep undercover thing where you entrap me by being so fuckin' stupid?"

"You want what I got or not, Joe?"

I sighed and crossed my arms, well aware I looked like a kid being forced to apologize to his sister. "Yeah, I want what you got."

"Okay, Kinneavy's gonna come to you, her and Lauder, the spook I told you about. They're gonna be asking around about Milazzo, and I know you don't know shit about who killed him, but be ready to lie if they ask you about what he got up to."

"Noted."

"Also, there's two red-on-reds on my desk that they're not talking about because of all this Judith shit."

"Red-on-red" was cop-talk for one criminal popping another.

"Yeah? Who?"

"Big-time Puerto Rican coke dealer and some Dominican pimp. I'll probably let it go cold but they were both in your area, so I figured maybe you'd wanna look into it."

"Send me some names, I'll see if it's anything."

Frankie O'Halloran sat down on the other side of me without a word. He looked over at Brickman. "Fuck off."

Brickman looked pissed, but like all bullies, he knew not to punch above his weight. I slipped him a hundred and he jogged down the sidewalk.

Unlike some other associates of the family, I didn't have any experience with O'Halloran, and I was happy to keep it that way. We operated out of different parts of town and, for the most part, in different businesses. I couldn't see any possible reason he wanted to talk to me that I would like.

"So, Joe," he said, "you're a smart enough guy to have already figured this out, but Judson Crowning is not a man you want to dance with."

"I did figure that out."

"Before or after you took his money to do a hit? You don't see anything off with a guy paying you five mil for doing nothing?"

"What are you trying to tell me? That he's trouble? I know he's trouble."

"First, clean the money. Do whatever you want. I dunno, go to Atlantic City, play a single hand with it and cash out. Whatever you want. Second, and here's where you can make some real money, anything else he approaches you about, you bring to me, and there's some real money in that for you."

"Frankie, seriously, why you breakin' my balls like this? Everybody's breakin' my balls, tellin' me what to do. I mean, not to sound like a little kid or nothing, but I'm not a fuckin' intern."

He lit a stogie the length of my forearm. "I'm not making you do anything, Joe. I'm makin' a proposition. Because if he approaches you again—and sure as you're born, he will—you'll want someone on your side."

"Frankie, our only connection is that you turned a colleague of mine into Terri Schiavo. Why the fuck am I supposed to believe you're on my side?"

He exhaled smoke over the river. "I need things to work the way they're supposed to work, just like you do, Joe. There's a ripple effect. We may not all be friends or partners, but all the cogs need to turn the same way. Crowning is a gremlin. He keeps things from working, at least in our world. And because he has no interest in things running as they're supposed to, I can't predict him. There is no one worse than someone you can't predict." Without warning, he pulled the cigar out of his mouth and pressed the lit end against his cheek.

I jumped up off the bench. "Jesus Christ!"

He laughed and threw the cigar into the river. "Sorry, Joe. Just making a point. So we got a deal?"

I nodded; I didn't want to speak because that would mean opening my mouth to the smell of burning meat.

"Great," he said. "Give me a call next time he gets in touch." He got up and walked off. I could still see smoke coming from his face as he disappeared down the sidewalk. I was starting to lose hope of ever doing business with anyone who wasn't shithouse crazy.

KINNEAVY

Donnie clawed at the fringe of dark hair sticking up near his hairline. That only made it stick up higher.

"You're making it worse, sweetie," I said from the passenger seat.

"Don't call me 'sweetie,' that's harassment."

"Oh, bite me, I call everyone 'sweetie.'"

Donnie spread his hands like he was envisioning a newspaper headline. "NYPD Vixen: 'I Harass Everybody.'" I punched him lightly in the shoulder.

We had a meeting with the mayor at three and both us of were dolled up to the best of our ability. I was wearing a skirt/blouse/blazer combo in various shades of blue, and I was wearing dark eyeliner, another thing I would normally never do. My mother always said it brought out my eyes, but I'm pretty sure it just makes me look like I'm stepping up to the plate. Donnie was dressed like a *GQ* model but was still carrying himself like a high schooler who was terrified to ask Jenny Wasserstein to homecoming, which kind of robbed the suit of its effect. Neville had volunteered to have us brief the mayor on how the case was going, another prong of her preemptive-strike school of PR.

We'd gotten there forty-five minutes early, and I didn't want to leave the warmth of the car until it was absolutely necessary. A gray, hateful cold had descended on the city over the past week. Cold makes me nervous. It's nothing to do with the actual temperature (bitch, please, I'm an Irish girl from the Northeast). My first collar after I got my shield four years ago was a gang leader who was rumored to have cartel ties. In my gung-ho greenness, I still insisted on being the one to escort him to his sentencing. We had just reached the courthouse's block when I noticed a man coming from the other direction as though he was heading directly for us. I couldn't help but notice that he was wearing a full-length coat even though it was June. In the second or so I spent figuring out what that might imply, I had the presence of mind to dive for the pavement just as he pulled a revolver from his belt and pointed it at my heart.

Because I dove when I did, the shot tore off a bit of my left breast rather than hitting me square in the chest. A ridiculous amount of blood and pain, but not a death sentence. (Captain Neville said they call that an Italian mammogram, but I think she made that up.) Donnie tackled the guy and cuffed him before he could get another shot off. Ever since that whole experience, I'm always jumpy when it gets cold. When everyone's wearing a coat, you never know what's coming.

Sitting in the car was getting to Donnie; he had longer legs than his car was intended for, and he couldn't sit still for long. He opened the door and we got a blast of cold air like someone had punched out an airplane window.

"Agggh, no, close it, you dick," I said.

"Nope. Not sitting here," he said. "I'll find a lobby to wait in. Join me or don't." He locked the door and Froggered his way around the cars on Broadway. I rolled my eyes, opened the door, and followed him.

My experience in city hall has been minimal, and I like it that way. We as people have a need to place each other in as few categories as possible. I'm a college-educated woman who loves Yeats and Blake, and I'm also a second-generation cop from a working-class neighborhood. People who want to know everything about me without having to, you know, talk to me don't know what to do with all of that, so they tend to cherry-pick whichever bits they like the least. At the station, to the cops who don't like me, I'm a smug bitch who thinks she's smarter than everyone. On the other hand, when I get shit at city hall, it's because I'm just dumb white trash who thinks the mayor owes her an audience even though she never quite lost the neighborhood accent. I know I shouldn't bitch too much about this—it'd be a thousand times worse on both levels if I wasn't white.

We went through the metal detectors and waited outside the mayor's office. Donnie said he wished he had brought a book at least twice. When there were about ten minutes to spare, a girl of about seventeen with a pixie cut sat down next to us with a sheaf of papers. She was breathing heavily and looked close to tears.

"Is . . . is Mr. Crowning here?" she asked the reception-ist. The receptionist nodded and buzzed him. The office door opened a second later, and the stiff-looking guy from the press conference emerged. The girl walked up to him in a sort of speed-stumble, like she expected to be beheaded and wanted to get it over with.

"Mr. Crowning, I'm so sorry!" she said. "I thought I had everything when I left this morning—I mean, I *know* I had everything—but now I can't find the transportation memo anywhere, and I think I must have left it on the train. I'm sorry, I'm so sorry!"

Crowning hovered his hand over the girl's shoulder without actually making contact. "Krista, listen to me. Calm down. It's fine. You're fine. Every memo I give to the interns, I make at least two backup copies. Just come by my office and I'll give you one. Just calm down."

Krista nodded and tried to steady her breathing.

"Deep breaths," Crowning said.

"Thanks, Mr. Crowning. Thank you so much."

"It's fine, Krista. It's fine. Go pick one up, they should be in the outgoing tray. I think they're at the top, but if you have to dig, please put everything back, okay?"

"Okay."

Krista disappeared down the hall. Crowning turned to us. "Ah, hello. You're early. Judson Crowning, chief of staff to the mayor." He pronounced it like one word, as if "Crowning" were his middle name and "Chiefofstafftothemayor" his last. "Please, come in. We're ready for you."

We followed Crowning into the mayor's office and took a seat in front of his desk. Crowning stood behind the mayor's desk and looked us both in the eye. The whole thing looked like a magazine ad for a political drama on a channel you had to steal from your neighbor.

"So," the mayor said, "how goes it? The investigation, I mean."

I spoke first. "Well, Mr. Mayor, we've got a running profile of Judith's members. They're predominantly white, at least one of them has extensive police or military firearms training, the others less so, there are between eight and ten members, they operate in areas with which they're intimately familiar—which suggests their membership is primarily Manhattan based, with some knowledge of Brooklyn. I'm afraid we can't tell you much beyond that." I glanced at Crowning and got a great, grinchy idea. "We're also trying to figure out specific people they may

130

target. We've obtained a laptop belonging to Russell Milazzo, the second victim, with his client list."

Crowning's eyes widened. I could see it, the mayor couldn't. Fuckin' A.

"Really?" the mayor said. "So who've you been looking at?"

"Well, a lot of the list is organized crime figures. We haven't had much luck with them, so we're considering expanding to the other names on the list."

"When you say other, who do you mean?"

Crowning was digging his fingernails into the headrest of the mayor's chair. The mayor was leaning forward, so he didn't notice.

"Well, they're mostly low-level city employees. I can't remember any names off the top of my head."

"City employees? That's a problem. I'm definitely gonna want to look at those names at some point."

"Well, Mr. Mayor, we're gonna be sitting on those names for the duration of the investigation. I know youse guys want to clean house—I get that, I do—but any action taken against them could compromise the investigation." The "youse" was deliberate, in case you were wondering.

The mayor looked a little pissed off, in the same way a person stuck in a crowded space looks pissed off—just because he didn't like it didn't mean he could do anything to fight it. The mayor, as it happened, had been a big booster of Commissioner Clarkson's more controversial initiatives, and fighting the NYPD on anything—particularly during an ongoing investigation—would fuck up their united front. He leaned back in his chair. Crowning saw it coming and removed his fingertips.

"The two of you are doing some fine work, and I appreciate you touching base like this," he said. He drew out the second "you." "Is there anything else?"

"Nothing major, sir," Donnie said. "If anything occurs to us that we think city hall should know, we'll definitely inform you."

"Great," he said, in a tone that suggested it was not particularly great. He rose from his chair; Crowning jumped back a bit. The mayor extended his hand. "Thank you both for coming in. You know your way out?"

"Actually, is there a ladies' room close by?" I asked as I shook his hand.

"It's unisex," Crowning piped up. "It's down the hall."

"Thanks," I said. I strode off down the hall until I reached the restroom. I washed my hands and studied my eyeblack-looking mascara in the mirror when I saw Judson Crowning enter the bathroom. He flicked the lock shut.

"Detective Kinneavy."

I turned around to face him. "Unlock that door right now."

"Detective, I'd just like to talk to you about a few things—"

"We're not talking about anything unless you unlock that door."

He sighed and unlocked it. "Are you proud of yourself for that?"

"For telling you to unlock the door?"

"For that foolishness in the office."

"Foolishness? It confirmed my hunch. Call me crazy, but when I hear something from a gangster, I look for confirmation elsewhere."

"How is any of this relevant to your investigation?"

"You don't think they'll target you?"

"I have a security detail, Detective. I get the sense that your interest is more in actively antagonizing me, and I don't fucking appreciate it."

"Mr. Crowning, antagonizing you is pretty goddamn low on my list of priorities. I was told to watch out for you and I wanted to confirm whether or not that was true. And if your reaction in there didn't confirm that for me, the fact that you thought this was a discussion best had in a locked room definitely does."

He moved over to the sink very quickly. He stood over me, again making no physical contact but getting very close to it. He wasn't invading my personal space so much as planting a flag and annexing it. "Detective," he said, "you need to forget about that client list, and you need to stop talking to that reporter. The investigation may be your first priority, but I assure you, it is not his."

"You know what you sound like, Mr. Crowning?" I said. "You sound like you have something to hide. I think maybe you should stop digging if you want my sole focus to be on Judith, because I don't like people who think they can intimidate me, even if they don't pay to rape Ukrainian teenagers."

"You are playing an unhealthy, unproductive game, Detective."

"Oh, I know exactly what I'm doing, Mr. Crowning." I drew myself up to my full height and leaned in even closer to him. "You think it scares me? I love this shit. This shit gets me wet."

He winced noticeably at my word choice. "Oh, I'm sorry, Mr. Crowning. Am I making you uncomfortable?"

He snatched back his composure. "My comfort is immaterial."

"So you say. You don't like to touch people, I notice."

"Physical contact is an act of intimacy. We as a people overuse it and rob it of that intimacy."

"So I guess Krista the intern's not your type, then."

He looked genuinely angry at that. "Krista is excellent at her job. I have no such interest in her beyond that."

"Thanks for the reassurance, Mr. Crowning. I'd like to leave now."

He stared at me for a second and then stepped out of the way.

As I walked to the door and opened it he turned around. "You look lovely, Detective."

"Aww, you're sweet. I'd thank you, but I think we have different ideas of loveliness."

"You should thank me anyway, to be polite."

"Yeah, I should. We know I'm all about politeness. Thank you, Mr. Crowning." I curtsied. God save the Queen.

Donnie had waited for me by the elevator. He was silent until we got to the car, at which point he immediately said, "So what the *hell* is the deal with the mayor's chief of staff?"

"Well, he appears to be literally psychotic."

"That doesn't sound exotic enough. He strikes me more as some kind of human-passing genie."

"Is that why you didn't want to talk about him until we were out of the building?"

"Yes! Tell me he doesn't seem like the kind of guy who'd come around the corner right when you were talking about him. Or not even come around the corner, like, fuckin' materialize."

"Turn the heat up, will you?" I pulled my peacoat on over my blazer. "Fuckin' winter, man."

"You could always transfer to Miami."

"I'd rather get shot again."

Contrary to what I'd told the mayor, we'd pretty much entirely dispensed with the client list. Our main focus was on the Rivette trial, on which Wendell was discreetly keeping me posted. Wysocki, meanwhile, had made the closest thing yet to a breakthrough. A friend of his in Narcotics had taken a piece off a dealer and, on a hunch, asked Wysocki if they could compare notes on ballistics. Sure enough, the gun was the same as one of those used in the Zhar-Ptitsa, which would seem to confirm my theory about them having a pipeline. That is, unless they had sold it themselves, but Wysocki's friend said that even though the guy wasn't talking in terms of where he got the gun, he'd repeatedly referred to the seller using male pronouns.

Donnie had to rejoin Lyndstrom and Torrio in their stake-out of Rivette as soon as we finished up at city hall. He dropped me off at the station and headed uptown. I went to the stairwell and called Wendell on my cell.

"Wendell, the prostitutes you talked to before all this started, for that earlier series you did . . . were any of them users?"

"A few. None of them were hard core. The ones who are like that, the pimps would never let them talk to press. Why?"

"Can you do me a huge favor and see if any of them know a Ricardo Tennyson from Fordham? They're not going to talk to a cop, and I really don't have the time to build up that kind of trust with anyone."

"Is this Judith related?"

"I can't tell you any of that."

"But I'm still expected to help you?"

"Well, I dunno about 'expected.' I guess I just figured your memory of me when I'm angry would do most of the arguing on my behalf."

"That is some lazy-ass intimidation."

"Like I said, strapped for time."

"I'll talk to some people after the Rivette verdict. If I come through, you have to buy my boss a drink whenever he wants."

"No."

"Oh, by the way, Kinneavy, I got another Judith letter."

"Oh shit, really?"

"Yeah, it talks about Gill and Augustine, but it just reached me yesterday. It, ah, it addresses you by name." He paused while he presumably scrolled through the letter. "Here it is:

'Detective Kinneavy should be monitoring men like Martine Rivette all the time, not only when it might give her an opportunity to catch us.'"

My heart was in my mouth. "Wendell, do me one more solid: please don't run that letter until we have a chance to talk."

"Huh?"

"Wendell, it's really important. And I'm sorry, but I'm gonna have to go at you with the full force of the department if you publish without us talking."

"Well, not for nothing, Kinneavy, but you're kind of asking me to compromise myself as a journalist."

"I'm asking you not to fistfuck our investigation. Okay? Please, Wendell."

I heard him sigh on the other end. "Okay, Kinneavy. As a favor. And if I come out of our meeting and I'm not convinced, I'm running it unedited."

"Do what you think is best." I hung up and walked up the stairs and didn't stop until I got to the series of cubicles arranged in a box shape in the corner of the bull pen. Neville had set it up after the restaurant massacre to serve as a de facto office until hers, now a crime scene, was cleared to use again. You could hear what people inside it were saying if you got close enough, but everybody knew not to. "Captain," I said, "we have a leak."

She sat bolt upright. "What?"

"We have a leak in the task force. Somebody knows we're sitting on Rivette. My guy at the *Septima* just got a letter from them confirming it."

Neville sighed and emptied her skull ashtray into her wastebasket, scraping a few stubborn ashes out of the rim with her little finger. Then she whirled around and flung the empty skull against the wall. "Mother*fucker*!" She turned back to me. "Have you told anyone?"

"No."

"Smart. Keep not telling anyone. Not even Klein."

"You don't think *Donnie* can be trusted?"

"I know he can be trusted. But I've got my share of experience in leaky divisions and we need to make sure no one else knows. Doesn't matter whether or not we can trust them. The leak stays between you, me, and your boyfriend."

"He's not my . . ."

"Kinneavy, seriously, pick your fuckin' battles. Do you like anyone for the leak?"

"Brickman, if I had to guess."

"No, you just think Brickman's a dick. Which is a totally valid, normal human emotion, don't get me wrong. Do you have *actual reason to believe* anyone specific in the task force is the leaker?"

"Not at present."

"You have any reason, let me know immediately."

"Will do."

It was getting dark. I got a text from Jalisa asking if I wanted dinner at her place. Ugh, yes, you angel of mercy and free food, that was exactly what I needed.

Jalisa lived in this amazing suite in Manhattan Beach. The commute to Centre Street was a pain in the ass, but to her mind, it was worth it to live that close to the ocean. I let myself in. Nina Simone's *Pastel Blues* was on Jalisa's stereo and she had just put fried eggplant in the oven. She offered me a beer from the fridge.

"I shouldn't," I said, before taking it anyway. I twisted the cap off. "So how goes the trial?"

"Uh-uh. No." She held up a hand. "This night is free of work talk."

"That bad, huh?"

"Nah, not that bad, but we're not down to the wire yet. Rivette and the vic both take the stand tomorrow."

I winced. "How do you feel?"

"K, we are not talking about this right now. We are here to unwind. You wanna take your work home with you, you can teach."

"I'm not at home."

She laughed. "You should be homeboy's lawyer." The food was done. Jalisa grabbed a floral oven mitt from the stove and pulled the pan out of the oven, scooping the servings onto sliced pita bread with a spatula. She set our plates down in front of us and clinked her beer against mine.

"*Sláinte*," I said, taking a sip and then trying the food. It was amazing, naturally. I don't know how she does it. My version of gourmet is something I have to rotate during the microwaving process.

"This is fantastic, Jalisa. Thanks so much."

"No need. Mind if I open a window?"

"J, it's like twenty-eight out."

"Just a crack."

"It's your apartment. I'ma get my scarf, though."

Jalisa cracked the window. The wind had calmed down, so there was still cold air, but it wasn't as actively hostile. Jalisa inhaled and smiled.

"You remember my uncle's place on the Cape?"

I nodded. I loved that house. I'd been up three different summers.

"Well," Jalisa said, "one winter Uncle Harold asked if I'd come up and help him install some insulation. And every night I was up there, I'd go up to the roof deck he had up there and just look out over Nauset Beach and smell the breeze off the Atlantic." She put down her fork. "I smell that smell, that sea breeze on a cold night, and I feel like that's what heaven feels like."

"Hm. I was raised Catholic, so I've put a lot more thought into hell."

"Yeah? What's hell?"

"I'd have to say it's the worst moment of your life, only it's transcended being a moment and becomes something else, something infinite."

Jalisa raised an eyebrow. "You *did* put a lot of thought into this."

"Oh, that wasn't just thought. I've been."

Jalisa sighed. "Katherine, are you doing okay? You haven't mentioned that in years."

"Yeah, I guess all this Judith shit has me thinking it over."

"You think that's a good state to be in?"

"Jalisa, you think I ever stop thinking about it? Because I don't. Never for very long, anyway. But I still function."

"You just functioning isn't good enough. It might be for you, but not for me."

"J, relax, okay? All I said was that the case made me think about it. If I grew up on a farm, and then I had to investigate the murder of a farmer, it'd make me think about it. It's the same thing. I thought you were the one who said no work talk."

"It's not work talk. I'm worried about you. You got enough of a temper when you're uninvolved. This is not an investigation for that Leeroy Jenkins shit."

"There will be no Leeroy Jenkins shit."

"If you say so."

The wind off the beach picked up, and Jalisa hurried over to close the window. We finished eating and stuck to safe bullshit for our topics of conversation the rest of the meal. I hugged her, thanked her for the meal, and headed home. I hoped I was right and the case wasn't getting to me. When I'm at my low point (and I have been, multiple times), the only comfort is a job I can lose myself in. Give me work that follows me home over a home that follows me to work any day. I got upstairs, flung my scarf and coat into the closet, and collapsed into bed.

ROANE

I still felt vaguely dirty over having withheld the letter at Kinneavy's request. Up to this point, I really didn't like to think of myself as the kind of journalist who does whatever the cops tell him, and it felt like a huge compromise—the bad kind, not the now-everybody-gets-candy kind.

I couldn't be too pissy about it. This was the nature of the beast with any reporter-cop relationship, which, to her credit, Kinneavy explicitly warned me about. My main question was, how much of this resentment was foolish professional pride and how much was that creeping sympathy for Judith that I was worried about developing. Did I resent Kinneavy for stepping on my reportage, or because she was doing it in service of busting Judith?

The last day of the Rivette trial, I had planned to go straight from my apartment to the courthouse, but Tony sent me an email telling me to stop by the office first. I didn't know what he wanted—the two were in opposite directions, which would make it a tight fit, schedule-wise—but I went in anyway, without arguing. Nothing had happened that made or broke the trial for either side: various bits of witness testimony, a lot of which supported the accuser's account, but we were still firmly in reasonable-doubt territory.

When I got to the office, there was a big red-faced guy in a suit with thinning white hair sitting in the waiting area. With him was a younger blond guy. As I walked past them, the older man shot me a look, and I suddenly recognized him. I stuck my head into Tony's office.

"Tony, why is Marvin Devaney in our waiting area?"

"Why, to receive your formal apology, naturally."

"Ain't nothing natural about a formal apology from me."

"Get all of this out of your system before we actually talk to him, okay?"

Rosalind stuck her head into the office behind me. "Did you tell Wendell about the formal apology to Devaney yet? I wanna come."

"No," I said.

"Only if you don't say anything," Tony said. It was hard to tell which response she seemed more upset by.

Devaney and his life partner, or whatever, walked into the conference room ahead of us as soon as they saw us coming. They sat down on the side of the table facing away from the window, which I would have guessed was a power play if it had been someone smarter doing it. Devaney looked confused when Rosalind sat down.

"Who are you?" he said. "Who is this?" he asked Tony, without giving her a chance to answer.

"I'm their bodyguard," Rosalind said. "Who's your guy?"

Devaney's guy spoke up. "My name's Harvey Gunderson. I'm Mr. Devaney's legal counsel."

"Um, okay," Tony said. "What's happening today that you need legal counsel present?"

Devaney glared at me across the table. "One never knows," he assholed.

Tony cleared his throat. "Well, now," he said. "Let's get down to it. Wendell, anything you'd like to say?"

I met Devaney's eyes, trying my hardest to make the eye contact seem more smug than contrite. "Mr. Devaney, I'm very sorry I told you to suck my dick. It was both sophomoric and unnecessarily homophobic."

There was an awkward silence. After about thirty seconds, we realized neither of them was going to get up and leave.

"Is there, um, is there something else we can help you gentlemen with?" I asked eventually.

"Well, we appreciate the apology, but it really doesn't address the underlying issue that prompted that epithet."

"And what underlying issue would that be?" Tony asked.

"Your publication's continual promotion of a bunch of feminist terrorists, obviously."

Tony looked back and forth from Devaney to me as though he was expecting to be let in on a joke. "What are you even *talking* about?"

"The Judith letters! The ones you keep publishing!"

"Mr. Devaney," Tony said, "I'm really not entirely clear on your objection to the publication of the letters we received, and I don't really care to parse it. I feel like we're getting off the subject. You were invited here to accept an apology from Wendell."

"And I appreciate that, but I want to address your publication of those letters as part of the apology."

"Hold on. No. 'Part of' the apology? Uh-uh. That's not how it works. The actual apology—the one you just got—is the only 'part of' the apology. That's what the word means."

"Well, I'm afraid that's not going to be sufficient."

"Oh, it's not going to be sufficient? What would be sufficient?"

"I'd like to review anything you publish specifically relating to these terrorists. You don't seem like you have a very firm grasp on what'll incite people, frankly."

The dragon was awake. Tony seemed to grow about a foot in his chair. "Mr. Devaney, are you asking for final cut on what I publish, here at my newspaper? We already have someone who does that. He's called an editor, and he's me. If you want to do some kind of *Trading Places* thing, that could be pretty funny, but no, you do not get long-term editorial control of somebody else's publication."

Devaney cleaned his glasses. "Well then, maybe we'll have to go back to the drawing board as far as a boycott of your advertisers."

"Oh, is that what you're gonna do? You're gonna boycott us for publishing letters—newsworthy letters—that we're sent? Let me tell you how things work, Mr. Devaney: I decide what my employees do, just like you decide what your employees do. And if anyone holds us accountable for what we publish, it'll be our readers, and as things currently stand, we're nearing a record high in terms of circulation. You make me sad, Mr. Devaney. You make me so unbelievably sad. Your ideology isn't even religious or political. You simply disdain information on principle. You don't want five-year-olds to be taught evolution or teenage girls to be told where they can get the pill or our readers to have newsworthy information they won't get any-where else. Your agenda is literally the reduction of knowledge. You *want* to be of negative value to the world at large. What a depressing *fucking* goal for anyone to have."

Devaney pushed back from the table, his teeth clenched so tightly it looked like his skull might cave in.

"You're going to regret speaking to us this way, Mr. *Mendelsohn*," he spat.

"Mr. Devaney, trust me, I already regret speaking to you," Tony responded.

Devaney stood up and stalked out the door. Gunderson gave us a semiapologetic nod of acknowledgment and followed him. As soon as they were gone, Tony let out a short, sharp breath.

"Wendell, it's my turn to apologize. I have never met someone more deserving of being told to suck your dick."

"But not to actually do it, right?"

"God, no. You are way out of his league."

"Aww, I thought he was a sweetheart," Rosalind said. "Call me crazy, I just think ill-disguised contempt for everyone you meet is precious."

"Okay, you're crazy," I said. I swung my messenger bag across my shoulder. "I gotta get to the courthouse."

I arrived too late to ambush Rivette as he got out of his Rolls, but then, I didn't represent that kind of publication. I represented the kind of publication where the reporters and the editors both told reactionary Catholic blowhards to fuck off.

The press gallery was predictably crowded. I was stuck next to a guy I was pretty sure was from the *Times* who smelled like rubbing alcohol, for some reason. Rivette took the stand first, a heavyset gray-haired guy resplendent in a full fuck-you-I'm-rich ensemble. Even his cuff links seemed precisely angled for the diamonds to catch the light. His lawyer was also French, but the best kind of French—a charming, good-looking guy in his midforties with an accent that wasn't thick or distracting.

As Rivette was sworn in, his lawyer walked him through the evening the accuser said the assault took place. Rivette denied anything nonconsensual took place; rather, he said, he had suspected the accuser was coming on to him and discreetly asked her to come up to his room later, telling her there was five hundred dollars in it for her. "She brought me up to six hundred before she agreed. She was . . . eager," he explained.

I decided I was not a fan of this guy. Even if he was telling the truth—and I wasn't there, so I didn't know—the scorn in his voice as he described a transaction in which he was a willing participant was infuriating.

After a little while of this, Rivette's lawyer had no further questions, and the ADA approached the witness stand to cross-examine. She was a poised black woman in pearl gray.

"Mr. Rivette, you said you told the accuser to 'come up later that evening' to take you up on your offer?"

"That is correct."

"Just . . . anytime?"

"Yes."

"Why, then, do the hotel call logs indicate that you called for room service just before the assault is alleged to have taken place?"

Rivette shifted his weight a little. "Of course. That was my signal to her."

"Your signal to her specifically was a call in which you said, quote, 'Please send a maid up'?"

"She had . . . we had arranged so that she would be the nearest available staff member."

"How does one arrange that in a hotel that employs two hundred full-time service staff?"

"She was maintaining a position close to the desk."

"She was maintaining a position close to the desk. And you didn't believe any of these details were relevant in your testimony five minutes ago?"

"The point of my testimony was that the encounter was consensual, so no, I did not believe these details were relevant to that point."

"And the bruising on her body, as annotated by a medical report, exhibit D, was this also the result of consensual sex?"

He gave her the most condescending half smile I've ever seen. "My dear, different people have different proclivities. Who am I to judge?"

My dear? Jesus Christ.

"Mr. Rivette, are you honestly telling me that you paid Ms. St. Cyr to perform oral sex on you, and the resultant oral sex was primarily concerned with *her* proclivities?"

"As I've told you, it was a consensual act. Why should a consensual act only involve pleasure in one participant?"

They went on like that for a while. The ADA was amazing, but Rivette had the best asset any defendant can have: the ability to sling obvious bullshit with confidence. Around nine, she finished and Rivette returned to the defendant's table.

Celeste St. Cyr took the stand at approximately eleven. ADA Jalisa Thorpe went over the events of the incident with her. Celeste gave an account consistent with her initial accusations. Rivette, she said, had struck up a conversation with her when she went up to his room in response to the call downstairs. About two minutes in, he had groped her and acted like it was an accident. When she got up to leave, he had stood in her path and forced her to her knees and forced her to perform fellatio on him. Celeste seemed shaken, but she kept her composure throughout. She was a West Indian woman in her early forties with a strong accent and a slight stutter. All of that can help you or harm you, depending entirely on the jury.

Thorpe stepped back as Rivette's lawyer came forward to cross-examine.

"Ms. St. Cyr," he said, "what is your motivation for making these accusations?"

"Pardon?"

"I mean, are you really seeking justice, or profit?"

"Objection!" Jalisa called.

"Mr. Chereau, make your point," the judge said.

"Ms. St. Cyr, for a woman distraught over her sexual assault, you displayed, dare I say, remarkable calmness in this call you made to your brother a mere four hours after you say the assault took place, in which you say you can 'get some money out of it.'"

Celeste's eyes widened. She didn't say anything and then realized he was waiting for her to proceed.

"Mr. Chereau, I don't . . . I make not much money. This terrible thing had just happened to me, but the amount of money I make, and the problems that causes, that is a terrible thing that happens to me every day. My family has medical bills, Mr. Chereau. I have a mother and a brother who can't find work. So before I made my accusations, yes, we discussed seeing if Mr. Rivette would settle out of court."

"So you tried to blackmail Mr. Rivette and went public with your accusations when that didn't work."

"I tried to blackmail no one!" She was yelling now. Which, I guessed, was the entire point. Of course, she hadn't said shit about blackmailing Rivette, but now she was agitated, especially compared to Rivette. Who are you going to believe?

"It's funny, Ms. St. Cyr. You've been talking for quite a long time about being brutalized and raped and you don't seem truly upset until I ask you if this is some sort of scam."

"Your Honor!" Thorpe thundered from behind him.

The judge gave Rivette's lawyer a dirty look. "That's enough, Mr. Chereau," he said. "The jury will disregard Mr. Chereau's last statement."

Except they wouldn't. Can't unring a bell, as they say.

"Ms. St. Cyr, is it true you've talked to literary agents?"

No answer at first.

"Ms. St. Cyr."

"Yes, I have."

"Now perhaps I'm making unreasonable assumptions, Ms. St. Cyr, but I'm guessing you would not be writing a book for free?"

"No, sir, I wouldn't."

"Ah. So is it really unreasonable to—"

"I wouldn't, sir, because I don't think it's shameful to admit I need the money. I am paid hourly, sir. I've been making half of what I usually make because I have had to be in court. I will still have to come up with money for the lawyer I retained before criminal charges were brought against Mr. Rivette. I want to tell my story. Condemn me for that if you like."

He smiled down at her with an almost kind expression, a benevolent god telling his children they were money-grubbing whores for their own good.

"No further questions, Your Honor."

Shortly after, Ms. Thorpe took her place at the front of the courtroom again for her closing summation.

"Ladies and gentlemen," she said, walking back and forth in a way that seemed too artful to be called "pacing"—it was more like a dance step. "Mr. Rivette is excellent at looking and sounding and seeming like he is above something as base as sexual assault. Mr. Rivette has an explanation for everything that seems amiss about this incident, and he hopes that you will equate these ready explanations with innocence. But Mr. Rivette cannot explain why crucial details of his story were only acknowledged when the city brought them up, and he cannot explain how Ms. St. Cyr came by her injuries beyond vague allusions to 'proclivities.' This despite the fact that the only possible time these injuries could have been inflicted is the time he claims to have been involved in a consensual sex act with her. The state offers bruises and welts that could only have been inflicted by him, and Mr. Rivette offers evasions.

Mr. Rivette has victimized this woman and believes he can charm his way out of being held responsible for it and charm his way into victimizing more women. As is so often the case in our justice system, ladies and gentlemen, people may lie, but bruises don't. And those bruises prove, beyond a reasonable doubt, that you must find Martine Rivette guilty."

Rivette's lawyer was still smiling as he stepped up. His accent seemed even less pronounced as he spoke. "Ladies and gentlemen of the jury, Martine Rivette does not claim to be perfect. He does not claim to have engaged entirely in model behavior during his stay in this beautiful city. All he claims is that he did not commit the terrible crime for which he finds himself tried. He has stood by his version of events from the start. And to this, the state responds that he omitted some details. Well, which omission is more suspicious—how a consensual sex act was arranged or the fact that the alleged victim sought to profit from this incident almost immediately? Mr. Rivette tells a story that absolves him of the crime of rape but never pretends that he is a saint among men; Ms. St. Cyr, meanwhile, sold you a story about a woman who works her fingers to the bone, asking nothing in return, and found herself victimized by a rich foreign villain—a story that completely omits the book deal she sought, naturally. When pressed on his story, Mr. Rivette offers explanations even if they do not flatter him; Ms. St. Cyr offers only further excuses and justifications. 'It was my fault' versus 'nothing is my fault.' Ladies and gentlemen, the facts are clear on which side deserves your credulity, and that is why you must acquit Mr. Rivette."

The jury deliberated for about three hours. During that time, I decided to stop being a brat and go ahead and look into Kinneavy's gun dealer. I gave Gabrielle, a sex worker I knew in Queens Village, a call regarding where a fella might get a hot gun. She was an independent operator, which put her in a position where she might need a gun quick. Her piece, she said, came from somewhere in Manhattan, but the guy insisted on going through two other people. Well, that narrowed it down a bit. She was able to give me the name of the second go-between, but strongly advised against talking to him alone. Whee, progress.

At 3:00 p.m., the jury filed back in and announced that they had found Martine Rivette not guilty of the forcible rape and sexual battery of Celeste St. Cyr.

I tweeted the result immediately. Everyone else was busy mobbing Rivette and his lawyer. Rivette was free to go immediately, but I had heard through the grapevine that he was being hustled back to his hotel under armed guard and then straight to a private jet back to France. Unfortunately for him, a private flight couldn't be chartered until eight that evening.

I typed up my story on my laptop on the train from the reserved-for-the-disabled seats. I only allow myself to be that guy once every few months, when it's really important. When I got back to the office, Tony waved me over.

"She wants to talk to you specifically," he said.

"Who does?"

"The foreign woman. The one who's still alive."

"How do they know?"

"She keeps asking for 'Newspaper Wendell.' That's all she'll say. She'll thank them and ask them for food or a new pillow or whatever, but whenever anyone tries to talk to anyone, she just says, 'I want talk to Newspaper Wendell.' Says it in both English and Ukrainian."

"Shit, they don't like me for it, do they?"

"No. Don't worry about that. You were here with me when it happened."

"I don't want to talk to her unless I can guarantee I won't be followed. I don't know if Crowning knows she's alive, but I'm not fucking her over again."

"Wendell, I'm not her manager. You'll have to figure this out yourself."

"Okay, fine. Tony, there's something else."

"What's that?"

"I think Devaney wants us to stop covering Judith for personal reasons."

"Ugh, Wendell, can we please just pretend he doesn't exist?"

"Ton', he was scared. I saw it in his eyes in the meeting."

"Yeah, that's not a basis for anything. Like, at all."

"There's more than that. Did you know Devaney's got a law degree?"

"Yeah. He started out handling litigation for the diocese. So?"

"Did you know he's currently retained by Worldlink?"

Tony leaned forward. "*Really?*"

"Yep. As of a couple months ago."

"Look into that. Compare notes with Rosalind. Good thinking, Wendell."

"There's another thing. Someone with the NYPD wants to meet with me to discuss the most recent Judith letter."

"That's fine. Do what they tell you. We don't need them fucking with us right now. Anything else?"

"That's about it."

"Sweet. Oh, and Wendell, we all really appreciate your punctuality, but our Twitter followers want to know what 'BREAKING: Martine Rivette found not guiltzxs' means."

"That's bullshit, Tony, we don't have Twitter followers."

"Yeah, you got me."

I headed back to my desk. Along the way, I stopped in the kitchen area for a cup of the really strong coffee that Dewayne thinks is hidden from everyone else. I was prepared to stay late tonight, because something told me there was going to be big fucked-up Judith-related news before the night was out.

CATALDO

You remember in *Goodfellas* when De Niro's crew has just pulled off the heist and De Niro's getting all pissed off because they immediately start buying shit like Cadillacs and mink coats for their wives? That's kinda how I am. Even since I made underboss, the only luxury I've allowed myself is the gym in my basement. It's nothing fancy, but it gives me solitude and an outlet for anger, two things I'd been sorely in need of lately.

I was at the heavy bag when the two cops knocked on the door. I knew to expect them, thanks to Brickman, but I still jumped when the woman yelled my name. I whirled around, still breathing heavily.

"Shit, lemme get my towel." I grabbed it off the top of the chin-up bar and pulled it around my shoulders. "What can I do for you?"

The lady was someone I'd seen before, I was realizing. She was the cop from the pier the afternoon Russell's body turned up. I'd never seen the spook before.

She badged me. "Katherine Kinneavy and Derek Lauder, NYPD. I assume you're familiar with the Judith organization, Mr. Cataldo?"

"I wouldn't say I'm familiar. I read about 'em in the paper, but I dunno anything about them beyond that."

"Mr. Cataldo, were you aware that your late associate Mr. Milazzo was involved in sex trafficking?"

"I know it now. I didn't when he was alive."

"That's funny, because plenty of his associates appear to have known about it. You had no idea one of your employees was moonlighting?"

"I heard rumors, sure."

"And you didn't see fit to investigate these rumors?"

"Hey, *sweetie*?" I said. "Do you even fuckin' know what my job involves? I know you think I just drive a muscle car around the block, order a cannoli, and whack a guy, but here's how it works: I wake up, I already got a line out my door. And that's not just people I do business with, that's people in my neighborhood who need a favor, people who need to borrow money, people who are in trouble. That's first thing in the morning. Then I gotta go all around first my neighborhood, then about a dozen fuckin' others not just on the island, but in Queens and the Bronx, and make sure everything's up and running. Then I gotta check in with all my crew chiefs one-on-one. Then I gotta get back to the club I own and take care of anything that needs doing there. And that's on a weekday—weekends I gotta touch base with *my* boss, which is a long fuckin' drive. So no, unlike certain fuckin' institutions, my job leaves me a little too busy to verify every single rumor I hear, okay?"

By the end of this little spiel I was pretty much yelling in her face. She didn't seem to mind.

"You talk about employees, Mr. Cataldo," Lauder said from behind her. "Could any of them have had more intimate knowledge of what Milazzo did than you did?"

I sat down on the bench. "You'd have to ask them."

"Okay, who's 'them'?"

"Paul Magliacci, Nicky Brunaldi, that whole crew. Don't act like you don't already know who all of us are."

"Oh, one more thing, Mr. Cataldo," Kinneavy said. "You said you didn't know for sure Milazzo was involved in trafficking until after he was dead. Did you mean when we told you, or before then?"

Jesus, this twat didn't quit. "I confirmed it for myself."

"How so?"

"I refuse to answer on the grounds that go fuck yourself."

She gasped and turned to Lauder. "Detective Lauder?"

"Yes?"

"Bring me my fainting couch immediately. This horrible man is being a meanie." She turned back to me. "So I don't suppose you had anything to do with the I-80 incident?"

"The which?"

"Jesus, Mr. C., I thought you said you read the papers. The women that got run off the road and shot. Undocumented immigrants, all. Thought you might know something about it, but I guess not."

"Why would I know anything about that?"

"Head shots in the middle of the night? Seemed like your style, is all."

I jumped up from the bench. "This is the first I'm hearing of any of this. And considering I just explained how you know Jacqueline Bouvier Shit about what I do for a living, don't fucking tell me what sounds like my 'style.'" I pointed to the door of the basement. "We're done. Both of youse get the fuck outta here."

Kinneavy smiled and raised an eyebrow. The two of them left the basement, Kinneavy closing the door behind her.

A little while after they left, my landline rang. I answered it and a voice that sounded like Barry White in a shitty mood said, "Mr. Cataldo, this is Cyrus Yale. We've got a problem."

Yale was the closest thing Harlem still had to a boss; like most of Manhattan, it had quieted down in the past ten or fifteen years, but Yale still made out like, excuse the term, a bandit when it came to numbers and blow. I hadn't seen him since around 1995, when the Dellapontes lent him some key support in the crack wars in exchange for an annual fifteen percent cut.

"Ah, okay," I said. "What problem is that?"

"I got a boy, name of Drexel Wilson," Yale said. "Pimp who works out of Hamilton Heights. Harbor Patrol pulled his ass out of the water today with a hole in his head, but he went missing a few weeks ago."

"Not to be rude, Cy, but what's this got to do with me?"

"You ever heard of Yaz Pacheco or Marco Clemente?"

"Rings a bell, but I'm not sure which one."

"They're both dead too. They were a dealer and a pimp, respectively."

Shit. Didn't Brickman say something about a dealer and a pimp?

"Anyway, all three of them operated within a twelve-block radius of your boy Milazzo, and all three of them did shit that he did too. Funny coincidence, don't you think?"

"It is pretty funny. What's even funnier is that Russell Milazzo's dead."

"Oh, I know. All three of them died before he did, though. I can't think of who'd want to besides Mafia, gangbangers, or customers. And not to stereotype, but all three were done pretty Eye-talian. One in the back of the head. Some saggy-pants-ass homeboy is never gonna stop at one shot, and I never met a basehead who could hold a piece steady enough to do the job with one. So I guess what I'm saying is, your Russell was, whatchoo call it, a captain, right?"

"Right."

"So if he's taking out rivals in the trade, he's probably not doing it personally. I'd very much appreciate knowing who else, if anyone, was involved."

"Way I remember it, Cy, you already owe me a favor."

"You think this is just a favor to me? Sheeeeit. We go to war, I couldn't touch you for firepower. But is it in your best interest to have free agents running around killing without permission?"

He definitely had me there. And so did the cop, for that matter. A whole lot of this shit could have been avoided if I'd made time to keep up with what Russell had been up to. Then a thought occurred to me: How did I know Judith had killed Russell? They sure as shit weren't the only people who used knives. Sure, the fucked-up way he'd treated the foreign girls made it understandable why they'd want him dead, but when you're also stepping on the toes of people who kill for a living, chances are they'll get to you first. I ended the call with Yale and gave Brickman a call.

"Howard, do you still have the stuff on those two red-on-reds?"

"Yeah, why?"

"You're a dirty cop and I give you money to be my dirty cop, that's why. Jesus."

"Okay, okay. What do you need to know?"

"Any eyewitnesses?"

"One for the Dominican, a couple for the Rican."

"What do they say?"

"Tall lean white guy fled the scene. Aviators. None of them saw him do anything, they just saw him running away and he wasn't from the neighborhood."

"You like anyone based on that?"

"Oh yeah, Joe, naturally, I'm casing the city for one of its five skinny white guys. His reign of terror putting down spic felons is at an end."

Certain people, no matter how useful they are, get to be such assholes that you start to wonder if it outweighs their usefulness. "You're still nominally a cop, aren't you?"

"Yes, Joe, I am. But you seem to have a pretty naïve idea of what that actually entails."

"Look, Howard, help me out here and see what you can find out about the two red-on-reds. Do you have anything besides the description of the runner?"

"No, Joe. When I have to divide my time between murders that are making *Nancy Grace* and murders that literally nobody but you gives a shit about, which one do you think I'm gonna end up spending more time on?"

"Okay. Jesus. Plenty of people multitask without being hard-ons about it, you know."

"Good for them." He hung up. I needed a new sleazebag.

Business takes precedence over personal issues, obviously, but I was anxious to get back to that church in Brooklyn. It took me a little while to find it again, but once I was in the general area, it was pretty hard to miss. An old priest or rabbi or whatever (he had a weird hat and a beard, so maybe he was a rabbi, I don't know) was sitting in the front pew when I got there.

"Uh, hi," I said. "You, ah, you speak English?"

He looked me over. "No, I don't speak any English because this is 1915," he said. "Can I help you with something?"

"Well, I'm Agent Collingsworth of the Federal Bureau of Investigation, and I got a tip-off about several young women who may have been in the country illegally."

"Ah, them. They're not here. You wanna talk to Father Mirzoyev."

"Where's Father Mirzoyev?"

"You sure you're FBI?"

"Hey, listen, friend, this is not a day to play games with me. I can have your veiny ass deported."

He looked annoyed. "I'm from Little Odessa. Also, I ask because you're here asking about illegal immigrants and threatening to deport me, so I think you may have meant you were INS."

"Ah, yes. Yes, that's what I meant."

He shrugged. "It happens. The other day I accidentally called myself an Imam. Let me get Father Mirzoyev and you can sit here and figure out for sure which institution you're with."

Jesus. I open my mouth, the whole world turns smart.

A younger guy came down the stairs a few minutes later, also with a funny hat and a beard. I walked down the aisle toward him.

"Father, my name's—"

"I know who you are, Mr. Cataldo. I wasn't born in this building. I understand you want to talk about the women."

"Well, yeah, I—"

"And you should know that if you had anything to do with them being taken, I'm probably going to hurt you very badly. I'm sorry I don't have anything more creative, but these are not circumstances I'm used to."

"What do you mean, taken?"

He sighed and waved me over to a bench against the interior wall of the building. He sat down and I followed suit. "How do you know about them?"

"I . . . I found them. An associate of mine brought them into the country without my knowledge, and after he died, I found them and brought them here."

"And you knew nothing about what he'd done to them?"

"I'd heard rumors."

"Rumors." He looked me over. Somehow, just repeating the word and making eye contact, he made me feel about a billion times more shame than the cop had. "Well, Mr. Cataldo, these girls, these girls from the rumors, were arrested by the real INS shortly after you left them here. I have no idea what happened after that, but I doubt it was anything good."

"Okay, are you sure they were real INS?"

"They had badges, uniforms, and guns, but then, I'm not the expert on INS impersonators here."

"Jesus."

"Please don't. This is a church."

"Listen, Father, I'm positive I wasn't followed. Did anyone else know about them?"

"There was a reporter. He didn't write about their location or anything, but he seemed to think *he* had been followed."

"What's his name?"

"Sorry, Mr. Cataldo, I'm not in the habit of telling gangsters where to find people they're angry with."

"I'm not gonna hurt him."

"Not in the habit of trusting their assurances either. No offense meant."

"Father, why would I hurt him? It sounds like he didn't have anything to do with it. I just need to find out what happened to those girls. Okay? I worry about them too."

"Mr. Cataldo, you're a murderer who dumped a liability and now you have slight pangs of conscience. We are nothing alike."

"Really? Even though you threatened me a minute ago?"

That stopped him for a minute. He pushed up his hat and ran his fingers through his hair. "Maybe you're on to something there. Forgiveness and mercy are pretty far from my mind since those women turned up. I'm not sure I believe in a god who asks me to love whoever did these things to them. But some part of me knows that even if we lived in some fantasy world where I could so much as hold a gun properly, any revenge I took would be for my benefit, not for theirs." He shrugged. "So I'm not sure what feeling I should strive for. Maybe that's the true human struggle. To find something that gives us more satisfaction than hate does."

He leaned back on the bench. "The reporter's name is Wendell Roane, Mr. Cataldo. He writes for the *Septima*. I'm telling you because you seem like you have some semblance of decency, besides which if anything happens to him I'll inform the police before you can so much as wash your hands."

I pumped his hand. "Thank you so much, Father. And for what it's worth, I promise you nothing will happen to Mr. Roane at my hands."

"Or your behest. I'm clergy, Mr. Cataldo. I know all the loopholes."

"Or my behest. Thanks again." I pulled on my overcoat and headed out.

KINNEAVY

It was 8:00 p.m. and colder than a witch's tit. From across West Forty-Fourth, I saw Martine Rivette emerge from the revolving door of the Sofitel and head toward his black limo, which was idling at the end of the block. Rivette staggered slightly as he approached the car. He'd probably been celebrating his victory, the fuck.

My gut told me Judith was going to try something tonight. I had a vest on under my peacoat, I'd given my gun more oil than a Texan stock portfolio, and I had the Action Girl mix Jalisa had made for me in my CD player. I know the CD seems like kind of a stupid thing for a grown-ass woman to have on the job, but it had sentimental value and it put me in the right mind-set. Officially, Rivette was heading for LaGuardia and getting the fuck out of Dodge before some women's rights heavy hitter could file a pro bono civil suit on Ms. St. Cyr's behalf. In actuality, he was headed for a Long Island safe house for the remainder of the week. Everyone in the task force was aware of this, but only Captain Neville and I knew just how much we were ramping up security, or that I was tailing Rivette in the first place.

My presence hadn't been part of the plan; it was supposed to be Donnie, but just after I'd finished dinner I'd gotten a call from Neville telling me Donnie's younger sister Angela had had an epileptic seizure, and he had to visit her at Beth Israel. I'd heard Donnie talk about Angela before. She sounded like a sweet kid, and Donnie was utterly devoted to her, so I was happy to spot for him.

I reached down and changed tracks on the CD. Rivette was almost to his car, and I was in the mood for my favorite song in the mix, a live recording of Nina singing "Pirate Jenny."

Then one night there's a scream in the night
And you'll wonder who could that have been
And you see me kinda grinnin' while I'm scrubbin'
And you say, "What's she got to grin?"
I'll tell you.
There's a ship
The Black Freighter
With a skull on its masthead
Will be coming in.

Rivette's limo glided away from the curb and toward the stoplight. I pulled out behind him as discreetly as possible. At the last second, some asshole in a Yugo pulled in between us. "Mother*fucker*," I said, swinging one lane over and pulling up at the light parallel to the limo instead. The windows were tinted, but I could still see the driver's profile. I couldn't figure out why, but something felt off. As the light turned green, I pulled slightly ahead of the limo. I looked in my rearview to make sure I never let him out of my sight. I briefly saw blond hair under a chauffer's cap, and then the limo accelerated and pulled out ahead as it turned onto Vanderbilt. Then it clicked: I remembered seeing Rivette's driver on TV when he left the courthouse the day of the verdict, and I remembered seeing him open the door for Rivette that afternoon when he dropped him at the hotel.

Rivette's driver was black.

I grabbed my radio and called Neville. "Captain, this is Kinneavy, do you copy?"

"This is Captain Neville, copy. Over."

"Captain, they've got Rivette. Judith does. That's not his driver driving the car."

"What the shit? Where the fuck are you?"

"I'm tailing them on East Forty-Sixth . . . ah, shit. Never mind, going north on First Avenue."

"Did the driver make you?"

"I can't tell. Looks like we're heading for FDR Drive."

"Kinneavy, do not let that rat bastard onto the bridge."

"I'll do my damnedest, Captain. Can I get an APB out on a late-model black Bentley limo with diplomatic plates? Driver is blond, Caucasian, short hair, indeterminate sex, wearing a chauffeur's cap."

As we screeched onto FDR Drive, the East River came into view, lit up by a high winter moon. I tried to pace myself, walking the line between not going so fast as to tip the driver off and staying on their ass. It was hell on the nerves, like trying to walk past an unfamiliar man on the sidewalk at night. We were nearly to the Fifty-Ninth Street Bridge when the limo made a sharp turn onto East Fifty-Eighth and then swung out back onto First Avenue.

Shit. They had made me. I stomped on the gas. "All units, currently pursuing suspect on the Upper East Side. Immediate assistance is requested. Heading north on First Avenue . . . no, fuck, never mind, east on East Seventy-Ninth. All units, I have resumed pursuit north on FDR Drive. Suspect appears to be heading for East Harlem."

I kept up my pursuit along the river's edge for the next fifteen minutes, threading its curve as it branched off into the Harlem River. The limo turned onto West 135th. I spun the wheel to follow it across Lenox Avenue when a tractor-trailer barreled in front of me, separating me from the limo for several vital seconds. By the time the rig had passed, the limo had disappeared into the night. I may very well have screamed, "No," skyward.

"This is Kinneavy. I have lost visual contact with the suspect."

"Jesus Christ, Kinneavy."

"I am proceeding to Adam Clayton Powell Jr. Boulevard to attempt to pick up the trail and wondering why *literally no one* has provided the backup I requested."

"Keep the editorial comments to yourself, Detective."

I pulled onto West 138th, and then my headlights washed over the limo as I did a double-take worthy of vaudeville.

"Suspects have abandoned the vehicle in a lot in the one hundred block of West 138th Street. I am pursuing on foot. I truly cannot overemphasize how appreciated backup would be."

"Three units on their way, Kinneavy. Nearest is coming from Morningside Heights."

"Request permission to continue pursuit?"

"Permission granted."

I parked next to the limo. I got out of the car and unbuttoned my coat so I could unholster whenever I needed to. I checked the back seat of the limo, which was unlocked. The spotlessness of the off-white interior told me Rivette was probably still among the living. It wasn't yet nine, and while the streets were less crowded than they'd be on a summer night, there were still civilians milling around. I stared down the sidewalk, trying to figure out what to do next. The position in which the limo was parked suggested they'd headed east. Right in front of me loomed the Abyssinian Baptist Church. I'd only been there once when I was thirteen, after spending a Saturday night with Jalisa. It was a completely new experience for me. Growing up around austere Mick priests and razor-faced nuns, it was strange to see people putting so much life into their faith. Jalisa said you had to be raised in it to really understand it, which made sense, since it's what I've been telling people about our music for years.

Next to the church, several stories shorter but just as impressive, was the three-story building that, back in the Jazz Age, was the Renaissance Ballroom and Casino. All the legends used to play there, your Ellingtons and your Basies and your Ellas. Today all the windows are boarded up, and the paint on the red brick exterior is faded and peeling. Not that many people south of Ninety-Sixth Street could tell you it was ever there in the first place. The only thing sadder than the death of something beautiful is when people didn't know it existed to begin with.

If this seems like a tangent, it's because while I was thinking all of this, I noticed a thin shaft of light coming from a second-floor window. I pulled out my walkie-talkie.

"Attention all units in the Harlem area, this is Detective Kinneavy. I am preparing to pursue the suspect into the Renaissance Ballroom located at the corner of Adam Clayton Powell Jr. Boulevard and Odell Clark Place."

I stowed the radio in my belt and clambered to the top of the fence between the church and the ballroom. Standing on tiptoes, I was able to hop over onto the brick ledge beneath the windows. I eased myself over to the window the light was coming from and tentatively felt the boards. They were old and would likely give easily. I unholstered my gun, drew back the butt, and caved in the boards until I had broken away enough to crawl through.

The windows were set on ledges high above a vast dance floor, now strewn with boards, splinters, and broken glass. There were scattered patches of mushrooms growing up from the floor. The starless sky was visible through a hole in the rusted-out ceiling. And there, surrounded by a ring of klieg lights in the center of the dance floor, was Judith.

There were six of them that I could see. They were all wearing red hoodies, red scarves over their faces, black jeans, combat boots, and sunglasses, just like in the original video. Rivette, his collar unbuttoned, was on his knees; one of the taller women had a snub-nosed revolver to the back of his head. Another member, standing next to the one with the gun, was yelling something, while a third manned the video camera. As her voice rose, I could tell I was running out of time. I crossed myself and leapt down from the window directly in front of the women.

The landing was a bit rough, but nothing broke. At the sound of me landing, all the women jerked their heads in my direction. Even the one with the gun had taken it off Rivette. I rose to my feet, took hold of my Glock, and pointed it at them.

"My name is Katherine Sheila Kinneavy, and I've had one rough cocksucker of a week," I said. "I'm walking out with at least one of you, all of you with some luck. You give me trouble, rest assured, there will be an equal and opposite reaction. I'll fire this thing until it clicks if necessary, and after that I suppose I'll have to get creative. So just let me know which way you want to go with this, and then we can get started."

None of them said anything. The two closest to me went for guns. I fired back twice and rolled behind a support column as the others continued shooting. I appeared to have drawn their attention away from Rivette momentarily, at least.

I was vaguely conscious of the sound of sirens getting closer. I peered around the edge of the column and ducked back down as another member fired at me.

"Stop shooting, you dumb fucks!" I yelled. "You're digging a *deep* fuckin' hole for yourselves." A trained negotiator I ain't. I looked back around the column, gun at the ready. The shooter aimed at me, then dropped the gun as blood burst from her throat. The one next to her, seeing this, turned to her compatriot and lowered her gun for a second. I used this opportunity to tackle her and take the piece.

Donnie strode into the center of the dance floor, his gun smoking, flanked by eight other cops. "Up against the wall, motherfuckers," he called. I made a mental note to tell him there was no possible way that could sound badass coming from him. He turned to me. "You okay, Katie?"

I nodded and got to my feet. The rest of the women quickly made for the back of the ballroom, firing their guns as they ran. Two of the cops grabbed Rivette and jerked him off his knees, pulling him out of the line of fire.

This saved Rivette, but it was just the opening the remaining members needed. Donnie already had bracelets on the one I'd tackled, and the one he'd gotten was pretty clearly dead, but the rest took the opportunity to make for a hole in the back wall of the building. The cops who weren't preoccupied with Rivette ran after them, but one of the women turned and shot out several of the klieg lights. The cops, at the sight of the gun, returned fire, and the ricochets sent the remaining members running.

"Around the front! Go!" I yelled. I pointed to one of the cops. "Detrolio, confirm TOD on the dead one."

Detrolio took the vitals of the one Donnie had shot. I dashed out the front door ahead of the other cops and around the back. There was no sign of any of the women. I cursed and met the cops around the other side.

"I need techs down here and around back and in Rivette's limo," I said. "I want roadblocks every way out of Harlem, with emphasis on exits to the south. Maybe they're local and they humped all the recording equipment here, but I kinda doubt it."

I ran over to Donnie, whose car was idling at the curb with the captured Judith member in the back. He'd removed her hood and glasses. She was a small Latina woman, no older than twenty-five, with limp black hair, large accusatory eyes, and a sardonic apostrophe of a mouth.

"Thanks for the big damn heroes bit," I said.

"Is that from something?"

"It's from *Citizen Kane*. How's Angela?"

Donnie sucked his breath in. "She's stable. She'll probably go home tomorrow."

"She's in my prayers."

"Thanks."

"Any ID on our new friend?"

"No ID, but she says she's Elba Borrero."

"How bad did I get her?"

"Minor scrapes. She's going straight to the station. Nice job."

The entire task force and Captain Neville were all at the station when I got back. There was scattered applause when I walked in. Neville pulled me aside and gestured for me to follow her back to the office, finally cleared for her use again. I could hear music emanating from her computer down the hall. As we got closer, I could distinctly make out Florence Welch exhorting me to run fast for my father, my mother, in a fox, with a box, et cetera.

"Pardon the music," Neville said as she opened her office door. "Keeps me alert when I have to stay late."

"Didn't peg you for a Florence fan, Captain."

"You kidding? She's the shit." Neville slid open the bottom drawer of her desk and pulled out a nearly full bourbon bottle. "You know what that is, Kinneavy?"

"Bourbon, Captain?"

"Wild Turkey Rare Breed. I bought this in 1993, took one drink, and put it away lo these twenty years."

"Why just the one drink?"

"I was working a bitch of a case and I wanted to incentivize it. That was right before the mayoral election, the very end of the bad old days. Story for another day. Anyway, when you close this Judith case, you and me'll have another glass." She put the bourbon back in her desk. "Klein and the Littlest Knife Nut are on their way. She's gonna be at her fuzziest right now. It's late, she's been in a fight, she's coming down adrenaline-wise, so I figure if we're gonna get anything out of her, now's the time. Have you got this? The interrogation?"

"Of course. She have any priors?"

"Nope. She's not in the system at all."

Down the hall, I heard the door open. "That must be them."

"Must be. You ready?"

I inhaled and crossed myself. "Yep. Give me just a second."

I stopped halfway to the interrogation room and shot Roane a text. *Look up elba borrero. Can't say why.*

I hung my vest up, unwound my scarf, and walked into the interrogation room. Borrero was still wearing the hoodie, albeit with the hood down. Despite her size and age, she didn't look at all intimidated to be sitting there, nor did she look defiant, itching to tell her friends on the block about how the pigs didn't have shit. She didn't just look at ease; she came across like she owned the place. She looked like the young Victoria on her throne.

I sat down across from her. "Good evening, Elba. I'm Detective Kinneavy. How do you feel?"

Borrero didn't say anything, she just gave me a look like a fifteen-year-old whose parents were trying to tell her that weed was totally uncool.

"My partner, Detective Klein, tells me that .22 you put on me had a shaved number. You know that's an automatic dime, right?"

"As opposed to trying to shoot your ass with it."

"Well, first things first. You may not believe me, Elba, but I want to help you—"

"You're right, I don't believe you."

"And I want to make sure you're not in too deep. Have you ever killed anybody yourself?"

She didn't respond.

"Elba, you don't think I know Martine Rivette is a piece of shit? And Martin Vickner? And Valery Degtiarenko? You think I'm only out to punish you or some shit? I understand where you're coming from, believe me. I'm a woman too, don't forget."

She sat up. "You're a cop. That makes you a collaborator, you Mick whore."

"That's interesting. You call other women whores and *I'm* a collaborator."

"Oh Jesus, spare me your PC Tumblr bullshit. You know why I do this shit, Clarice? Because men like that got to get got. Don't mean every woman I see, I'm gonna join in a drum circle and eat her pussy."

"Well, that makes sense. I mean, doing both at the same time sounds like a logistical nightmare."

She smiled at that, but it seemed less like she was amused by what I'd said and more like she was having a conversation I couldn't hear.

"You talk like that with the boys?" she asked. "You sit around playing cards and slamming beers and yelling at the TV when Sanchez fumbles and telling yourself they think you're just like one of the guys and not just a prissy little token bitch? I guess you can take some comfort in the fact that you know they don't just keep you around 'cause they want to fuck you. Well, maybe the black guy."

I smiled. "You're wasted with a gun. You should be their press secretary. So tell me, Elba, if you guys are Judith, why do you cut throats? Judith cut off Holofernes's head."

She sat back again. "What makes you think we've gotten to Holofernes?"

"You know what I noticed just now, Elba? You lose your accent when you say 'Holofernes.' You don't say it like a Puerto Rican girl."

"Have you heard a lot of Puerto Rican girls say 'Holofernes'?"

"You just did it again. You pronounce the *e*'s and the *r*'s a completely different way. I think you're playing a character, Elba. I think you're just fucking around with me and I don't think you should, because you tried to kill a cop and kill a diplomat and you've conspired to kill at least eight other people. You can get cute with me all you want, but just know that if you don't play ball, and I mean 'all the rest of them on a silver platter' play ball, you're going to spend the rest of your life in the kind of women's prison *men* are afraid to go into." I felt my phone buzz in my pocket and backed toward the door. I checked the ID. It was Wendell. "I'll be right back," I said, stepping out of the interrogation room.

I answered the phone in the hall. "Anything?"

"Yeah, Elba Borrero was a nurse in the Brooklyn area. She was walking home one night and a guy jumped her and tried to rape her. She was able to get him off her before a cop showed up. NYPD ended up pulling in a black kid from Jersey named George Whitmore and forced him to sign a confession. He was convicted on the basis of the confession, but eventually he was exonerated and released."

"Would she have any way of knowing who the real perp was?"

"Would who have any way of knowing?"

"Elba Borrero."

"Huh? Kinneavy, this happened in 1964."

I chuckled in spite of myself. "Oh, that clever little bitch. Thanks, Wendell. I'll talk to you later." I hung up and went back into the interrogation room.

"What's your real name, Elba?" I asked.

"That is my real name."

"Really? Your barely-drinking-age ass was sexually assaulted in '64?"

"You think only one Elba Borrero's ever lived in New York?"

"No, but I kind of doubt a woman who murders rapists just happens to have the same name as a woman whose rapist was never caught."

"Fine, you got me. Kitty Genovese."

"Oh, come on, sweetie, everyone knows who she is. Don't insult me."

"Okay, you got me. My real name is . . ." She extended her finger and crooked it inward. "Come closer."

"Or you can tell me right here."

"Okay, fine. Paul Hudson."

It was like the world had stopped, and everything around us had vanished, leaving just her and me in the void. There was a noise like a train in my ears. I tried to yell, but I could only whisper. "How do you know who Paul Hudson is?"

"You oughtta read the paper, chica. We do background on all the principals. Targets, investigators, that guinea who's looking for us . . . you still have plenty of college buddies in the area. Him too."

She said more after that but the train noise had almost completely filled my ears by now and I couldn't hear a word she was saying.

I hadn't had anything close to a proper boyfriend in high school. I'd made out with a few guys and very briefly let Mikey Corrigan get to second base the night of graduation, but Paul Hudson, like college in general, had been a wholly new experience.

We met in a sophomore-level chem lab. We'd been paired off and we bonded over how utterly useless the class was for a lit major (mine) and a business major (his). I was kind of amazed by how easy I found it to talk to him. Of course, even at that point, I never imagined we'd end up dating. He was about five ten with thick dark hair, deep green eyes, and a jaw and cheekbones straight out of a superhero comic. Like me, he was a big reader, albeit newer stuff like Michael Chabon. The closest thing we ever had to an argument before we started dating was when he said Bret Easton Ellis was superior to Faulkner.

We'd gone for dinner with some friends one night and were walking back toward campus when he asked me out. My first instinct was to feel hurt, because there was no way he wasn't making fun of me. No matter how much my parents and friends told me I was beautiful, no matter how little I cared about what guys thought of me as long as I was good at what I did, there was still a little insecure part of me that was utterly convinced guys who looked like Paul didn't have any interest in girls who looked like me. I was about to leave him there when he looked in my eyes and just told me that he liked me a lot—he liked talking to me, he liked being with me, he liked the sound of my voice, and he would really like to be a bit more than friends.

The first couple months are among my happiest memories. The whole city seemed to have a brighter sheen to it. I, little Katie Kinneavy from Inwood, had a hot boyfriend. Hell, even my dad, who Ma always joked didn't even like the way the boys looked at me in the hospital nursery, liked him. Even the weather seemed nicer. I felt amazing and beautiful and like I was finding my place in the world, even if I'd hardly seen any of that world outside of the tristate area. I felt that way almost without fail up until the evening of March 12, 2000.

My twenty-first birthday was still a couple months off, but I figured what the hell. We'd done shots in the Village and then had a couple beers before heading back to our dorm. Strictly speaking, I wasn't supposed to be on the boys' floor, but we were already drunk. Again, what the hell.

I don't know why I stonewalled Paul. We were already in his room at twelve thirty in the morning. Maybe some long-buried Catholic instinct still made me think only bad girls went all the way. But regardless, I told him I wasn't interested, and was about to fall asleep on the beanbag chair at the foot of his bed when I realized he was standing over me rather than lying in his bed. I tried to stand up to leave, but he placed a hand on my shoulder and—"forced" is the wrong word, he more guided me back down on the beanbag chair. I heard the dull clack of his belt buckle dropping onto the tile floor.

"Please don't," I said. But of course by then he already was. I know, on an intellectual level, that it was over in under a minute, but I felt myself age years. I was sure I would walk out of that room an old woman, that once I reached the street I'd barely even recognize the skyline. Then Paul braced himself against the floor and pushed off the beanbag chair. He leaned against the footboard of the bed.

"Jesus, Katie, I'm sorry," he said. "I . . . I'm really drunk. Shit, I'm sorry, Katie. I just got . . . kinda backed up, you know? I thought you knew the plan." He looked at me in the darkness, and after a while, I guess he realized I wasn't going to say anything. "I mean, you seemed okay. You didn't scream or anything."

No, I didn't. I wanted to. Jesus, Mary, Joseph, and all the saints, did I want to. But I couldn't force a scream out, because even as I felt like dying, I knew that to scream would make this experience irrevocably what it actually was, and I felt like as long as I didn't, I could pretend it was something else.

Two days later, I was eating in the dining hall with Jalisa when, apropos of nothing, I broke down crying. She asked me what was wrong, and the whole thing came spilling out, semicoherently. Jalisa, who was in prelaw, hugged me until I stopped crying and then marched me straight to the School of Business's honor code board to explain the situation. Paul was never called up before the board. The next week, I received a letter from them saying that, unfortunately, my claim had been ruled without merit since there was no corroborating evidence and that I had been engaged in activity that was in violation of university policy at the time. That very afternoon, Jalisa saw Paul in the student commons and walked over to him, flipped over the chair he was sitting in and kicked him several times in the ribs. No charges were filed, on the condition that she write a letter of apology (which she was going to boycott but for my insistence).

I didn't tell my parents. I don't know how long I intended to keep it from them, but my dad noticed my calls and visits had dropped off over the next month. He asked if we could meet in the park, and I agreed. I awkwardly tried to make conversation for a few minutes, and then I told him everything. I wasn't sure what to say when I finished. All I could think was "Please don't be angry at me." Dad's brow furrowed, and I saw storm clouds behind his normally warm, kind Henry Fonda eyes. He wound his arm firmly around my shoulder.

"Katherine," he said, his voice ragged at the edges. "Why the *hell* would you ever think I was angry at you?" He hugged me tight and I didn't start crying until I realized that he had.

There wasn't much for me to do past that point. I was terrified to go out alone for months and eventually had to take a semester off. I was able to get PTSD counseling through the university, and that was probably all that kept me from a complete breakdown. I never saw Paul again. He graduated, got his master's, and got set up on Wall Street through a family friend. So I hear.

I tried to mentally force myself back into the interrogation room. I clenched and unclenched my fist several times, and tried to find what they called a "mental focal point" in counseling—picking something to fixate on to stay tethered to the present. For me, in most instances, that's been "I'll Tell Me Ma," an old folk song my dad used to sing. *I'll tell me ma, when I go home, the boys won't leave the girls alone, they pulled me hair, and stole me comb, but that's alright, 'til I go home . . .*

I noticed a hand on my shoulder. I grabbed the wrist and was about to twist when I realized it was Donnie. "Katherine," he said. "Are you okay?" He looked more concerned than I'd ever seen him look and that made me feel a thousand times worse.

"Yeah," I said. "Y . . . yeah, I'm . . . I'm . . ." I couldn't get the words out without sounding like Porky Pig.

Wysocki stepped into the room behind Donnie. "I got this, Kinneavy," he whispered. "It's okay."

Donnie helped me out of the room and down the hall. Neville was the only person in the bull pen. She shooed Donnie away once we reached her.

"Who's Paul Hudson?" she asked, as soon as Donnie was out of earshot.

"Huh?"

"Don't fuckin' 'huh' me, Kinneavy. She mentioned that name and your entire interrogation goes sideways. Who the hell is Paul Hudson?"

I found my voice, even if I couldn't bring it much higher than a whisper. "He was my boyfriend in college. He sexually assaulted me in the spring of 2000."

She smiled mirthlessly and ran her red-nailed fingers through her hair. "That's great. That's just great. Well, you are right the fuck off this case, little girl."

"What?! Captain, you can't—"

"Do not fucking tell me what I can and cannot do, Detective!" She ground her cigarette into the carpet with her heel. "Do you not realize what it does to this entire case if my lead motherfucking investigator has reason not to protect someone Judith is targeting? What the hell were you thinking not telling me this shit from the outset?"

"His name never came up! Captain, please, it's not fair to pull me off over—"

"But, like, O-M-G, Captain, you can't, like, pull me off over something like a massive fucking conflict of interest an' shit!" Neville said in some kind of grotesque teenage-girl voice. "Jesus, Kinneavy, if it's not affecting your handling of the case, why'd you just go fucking catatonic in there?"

"Captain, I don't know. I'm sorry. Please. I can do this. I found them in the first place, didn't I?"

Neville sighed. "This whole thing is turning into a fucking nightmare. I can't have you compromised on top of a leak,

Kinneavy. I'm a cunt-hair away from finishing out my twenty-five with the Transit Bureau." She leaned backward against a desk. "You're still on the case through this week. I'm going to explain the situation to the commissioner and leave the final decision to him."

"And you think he's gonna keep me on?"

"I have no idea whether or not he'll keep you on. But you can take a chance on him, or I can remove you from it right now."

I rubbed my temples. "All right. That's fine."

"Kinneavy, seriously, you look like shit. Go home and sleep. No matter what happens, you did good tonight."

I nodded wordlessly and drove home. The rest of the night, I had the kind of nightmares you can never clearly remember.

ROANE

Oksana was being kept in the TBI ward at Bellevue. An armed guard at the door told me I had fifteen minutes and on minute sixteen he was hauling my ass out in cuffs. Everyone was so nice here.

Oksana was sitting up in bed. She looked like she'd been expecting me for a while. A good bit of the hair on the left side of her head was shaved, and one of her eyes was rimmed with blood. She gestured for me to sit.

I wasn't sure where to start. "Um, Oksana, I don't . . . I don't know how much you—"

"I speak English, Mr. Wendell," she said.

"Yes, I know."

"How?"

"I don't speak a word of Russian but even I could guess 'navy' and 'navy blue' don't have the same literal translation. You speak English before you came over?"

She nodded. "Not perfect, but better than anyone here knows. I'm sorry for not being honest, but once I realized what I'd gotten myself into with Mr. Russell, I knew he'd kill me if he knew. Father Mirzoyev is the only one I told."

"So why keep it up with the hospital staff?"

"I'm an illegal immigrant with a metal plate in my head and the mayor's Cossack wants to kill me. I am on borrowed time and it will be worse if he thinks I can tell anyone what happened to me."

"Not for nothing, Oksana, but I'm a reporter. If you don't want something to be public knowledge, I may not be the person to tell."

"You've done your reporting, Mr. Wendell. Right now I need someone to talk to. Is that all right?"

I laid my messenger bag at my feet. "Yeah, that's okay."

She shifted her weight in the bed, sitting higher up against the pillows. "I didn't tell you everything, you know. About the mayor's man."

"How do you mean?"

"About a month before all this started, he asked for someone new. Russell put him with one of the Laotian girls. She'd had a bad experience, I'm thinking, and she had an attack of some kind when he brought the razor out. He kept screaming at her to shut up but she was too far gone to understand. Eventually, he starts trying to hold her down, then he put his hands over her nose and mouth trying to get her to stop and I suppose he just lost control."

Jesus. "Did Milazzo know about that?"

"He has cameras hooked up. He came in to try to stop it but it was already too late by then." She looked at me with what looked like concern in her eyes. I didn't understand why until I looked down and realized I was shaking violently all over. "You okay, Mr. Wendell?"

I thought back to my conversation with Tony. "How do you live?" I asked. "How do you keep going after all this?"

She looked confused. "What else am I going to do?"

I looked at my watch. My time was nearly up. "You say he recorded everything. Do you have any idea where those recordings might be?"

"No, sorry. I'd guess he has a safe deposit box somewhere."

"But you're sure he recorded what Crowning did to the Laotian girl?"

"I saw the red light. I had to focus on it to keep from passing out."

I got to my feet and handed her my card. "Thank you, Oksana. Listen, you ever need anything, you get in touch with me and I'll come to you. I promise. Okay?"

"Thank you, Mr. Wendell. Please look after yourself too."

It had warmed up a little over the past few days and now it was pleasantly brisk, so I decided I'd walk back to the office. A few blocks in, I realized the same gunmetal Caddie had been beside me the entire time. My first thought was Crowning, but it occurred to me that his focus would be on Oksana, not me. I tried to get a good look at it but the windows were tinted. The light ahead of us turned red and I was about to jog across the intersection when the car's window rolled down.

"Wendell, right?" said the guy who'd rolled down the window. "Come in for a second, we got shit to talk about."

"All due respect, I'll pass," I said.

"This shit we got to talk about?" said a deeper voice from the other seat of the car. "It involves that Russian girl. You don't want to talk about her?"

Oh, fuck a duck. I got into the car.

Sitting opposite me was a broad-shouldered guy in his midforties in a dark pin-striped suit. He held out his hand and shook like he was kneading dough. "You know who I am, Wendell?"

"Yeah, Mr. Cataldo, we actually met once."

"Did we? I'm real sorry. Look, Wendell, you strike me as a guy with a lot to do, so I'm gonna do you the courtesy of being blunt: Did you tip Immigration off about the girls my late associate was employing?"

The self-aware bullshit euphemism made me want to get in his face, but I restrained myself. "No, Mr. Cataldo, I didn't."

"Good, that's good. I'm glad to hear that. I liked those girls. How 'bout this, do you know who went after them?"

I'd been thinking a lot about my decision not to report my (eventually proven entirely correct) suspicions that Judith had been about to pull something. Whether or not Cataldo was being honest about having "liked" the women, when a man like that asks you for a name, it's only for one reason. So essentially I had a shot at making Judson Crowning's raping, murdering ass vanish from the earth . . . at the low, low price of being an accessory to murder and giving a mob capo something to hold over my head. I sighed and said, "No, no idea."

Cataldo smiled. "You've never taken a polygraph, I'm guessing, Wendell," he said. "What they do is, first they ask you something they know you'll answer honestly, so they know how you look when you're telling the truth. And Wendell, you answered that first question a fuck of a lot quicker than the second one." He leaned forward and fiddled with the ring on his little finger. "So I guess my question is, which one are you lying to me about? Because both of those are questions I kind of need to know the answer to."

Dear Mom, my day was okay. Today I visited a Russian prostitute in the hospital and then gangsters kidnapped me and accused me of lying to them because of some ridiculous *Mentalist* bullshit. How about you, how've you been?

"Mr. Cataldo," I said, "if I paused it's because I needed to think about whether or not I had any ideas on who went after them. I know without having to think about it that I didn't tip anybody off."

He leaned back slightly in his seat. "Wendell, you're a reporter, right?"

"That's correct."

"Tell me, in your words, what I'm responsible for. Professionally."

"Well, you're essentially acting boss of the Dellaponte family in everything but name. Various regional captains handle the action in their respective territories, but in addition to handling almost all the family's Lower East Side business, you're also responsible for consolidating payoffs city- and statewide, and you're in charge of all the construction contracts and the drugs coming up from Baltimore and Mexico and down from Toronto."

He looked pleased. "And, allowing for your lack of first-hand experience, does that strike you as the level of responsibility you get by being a dumbass?"

"I doubt it."

"And yet, you expect me to believe what you just said?"

"It's totally up to you whether or not you believe it, Mr. Cataldo, but it's true. Like we say in the business, truth is an absolute defense."

He looked out the window like he was considering it. "Can I ask you a personal question, Wendell?"

"I'm on the Williamsburg Bridge in your car, Mr. Cataldo, you can do whatever you like."

"Are you . . . what are you, black? Arab, what?"

"My dad's black. Mom's Italian. Indelicato."

"Shit . . . hold on, is your mom Maggie Indelicato, from Arthur Avenue?"

"I guess. That's her name, and she's from Arthur Avenue."

"Shit, man. She was three years ahead of me at Monsignor Scanlan. I thought she was the hottest girl in New York, growing up."

I sighed. "Are we . . . are we supposed to be bonding over this, Mr. Cataldo? Because I know you don't want me to lie to you and this is really not something I'm capable of shooting the shit over."

For a minute, I thought I'd gone too far. Then Cataldo burst out laughing. He turned to the other guy in the backseat. "This kid, Paulie," he said, still laughing. "This kid is definitely Maggie's son, am I right?"

This kid is in his thirties, you patronizing douchewhistle.

He turned to the front of the car. "Hey, Dom, pull over up here, huh?"

The Caddie pulled up to the curb and Cataldo flicked the lock open.

"You keep fightin' the good fight out there, huh, Woodward?" he said. I nodded as I got out.

Once I got upstairs to the office, Rosalind rapped on the outside of my cubicle and pulled her chair inside.

"So Tony told me what you found regarding Devaney and Worldlink. Now, that struck me as odd, because, y'know, a brokerage firm is already gonna have a ton of lawyers, so why the fuck do they need one more whose expertise isn't even in finance law? *Well.*" She flipped through her iPhone and pulled up a pdf. "That right there is an incident report by the NYPD's Quality of Life boys."

"It's a redacted-halfway-to-hell incident report."

"Nothing that matters is redacted. See, apparently in October, an unnamed partner in Worldlink got fresh with a hooker. And by 'got fresh with,' I of course mean 'beat the shit out of.' This happens within a week of Worldlink retaining Devaney."

"So what's the connection?"

"Um, maybe you forgot, but I'm not a crime reporter, because crime reporters aren't allowed to be this hot. This is where you come in."

Quality of Life being Quality of Life, they had redacted the name of the employee but not the prostitute. Her name was Tanya Bledsoe and she was an associate of my source Gabrielle's, as luck would have it. I called Gabrielle and asked how to get in touch with Tanya.

"Wait for her call," Gabrielle said. "Don't call me again for a while. I'll make sure she gets up with you soon."

About an hour later, I got a call from a blocked number. Tanya explained what had happened that night: the john (he hadn't given his name) had been booked for soliciting, but the beating had been vicious enough that she was determined to file charges as well. While she was in holding, however, she was visited by a big older guy with thinning white hair and a loud, abrasive voice. The man explained that no, actually, she would not be pressing charges against the trick, and if she wanted to go ahead with it, it would be the easiest thing in the world to not only produce evidence that she was a fan of consensual rough sex, but to make sure that any relatives of hers who *had* managed to become productive members of society would be tied to her in the press. He said all of this while getting in her face, raising his voice at completely random times, and addressing her as "whore."

After about an hour of this, Tanya informed the police she would not be pressing charges. There was no record of the john being arrested for soliciting either, so presumably Devaney had worked his magic there as well. I thanked Tanya for her help and promised her nothing would be published that could compromise her safety before hanging up.

I walked to the other end of the office and stuck my head into Rosalind's cubicle. "Oh my God, he's a fixer," I said.

"What, like for pets?"

"No, he . . . Worldlink has a partner with some fucked-up proclivities. They bring in Devaney to bully the victims out of pressing charges. It works perfectly because he's retained by them without being part of the team, so there's a buffer between them, and he's also a mean-ass old creep who can twist vulnerable people's arms. *That's* why he's so hot under the collar about Judith. It's nothing to do with the 'promoting terrorism' bullshit, he's shitting his pants they'll publicize one of his clients."

Rosalind angled her chair to face me. "Okay. So what is any of that, practically? There's nothing putting him there but a hooker's description with no name."

"For now. First rule of Fight Club, Roz, everyone leaves a trail some way or another. And if he was this sloppy about being on the defensive, it shouldn't be that hard to find."

Rosalind stood up and met my eyes over the top of her cubicle. "Wendell, you're gonna do what you're gonna do. I know you that well. But these finance fuckers don't play. Especially when there's something like this at stake. Look at me!" I must have still looked smug because she was barking now, as serious as I'd ever seen her. "These are nasty people if they don't like you. I can't stress that enough."

"I hear you, Roz. Thank you. You're sweet to be worried."

"I am neither sweet nor worried, pal of mine. I (a) take care of my own and (b) don't want this pub to get a reputation among the people I need access to."

"Potato, potahto."

A couple hours later, I put on my coat and headed downstairs. As I walked past the alley that separates our building from the sandwich shop next door, I felt something press into the base of my skull.

"You know what that is?" said a modulated voice behind me.

"Can't say for sure, but I can guess."

"There are a couple of things you need to know. First, the Worldlink partner's name is Paul Hudson. Second, Tanya wasn't the only one. You need to talk to Detective Donna Torres in the Twenty-Eighth Precinct. She made an unredacted report. It was suppressed, but she still has it."

I didn't say anything, and for a while I wasn't sure if they were still there.

"Nothing to say, Mr. Roane?"

"Well, not for nothing, but I'm not in a hurry to be in your debt."

"We have mutual goals, Mr. Roane. This isn't a question of debt. If you want the law to give Mr. Hudson his comeuppance before we do, I suggest you act on this information."

"What happened to emails? Emails were nice."

"Mr. Roane, the most militarized police department in this country is looking for us. They've been hacking your computer for two weeks."

Fuck. "So it's guns and alleys from here on out?"

"There won't be much 'from here on out' to speak of, Mr. Roane. We're building to a crescendo."

"That's interesting."

"I'm flattered you think so. I'm going to leave now. You're to count to thirty, and if I see the front of your face any earlier, I'm putting a bullet through it."

I counted to forty and then walked straight ahead.

CATALDO

B rickman hadn't touched his *cotechino di puledro*, and it was starting to bother Cyrus Yale.

Yale had made a rare appearance on the Lower East Side today. He was about sixty and bald with a salt-and-pepper goatee and tinted glasses. He was wearing a black suit, shirt, and tie under a fur-collared overcoat. His black homburg rested on the table.

"Man can't eat when he's afraid," Yale said conversationally. "Met a whole lot of men who could hide when they were scared pretty well, but none of 'em ever could make themselves eat. You scared of me, Detective?"

"What? No!" Brickman said, sounding like the worst actor in a high school drama club.

Yale pushed his hat aside and tented his fingers. "Well, that ain't particularly respectful," he said. "My line of work, a man tells you he's not afraid of you, he's telling you he doesn't take you seriously. You don't take me seriously, Detective?"

Brickman's eyes were practically popping out of his head. "Jesus Christ, he's *fucking with you*," I said to him. "Can we cut out this bullshit?" I turned back to Yale. "Cyrus, you wanna tell Detective Brickman why we're here?"

"Yeah, here's why I came down, Detective," Yale said, taking a sip of his wine. "I had an associate of mine meet his end recently and as I understand it, the case crossed your desk."

"Which, the pimp?"

"That's correct. Now, our mutual friend here, Mr. Cataldo, he says he asked if you could, as a personal favor, look into those a little further. Now, I also understand you were not particularly receptive to that request, so I figured maybe if I came down and asked you personally, you'd be a little more moved. Drexel was a dear friend, you understand."

Brickman was starting to get his swagger back. He rose slightly in his seat and pushed his chair back as though preparing to leave. "Okay, look, Mr. Yale, I'm sorry for your loss, but I'm just about done here, so . . ."

I nodded over Brickman's shoulder at the guy tending bar. He came around the bar and locked the door. Brickman's posture deflated in a second and his eyes darted back and forth between us like he was at a tennis match.

"I'm a cop, you fucking idiots," he hissed.

"Yeah, we got that, Howard. We're not gonna ask someone about a murder investigation if we think he's a bus driver. But Sal over there? He knew you're a cop too. You give off the vibe, no disrespect. And he still locked that door without me having to tell him. That's where you are right now, Howard. I'm the guy people lock doors for. Even on cops. And let me tell you something, Howie, you are wearing, snorting, and driving way too much of my money to think that when I tell you to do something, you do anything but exactly fucking that. You think anybody gives a solitary fuck when someone like you gets killed, you greasy little Internal Affairs jerkoff fantasy? You ain't Danny fuckin' Faulkner, you're my fuckin' piece on the side, and if I kick you out of bed, you'll land hard. Is that clear?"

Brickman gave a weird little cough. "Yeah, that's clear."

"Magic. Now, Howie, you're gonna look into the Drexel Wilson homicide for my friend, and you're also gonna text me the second anything weird happens down at the precinct, be it homicide related or Judith related. Got me?"

"Yeah, I got you."

"Great." I clapped him on the shoulder and nodded to Sal, who unlocked the door. Brickman pulled the lapels of his coat so they were aligned, gave us both a cursory glance and walked out onto the sidewalk.

Yale gave a chuckle that sounded like he was telling a scary story. "You love your theatrics, don't you? Weren't you just saying you were worried the Old Man had it in his head to kill a cop?"

"Please. I'm not gonna kill Brickman. No reason he needs to know that, though."

"Not sure that's the best strategy, Mr. Cataldo."

"No?"

"Maybe if he was muscle. But here's the thing: a guy you need for information, worst thing you can do is make him think you a madman."

"Why's that?"

"Because then he won't come to you with bad news. And a guy like that, you need for bad news. Ain't nothing less useful than a snitch who self-censors."

It was a fair point. "Look at this Machiavelli motherfucker over here." It was the weirdest damn thing, but I'd missed this guy. "How you been, Cy? How hangs the crown?"

"Not too heavy. You remember being young? Young bucks ain't want anything they have to spend longer than a day on. Anyone who comes at me is gonna try to do it hanging out of an Escalade, throwing up some stupid-ass sign with one hand and holding a piece bigger than they dick sideways in the other. Nobody singin' songs about the fool who tried to kill the king and got shot up the next day in their weak-shit safe house." He rubbed his index finger against his temple. "We some lucky motherfuckers. Rose to the top just as war became obsolete."

"Is that lucky, though? Look at us now. Philosophizing in the back of an Italian restaurant. When did I turn into a fuckin' college student?"

He laughed again. "Way this city's going, we'll all be college students eventually. It's like a virus. It'll spread all the way out here. You thought the yuppies were bad, wait until this place is full of white girls in Uggs singing Beyoncé off-key after finals."

That made me laugh too. "I'll die first. I'll be standing on the roof with a fuckin' rifle and a coonskin cap."

Yale's face went mock-stern. "A *what*-skin cap, now?"

"Get off my balls, Huey Lewis."

"Newton."

"Sorry, Newton Lewis."

Yale thanked me for dinner and headed out.

It was Friday, so the next day I had to make the drive up to Ithaca. On my way home from dinner I got a call from a voice I didn't recognize at first. It took me a minute to realize it was Soldato.

"Listen, Joe," he said. "I know it's a pain in the ass making this trip every weekend. The Old Man has his ways. I dropped a car at your place, so you don't need to worry about gas or nothing."

"That's great of you," I said. "Thanks so much." It was fucking weird, was what it was. I never figured Soldato to worry about someone's convenience. I never figured him to worry about anything other than what, or who, the Old Man wanted taken care of. The car, a dark blue Continental, was in my driveway when I got back, the keys under my mat.

As I stepped inside, I got a text from Frankie O'Halloran. *Call on burner.* I kept a couple in my garage, so I went out, grabbed one, and called him.

"I hope you're not actually thinking of getting in that car," O'Halloran said when I called him back.

"Not very eager to. Why?"

"Because it's got enough C-4 under the hood to make bin Laden's corpse come."

Holy shit. "How do you know that?"

"Because Mr. Soldato paid me to wire it. Need a car bomb, ask the Irish guy. Racist guinea motherfucker. No offense."

"Well, thanks for the heads-up. I guess I'm taking the bus. So what's in it for you?"

"What do you mean by that?"

"Frankie, I'm not a fuckin' child. The last time a guy did something for me out of the kindness of his heart, he was trying to blow me up. What's in it for you?"

"The mayor has eyes in the police department. He thinks he does, anyway. They're actually Mr. Crowning's eyes. When Detective Brickman comes to you with that interesting information you asked for, Mr. Crowning is going to want in. You're going to let him in, to further the arrangement you and I made."

"Fair enough." It wasn't, really—I didn't want to talk to either of these two creepy fucks ever again—but when a guy who could have blown you up decides you owe him something, you nod and agree until you think of something better.

The only bus I could get the evening before left at six in the morning and had me in Ithaca by five. I didn't call the lodge because Soldato would probably be the one who picked me up, so I booked a cab the rest of the way, which ended up costing me more than I would have spent in gas. Fuck small towns.

Soldato answered the door, naturally. He made this face like his jaw had been about to drop like a cartoon character, but he managed to pull it inward at the last second.

"Joe," he said, not letting me in the door just yet.

"Soldato."

"How was the car?"

"You ever order a meal that's too pretty to eat? That's how I felt about that car. It was some beautiful thing, and I didn't want to fuck it up on these valley roads."

He looked me up and down, like he was hoping I'd blown up and there was some kind of delayed-action thing going on. "Yeah, I get that. At the same time, you know, we did take the time to get that car down there for you. Doesn't do anyone much good sitting in a driveway in Manhattan, you know?"

"And I appreciate it, like I said. I'll drive it another time. Understand? Another time."

Soldato unbuttoned his cardigan. "I don't see why it has to be another time. I think right now works okay."

I moved to the top step. "In the Old Man's house? You think he'd like that idea?"

Soldato reached toward the small of his back as casually as if he was scratching an itch. "To be honest, Joe, I don't think I would have gotten as far as I did unless the Old Man liked the idea."

"Giuseppe! Come in, come out of the cold." The Old Man was hobbling out of the den, in an uncharacteristically good mood. This was either a good sign or a terrible one.

Soldato gave me the least human-looking smile I've ever seen, like a straight line bent and curved until it was vaguely recognizable as one, and then turned to let me in.

Old Man Dellaponte took a seat in his armchair and gestured to the love seat. "So how are things in the kingdom?" he said.

"Pretty good. Those crazy bitches have been pretty quiet since the business with the French guy."

"You know how they are. They're not out to accomplish shit, just to make sure you know they're there. I doubt you'll hear from them again. How about the cops?"

It went on like that for a while, him asking for updates on a bunch of things there were no updates on, with that weird cheeriness the whole time. He realized everything was pretty much the same just in time for me to miss the last bus back to New York until the next day.

I got a motel room a few blocks from the station, set an alarm, and wished to God I had a company credit card. Around ten, I went out front for a smoke. Soldato was out front, leaning on the hood of his car like a high school bully who'd promised to get me after last bell. I pulled up my shirt a bit to show him the .45. I pointed to the car with my cigarette.

"Oh good, you got another car. I was worried. You seemed pretty upset."

He smiled. A real smile, not that thing he'd done in the doorway.

"Can I ask what the plan was?" I said. "Were you really going to drop me on the front porch, without approval?"

He strolled in my direction, casual enough that I didn't pull on him. "Well, see—and you should take this as a compliment, Joe—I'm more concerned with killing you than the details beyond that. I'm what you call goal oriented. Maybe you pulled on me, maybe you were waving your piece around saying you were going for the Old Man—I'd have figured something out, is my point."

"Speaking of the boss, what are you giving him? Uppers?"

"Just Valium. Makes him nicer to be around."

"And what's he think they are?"

"Heart pills. Neither of them mixes with the amount he drinks, but Valium mixes a fuck of a lot worse."

"Soldato, I'm not just saying this to be a dick, but do you really think you're boss material? Like, do you know what actually goes into it? Long as I've known you, you've been muscle. It takes more than that."

He smiled and shook his head. "You poor fucks," he said. "I'm the only one who gets how Our Thing even works anymore. I'm not campaigning, you pussy. It's my fucking *turn*. He's a senile old fuck who can't find his asshole with a flashlight and you're young enough to be my kid."

This was the most I'd ever heard him talk. "Listen to me, seriously," I said. "This is a terrible fucking idea. You're gonna make things harder for everybody, yourself included. Look, walk away from this and it's over. I swear to God, no grudges. But the two of us kicking each other under the kiddie table right now is the worst possible fucking thing we could be doing right now. Seriously."

He came closer, until he was only a few feet away from me. "Joe," he whispered. "If I gave a fuck what you thought was a good idea, I wouldn't be trying to kill you." He turned around and walked back to his car. "Have a nice trip back," he called over his shoulder as he got in his car and drove back down the road.

KINNEAVY

A ware of the genes I'd gotten from my mother and her father before her, I developed a system for myself early on:

If you go out, don't drink.
If you drink, don't drink whiskey.
If you drink whiskey, don't drink it alone.

The weekend after the interrogation, I started drinking whiskey alone. I wasn't so much in denial as in apathy.

I'm a bitchy drunk, and against my better judgment, perhaps with Paul in mind, I started drinking whiskey alone in Wall Street bars. They were overpriced as hell and their volume never dipped below that of a crowded airstrip, but the thought of shutting down people who didn't like to be told no gave me a certain satisfaction.

I got my first bite Sunday night. He sat down next to me at the bar when there were three other open stools, and the thunder in my head started.

"Looks a little strong for a lady to handle," he said.

"Sweetie, if you didn't think people should have what they couldn't handle, you wouldn't be hitting on me."

"Hey, no offense meant, sweetheart. I like a strong woman."

"In what fucking universe does a 'strong woman' like strangers calling her sweetheart?"

"Jesus. Daddy issues over here."

I stood up behind the stool, leaned in, and poured the entirety of my drink directly over his head. "You do not know *shit* about my dad," I said, grabbing my coat and scarf and walking out the door.

On the train home, I got the call I'd been waiting on for a while. Ever since the incident with Rivette, I'd been trying to get in touch with his entourage to find out the name of his driver when he was in New York, but he'd been whisked back to France immediately after we'd busted up Judith's party, and he was such a wreck, it was all but impossible to get anyone associated with him to talk to me. I'd finally gotten the guy's name, Melvin Bright, and it was him calling me that night.

"Okay, first things first," I said, "I saw you out on the curb an hour before court let out every day of the trial. What changed?"

"What changed was I was told not to," he said.

I had been feeling the effects of the whiskey, but this was like a bucket of water over my head. "Told not to? Who told you not to?"

"One of y'all. He said they were giving Mr. Rivette a police escort for the transfer."

My voice was shaking. "Which cop told you that?"

"Dark-haired skinny white boy. Man, sorry. Clyde or something."

I could hear the train roaring as it neared my stop, but the roaring in my head was starting back up as well, and the two blurred together like a roomful of screams.

I called Donnie when I got home and told him we needed to talk the next day. He began to say something about having to check his schedule, as I'd figured he would.

"Donnie," I said, "I'm not having any of your bullshit. I'm telling you we need to talk. Not at your convenience, not let's meet up sometime, we need to talk as soon as humanly possible."

"I mean, is everything okay?"

"No, Donnie, we are an ocean away from okay. I wouldn't insist on meeting in person otherwise." I hung up.

I met Donnie in Battery Park the next day, in the afternoon. After a brief warmer period, it had gotten colder than ever. Donnie sat down next to me on the bench, clearly aware something was wrong but trying to be casual.

"What's up?"

"Donnie, where were you the night we saved Martine Rivette?"

"I told you, I was seeing my little sister in Beth Israel."

I turned to look him in the eye. "Your little sister Angela?"

"Yeah."

"Donnie, there was no Angela Klein checked into Beth Israel that night. There was no Angela anything. And I just heard from Rivette's driver that you told him not to show up after the verdict. So you need to drop this bullshit about your fictional sister and—"

"She's not fictional!" Donnie said. He inhaled and ran his fingers through his hair, wet and spiky as though he'd just showered. "I do have a sister. Three years younger. She . . . we were close. Very close. When she started dating, she figured I'd get protective. Which, you know, I probably would have, but nothing crazy. Anyway, I found out she was meeting this guy on the night of August 15, 1996." He tapped his temple. "I remember that part. I always remember that part. I caught her sneaking out and I asked if she'd at least tell me his name. She says no, maybe she'll introduce me eventually but it's way too early and she doesn't want to send him the wrong message, scare him off. Well." He stopped there and blew out several short breaths. "Angela . . . Angela doesn't get home until after midnight. Mom's about ready to rip her a new one but then we both see her and . . . her face is all beat to shit, she's got bruises all over her throat and on her thighs . . . there's . . . blood everywhere. Angie won't say anything about what happened. She still won't name him. She just goes to her room and locks the door. Won't answer, won't eat. Three days she's in there, and then finally I kick the door in and she's . . . she's hanging from the ceiling fan by a belt." He was hyperventilating now. "I don't know how they knew, but they knew. A little while after the restaurant massacre, they got in touch with me."

"Got in touch with you? What does that mean?"

"It means someone pulled me into an empty building, pitch-dark, and said they would give me his name if I helped them."

"And what did you tell them?"

"I told them the plan for moving Rivette. I got his driver out of the way. That was it."

"Oh, that was it? Thank God. I was worried. What were you going to do when they gave you the name? Were you gonna kill him, Donnie? Was that what you were gonna do?"

Donnie didn't say anything. He just stared straight ahead at the statue across the harbor.

"Fuck you," I said, after a while. "Fuck you, Donnie. I'm your partner, you piece of shit. Jesus Christ, does that mean nothing to you? You fuckin' hang me out to dry because you feel bad you didn't put a nanny cam in your kid sister's hair?"

That made him smile. "I could have, you know," he said. "You think mine's bad . . . she had the longest, tangliest black hair you ever saw. She could never do a thing with it. She didn't mind, though. She didn't mind." He laughed a few more times and then it gave way to sobs. "I'm sorry, Katie. I'm so sorry. I know that means fuck-all at this point, but I really am."

"Donnie, I'm touched and all, but you didn't tell me my dress makes me look fat, you sabotaged this entire investigation and probably cost me my career. You want to take the first step in the hundred-fucking-meter dash of making this right? Give me something I can *use*."

"Katie, I—"

"Donnie, as of right now I am Detective to you or nothing."

He sighed. "Look, I . . . the voice . . . they had one of those modulator things. I couldn't hear an accent or anything. But here's something I noticed . . . she . . . bit down on the pronunciations, you know? No one without an accent talks like that."

"So, what, British? Australian?"

He shook his head. "Nah, it . . . it sounded kind of unsure of the words. If I had to guess, I'd say English was their second language, but they're from somewhere lots of people speak English. France, Germany, Israel. Places like that."

I pulled the handcuffs from my belt. "Thank you, Donnie. I mean it."

He nodded, not looking at me. I leaned in and cuffed him. "Theodore Donald Klein, you are under arrest for conspiracy to commit murder in the first degree," I said. "You have the right to remain silent when questioned. Anything you say or do may be used against you in a court of law. You have the right to consult an attorney before speaking to the police and to have an attorney present during questioning now or in the future. If you cannot afford an attorney, one will be appointed for you before any questioning, if you wish. If you decide to answer any questions now, without an attorney present, you will still have the right to stop answering at any time until you talk to an attorney. Knowing and understanding your rights as I have explained them to you, are you willing to answer my questions without an attorney present?"

Donnie just nodded again.

We drove back to the precinct in silence. When we got there, I was vaguely aware of noise from other cops as I walked him through the station and into the holding cell, but I didn't hear any of it. I got back to my desk, reached for my flask, and began typing up the arrest report.

"Jesus, Kinneavy, it's three o'clock," said Captain Neville, crossing the floor and sitting on my desk.

"Captain, all due respect, I just arrested my partner," I said. "I think I'm entitled to a drink."

"Well, by that logic, you must arrest your partner pretty regularly," she said. "Klein says he's not going to give his confession to anyone but you."

"Fuck that. Let him fight it if he doesn't want to give a confession. I'm not playing Donnie Christ Superstar with him."

Captain Neville frowned. "With me, Kinneavy," she said. I followed her down the hall toward the interrogation room.

"Not to put the cart before the horse, Captain, but what happens with the task force now?"

"Officially? We dismantle the task force and give everything we have to Org Crime."

"Unofficially?"

She turned on her heel. "Unofficially, you stay on this like it's Noah's fuckin' ark. I'm not dumb enough to take this from the only person who could find any of these bitches in the first place. You report directly to me and don't say shit about this to anybody else. Okay?"

"Yes, Captain."

We had reached the window of the interrogation room. Donnie was staring straight ahead, his eyelids looking heavy. I sighed, gave the captain a salute, and opened the door.

Donnie's confession was short and straightforward, a slightly longer version of what he'd already told me. When he reached the end of it, he looked up and finally met my eyes for the first time since Battery Park.

"I'm sorry, Detective," he said again.

I pushed the confession aside. "What was Angela like?"

"Huh?"

"If you don't mind talking about her."

"No, no, I don't mind. She was . . ." His face twisted up, like he was stuck on an essay question. "She's so impossible to, to explain, you know? She was the sweetest girl you'd ever meet, and the toughest, all at the same time. When we were in high school, it was . . . it was common knowledge she was tougher than I was, and sometimes kids gave us shit for that. Mostly boys, you know how that goes. Mikey Ebdus, in particular— this one time he goes, 'Your kid sister probably fights better than you, you fuckin' pussy!' And Angie just walks right up to him and beats the crap out of him, and goes, 'Yeah, probably,' and walks off."

I laughed in spite of myself. It was a funny fucking story.

"What'd she do for fun?" I asked.

"She read a lot. Had a guitar too. She couldn't play anything too complex yet but she was working at it. She was someone who worked at things. I think if, you know, if she'd grown up, you two'd have been great friends."

I smiled, just a little. "Sounds like it."

We went on in that vein for a while, me asking questions, him summoning the happy memories he'd buried in his sense of obligation years ago. It was around nightfall before I realized.

I looked at the time. "Donnie, you have to go to the Tombs now. I'm sorry."

He shrugged. "Will you drive me?"

"I can, yeah."

He got to his feet. "I'm glad it's you."

I walked Donnie down the front steps and toward my car at the curb. I was about to open the back door when a shotgun barrel jabbed me in the belly. It was in the hands of a (presumably) man of about six feet wearing a black jacket and dark goggles over a dark gray balaclava. Behind him, a similarly dressed guy flanked Donnie.

"Hey there," I said. "Who the fuck are you?"

"If you needed to know, would I be dressed like this?"

"I dunno. I figured you probably wouldn't talk to me either."

"Detective Klein is coming with us."

"Is he?"

He lifted the gun and pressed it to my temple. "This is not a conversation we're having, cunt. This is me telling you what's going to happen."

I leaned in. "Let me respond in kind. I'm pretty sure I know who you are. I don't know what you want with him, but I promise you, if anything happens to that man, there won't be anywhere in this city, this state, or this country you can hide from me."

"I'm sure," he said. "Please understand that if you follow me, I'm going to shoot your partner in the face." He kept the gun on me as they got in the car and sped off down the street.

ROANE

I extended my hand to Donna Torres's tortoiseshell cat. It hissed and backed away.

"He only likes me," Torres said as she brought two cups of green tea back to her kitchen island, pushing one to me. "Sorry."

"No worries."

She sat down across from me, picking up the manila envelope she'd laid on the island. "So Paul Hudson, huh? Nasty bastard. Bastards you meet every day, but our Mr. Hudson is a *nasty* bastard. Understand?"

"Sure," I said, not altogether truthfully.

She opened the folder. "I want you to understand something, sweetie. They told me not to file this in the first place. When I did anyway, they transferred me to Drugs. See, they woulda busted me down, but if you demote a Latina and won't tell anyone why, you're gonna reap a whirlwind of shit. So if I give this to you, it needs to land hard, because the only way I don't lose my job altogether for giving this to you is if there's too many eyes on my superiors to get away with it. We clear?"

"We're clear, absolutely, Detective."

"You're gonna make sure it lands hard, then?"

"I promise I'll do everything I can to make sure it does, and if that can't happen, I won't publish."

She slid the folder over to me. "Paul fuckin' Hudson . . . ," she said. "I'll always remember, I go in to talk to this boy and he immediately starts trying to talk his way out of an arrest. Turning on the charm, you know. Only the more he talks, the more I realize, he thinks he's in there for solicitation. It's not even registering with the motherfucker that he might be in trouble for making her face look like hamburger. And eventually I stop him, I tell him I'm not Vice, I'm Special Victims Division. He just stares and goes, 'What the fuck for?'" She sipped her tea. "I welcome the transfer, honestly. Maybe it'd be okay if it was the first time I'd seen that attitude from a perp but I saw it all the time. Never entered into their heads that it was wrong to hurt a woman. Even if they knew it was a crime, you know, they never thought of it as wrong." She tilted her head. "You're the one who writes about those ladies, aren't you? The ones who kill rapists."

"I've written about them, yes."

She shook her head. "I've never in my life been so sympathetic to people I knew I couldn't defend. If they'd caught me when I was younger and cared less, I'd be blasting away with them right now. They shoulda talked to me. I probably cook better than any of 'em. Pick all their meetings right up."

She noticed I'd finished my tea. She killed hers, grabbed both mugs, and took them over to the sink. "Thanks for coming to me about this, Mr. Roane," she said. "You remember what you promised me."

Now that I had the police report, I was in a bit of a tricky position. I couldn't very well write the story without giving Paul Hudson a chance to respond, but I also didn't want to make Rosalind's job any harder. I had a plan I was pretty sure would work, but I was entirely sure that if it didn't, I had no idea what I was going to do. I dug through various dead-end contact pages at Worldlink before I finally found Hudson's office number. He answered on the third ring.

"Paul Hudson, Worldlink."

"Hi, Mr. Hudson, I'm working on a story on violence against sex workers in the finance sector, and I was wondering if you had any response to this police report I've obtained that puts you at the scene during an incident of solicitation and sexual battery?"

"Go fuck yourself," he said, and hung up. Hell yes.

"Hell no," Tony said. "We don't run blind items, Wendell. Jesus. This isn't fucking TMZ."

"Tony, come on, it's not like that."

"Yeah, what's it like?"

"Baiting the hook, is what it's like. Look, I know there's a lot missing. That's why I don't want to run it with any names. But if we put this out there, the people we can't name yet are going to get paranoid, and they're going to get lazy. Then they'll come to us."

"Wendell, I don't want them to come to us. Have you not talked to Rosalind about this? These people are scary."

"Who's going to sue if we don't name names? Wouldn't that defeat the whole purpose?"

Tony sighed. "One of these days you're going to be such a pain in my ass that it won't matter how many good stories you bring in. Not today, though."

I went back to my desk and prepared the story for submission. A little while later, Rosalind came by again. She looked angrier than I'd ever seen her, which wasn't particularly angry by most people's standards, just annoyed.

"What did I tell you?" she said.

"Many, many things, most of them some variation on 'You're always late and I'm not, ha-ha-ha.'"

She stepped inside. "I'm serious, Wendell. If you rattle my sources' cages, they're not going to talk to me anymore. Did you consider that for even a second?"

"I don't name anybody."

"It doesn't matter. That feature reads like an indictment of trader culture and they're going to take it personally if you're not careful."

"Roz, I'm not indicting anything. This is a he-said, she-said in which he declined to comment."

She rolled her eyes. "Jesus Christ. You know, you have really mastered the noble art of dancing on the fine line between irritating me and outright pissing me off."

"I haven't outright pissed you off yet?"

"Honey, you will know. Take that to the fuckin' bank and smile at the cute redheaded teller. You will *know* when you've pissed me off." She looked around the office like she was expecting someone. "Oh, as long as I'm here, maybe this is weird, but do you want to grab a beer sometime?"

I turned my chair around to look at her. "You're asking me, huh? Is that normally how it goes?"

"Oh, Mr. Lord High Enforcer of Gender Roles over here all of a sudden."

"I never said that."

"Then just tell me if you don't want to, ya fuckin' baby."

"Oh no, I'd like to."

"Sweet." She stepped out of the cubicle and headed back toward her desk. She turned to look over her shoulder. "That took way too long, incidentally. I don't pay by the word."

"Coulda fooled me." This was unexpected, if not unpleasant. I hadn't been on a proper date in several years, simply because on a journalist's salary, I really didn't feel like experimenting with any kind of relationship if it might all have been for nothing. Besides that, I was, if not married to my job, at the point of moving in with it and making her promise not tell my mother or she'd start yelling about "living in sin." I was grateful Rosalind had taken the initiative, because whatever hints she might have been dropping were exactly the kind of thing I'd be too oblivious to catch.

I was still fine-tuning the article at home when I got a call from a number I didn't recognize. It was Oksana.

"Oksana, how are you calling?"

"Father Mirzoyev was here a little while ago. He gave me a burner phone, but the doctors don't know. Wendell, I am probably going to die very soon," she said, "and I just want to thank you for everything in case I don't have another chance." Her voice was emotionless and fearful at the same time, like a shy child giving a presentation in class.

"Wait, Oksana, hold on, are you still in the hospital? What's going on?"

"I'm still in the hospital for now. They finally found an interpreter for me."

"Okay, and?" I said, sounding ruder than I meant to.

"And when they told him to ask me if I remembered how I got there, what he actually said was, 'You're going to die soon, you useless cunt.'"

"Oksana, there are armed guards outside your door—"

"So what? They won't keep him from coming in. They know what he's supposed to be there for."

I sighed. "Oksana, how hard would it be for you to get out of there on your own?"

"They're letting me use the bathroom by myself now. I could probably run during that."

"Oksana, I need to make a call for you. It'll only take a minute. Can I reach you on this number after I do that?"

She said yes, and I called Gabrielle.

"Wendell, you are already way the fuck in hock to me favor-wise, if you remember," she said. "Now you want me to, what, take in someone with heat coming down on her? I got other girls to take care of. That don't sound like much of a trade-off."

"Gab, I'm sorry. I'm really, really sorry. If I knew anyone else I could ask, I would ask them. This girl has already been through hell and it's all my fault, and I'm just trying to make it right. I really don't think I can trust anyone on the other side of the tracks anymore."

"Ugh. Your ass knows I'm not gonna say no to that, but you sure as shit better be nice to me. Shit, I'm entitled to a free full-page ad at this point."

"I'll send you a nice gift basket for Christmas."

"No, uh-uh, you're not just sending me a 'nice' one, you're sending me one so motherfuckin' huge I need movers to get it up to the bathroom."

"As she commands."

"Tell her to wait for my call."

I called back the number Oksana had called from. "Oksana," I said, "a woman named Gabrielle is going to call you in a little while. She's a friend of mine. Trust her and do what she says. Do not trust anyone else, do you understand?"

"Yes. Thank you, Mr. Wendell. Thank you so much." Her voice sounded like she was close to tears.

"Oksana, please don't thank me. So much of this is my fault. Just please stay safe. Do what Gabrielle tells you to. She's one of the best women I know and I trust her completely. And whatever you do, don't get back in touch with me unless it's an emergency. I don't care how safe you think you are. And Oksana?"

"Yes?"

"You are tough, you are smart, you are brave, and by any reasonable expectations you should be dead about three times over at this point, but you're not. Trust your instincts, like you did when you got in touch with me, and you'll be okay."

I hung up and hoped to God I hadn't signed her death warrant yet again.

CATALDO

After Brickman texted me that Kinneavy had just arrested her own partner for leaking information to Judith, things started happening really fuckin' fast.

My initial reaction was to sit on the information, but not ten minutes later, who should show up at my door but King Creepy Fucker. We would be intercepting the perp, he said, and in case I was thinking of being uncooperative, he did still have the severed hand of a guy I was the last person to be seen alive with.

So that was how we found ourselves dressed like home invaders, pulling into Crowning's driveway in Long Island with a cop in handcuffs in the trunk.

Crowning popped the trunk, jerked the cop to his feet, and frog-marched him across the driveway, into the house, and up the stairs. I followed, both of us with our masks still on. Crowning marched the cop into his bathroom, a sparse gray-walled room with a shower that looked way too big for one guy. Crowning ripped down the curtain with one hand and gestured for the cop to sit. Once the cop was seated, Crowning disappeared into the bedroom and laid the shotgun on the bed. He walked over to the far wall, where one of those iPod boom box things was plugged into the wall next to the bed. He flipped through it before an instrumental piece filled the room. It sounded vaguely familiar, like that song they had played at my niece's high school graduation a few months back.

"What are your thoughts on Pachelbel?" Crowning said.

"Not many."

Crowning smiled, or more accurately stretched his lips upward instead of horizontal for a second. "He focuses me, I find."

I followed him back into the bathroom, where he dropped to a crouch in front of the cop.

"Detective Klein, if you cooperate with me, this will not take long at all and you will be okay," he said. "If not, things are likely to go in directions I don't want them to go, and you even less so."

As he looked in Klein's eyes, I saw a light of recognition go off in the cop's face, and the familiar struggle to suppress it before Crowning noticed.

"Detective Klein," Crowning said, "the reason you find yourself in handcuffs at present is because of your collusion with a criminal enterprise called Judith. I am very interested in the identities of this group's members. Please tell me who they are."

"I don't know," Klein said.

Crowning shook his head under the mask. "You know, I thought this might be the way you wanted things to go." He took off his right glove and slammed his fist into Klein's nose. I heard his nose break and the cop cried out. "Who are they, Detective Klein?"

"I don't fucking know!"

Crowning sighed and turned to me. "If you open the medicine cabinet, you'll find a razor on the middle shelf. Will you please bring it to me?"

I walked to the cabinet without a word and brought him the razor. Crowning unfolded the razor and then slipped his glove back on, then turned to Donnie and yanked his mask off. I was right on the edge of demanding to know what the hell he was doing, but I knew it would only make things worse if the cop heard my voice.

"Detective Klein," Crowning said, "I am no slouch with this razor, but you should know that my skills will take a substantial hit if I have to wear gloves while using it, which, because of fingerprints, I of course have to."

Klein didn't say anything. Crowning pressed the squared-off outermost edge of the blade against his forehead until a small bead of blood appeared. "Who are they?"

"I don't know."

Crowning held the razor against the spot where he'd drawn blood and dragged it in a question mark shape across Klein's forehead and down the right side of his face.

"Tell me who they are," Crowning said. "I assure you, Detective Klein, you have not yet seen me at my worst." This time the cop didn't say anything at all. Crowning snapped his fingers at me. "Under the sink, you'll find a jug of bleach. Bring it to me, please."

I eased open the cabinet with the heel of my boot, found the bleach, and brought it to him. I was trying to avoid talking, but I couldn't help myself. "Why do you have a thing of bleach in your bathroom?" But there was no real reason to ask. Just like there was no real reason to ask why there was a straight razor in a medicine cabinet full of safety razors, or why Crowning had taken us to his bathroom with zero hesitation, or why the shower looked large enough for several people.

Crowning didn't answer. He unscrewed the cap, set it on the edge of the shower almost daintily, and dipped the blood-ied razor in the bleach. He bent over the cop and wiped off the excess bleach on the cut he'd made. The cop hadn't screamed when the cut was made, but he was screaming now. Crowning leaned even further in, his nose and Klein's nearly touching, and spoke in a low whisper that was entirely different from his normal speaking voice. It sounded weirdly comforting, except you got the sense that anyone who heard this voice had already seen the side of him that broke noses and carved up faces.

"Donnie," Crowning said, "your partner brought you to the station at two forty-five. We intercepted you at five fifteen. That's two and a half hours, and yet you expect me to believe you know nothing—nothing at all—that could lead me to Judith. That's insulting, Donnie. That's insulting that you think that of me. Because I'm not stupid, Donnie. I knew you recognized me as soon as I looked you in the eye, or I'd never have shown you my face. Now, Donnie, if you tell me what you know—any useful information at all—I promise you, I *promise* you, this will all end, and I'll have you taken somewhere safe. But Donnie . . ." He grabbed a fistful of the cop's dark hair. "Donnie, if you keep playing these *games* with me"—he pulled a revolver from the small of his back and pushed it under Klein's chin—"then I'm going to kill you. Do you believe me?"

Fuck this. I slipped the .45 out from my waistband and pressed it to Crowning's spine. "You need to step into the other room with me for a second," I said.

Crowning lowered the gun and rose to his feet. I put my own away and we walked out into the bedroom, Crowning closing the door behind him. The Pachelbel was still playing. I raised my gun to chest level. "This is way the fuck out of hand. I don't give a shit what you think you have on me, I'm not helping you kill a cop. We're turning him loose or I kill you right now."

He made that goddamn nonsmile again. "Will you, Mr. Cataldo? Will you kill me?" He opened and closed the razor idly as he talked. "What, then, do you think the police will think when they look in the appointment book on my desk and see that the last entry is a meeting with you?" He raised his hand without batting an eyelash and guided my gun hand back to my side. "I worry for your adaptability, Mr. Cataldo. Let's finish what we set out to do without further interruptions, please." He reopened the bathroom door and beckoned me inside with the gun.

Crowning crouched down in front of Klein again. "Donnie," he said, "I hope very much that you have something to say to me now. As I said, you haven't seen me at my worst."

A low throaty sound filled the room. I grabbed my gun, not sure what it was, and I realized after a second that the cop was laughing. "Sure I have," he said. "I saw you at city hall trying to pretend to be social."

Crowning shot the cop in the face, about an inch below his left eye. Klein's head thumped hard against the wall of the shower and Crowning jumped back as his feet kicked out. I looked down at the cop. The entry wound was weeping blood but he was still wheezing and his eyes were twitching.

"He's not dead," I said. "You have to finish it."

Crowning didn't respond for a second, then looked at me, as if he'd just figured out it was him I was talking to. "What?" he said. "You said yourself, I can't kill a policeman in my home." He held out the gun. "You can finish him if you like."

I took the gun from him. I looked at Klein again. He was already death-pale even as he clung to life. If I didn't do anything, he had maybe two minutes, tops. That's not very long to set your affairs in order but it's a hell of a long time to spend bleeding out from the face. I pulled off the mask and placed the barrel of the gun between his eyes. "I'm sorry," I said.

Crowning was sitting on the toilet, seat down. Other than a slight flinch when I pulled the trigger, he hadn't reacted at all. I backhanded him across the face.

"You know what you've done, you stupid piece of shit?" I said. "Do you even know? Do you know dick about anything but your fuckin' bleach and Pachelbel and all this bullshit you use to disguise the fact that you're the kind of fucking idiot who'll kill a cop for not knowing what you want him to know?" I raised my hand again. He caught my wrist and forced it backward.

"Mr. Cataldo," he said. "There's still work to be done. I can handle the body. With regard to the gun, don't you know a gentleman who can make it no longer a problem for us?"

"I know a guy who can clean the gun. That's not gonna make this shit not a problem for us."

Crowning ignored me and pressed the gun into my hand. "I have a second car in the garage. The keys are by the door. Burn what you're wearing, sooner rather than later."

There was a full moon with a ring around it over Manhattan when I reached Frankie O'Halloran's chop shop. O'Halloran was the only one there. Some weird-ass opera-sounding German thing was playing on the garage's sound system. *Madonn'*, am I the only one who listens to normal music?

"Ah, Joe, how are you tonight?" O'Halloran said when he saw me.

"Truth? I'm not great, Frankie. I'm way up Not Great's asshole."

He came around the table. "Do tell."

I did tell. O'Halloran's expression didn't change, that I could see, but the sunglasses concealed a lot. When I was finished he said, "I told you, didn't I?"

"No disrespect, Frankie, but I knew before you told me. Crazy leaks out of that motherfucker's ears when he shakes his head."

He stroked his chin. "This . . . this is interesting. Even for him." He crossed the garage floor and opened a strongbox. "I told you there was money in keeping me abreast of what our friend was up to, and I'm a man of my word."

"Keep it," I said. I held out the gun, wrapped in a rag. "Just get rid of this for me."

O'Halloran walked back over to me and took it. He looked vaguely like he was smiling, but it was impossible to tell.

I turned to go and then, completely on a whim, turned back around. "Hey, Frankie, what song is this?"

He sat back in his chair. "This, Joe, is Schubert's 'Erlkönig.' I like to listen to it when it gets late and there's no one else here." The vocals intensified and O'Halloran translated.

"I love thee, I'm charm'd by thy beauty, dear boy!
And if thou'rt unwilling, then force I'll employ."
"My father, my father, he seizes me fast,
For sorely the Erl-King has hurt me at last."

The father now gallops, with terror half wild,
He grasps in his arms the poor shuddering child;
He reaches his courtyard with toil and with dread,—
The child in his arms finds he motionless, dead.

I tried to disguise my shudder and mumbled something vaguely resembling a good-night. I drove home, but I wasn't sure why, because I knew I wouldn't be able to sleep.

KINNEAVY

The morgue attendant slid open the drawer, and for the first time in my career, I nearly had to look away.

The two perfectly round holes in Donnie's cheek and forehead had been cleaned, and that somehow made it worse. They didn't look like wounds anymore, but like small sections of him had been erased. Even his hair, that untamable hair, somehow looked deflated in death. It wasn't even that he was dead that was fucking me up so bad, it was how many little parts of his body were just a tiny little bit wrong. My partner no longer existed; his body was something else entirely.

An APB had gone out on the car that took Donnie as soon as I had gone back into the precinct and described it. Physically, I felt fine, but Neville had insisted I take medical leave for the next few days. On the third day, a man walking his dog in Seward Park, where this whole mess had begun, stumbled on a body and called it in. They'd initially called his mother to identify the body, but called me instead when they found out Mrs. Klein hadn't seen her son since 1996.

My throat felt swollen. "That's him," I said. The attendant slid the drawer shut.

I knew Captain Neville wanted me to take a break, but I drove back to the station for lack of anywhere else to go. Neville was at her desk, with Commissioner Clarkson leaning against the back window, as though they'd been expecting me.

"Donnie's . . . ," I said, and once again the words that would take things past the point of doubt or deniability, that would make them irrevocably as they were, burned coming up and wouldn't come out.

Neville nodded. Clarkson didn't respond.

"Kinneavy, Commissioner Clarkson wants to speak with you for a minute," Neville said.

"What about?"

"If he meant for me to know that, I'm guessing he'd have asked to speak to both of us." Neville got to her feet and left the office with the brisk stumble of someone resolved to keep their composure until no one was watching.

Clarkson sighed, crossed his arms and leaned back against Neville's desk, the alpha male marking his territory in one of many socially acceptable ways. "Kevin Kinneavy's your da, isn't he?" he asked.

"Yes, sir." I can't stand Irish-Americans who say shit like "da" and "grand." People will have their affectations, no matter where they come from, but I always associated it with a certain kind of old-school New York Mick, the kind who thinks the Mafia kept drugs out of the neighborhood and that never having "needed" to go on welfare makes them nobler than those who do.

"Well, I don't know if he ever told you, Detective, but Kevin and I came up together. We started at the academy and we didn't part ways until I made sergeant. Your da wasn't a man who wanted to advance. He just wanted to find what he was good at and plant his feet. There's nothing wrong with that, of course."

I was starting to wonder where this story was going, and maybe it was visible on my face.

"Anyway," Clarkson said. "Your da told me what happened to you in school. Back in 2000."

I took a step back. Clarkson held up one hand. "I'm sorry, Detective," he said. "That was . . . indelicate."

"He just came out and told you?"

"We were out drinking. He was further in the bag than I'd seen him in a while and at a certain point I could tell something was bothering him. I was a little lit too, so I asked him what was up and it all came out." He dropped his voice a little without actually whispering. "Now, like I said, I was going places at that point. And I told Kevin we take care of our own, and that means families too. I said—and I was serious as a heart attack—I told him that it would be the easiest thing in the world for one Paul Hudson to be caught with child pornography. All I'd have to do would be to make a phone call."

"What did he say?"

"He said thanks, but no thanks. Said he wanted Paul Hudson to burn for what he did, not for something he didn't." He stood up, looking almost apologetically toward the captain's desk. "That was your da. From the day you joined I always hoped you had his integrity, even when it got hard, and when I heard you perp-walked your partner—especially knowing what I know about you—I could tell that you did. That's why I asked Neville to keep you on the investigation."

There was a weird sort of emotion in his voice. Assholes are, for the most part, unwilling to appear vulnerable, and I never know how to react when they do. "Commissioner," I said, "I have a request."

"What's that?"

"I want Donnie Klein to have a police funeral."

"Detective, Donnie Klein's last act on this earth was to confess to sabotaging his own investigation."

"No, Commissioner, his last act on this earth was to hold out as he was being tortured. As far as I'm concerned, he was killed in the line of duty."

"You don't think the room full of detectives who saw him come in in cuffs will wonder?"

"They can wonder if they want. It's not their call."

"Can I ask you something, Detective? Why are you going out on a limb for a guy who didn't think anything of fucking you over?"

I looked at my feet for a second. "When you stand in someone's corner, you stay there, sir. That's how I was raised, anyway."

"I know it was, Detective. You're dismissed."

The day we buried Donnie, it snowed. It started out as a clear gray day, and then without warning the sky broke open, like the first time you cry when you realize someone is truly gone. What remained of the Judith task force was asked to carry the casket. Captain Neville was in attendance, as were the mayor, Commissioner Clarkson, DA Suarez, and Jalisa, and what looked to be a small goombah contingent, including Paulie Magliacci, Nickie Brunaldi, and Steve Moretta. Joe Cataldo wasn't among them. Print and TV reporters ringed the mourners, including Wendell, who was dressed like part of the procession even if he wasn't there in that capacity. Next to Neville sat Donnie's mother, Christine, a tall thin woman with gray-streaked dark hair who looked like she was crying for the first time in years.

We lowered the casket at 12:00 p.m. as a six-gun salute was fired and the NYPD Emerald Society played "Scotland the Brave." I couldn't help but smile at the thought of what he'd say if he saw all the resolutely gentile touches the department had brought to the table, from the bagpipes to the Irish tricolors. It was a marked contrast to the rabbi reading the funeral rite and the Hebrew proverb we'd chosen for his tombstone: "Say not in grief 'he is no more' but in thankfulness that he was."

I lingered behind as the mourners left. When the last of them had dispersed, I sat on a bench next to the grave, unbuttoned the collar of my dress uniform, and drank from my flask as the snow fell. I tried to process the idea that he was gone forever, and I began to wonder if I would forget what his voice sounded like, given long enough. I realized I couldn't quite remember the sound of my father's, and I started to cry.

I don't know how long I sat there, but Wendell joined me after a little while. He didn't sit down next to me until I told him he could.

"I'm sorry about your partner, Kinneavy," he said. "He sounds like a good man."

"He was," I said. "He cared more about being a good person than being a good cop, I think. We all should, but I don't know that I do." I was more than a little drunk at this point, but I needed the release too badly to wait until I was safely alone. I lifted my flask. "Mother of all our joys, mother of all our sorrows, intercede with him tonight, for all of our tomorrows," I sang, a little embarrassed at the audible slur in my voice.

Wendell didn't seem sure how to respond, which I guess is understandable. Bereaved, sloppy-drunk cops are not a situation many people prepare for. "Is that biblical?"

I snort-laughed, which, to that point, I hadn't done since I was about fifteen. "It's a Pogues song, dumbass. 'Lorca's Novena.'" I lifted the flask again.

"Kinneavy, it's none of my business, but should you be hitting it that hard?"

"You know, you're right," I said. "It isn't any of your business." I finished the whiskey. "I mean, who the hell are you, man? Shit. My partner's a rat, and then he's dead, and then I'm thinking about fuckin' Paul fuckin' Hudson again, and—"

"What? What's Paul Hudson got to do with this?"

My filter was done for the day. "The motherfucker who raped me in college. Jesus, read my biography, *Shitty, Disappointing Men I Have Known*. The fuck do you know him?"

"I read the name somewhere. I don't remember who he is."

"Well, now you know, I guess. You're welcome."

He got to his feet. "Look, Kinneavy, I'm sorry I was out of line. Just take care, okay?" He left me alone.

I had the presence of mind to fall asleep in my car rather than try to drive it home. I woke up sober at about eleven that night; when I drove home I couldn't sleep. Around dawn, I drove to work to shower and then got to work on consolidating the Judith files. A few hours in, Brickman came by my desk. I wouldn't have given a shit what he wanted even if I hadn't been hungover.

"What happened to Klein was wrong," he said.

I didn't look up. "Thanks for informing me of that, Detective, I'll look into it when I get a chance."

Brickman brought his palm down on my desk. "Listen to me, please. I have to tell you something. It's important."

I sighed and looked up. "What do you have to tell me?"

He leaned in a little. "Look, Kinneavy, just before you were about to take Klein to the Tombs, I . . . I texted somebody. I told him you'd arrested Klein."

I stood up. "Who did you text, Detective?"

"Joe . . . Joe Cataldo."

I walked around my desk. "Detective Brickman, will you please step outside with me for a second?"

He followed me into the hall. Once we were clear of the bull pen, I grabbed him by the lapels and slammed him against the wall.

"You unbelievable piece of shit," I hissed. "I should fucking kill you. Jesus Christ, dirty is one thing. I always knew you were dirty. This is something else. You got another cop killed, you cocksucker. The unpardonable sin."

The vague contrition I'd seen in his eyes was crowded out by petulance. "Oh, says the cop who ran him in."

"I arrested him for committing a crime. You set him up to get a bullet in the head. Are you seriously fucking comparing the two?"

"Oh yeah, a cop—a *white* cop—is gonna have such a great time locked up. Nailed it, you dumb bitch."

"Do you even really care about this? Or did you just think I was going to say, 'It's okay, don't feel bad'?"

"Kinneavy, I came to you because I fucked up. Okay? I fucked up as bad as it's possible to fuck up. I'll do what you think I should do. Fuck, I'll turn myself in if I have to."

I took my hands off his jacket. "Why did you text Cataldo about that? I know you're on the take but why did you think he'd care?"

Brickman smoothed the part of the lapels I'd grabbed. "He told me to text him anything unusual that happened."

"Why?"

"Because . . . because there were a bunch of red-on-reds on my desk he was interested in."

"What was interesting about them?"

Brickman licked his lips, like he was worried the words wouldn't come out on the first try. "They were all business rivals of that guinea who turned up dead when all the Judith shit started."

"Is that all?"

"No, that's not all. I looked through them when he told me to. And . . . every one of them was done with an NYPD-issue gun."

"Tell me what you're thinking, Brickman."

"I'm thinking someone had a debt to settle with Milazzo. Someone with pull. And I think he settled it by having cops kill his competition."

"The police-issue guns . . . can you document that part?"

"Yeah."

I dug into my wallet and pulled out Roane's card. "Don't talk to me about this again. Get in touch with this guy. Be fucking discreet. More discreet than walking up to my desk and telling me who you've been texting. And if this is some attempt at playing me, Brickman, I swear to God I will fuck you up in ways you didn't think physically possible."

ROANE

I generally try to stay out of loud, hot crowded bars. If that was what I wanted (and it's not), I'd go to the club. For the most part, I keep to quieter places where people tend to cluster at the edges, and if what you're drinking isn't too strong, you can get some reading done. But tonight I'd made an exception for Rosalind, who wanted to hit a place in South Street Seaport called Ninotchka. We talked and nursed our beers, and I found myself feeling a little bad about how much I was learning about her. It's one thing to get all Howard Hawksy with a woman and trade barbs with her while you fuck with the Keurig machine. That's not who she is, that's what she is in relation to you.

Rosalind was from the Loch Raven neighborhood of Baltimore originally and had gotten a scholarship to NYU based on an essay about the death of her father. A stevedore and a union vice president, he'd been killed in an accident caused by faulty equipment he'd been trying to alert his bosses to for months. His death had been the start of her drive as a journalist and an even stronger drive to bring down the kind of people responsible for his death ("Like Batman," she said, killing her beer), and finance reporting left her with no shortage of them.

"The most loathsome of all God's creatures are men in ties who pat you on the head, smack you on the ass, and tell you they'll take care of it," she added.

Counterintuitively (her word), Rosalind's father's death had also inspired in her a deep, abiding love of the sea, or at least the oceanfront. It was that that led her to hold out after getting a scholarship to Northwestern, even before she heard back from NYU.

"Lake Michigan doesn't count?" I asked.

"No, nudnik, Lake Michigan doesn't count as the ocean. That's why it's called *Lake* Michigan." She was turning to ask the bartender to hit her again ("again," that was the turn of phrase she kept using) when her grip on the glass slipped and she leaned in to the bar to make sure she lowered it gently enough that it didn't shatter.

"You okay?" I said.

She nodded to a man, a couple years older, by the looks of him, standing further down the bar. He was tall and broad shouldered, with medium-length dark hair, high cheekbones, and green eyes, and he looked familiar somehow.

"That's Paul Hudson," she said. Ah, fuck, there it was.

It was at this point that Paul Hudson looked to his right and saw Rosalind. He maneuvered around the people between us until he reached her, standing with a slightly off-kilter gait.

"Hey, reporter girl, right?" he said. "Talked to you 'bout all that good shit last week. You make me sound good?"

Rosalind gave an odd tight-lipped smile. "I did my best to be objective," she said. "Hope you liked it."

Hudson laughed. "Sorry, honey, I don't really read that shit," he said. "Could be persuaded if they run your picture, though. Do they?"

She smiled again and shook her head. He was clearly making her distinctly uncomfortable, in a way I'd never seen her before. Her posture was the kind I'd seen on a hundred subway cars and park benches: *I'm hoping my posture will tell you to go away, because I don't know what will happen if I tell you to.* The hell with this.

"He bothering you?" I said, loud enough for him to hear.

"It's fine, Wendell," Rosalind said, but now Hudson was focusing on me.

"Hold on, the fuck is this?" he said. "Who the fuck you think you are? You know who I am?"

"Well, she seemed like she didn't want to be bothered, no matter who you are," I said.

"Wendell. No." Rosalind said.

Hudson took a step closer. "You sound like maybe you're the one with a problem."

"I'm getting kind of bored repeating myself, but that's a pretty minor problem. Why don't you go back to whatever drink you handled way better in college?"

Another step closer. "You think you're gonna tell me what to do, we really do have a problem," he said.

I loosened my tie. "Shit, man, it's Friday night. I don't got no place to be in the morning."

Rosalind grabbed me by the arm and yanked me by it out the door. I was reminded of an ant carrying a crumb triple its size. Once we got to the sidewalk by her car, she let me go with a flourish like she was cracking a whip. She was angrier than I'd ever seen her.

"What the fuck did I tell you?" she yelled. "I need access to people like him to do my fucking job, access they will deny if people say I bust balls. Did I not *tell* you all this? Jesus Christ, does a woman have to suck cock for money for you to listen to what she says?"

"That's not fair," I said softly.

"Fuck you, Wendell," she yelled, sounding close to tears. "Fuck you and fuck fair. That guy stared at my tits the entire damn time I interviewed him, when I put the end of my pen in my mouth he asked if I was 'practicing,' and none of that was even out of the ordinary for me. And I didn't say shit. I didn't say shit because I had a story to write. You can't keep it in your pants when you have to sit near him for ten fucking minutes? And you're telling me what's fair. Fuck you again."

"It's not just you," I said.

"The hell does that mean?"

"He . . . he raped a friend of mine, years ago. I mean, maybe she's a friend, I don't know. Someone I met who I admire."

She squinted at me. "Wait, are you talking about that cop?"

"Huh?"

"The detective, the one working Judith, big girl?"

"I guess."

She paused as though processing the new information. "Did she ask you to hit him or whatever?"

"No."

"Yeah, that's what I fuckin' thought. Because I know I didn't either. So don't give me any alpha-male bullshit about how that was for us if neither of us wanted you to do it. We can handle our own shit, and this is real life and I can't just go off on every douchebag like I'm Black Canary."

She paused as though waiting for a cue.

"Actually," I said after a little while, "you couldn't be Black Canary anyway. She's a blonde."

"No, she's not, she's a brunette in a fucking wig. Don't try to come at me on comics, Wendell, because you will lose." She flung open the door of her car and got in on the driver's side. "In," she said.

She drove in silence for a while.

"So what happens now?" I asked.

"We are going home and you are getting fucked consensually and angrily."

"Your home or my home?"

"Yours, Jesus, were you raised by wolves?"

I hadn't had a chance to straighten my apartment up, but Rosalind didn't mind much. Or if she had, she put it into the angry fucking. By the end of the night, I was yelling her name and vowing never to question her knowledge of female superheroes again.

My bedroom windows face east in such a way that, no matter how tired you are in the morning, the sun is going to wake you up and keep you from falling back asleep.

"Ugh, what the shit, no," Rosalind grunted as she encountered this phenomenon for the first time.

I rose from the bed and pulled on a T-shirt from a Fugazi concert I didn't actually attend, unsure if we were at the stage where I wanted to wear the one from the Katy Perry concert I did attend in front of Rosalind.

"You want breakfast? I can make breakfast," I said.

"Yeah, awesome, fry me up a solar eclipse," she said. "This is inhumane. It's Saturday. If you can't trust the sun to keep Shabbat, who can you trust?"

"Roz, that started at sundown and you spent last night drinking, cursing, and fucking a Catholic, not that I'm complaining."

"I'm a half-goyish agnostic, the sun is the damn sun. I hold her to a higher standard."

"Can I at least make us some coffee?"

"Coffee sounds wonderful, thank you."

"How do you take it?"

She clawed her way out of my bed. "Black and bottomless, like my depravity." She walked over next to me and spotted the Katy Perry shirt. "Is it cool if I wear this?"

I was able to convince Rosalind to have some eggs after making way more than I could eat.

"So hey, maybe it's none of my business," she said, "but Judith seems pretty quiet these days."

"You don't think they did that cop?"

"Well, they're your white whale, not mine, but that doesn't sound like them. What's the percentage?"

"They killed two cops already."

"Yeah, rapists. No reason to think that was the case with this one, was there?"

I shrugged. "Yeah, it probably wasn't them. But I think it's all part of the process."

"Say what now?"

I freshened my coffee. "I don't think Judith is just about killing these guys," I said. "They're out to dismantle the system that let them thrive. I mean, shit, look at this." I flipped to page 8 of the *Times*'s Metro section. "Three gangbangers arrested for executing their crew chief. All three of them told the cops in independent interviews it wasn't a coup d'état or anything; they'd just found out he was a rapist." I scanned the brief. "One of 'em says, 'That's not us and we had to send a message that's not us.'" I laid the paper down on the table. "This is what they want. To make themselves unnecessary through fear. And who-ever killed that cop, wouldn't surprise me at all if it's someone they're going after starting to get paranoid, wondering when his number's up. Make examples of a few, give the rest enough rope to hang themselves."

After we finished breakfast and cleared the table, Rosalind decided to head home. I walked her to her car, which was parallel-parked four blocks away at an angle indicative of last night's presex rage. Walking back toward my building, an idling maroon sedan at the curb honked as I passed by. The driver looked familiar; after a minute I realized he was one of the cops who'd been a pallbearer at Detective Klein's funeral. He rolled down his window and I leaned in.

"I help you with something?"

He tried to keep his voice low and still audible on the street. "Katherine Kinneavy told me to talk to you."

"About what?"

"Get in the car."

"Yeah, I've gotten into enough cars with strange men this week already."

He looked pissed off. "Look, call Kinneavy if you want. But this is important and I don't have time to make an appointment."

I kept my eyes on him and climbed into the passenger seat. "I'm texting my coworker the make and model of your car and the time and place I'm getting in," I said.

"That's fine," he said. He reached into his glove box and pulled out a notepad and a pen and handed them to me.

"What are these for?"

"I have some shit to tell you. I told you I only had a minute, and I figured you wouldn't be carrying your own."

"Okay, so what's the story?"

He put his hands on the wheel and stared straight ahead. "You familiar with the King's Men?"

I readied the pen. "Can't say I am."

"How old are you?"

"Thirty-two."

"Do you remember back when John Minetti was mayor?"

"Sort of."

"Okay. Well, before 9/11, it came out that he'd been using a ring of cops to chauffeur him and his girlfriend around, make sure she got home safe, shit like that. Looked pretty bad when it came out, but a little while after, the towers came down, he's Captain America, all the indictments go away. Ever since then—maybe before—there's been a group of cops within the

NYPD who answer to the mayor and do personal favors for him. In exchange, they pick up an envelope every couple weeks and find good things happen to them maybe a little faster than you'd expect."

"These are all the same guys who were doing favors for Minetti?"

"No. They rotate. I think maybe two or three of the Minetti-era guys are still cops. Basically, though, if you want in, you just let the right person know and after they decide you're cool, you're in."

"Can you document any of this?"

The cop pulled a manila envelope from under the seat and took a photo out of it. It showed the current mayor in a bar or club posing and smiling with several off-duty cops. The cop placed his finger on one's face, a tanned guy of about forty with light brown hair. "This is Tom Mazursky from Burglary," he said. "He had one of the shittiest clearance rates in the division when this picture was taken. But if you look in NYPD records, he made detective within a month of it being taken. You got a smartphone?"

"Yeah, why?"

He held out his hand and I handed it to him. He navigated to Facebook and pulled up what appeared to be Mazursky's page. He handed the phone back to me. On it was a picture of Mazursky standing in front of an old-school blue Cadillac, with the caption 'BITCHIN.'"

"That's from a week after making detective. Trust me, it's not that much of a pay bump."

"Jesus, this is pretty reckless. Nobody noticed?"

"Oh, people noticed. That's why he got what they call 'work detail' in the business."

"And what's that mean? He had to do the mayor an extra favor?"

The cop shook his head. "Not the mayor. The mayor's a fuckin' empty suit. Most of the King's Men don't work for him, they work for his chief of staff."

"They work for Judson Crowning?"

"You know him?"

"We've met."

"Anyway," the cop said. He pulled a cassette player out of the envelope. "We've got this really old-school call recorder down at the precinct. All tapes are supposed to be checked with the desk sergeant when they fill up. But I found this one in the evidence room. It's from the week before Russell Milazzo died."

He pressed play on the recorder, and I heard a scratchy voice with a Queens accent.

"Mazursky, who's this?"

"This is me." I heard Crowning's stick-up-the-ass typewriter voice on the tape, patchy but distinct. "Is it taken care of?"

"Is . . . huh? Oh! Oh yeah, that fuckin' yo in Hamilton Heights. Tell our friend you don't got to worry about him no more."

"Keep your damn voice down. What's the status of the . . . screwdriver?"

"Pursued a juvenile, believed to be armed, through a vacant lot. Juvenile turned with hand to waistband, fired a shot to disarm."

"Did that wash with Internal Affairs?"

"I still have the screwdriver, so I guess so."

The cop stopped the tape. "This is from two days after the murder of Drexel Wilson. I have the write-up on the murder in here too. He was done in the back of the head with an NYPD-issue gun."

"Nobody ever checked to see if the gun was a ballistics match?"

"Why would they? Mazursky was cleared on firing at the runner."

"Was the runner even real?"

"Yeah, he was real. Mazursky probably just rousted some corner boy he knew was gonna be there so he'd have an alibi for the shot fired." He placed the folder on my lap. "Anything else you need should be in there."

I picked up the folder and stared at it for a second. "I don't even know your name."

"Detective Howard Brickman, Homicide," he said. "You can use my name."

"Shit, man, are you sure about that?"

He sighed. "Yeah," he said. "I got . . . I just got a lot of shit to make up for." He sat back in the driver's seat. "You believe in atonement?"

"What, like, conceptually?"

"Yeah. I mean, can we offset our sins? Does it mean anything if we're still the same we always were?"

I shrugged. "Haven't thought much about it."

Brickman turned and looked me in the eye. "I'm the reason Donnie Klein is dead," he said. "Me. I'm in way too deep to do good the regular way, so pretty much all I can do now is pull the columns down." He tilted his head back again. "You can go now if you want."

I put my hand on the door. "Where can I reach you if I have any follow-up questions?" I asked, gathering up the material he'd given me.

"You can't," he said. "And you shouldn't try." As soon as I opened the door and stepped onto the curb, he sped on down the street.

CATALDO

I've talked about how I don't like people who wish they'd lived in the past. But there's one exception: I would give my immortal soul to have been present at the Atlantic City Conference in 1929.

It was the first attempt at getting all the big shots into one place to discuss how to avoid the heat that the violence in Chicago and New York had drawn and to come up with alternatives to the booze business now that the writing was on the wall for Prohibition. It was Meyer Lansky's idea, but all the big guns were there: Lansky, Lucky Luciano, Capone, and Nitti down from Chicago; Owney Madden from Hell's Kitchen; Longy Zwillman out of Newark, with Nucky Johnson, the boss of AC, hosting.

I couldn't help but think of how I pictured it as I looked over the back room at Rao's. I'd called everyone I knew, practically, but I'd gone outside of Our Thing. My inner circle—Paulie and Nicky and Steve—was there, but we were the only Italians at the table. Cyrus Yale and Frankie O'Halloran had both turned up, O'Halloran in a suit, which was as freaky as it sounds. Next to them was Elena Quintero, a petite woman in a black leather jacket and short skirt with a Puerto Rican flag pattern who was the maximum leader of the Ñetas gang. She was accompanied by her boy toy Enrique, who served as her number two and knocked a couple teeth out of any homie who said he didn't take orders from *putas*.

Sitting next to her was a small man in a sharkskin suit with curly graying black hair. His name was Saul Abramowitz, but the FBI had no name for him beyond "The Cantor," a nickname they came up with based on his deep, sonorous voice in wire recordings. Saul mostly kept his heroin and construction interests in Flatbush, but various people of various ethnicities called him in as an adviser or mediator from time to time.

Next to him was Mikey Chu, the public face of the Triads in Chinatown as well as a prominent local business owner and one of the major string-pullers in the Chinese community. His presence was pretty encouraging, as he had a reputation for not showing up to anything that didn't interest him. "I don't like to get people's hopes up," he said once.

Once everyone was seated, I stood up at the head of the table. "Gentlemen, lady," I said. "Thank youse all so much for coming out this evening. I have something I need to talk about. A little while ago, an associate of the boss of my family made an attempt on my life. He's made clear he wants a war. Now, this guy is high up. Probably about my level, to be honest. I don't know who within My Thing I can trust besides the men you see here next to me. So my proposition is this: if youse back me in this, I'm going to win. And when I do, you'll have a friend in the head of a family. Any debts you have to me or the family will be forgiven . . . or, if you like, we'll make you partners. I remember my friends. Now, alternately, you can sit this one out, and if my acquaintance comes out on top, a guy who's never given a shit about you will be in charge. If I win this without your help, I'll remember that too."

"So, what, you called us in here to threaten us?" Elena piped up.

"Miss Quintero, I don't think 'I remember who was there when I called and who wasn't' is all that threatening a sentiment," I said. "Alls I'm saying is, whether you want to be my friend or you think I can go fuck myself, when the smoke clears, the feeling's gonna be mutual, so do what you think is right."

"Joe, we go back," said Yale. "And yeah, you been a friend in need. But do you understand what you're asking some of us to do? You're asking black folks and brown folks to commit to a war with white people. Now, I know you're good as your word, but that's something other people are going to notice."

"Cy, I'm glad you brought that up," I said, "because that's where my friend in Homicide comes in. There's no heat unless he says so, and he won't."

The table processed this information. O'Halloran was the first to speak. "What the hell," he said. "You got me for the duration, Joe. You make me regret it, I'll fuckin' kill ya." He said it in a jokey tone, but I didn't doubt for a second he was serious.

Yale nodded. "Goes for me too."

Saul Abramowitz nodded. "This ought to be interesting," was all he said.

"Fuck it, we're in too," said Elena.

Chu just nodded.

I clapped my hands. "Great," I said. "Fuckin' great. None of youse are gonna—" I felt my phone ringing. "I gotta take this," I said, stepping out the back door. It wasn't a number I recognized, but it was definitely a voice I recognized.

"What the fuck is going on?" Judson Crowning yelled.

"I'm having dinner with some friends, is what the fuck's going on. What are you talking about?"

"Your cat's-paw is talking to reporters. We need to deal with this."

"My who?"

"Your cop, you fucking ape."

"Hold on, what?"

"Your Detective Brickman is talking to a reporter with the *Septima*."

"What the fuck? About me?"

"Does that matter? Is a man who knows the kinds of things he knows about you someone who needs to be going off the reservation? You need to contain this, Mr. Cataldo."

"Hey, how 'bout this?" I said. "How 'bout fuck you, considering what happened last time we got together? You weren't too worried about containing shit then. I'm gonna go back inside and finish entertaining my guests, and then I'm gonna go contain it. You go to bed if you're this upset." I ended the call, slid the battery out of the phone, and went back inside.

Maybe I was just desperate for a break after how stressful shit had gotten lately, but the coalition I'd assembled really was pretty fun dinner company, with the exception of O'Halloran, and Abramowitz, who was at least an excellent listener.

Around ten that night, I took care of the tab, and the rest of the group headed for the door. Noticing how much colder it had gotten after sundown, Enrique offered his chinchilla coat to Elena. They were pretty cute. I wished them well.

I went home first to pick up my car and my gun, then drove to Brickman's place in Forest Hills. I had a feeling in my gut I might need to get out of there quicker than I could on foot.

Brickman didn't answer the first two times I knocked.

"It's goddamn open," I heard him yell after the third time.

I pushed open the door with an open palm. Brickman was sitting in an armchair parallel to the door. There was a tumbler of whiskey on an end table next to it, and he was holding his Glock, which he leveled at me when he saw me in the doorway.

"Jesus, Howie," I said. "What are you waving that around for?"

He gave me a sideways smile. "Case some fuckin' goombah comes knockin' at my door, why do you think?"

"I'd feel better if you put it on the table."

"Yeah, I bet you would."

"Howie, come on."

He rolled his eyes and laid the gun on the end table, picking up the tumbler as he did so.

"Howie, why the fuck are you talking to reporters?"

"Why the fuck are you killin' cops?"

"What? Who says I'm killing cops?"

"Joe, come on. I text you about Donnie, that's the last anyone sees of him alive. I'm not retarded."

"So you talk to a fuckin' newspaper?"

He sat up in the chair. "Yeah, so I talk to a newspaper, Joe. Because I fucked up worse than I've ever fucked up, and a cop is dead 'causa me, and maybe you could just go to bed on something like that, but I can't."

"Listen, Howie," I said, "I got something else we need to talk about. It's good news."

"Oh, it's good news. Whee. Let's hear your good fuckin' news."

"Howie, I'm going to war. I'm gonna be blunt about that. Soldato isn't letting this go and it's gonna get bad before it gets good. And when it gets bad, there's gonna be some heat coming Homicide's way. I need you to steer it away from the people I've enlisted."

He snorted. "Enlisted? Shit. So that's your good news? You want me to do more of the same shit that got Donnie killed? You spoil me, daddy."

"Let me finish, okay? After that's done, we're through. Okay? I got nothing to hold over you. No more connection between us. You want out? You're out. We never have to talk to each other again. This one last favor and you're free."

Brickman's eyes had looked bleary and unfocused up until the last word. At that point he looked straight into my eyes. Brickman normally had sort of a male resting-bitch-face thing going on, with his default expression vaguely petulant no matter what mood he was in. But when he turned to look at me, I felt pure contempt radiating from him beyond any expression I'd ever seen on his face. He just stared at me like that for a while. I wasn't sure what to say, and I was a little afraid to move, like I was charming a snake. Finally, he started laughing.

"Free?" he said. "Come on, Joe. I'll never be free. I'll be your man for the rest of my life." He snatched the gun off the end table, wrapped his lips around the barrel, and pulled the trigger.

"Fuck me!" I yelled before I could stop myself. I had jumped back just in time to keep the blood spatter from hitting my coat. My ears were ringing and I thought I heard someone coming down the hall to see what the noise was. I threw open the door, slammed it behind me, and ran down the sidewalk.

I called Paulie to let him know I was coming over to his place. I paced while I explained the situation, trying to keep from panicking.

"This is not good, Joe," he said when I was done.

"No fucking shit!" I said. "I'm gonna lose the fucking coalition, and the Old Man is probably gonna clip me for letting this happen."

"Joe, come on, let's not get crazy," Paulie said, using the soothing tone he used to put on whenever I was trying to go back for more after I lost a fight when we were kids. "Let's think. What are our options?"

"Option, Paulie. Singularity. We have one option."

"Okay, we have one option. And?"

"We gotta nip this shit in the bud before we need Yale or the Puerto Ricans' help."

"And how do we go about doing that?"

"I'm still working on that."

"Okay, well, I dunno how long we have, Joe. When Soldato finds out about Brickman, he's gonna escalate."

"Yeah, no shit." I sunk onto the couch and ran my fingers through my hair, staring at the ceiling and waiting for this to all turn out to be a bad dream in the way you only do when you're fully awake.

"You gonna dress any different?" Paulie asked.

"Huh?"

"When you're the boss. I mean, you dress okay, but you gotta dress like the boss."

"Get the fuck outta here."

"Hey, I'm serious, you gotta figure this stuff out. I mean, look at what you got now. Open collar, blue scarf, that's under-boss shit. Come on, what are you gonna wear?"

I laughed and straightened up on the couch. "I think 'boss,' I think more reds. Gotta get a red tie, like, blood red, silk, white shirt, everything else black. Black Armani with the pinstripe, black pocket square. Really go balls to the wall with the blacks and reds, like, I dunno, fuckin' Dracula."

"Or a Nazi."

"Blow me."

"How about the car?"

"The hell is wrong with my car?"

"Nothing, if you're an underboss. Show up in that shit at a meeting with the heads of the other families, they'll all hand you their coats."

I laughed again. "You little fucker. Okay, fine. Black '76 Continental. Fuck it, let's get a red leather interior for that too."

It started to rain outside as the night wore on, and we kept talking about the reign of King Joe, like kids at camp talking about a girl's boobs. I still didn't know what I was going to do in the morning, but for a while, I felt okay.

KINNEAVY

So it turns out that if you manhandle a fellow detective, even if it's in the hall, people will start to wonder about you. Captain Neville, uncharacteristically, seemed more concerned than pissed off as she called me into her office.

"Kinneavy," she said, "what happened to Klein is fucking with your head. And I understand that. But you can't bring it in here. You're hungover every other day, you always look like you slept in your clothes, and now you're getting in fights like some fuckin' high school girl?"

"Captain, I apologize for losing my temper, but—"

"Katherine, please," she said. "A week paid leave. This isn't a suggestion."

"All due respect, Captain, I really don't think I need—"

She stood up. "I'm gonna be blunt, Kinneavy, I think you've spent your life thinking you and you alone know what's best for you, and look at the state it's left you in."

For the first time in a while, I didn't have a response. I unstrapped my gun and handed it to her.

It was hard to tell one day from the next during my week's suspension. I didn't leave the house much. I went to the bodega around the corner to buy some soup. I cleaned out my walk-in closet. I thought long and hard about calling my mother before deciding not to. Mostly I drank. When I stopped, it was only because of how far I would have to go to get more. I was informed of Brickman's suicide on Friday, shortly before it was hastily shoved into the eleven o'clock news. The pang I felt for him surprised me a little. Maybe he'd wanted to make things right more sincerely than I gave him credit for.

Jalisa came to visit Saturday night. She'd probably told me she was coming earlier, but I'd forgotten somehow. She leaned in for a hug as I opened the door. "Aw, honey, you look like shit," she said as she pulled away.

"Love you too, J."

"Hey, I'm a friend. You want someone to tell you what you want to hear, get an employee."

"Benjamin fuckin' Franklin over here."

"Ben, please. Benjamin Franklin is my father."

We sat down next to each other on the couch. "K, how often are you drinking?" she asked, her brown eyes wide and talk-show-host earnest.

I rolled my eyes. "When I'm thirsty. Jesus."

"Katie, I'm fucking serious. You have a problem. I'm frankly not sure why someone as smart as you hasn't looked for help yet."

"Well, fuck, Jalisa, maybe it's because I was raised to believe adults sorted out their own shit. Maybe I wonder if the very few men who take me seriously as a cop would stop if they knew I was seeing a shrink like some Upper West Side wife who can't stop crying over those Sarah McLachlan ads. Maybe because even if I do have a problem, drinking made me feel more comfortable with who I was and the shit that's happened way more effectively than any doctor or pills or meeting ever did."

"Katherine, we're friends. You need to stop shouting at me."

The quiet, deliberate tone stopped me dead. "I'm . . . I'm sorry," I said. "I'm not great right now, J. I don't know what's going on. I carried this for so long and it's just now fucking me up just like when it happened, and, like, I don't fucking know, is this going to keep happening? How long am I going to have until it happens again? Or what if it just goes on like this the rest of my life? Jalisa, what . . . what happens if I never get better?"

I realized for the first time that Jalisa's hand was on my thigh.

I reached out and wrapped my arms around her like they'd never been anywhere else and we leaned into a deep kiss as she undid the buttons of my blouse. I felt that rushing in my ears again, but it was another kind of train entirely, not approaching me but carrying me away, carrying me to her, and I had my head out the window with the wind whipping my hair across my face, and I was laughing and singing as it swerved out of the station and into the sunlight.

Do you know what it's like to realize you love someone? And more than that, that you've loved someone for a long time? It was such an indescribable, amazing feeling of *finding*, and there were times that the feeling of our bodies against one another made me want to cry because I knew in my heart this would eventually end. That was the kind of pleasure I was feeling: the kind whose only flaw was its finiteness.

But when it was over, I didn't want to cry. I just wanted to lie there on the couch with her and feel the love that I had spent years finding a name for. I loved this woman. I always had. That was something I could rest on, no matter how hard the world and my own memories got.

"Now what?" I said after a while.

"Huh?"

"I mean, what are we now?"

"Well, I'm gay, but I've seen you with plenty of dudes, so I'm guessing you're bi, so—"

"That's not what I meant. What are we together?" I pressed the palm of my hand against her cheek. "This isn't something we can be public with. Not now."

"You don't think so?"

"Jalisa, your star is rising. This is shit they'll use against you."

"Um, honey, you're not the center of the universe. I'm thirty-two. There were other girls."

I sat up and pulled my blouse on, but didn't button it. "Look, J, I'm saying . . ." I grabbed my forehead. "I love you. Okay? There it is."

She sat up next to me. "I love you too. What's the problem?"

"Problem is right now I'm gonna be the worst version of myself, and I just . . . I can't need you the way I know I'm going to, because I'm going to be bad for you until the Judith thing is resolved."

"So what are you saying?"

I held her hand in mine for a second. "If I put you and me on pause, will you wait for me?"

She smiled at me and I was back on that train. "Honey, I've been waiting since those hips and tits came in. I'm good at waiting."

That Saturday evening was the reason I was strong enough to go back to work on Monday. It wasn't a cure-all. I still felt the frayed nerves and cold sweats and random triggers that had been haunting my steps since I interrogated Elba Borrero. But I could feel the ground beneath my feet, and sometimes that's all you need.

Monday afternoon, a beat cop I knew by sight but not by name came looking for me at my desk. He introduced himself as Officer Hargrove.

"I was told to take this to Ciorra, but he said talk to you instead," he said, sounding nervous and proud all at once.

He drove me to the next precinct over. We were met at the door by Jim Ciorra of the NYPD Organized Crime Bureau, tall, dark, forty-five-ish, and first-male-teacher handsome. Ciorra beckoned us to follow him down the hall to the drunk tank, where a man with a black eye and a split lip was sitting.

Ciorra knocked on the bars. "Jimmy, this is my friend Detective Kinneavy."

"Mmmkay, and?"

"Jimmy, tell my friend why you're in there."

"'Cause I took a swing at a Jew broad and got fuckin' . . . *brutalicized* for it." He pointed to his eye. "I'm a fuckin' hate-crime victim and fuckin' Obama ain't gonna do shit because Mossad won't let him—"

"Yeah, yeah, yeah, cut the bullshit and tell us specifically what happened," Ciorra said.

Jimmy rolled his eyes. "My bitchhole upstairs neighbor is takin' forever on the stairs, right? So I give her a kick in the ass and she turns around and whales on me. She . . . fuckin' . . . she looks fine, so I don't know where they get off with the self-defense bullshit."

Ciorra turned to me. "Jimmy's upstairs neighbor, as it happens, is in the system," he said. He snatched a file from on top of his desk and opened it to a mugshot of a woman who had to be at least six two with a thick muscled neck and short, spiky blond hair. Annie Lennox as a bodybuilder.

"Rachel Litvak," Ciorra said. "Born in Borough Park but moved to Tel Aviv with her family at two. Commando in the IDF, moved back to New York four years ago. Two years ago she was arrested for aggravated assault for beating up a man who groped her on the subway."

I was starting to see where this was going. "What does she do for a living?"

"She reads meters for Con Ed."

"So she can drive all around the city to pretty much any address."

"Yep."

A lot of cops are ashamed to admit how much of clearance is lucky breaks: a guy gets picked up with a hot gun or a bag of weed, panics, tells you his cousin killed a guy, bang, cold case closed. I was sitting on my biggest break in a while: military experience, ability to move about the city incognito, a documented history of fucking up men who didn't keep their hands to themselves.

"Thank you, Lieutenant," I said. He nodded, while Jimmy whined about how people should be thanking him instead.

Rachel Litvak still lived in Borough Park, on the third floor of a brownstone. I explained the situation to Neville and asked for permission to go over and make a friendly visit to see how much was coincidence.

She clapped me on the shoulder. "Welcome back, kid," she said. "Take someone with you. That's an order."

I brought Wysocki, a big guy with a reputation throughout the precinct for being fast on the draw. Borough Park is one of the more heavily Orthodox neighborhoods in the city, and Wysocki looked a little overwhelmed by the sheer amount of bearded men in black fedoras and side curls and demure bewigged women pushing old-fashioned baby carriages.

"Is she, like, one of those?" he asked in a low voice, jerking his chin in the direction of one of the Orthodox women.

"Nah, I heard she's Reform," I said. "Does it matter?"

"I guess not, I just hate the idea of cuffing a woman in a dress. Seems like overkill."

"Stan, trust me, she is well acquainted with overkill."

We knocked on Rachel's door as a bright orange winter sunset was seeping through the windows at the end of the hall. When no one answered, I tried the buzzer, which worked. Rachel was wearing an unbuttoned work shirt over a solid gray T-shirt.

"Can I help you?" she asked.

I took out my shield, Wysocki following suit. "Detective Kinneavy, Homicide," I said. "This is Detective Wysocki."

She frowned. "Everything alright? I didn't hit that prick *that* hard, did I?"

I smiled. "It's nothing to do with that, Miss Litvak. We're not here to arrest you, we just have a couple of questions. May we come in?"

Her expression softened. "Sure."

Her apartment was modestly furnished. There was no couch or TV, just a few folding chairs, a card table, and a bookshelf. There was a computer desk in the corner, parallel to the kitchenette.

"Sit, please," she said.

We sat and she filled two glasses with ice water.

"All I have at short notice, I'm afraid," she said.

"That's fine," I said. "Miss Litvak—"

"Rachel, please."

"Rachel, until recently, we were assigned to the Judith case."

"Ah, yes."

"Now, you work for Con Ed and you live around the general area of several of the victims. Did you ever see anything odd while you were making your rounds, particularly in the evening?"

She frowned again and shook her head. "I'm afraid not. I don't pay much attention to anything but the job when I'm working."

Time to turn up the heat a little. "Okay, now, Rachel, can you tell me what you were doing on the evening of November twenty-fourth?" It was the evening Judith had nabbed Rivette.

Rachel paused, but that didn't mean anything. It gets harder to remember what you did on any given weeknight once the week is past. Then she looked up. "Ah," she said. "On the job in Red Hook."

"Okay, well, we actually talked to your supervisor, Rachel, and he says that was your night off."

She furrowed her brow. "Well, that can't be right. I have the printout by my bed. Can I go get it?"

"Mind if we come with you?"

"Of course not."

We followed Rachel down a short hall to her bedroom. She held up her index finger for patience and walked around to the far side of her twin bed, rummaging around underneath. "Ah," she said, then whirled around, a sawed-off shotgun with a pistol grip in one hand, and shot Wysocki in the stomach. I quickly returned fire and dove behind the bed as I fumbled for my radio. "Officer down at 5313 Ninth Avenue, unit 346!" I said. "We need immediate backup, officer down!"

Litvak discharged the spent shell from the gun and came around the side of the bed, pointing it at my head. I raised my gun and fired in the general direction of center mass, getting her in the right shoulder and knocking the gun to the floor. She fell into a pushup position. I stepped on her hand as she reached for the gun and flattened her back with the other foot.

"Rachel Litvak," I said, holding the gun on her with one hand while I pulled the cuffs off my waist with the other. "You're under arrest for—"

I didn't get to finish because it was at this point that she pulled a knife from the sleeve of her work shirt and sunk it into the right side of my belly. My breath caught. I saw her move her arm as if to drag the blade directly across and grabbed her wrist with my free hand, holding the knife—a big, wicked-looking thing, with brass knuckles welded into the handle—in place as she struggled to get control of it. With every iota of strength, I held the knife in place and shot her in the clavicle. Her grip slackened and she fell forward on her face on the hardwood floor with enough force to break her nose. I could still hear low rattling breaths coming from both her and Wysocki, and sirens were visible from the bedroom window. I sat on the bed and held the gun on her while I held the knife in place as I finished Mirandizing her.

"Fuuuck . . . I liked this sweater too."

"Fuck you, I liked that shotgun," Rachel said.

I turned to Wysocki. "How you doin', Stan?"

He wheezed from the floor. "Not great, Kathleen."

"I know. Stay with me, buddy, you're doing great. They're coming. They're coming. Ah, shit, this hurts." I shifted my weight slightly, to see if that would make it hurt any less. It didn't. "It's Katherine, by the way."

"Oh shit, sorry."

"No need to apologize."

"I musta just figured it was Kathleen 'cause it sounded more Irish."

"I mean, nothing wrong with Kathleen. It's pretty. Just not accurate."

"Will you two shut the fuck up?" Rachel groaned.

"Okay, you know what, we would have been gone ages ago if you hadn't decided to be a cunt, okay?" I said. "So, y'know, suck it up."

I was starting to see spots swimming around in my field of vision, but I'm proud to say I didn't pass out until I was in the ambulance.

ROANE

One of my worst tendencies as a journalist is realizing I have an important follow-up question immediately after I've finished the interview. It wasn't until I was in a coffee shop typing up what Brickman had given me that I realized I didn't have the name of the restaurant where the picture of the King's Men had been taken.

As luck would have it, a corner of a menu was visible in the picture. I could make out "KY'S" when I held the picture upside down. I looked up Nicky's, Macky's, and Franky's before finally trying some nontraditional spellings and finding a picture of the interior of Micky's in the Theater District on their website that matched the picture.

Micky was still there, a gray-haired, red-faced Irish guy in his midsixties. I told him I was working on a piece about restaurants with a large cop clientele, which made me feel like an asshole, and I made a mental note to actually write the article once all this was over. I showed him the picture and asked if he could identify all the cops.

"Yeah, yeah yeah yeah," he said, dragging his finger over the picture like it was a tablet. "Lessee here, we got Tom Mazursky, Jack Dragna, Eddie Wexler . . ." He paused and thought about the remaining ones. "Mike . . . no Mark Stamper, Al Cavuto, and . . . I don't remember that one's first name, something Dellinger." I entered the names into my phone as he recited them. He handed the picture back to me. "How'd you get that picture?"

"Friend on the force. Why?"

"I just . . . I remember 'em all, and I remember they were all big tippers. Like, not generous. Like, fuck-you money. They had something to prove, you know? It felt . . . felt kind of dangerous. I don't know how else to describe it."

I nodded and thanked him for his help. Once we were finished talking, I found a table by the window and ordered a sandwich. I wanted to, at the very least, make sure the place didn't suck if I'd roped myself into writing about how underrated it was. As luck would have it, the sandwich was delicious.

I looked at the list of names and wondered how afraid I should be. I've never really been afraid of the people and things I probably should be, even as I know in the back of my mind they're a threat. It makes for good journalism and, on occasion, bad health. I realized this was probably information Kinneavy could use too. I knew she was on Crowning's radar, and I knew how he reacted when he felt cornered. I called her, but I didn't get a response. I texted her the list instead.

I looked at the picture again and was struck with the normality of it all. They may have been flashing fuck-you money and celebrating their good fortune in becoming a bought and paid-for Praetorian Guard, but they were wearing cheap suits and looked like they were still getting their hair cut by a guy they knew from church or temple. I felt like I could see a process playing out in this single instant preserved in the photo: these were still blue-collar guys who needed a break, maybe had a sick wife or a kid stuck in a shitty school, but by the time the check came, you could already see that need for a leg up giving way to active greed, and whatever was happening inside of them just kept happening until these men would kill in cold blood if given the order. It was the banality of evil in microcosm: fallen man having fun on his evening off.

After I was finished eating, I called Tony and asked if we could meet up. He met me at Pier 84 about an hour later. I was thinking he'd be pissed I'd wanted to do this on a weekend, but he said he was happy to get out of the house. I sat down and showed him what Brickman had given me, explaining the situation with the King's Men and what I'd found out from Micky. He looked over the files and didn't say anything for a while.

"Wendell, I need you to understand how dangerous this is," he said.

"I do," I said.

"No, I really don't think you do," he said. "I think you think you know because you've annoyed the big boys before and you think this is the same thing. It's not, Wendell. This is the kind of thing people will try to hurt you for."

"So what are you telling me?"

"I'm asking you, Wendell. Please. Let me send this to someone else, to the *Times* or somebody higher-profile. The story still gets out there without your name on it. Will you get the credit? No. Will you be safer? Yes, and that's my priority."

"Tony, come on, we're both adults—"

"Fuck's sakes, Wendell, I'm responsible for you. You and everyone else in the newsroom. I can't stop you from sticking your neck out like this, but I'll be damned if I'm going to enable it."

I'm an only child and I don't see my parents with any kind of regularity. In the time I've spent at the *Septima*, I've learned how families are made by circumstances just as much as by genes. And more than that, I've learned that sometimes our instinct is even stronger to fight for our found families. When a sister or a brother or, hell, a father appears in your life out of nowhere, you know that's a rare thing, and you feel a different kind of responsibility for them. This was what I felt for the people I worked with, and I guess, to some extent for Kinneavy, in an aloof-cousin sort of way, and what I was now realizing Tony felt for me. As much as the King's Men story meant to me, that's not something I believe in lightly casting aside.

"What are you proposing?" I said.

"If you want me to run this, you have two choices: I can pass it on and have it run under someone else's byline, or I can hold it until the winds are fairer."

"How do you mean?"

He leaned in. "Look around, Wendell. People are snatching cops off the street and killing them. You know who does that? People who think they're untouchable. Now, whoever did that, they're gonna escalate until they burn out. And when that happens, this will finish the job. But right now, if I run this, I'm exposing you to someone who has the power to fuck you up. Do you understand?"

I nodded. I didn't like it, but that's not really the same thing.

"You're a good fuckin' reporter, Wendell," Tony said. "You always were. And I think you and Roz are cute as hell."

"Wait, who told you about me and Rosalind?"

"My good friend Not Being Blind. He told me a long time before you. He must just like me better."

I got home at dusk and decided to work on an ongoing feature on our editorial calendar. I had my headphones in and was listening to music as I worked, which was probably why whoever was at my door had to hammer on it before I noticed. I popped one headphone out to make sure it was coming from the door.

"Open up. Police." Yep.

I have never been sorrier not to have a peephole, because when I opened the door it took me a few seconds to realize I was looking at Tom Mazursky. My amateur evolutionary biology theories had been right. He now had a top-shelf haircut and was wearing a gray Ike Behar. He stepped inside before I could close the door, followed by Judson Crowning, who closed the door behind him.

Crowning walked over to my computer and yanked the headphones out of the jack. Jessie J's "Domino" filled the apartment. Credit where due, it was exactly the kind of song that would cover up the sounds of whatever they were going to do to me. I wondered if he was a fan.

Crowning sat down on my couch. "Where are the documents Detective Brickman gave you?" he asked.

"I don't know what you're talking about," I said, too quickly for it to sound like anything but a lie.

Crowning nodded to Mazursky, who walked over to my kitchenette, wrapped a dishcloth around his hand and punched me in the face. I spit out some blood but no teeth.

"Mr. Roane, I don't appreciate being lied to," Crowning said. "If you want to pretend you didn't meet with Detective Brickman, he shouldn't have parked within range of a stoplight camera. Now, where are the documents he gave you?"

I flipped him the bird. Mazursky went to work on my ribs and stomach, this time not even waiting for Crowning's nod. Crowning let him continue for a little while before raising one hand, palm up. Mazursky stopped immediately, like Crowning had unplugged him. Crowning motioned for Mazursky to step aside and sidled up to me, backing me against the wall.

"Mr. Roane," he said, "I want to be clear, I'd very much like what Detective Brickman gave you, but that's not our primary purpose here tonight. I'm here to let you know where things stand. You can laugh at this if you like, but I am a fairly patient man, all things considered. I feel like I've given you every possible opportunity not to antagonize me, not to go down tunnels you couldn't necessarily find your way back out of. But at this point, you are trying my considerable patience, Mr. Roane. You are at the banks of the Rubicon, and if you cross it, your only remaining choice will be whether Ms. Garwood dies with a dick in her ass and a gun in her mouth or the other way around."

"Fuck you," I spat before I could stop myself. He slammed the toe of his wingtip into my balls, backing me further against the wall as I slid down it. He held his face a few inches from mine and grabbed a fistful of my hair.

"I know you're still protecting that Russian whore," he said. "The blond one that got away. That keeps getting away. Have you noticed yet that I don't care? Do you want to know why?"

I didn't say anything.

"I already told you I'm not from this city. I've worked in several others. Chicago. Pittsburgh. Cleveland. Do you have any idea how many others there have been in those cities? How many families in Kiev and Phnom Penh and Sofia are never getting another letter from America? I want you to think about that. I want you to despair in the knowledge of how little men like you can ever do about men like me. I've done a great many things to upset a great many people, Mr. Roane. Maybe one or many of them will bite me in the ass someday. I'll take it as it comes. But I triple-fucking guarantee you"—he twisted my hair in his fist—"nothing will ever happen to me over those girls. Because no matter how many bleeding-heart stories you write, no matter how many campaigns you mount, no matter how many pictures you publish, you will never, ever make the world care about dead whores. Understand that, Mr. Roane."

He gave me an open-handed slap across the face and then stood away from the wall. Crowning beckoned to Mazursky and the cop followed him out of the apartment as the song ended and Katy Perry's "Firework," the next song in my "Beat Reporting" playlist, started. (I thought the name was pretty clever at the time I made it.)

I didn't contact Rosalind until the next day. I wanted to tell her what I had to say in person. I explained my black eye to her, as well as Crowning's visit and what he had said about her if I continued pursuing my line of inquiry.

She looked down at the kitchen table and didn't say anything for a little while. Then she looked up at me, the same dangerous Jewish-American Warrior Princess look I'd seen when she was yelling at me dancing frenetically in her eyes.

"Stay on the fucker," she said.

"But Roz, he said—"

"I heard what he said. I'm assuming you told me to ask what I thought you should do and I'm telling you, you should stay on the fucker."

"Rosalind, he threatened you."

"People threaten me all the time, Wendell. Usually anonymously. Once someone emailed me a rape threat for writing up someone's arrest for insider trading."

"Yeah, but this is something else. This isn't some Internet dipshit, this is a guy who could actually do it."

She shook her head. "Jesus Christ, Wendell, you are such a *man* sometimes. All of them could actually do it. Tell me you could get something like that at eleven fifteen at night and just say, 'Oh, it's just the Internet.' I've been threatened before, Wendell. If it's up to me, I say do it. You already made that Russian girl a promise. Don't fuck it up because you think you have to be my white knight."

"Half-white."

"Knock it off."

I moved my hand forward on the table. She reached out and took it, gripping it tight like she'd found it after thinking it was lost forever. "Thank you," she said.

"For what?"

"For trusting me enough to keep me in the loop and not doing some bullshit macho Spider-Man thing where you just push me away without explaining anything because that's what Real Men do."

I shrugged. "You told me to listen to what a woman wants before I do anything on her behalf."

"And you took that advice and ran with it? Wow, I'm sorry about that whole 'you're such a man' thing now. I should make you cookies."

"Please do. Please stay over and dote on me and my poor black eye and bruised ribs."

"I was goofing around, my cookies suck."

"I don't know good cookies from bad."

"I'm not fuckin' making you cookies, Wendell."

The next few days passed without incident, although Tony's expression when he saw my face on Monday made me feel a thousand times worse than the actual beating had. After deadline Tuesday, I got a call from a number I didn't recognize. When I answered it, I heard Kinneavy's voice.

"Wendell, how've you been?"

"Kinneavy! Where you calling from?"

"NYU Langone."

"Shit, what happened?"

"Long story. No it's not, I got stabbed."

"What? By who?"

"Not important. Look, when I get out of here, I have a proposition for you."

"What kind of proposition?"

"So way earlier in the investigation, I tailed Frankie O'Halloran for a while. After we stopped, I had one of my snitches stay on him for a couple more days, just to be sure."

"Okay."

"Now, everywhere Frankie stops, he makes a pickup, except for one bar on 110th where he makes a drop. The owner of that bar takes the package to 130th to a woman who drives it downtown and across the GW Bridge. I have a hunch I'm working on, but I can't leave my jurisdiction on a hunch. If I give you the address, will you follow her and tell me what you find?"

"You said it was a proposition. Do you have something to trade?"

"Yeah, as it turns out. When they were searching my stabber's apartment, they found a folder full of fake passports and IDs in her couch cushion. One of those names is listed as the owner of a rural property in North Jersey. Now, this lady having attempted to murder two cops, I *am* allowed to leave my jurisdiction to investigate that if I kiss the staties and the local cops' asses, and I have an entirely separate hunch about what I'm going to find on that farm. You follow the O'Halloran's package for me, you get exclusive access to whatever that turns out to be."

"When would all this be happening?"

"Ugh, these boners want to keep me here at least two more days. Can you do Friday morning?"

"I'll make time."

"Fantastic. Thanks."

CATALDO

Two nights after Brickman blew his gun, five high-ranking Dellaponte soldiers—all of them with close ties to Soldato—were playing their weekly card game in the back room of a bodega in Little Italy. About an hour in, a white man, two black men, a Puerto Rican woman, and a Puerto Rican man entered the room, all with guns drawn. All five of the soldiers were packing, but only one of them had a chance to so much as draw before the interlopers sprayed the room with bullets. Once they were sure everyone was dead, they shoveled the nonbloodstained portion of the pot into a valise and left the way they'd come.

At least, that was what Frankie O'Halloran told me when we met the next morning. It was weird to see him by daylight. I guess I'd figured he had a casket he slept in somewhere in the Kitchen during the day with rocky, inhospitable dirt from County Bumfuckigan piled up at the bottom. The crime scene looked enough like a botched robbery that it was being treated as such, according to O'Halloran.

"The hell do you know that?" I said.

"I know all sortsa shit, Joe, because I have a lot of people who owe me favors, and those debts are payable in information. It's a good trade to be in."

"That why you want me to keep you up to date on Crowning?"

"Shit yes. A bead on the wild card? That's gold."

"Glad to hear it, because he was in touch with me last night."

"Saying what?"

"Fuck, man, he's . . . the wheels are comin' off that *stronzo*. He roughed up that reporter Brickman was talking to, the *moulinyan*. Thinks he knows shit about 'all the king's men' or something."

I couldn't see the big Mick's eyes behind his shades but his eyebrows jumped a mile. "You're sure he said 'the King's Men'?" he asked, sounding more surprised than I'd ever heard him.

"Yeah, why?"

"Do you know who they are?"

"Dirty cops, right? Like, not individuals, a gang, like those Rampart guys in LA."

"That's part of it. Other part is, they report directly to the mayor. Except apparently not, if Crowning is concerned about them. That's . . . that's very interesting." He reached into his coat and slapped an envelope down on the table. "You earned the shit out of this, Joe."

"Hey, you know what?" I said. "Keep it. I got something else I want to ask, if that's okay."

He put his hand on the envelope. "Oh?"

"Yeah. Remember that car you wired for Soldato?"

"Sure."

"I like that car. What do you say you unwire it?"

I had a missed call after we left our meeting. I recognized Cyrus Yale's number and gave him a call back as I walked home.

"What's up, Cy?"

"Well, not to put too fine a point on it, but you curious at all why you got zero cops in your pocket and five points on the scoreboard?"

"I figured they hadn't been informed."

"Oh, they been informed. They been informed by yours truly, after which yours truly sold the fuck out of you and told them they'd regret it the rest of they lives if they pulled out on you."

"Shit. I mean, *shit*, Cy, I don't know what to say."

"Say, 'Thank you, Cy.'"

"Thank you, Cy."

"Thank you, Cy, and also your tribute goes down to ten percent."

"Twelve."

"Five."

"Fine, fine, ten. Ten's fine, ya chiselin' fuck." But I was laughing as I said it.

I got my money's worth over the next week. On Thursday afternoon, Tommy Visaggio, an old-timer who'd come up in the ranks alongside Soldato, was shot five times by two men in a barber shop on Vernon Boulevard. Tommy's son Harry, who'd been a sprinter in high school, pursued the shooters down the street and got one in the back. As he approached him to finish the job, the second shooter stepped out of the alley and shot him in the temple.

Friday evening, three more enforcers were leaving a club on West Broadway after a business meeting that somehow ended up incorporating lap dances and cocaine. One of them noticed a black Escalade coming alarmingly fast toward them and had the presence of mind to pull his gun and get off a few shots through the window, but that didn't stop its inhabitants from aerating all three men. The Escalade was found burned out across the river with the plates hacked off the next after-noon. Elena sent me a text to let me know when the car had been dumped and a second to inform me that I was buying her a new one once the bullshit blew over.

The Russian had been right, I was realizing. In a war, all we really had was the power people perceived us to have. And certain people, like carloads of jacked, crazy Puerto Rican motherfuckers, didn't give a shit about perception. It was like King Kong trying to swat away airplanes.

Soldato met me off the bus Saturday morning. His jaw was clenched so tight it looked like his face would shatter if you tweaked his nose.

"How's your week been, *paisan*?" I asked as I opened the passenger side door.

He put the car in neutral. "You think you're clever, you cocksucker? Huh? Think you're goddamn smart? I got a break-ing news bulletin for you, even if you come out on top, you think anyone's gonna accept you as boss after you set spics and niggers on your own family? You're a fuckin' disgrace."

"Yeah, well, I doubt they want to work with a sore loser either." I turned my head to look at him. "Here's the thing: everything happening right now was your decision. Maybe you forgot, I'm not the one who tried to blow up your car like some Hamas motherfucker. And frankly, I'm okay with giving you one last chance to walk away from this shit, because I don't like talking to you. So you tell me: You want to end this today, yes or no?"

"Fuck yourself," he said. "The Visaggio kid? That was my godson, you son of a bitch. This don't end any other way but me fuckin' curb-stomping you, understand?"

"I don't understand, but I acknowledge, how's that?"

"Little Joey C., always got a fuckin' answer. Enjoy it while you can."

We made the rest of the drive in silence. The Old Man was in the same weird, ebullient mood he'd been in last week, even as I described the killings (leaving out the incidental detail that I had ordered them).

"That's unfortunate, huh?" he said, pouring two fingers of brandy into a tumbler. "You got that under control?"

"Oh yeah, got some leads already. They're small-time. Probably borrowing the fuckin' cars from their parents."

The Old Man gave what he thought was a subtle glance in Soldato's direction. "Soldato, give us a minute, huh?"

Soldato looked around. "Out . . . outside, Mr. D.?" he said, pointing both thumbs over his left shoulder like he was trying to walk a dog.

"Yes. You. Outside while I talk to our friend. At the present-most time."

Soldato opened the door, grabbing his topcoat from the rack as he did, still looking confused.

Dellaponte turned back to me. "Is there anything you want to say to me about Soldato without him in the room, Giuseppe?"

I hesitate for a second. "Well, Mr. D., I mean, we're all adults here."

"What's that you say?"

"There's just shit people have been saying."

"What people? What are they saying?"

"Well, what, do you want to know what people, or what they been saying?"

"Both."

"Well, Mr. D., you know Cyrus Yale, yeah?"

"The *titsun*? Outta Harlem?"

"Yeah. Well, he said Soldato reached out to him about clipping the friends of ours. Middleman-like."

The Old Man's drink sloshed around the edge of his glass as he put it back on the coaster. "That's what he told you?"

"That's what he heard."

"Why, though? Clipping friends of ours . . . what's that get Soldato?"

I leaned in. "He didn't say, but I mean, it kinda makes sense, you know? Manufacture a crisis, fix it, look like a big shot."

"What's he want to look like a big shot for?"

"Mr. Dellaponte, he wants to be boss. And that's not hearsay, that I know. So all of a sudden we got a problem in the jungle, our Mr. Soldato makes some calls and cleans it up, he looks like boss material. Understand now?"

The Old Man stared at me for a while, his glasses too thick for me to tell what he was thinking.

"He isn't, though," he said eventually.

"Sorry?"

"He isn't boss material. Never has been. If he was, he wouldn'ta had a dumbshit idea like this."

"But see, I don't know that he did, Mr. Dellaponte."

"It doesn't matter if he did or not. It's the kind of idea he'd have, is what matters."

"You think so?"

"Shit yes. You see him when I told him to step outside? He's a fuckin' moron and he's the only one who doesn't get it." He sighed and sat back on the couch. "This is bad. If he was further down the totem pole this is something that would self-correct, but . . . no. No no no." He finished his tea. "I'd like you to do it."

This might seem like things were lining up perfectly for me, but I was really not ready to kill Soldato. I had counted on the boss still being paranoid, even while medicated, but if he was paranoid enough to kill his nursemaid on nothing but gossip, I was in danger too, and I needed Soldato between me and him. If there's one thing this business teaches you, it's that the guy who sends you to put one in the back of someone else's head will eventually do the same to you.

"Can I speak freely, sir?"

"What do you have to speak freely about? I didn't ask you for any feedback, Giuseppe."

"Mr. Dellaponte, I want you to really think about this. I want you to think about what a good earner Soldato's been, how much he's helped since you moved up here. Lemme talk to him about it. Look, you're right, he thinks he's hotter shit than he is. He doesn't think enough of me to lie. But let me discuss it and see how he reacts. If I think the stories are just stories, we both walk away. If I think they're true, he doesn't."

Dellaponte drummed his fingers on the arm of the sofa. "And what if you come away thinkin' they're stories and it turns out they're not?"

I shrugged. "Then I've fucked up and you know where to find me."

He looked me over. "You are so fuckin' hard to figure sometimes, Giuseppe."

"I wouldn't say that, Mr. Dellaponte. I'm just a man who looks out for his own."

Dellaponte and I sat in silence for a while as he finished his tea and for a few minutes after. He gave me the okay to go home afterward and let Soldato back in to drive me back to the station.

"So what did you and Daddy talk about?" Soldato said as we walked toward the car.

I pulled my gun from my coat and put it to his head.

"Hoooo, what the *fuck*, Joe?" he said.

"We're not going to the station just yet," I said. "Let's take a walk."

I put the gun against his spine and frog-marched him into the woods on the edge of Dellaponte's property. They weren't too thick, but it was cold and windy and overcast, and all the trees around us looked taller for it.

"On your knees," I said, when we reached a small clearing.

"Hey, fuck-stick, you don't think he's gonna know what happened?"

"On your fuckin' knees."

He sunk to his knees, still with that confused, incredulous, where's-the-hidden-camera air about him. I placed the barrel of the gun behind his left ear.

"I'm serious," I whispered. "This war bullshit ends right now. You know why? Because the Old Man thinks all the bodies from this past week are on you."

"You fuckin'—" He was about to try to get back up, but I pushed the barrel into his back and forced him back down.

"So here's the thing," I continued. "He wants me to kill you. Bought the whole thing hook, line, and sinker. But I said no, there's no need for that. Let me feel him out, I said. Maybe it's bullshit. Gotta make sure. In other words, Soldato, I got the Old Man's blessing to wish you into the fuckin' cornfield and make sure no one sees or hears from you again until aliens pave over you to build a parking lot seventy fuckin' years from now."

"Wait, aliens?"

"'Cause it's . . . 'cause it's the future."

"Just 'cause it's the future don't mean there's fuckin' aliens, dumbass. What the fuck do aliens want to build a parking lot in Ithaca for?"

"Jesus, I dunno. Point being"—I thumbed back the hammer—"I just pleaded for your life, you ungrateful prick. So your options are, drop your bid and drive me to the fuckin' bus station, or don't and I drive myself."

Soldato was silent as the wind blew around us and I found myself hoping I wouldn't have to do it, because as much as I loathed the fuck, this just seemed like a terrible, lonely place for anyone to have to die. Empathy is an inopportune son of a bitch.

"If I call a ceasefire," he said at last, "that doesn't mean we're through. It means this war in particular is through. I hope you don't think if you let me walk out of here, I'm never your problem again."

"Yeah, I'm not that stupid, friend. I'll cross that bridge when I come to it. I just don't feel like coming to it now."

"Alright. Truce, then."

I lifted the gun. He stood up, and we walked back to the car. We were silent the rest of the drive, and as I got out and onto the platform, I texted Yale, Abramowitz, and Quintero that I owed them dinner.

KINNEAVY

G od, I hate hospitals.

I regained consciousness shortly after I was admitted to NYU Langone Medical Center. My ears were still ringing from the little matter of all those close-quarters gunshots. The doctor told me they'd gotten the bleeding under control and that I was still alive chiefly because (a) I had left the knife in my stomach rather than immediately pulling it out and (b) I had been stabbed in a "well-insulated region."

"You can say I'm fat, I don't mind," I told the doctor, who didn't respond.

He didn't know what Wysocki's status was, which made me feel awful. They insisted on keeping me through the next week, which was bullshit, me just now getting a second wind on the case and all.

Internal Affairs took a statement from me on the second day, once they were sure I was lucid, breaking down the events that led up to the guns coming out. I was familiar with the process from when I'd been shot, and I'd followed procedure, but I didn't care for their tone and the way they seemed to be deliberately looming over my bed. I tried to passive-aggressively fight back by looking as pathetic and bedraggled as possible, but I don't think it worked. Ma always said I had a "defiant chin," whether my expression was actively defiant or not, and it made it hard for me to fake it when I wasn't in the mood for somebody's bullshit.

Captain Neville visited me later that afternoon, carrying what looked like a golf bag over one shoulder.

"How you doing, Kinneavy?" she asked.

"Better than I've been," I said, not entirely sarcastically.

She dug around in her coat pocket and pulled out a small felt-covered box. Inside was an NYPD Medal of Valor. "There'll be a ceremony when you get out, but just so you have it now," she said. "What's the doctor say?"

"He says, ah, he says I need to not run around and overexert myself in my usual badass bitch fashion."

"He said that?"

"Something like that. And he says to use a cane or a walker the first week the stitches are in, and that I should drink less and lose twenty pounds."

"You need to lose twenty pounds and then you won't have been stabbed anymore?"

"Apparently. He's very smart."

"Well, I actually heard about the cane thing," she said. "That's why everyone in Homicide chipped in for this." She reached into the golf bag and pulled out a thick black rod about the size of a baseball bat with a large knot at the head. "A shillelagh for the NYPD's wild Irish rose."

"Awww. I mean, I'm touched but not so touched that I'm not gonna let a line that cheesy go unmocked."

"Yeah, yeah, injured in the line of duty and you think you get to be a wiseass now."

"I thought that way before I got stabbed."

"This is true." She sat down in the chair across from the foot of my bed. "Never thought I'd say this, but thank God for Brickman."

"Huh?"

"Maybe you don't remember, Kinneavy, but you are not officially on this investigation, so it's kind of hard for me to explain what the hell a murder police was doing questioning a woman involved in an agg assault. Long story short, the only reason Clarkson isn't up both our asses right now is because he's already got a second dead cop on his hands and they're saying he killed himself after leaking some big bad shit to the press."

"How do you mean?"

"Departmental corruption. Like, hard core."

"What, like, *Serpico* shit?"

"Please. *The Shield* shit. Nothing's been published yet, but it's still all anyone's talking about, as these things go. Going after a hero cop would be poison for Clarkson right now."

"Is that what I am? I figured I was more of a classical anti-hero cop."

She laughed. "You are still such a fucking college girl."

"You can take the girl out of the Ivy League, but she'll still never pay off her student loans."

"Catchy."

"Have they told you anything about Wysocki?"

Neville sighed and ran a hand through her hair. "Wysocki's gonna need a wheelchair. Maybe short distances with a cane."

"Oh my God. Oh God."

"Don't get Catholic on me, Kinneavy, he's a grown-ass man and he knew what he was getting into. He and his family will be well taken care of. I forbid you to beat yourself up over this, and if you do, I will literally cite you for insubordination."

I sighed and shifted my weight on the bed as best I could. "What about Litvak?"

"Litvak is fine because *someone* is a goddamn ace at disabling shots."

"She name any accomplices?"

"You met her, do you think she did?"

"I guess that's a no."

"However," Neville said, "we went through her apartment looking for other weapons, and not only did we find them, it seems our Miss Litvak was planning on making a little trip fairly soon."

"Huh?"

"She had about ten passports, driver's licenses, and military IDs under different names. And one of them, Magda Rothstein, is also on the deed to a farm in North Jersey."

"Have you been up there yet?"

"Nah, Suarez's breaking our balls on the warrant. Wants us to be damn sure there's no real Magda Rothstein before we go for it, so we've been playing phone tag with Realtors this whole time."

"Ugh."

"Well, I'd think you'd be happy. At the rate it's going, you'll be out by the time we go for it."

"Fair enough. Thanks for coming out here, Captain."

"Thanks for the gift-wrapped psycho, Kinneavy."

After dark, I headed out to the stairwell to think. I hadn't had a drink since the last day of my suspension, and I was getting headaches and night sweats, so sleep wasn't really an option. Lauder, the dear, had sent a Don Westlake novel I hadn't read yet along with Neville, so I had something to read, at least. I'd been out there for a little while when Wysocki wheeled onto the stairwell holding his IV stand aloft like he was jousting. I shuffled over to him and we did the best we could under the circumstances to hug.

"How do you feel?" I said once we'd untangled from each other.

"Uh, better than you'd think. This . . . this is gonna take some getting used to, but they don't hurt or nothing."

I looked at his legs, unable to help myself, and then looked away. "Stan, I am so, so sorry."

He waved his hand. "The fuck outta here. I'm alive because of you."

"And in a wheelchair."

"Katherine, my wife's got a good city job and the disability pension's gonna help a lot. I got three kids. I need to be around in some form or another. Not to be a dick, but you're too smart to act like a spinal means I'm better off dead."

"Oh God, no, no, Stan, I'm sorry, I didn't mean it like that." I laid the book on the floor. "I just . . . look. When I was younger, I had a bad experience." I paused for a second to give him a chance to ask what it was. I wasn't prepared to tell him, but if he was too curious to pay attention to the rest of what I was saying, I wouldn't be able to make my point. When he didn't say anything, I continued. "Maybe this is me or maybe it's a lot of people, but when something like that happens, even through no fault of my own, I try to think—I tried to think— what I could have done differently. I guess I've spent my life since then wondering how much faster, how much harder, how much stronger I'd have to have been to keep it from happening. So I guess as an extension of that, I developed this fear of not being able to move. That's my thing, though, not yours. I'm so sorry."

"Nah, that makes sense," he said. "I was growin' up, my ma had muscular dystrophy. I don't think we knew to call it that, but that's what it was. It got tougher and tougher for her to move, so she found new ways to do what she needed to do, look out for herself and for me and my sisters. I guess she kept me from ever thinking not being able to move meant you couldn't do what you had to do."

"Your mom sounds like kind of a badass, Stan."

"Hey, you raise two girls and a boy in the same house, you're a badass no matter what."

I mimed lifting a glass. "*Sláinte* to that."

My phone woke me up the next morning—mine, not the wall-mounted hospital one. It was Neville.

"So we got ballistics back from Rachel Litvak's favorite toy," she said.

"Okay."

"And I talked to a friend at the FBI, and check this shit out—that shotgun was part of a bulk straw purchase in Virginia that the DOJ lost track of on its way up the East Coast until it ended up in New York. Then once they figured out who the buyer was, they couldn't bring charges because the guns went missing again."

"Wait, who was the buyer?"

"Frankie fucking O'Halloran."

"No shit."

"That was the closest they've ever come, apparently. Thought it was gonna be his Capone moment. More blue balls than a smurf orgy."

I got it now. I got it. Yes. Of fucking course. "O'Halloran is their gun pipeline."

"Huh?"

"When I talked to him about Judith, he acted like he sympathized with what they were doing. I'm so fucking blind, it's because they're his clients."

"Kinneavy, we can't prove any of this, you understand? They never tied the guns to him in any way that would stick in court."

"Then I'll have to find something to brace him with."

"Yeah? How do you imagine you're going to do that?"

"Can you bring me my O'Halloran notes from the Judith file?"

"I'll bring them at lunch. I dunno how soon that's going to be."

Neville dropped the notes by around one. I read through them and noticed something I'd forgotten. I pulled up Wendell's number on my phone and gave him a call.

Jalisa finally got a chance to visit later that afternoon, and because she was also a dear, she'd brought some of my non-bloodstained clothes for me to change into once I was good to go home. As soon as she came in, she closed the door behind her, advanced to the bed, and kissed me gently on the cheek.

"Don't you *ever* fuckin' scare me like that again," she said. "Got me feeling like Ben Cartwright over here."

"Who?"

"From *Bonanza*."

"Damn, if we are gonna be in love, you have got to get your pop culture current."

"Oh, la dee fuckin' da, Miss All-my-music-was-recorded-when-I-was-about-five."

"That's not fair, I like Florence."

"You listen casually to Florence. You don't spend an evening in a locked room blasting your ears with her like you do them Dropkick Mollys or whoever."

"It's the Dropkick Murphys and Flogging Molly. What, we all sound alike to you?"

"Um, yes, K. Not only is it all the same band, it's all the same song. Accept it and deal with it."

"Racist."

Jalisa's presence reminded me of something I'd forgotten to ask her while she was at my place. "Jalisa, I need Howard Brickman's phone."

"Huh?"

"I have reason to believe Brickman was in touch with Joe Cataldo, and if I have his phone, I may be able to tie Cataldo to Donnie Klein's death. Can you help me get a warrant for that?"

She shook her head. "'Fraid not, K."

"Wait, what the hell do you mean, 'fraid not?"

"Feds are building a case against Old Man Dellaponte. They have a snitch high up in the family. We were gonna try to indict Cataldo as an accessory in the Milazzo business and they swooped in and said nobody touches any of the upper-level Dellaponte guys or it'll rattle the cage."

"He killed a fucking cop!"

"Katherine, it's not my call."

"Oh my *God*." I threw up my good hand in frustration. I tugged my phone off the end table, stuck out my bottom lip, and widened my eyes as much as I could, then took a selfie. I handed the phone to Jalisa. "Can you send them that, see if it changes their mind? Look how sad and pitiful and stabbed I am."

She smiled in spite of herself. "You really think Cataldo was involved? What's he gain from killing a cop?"

"I don't know. All I know is Brickman told me he texted him when I brought Donnie in."

"K, do yourself a favor and don't try to juggle so much. I mean, my God, it's perfectly okay to prioritize the case that got you stabbed."

"Yeah, I'm gonna take advice on priorities from someone who hasn't updated her TV references."

"I hope the next person who stabs you gets you right in the sarcasm and they have to remove it."

"You want me to be stabbed boring? You're mean."

She smiled, then leaned in and kissed my forehead. I angled my head up and caught her on the lips. I looked up and noticed Wysocki wheeling by the door.

"Hey, mister," I said, "she's my sister." He rolled his eyes and continued down the hall.

As Jalisa straightened back up, she took my hand in hers. "Soon, okay? Soon."

I nodded.

"I love you, Katherine."

"Yeah, you too."

Two days later, they finally cleared me to go home. Well, not home per se. As soon as I had a time frame of when I'd be out, I'd insisted on scheduling my psych eval and shooting exam immediately thereafter.

At about two in the afternoon, I was dressed, packed, and secure in the annoying mandatory wheelchair when a cop I didn't recognize came into the room. He was tallish and skinny with red-brown hair and wearing a suit that made him look more like he should be selling stock or accepting a Grammy. He extended his hand when he saw me.

"You Kinneavy? I'm Detective Mazursky."

"Nice to meet you. To what do I owe the pleasure?"

"They wanted me to give you a ride back to the precinct."

"Wait, you're not Homicide, are you?"

"Burglary. It's a courtesy. You're kind of a legend now."

"For getting stabbed?"

He laughed. "Yeah, like that's all you did. Fuckin' Wonder Woman over here."

I dug under the cane across my lap and checked my phone as Mazursky wheeled me to the curb. I'd missed a text from

Wendell, but I wasn't even sure he'd sent it to the right number because it made no sense. It read, in its entirety,

KING'S MEN
MAZURSKY
DRAGNA
WEXLER
STAMPER
CAVUTO
DELLINGER

I recognized Mazursky's name but I had no idea what it meant in this context. I got into his car on the passenger side, still holding the cane.

"You want me to put that in the back?" he said.

"Nah, I can hold onto it. Thanks, though."

I reread the text as Mazursky drove, seeing if there was anything in it I was missing that made it make sense. I texted Roane back to let him know I'd just gotten it and asking if he could clarify. Just as I was about to hit send, something out the window caught my eye.

"So where you from, Mazursky?" I asked.

He seemed surprised I was talking to him. "Philly."

"Philly, okay. So close and yet so far. Were you a cop there too?"

"Nah, family moved here when I was twelve."

"Ohhh, gotcha." I put a hand under my chin and stared out the window. "Manhattan born and raised. I've never lived more than half an hour from the block I grew up on. Never really want to, even when this city gets particularly loud or cold or violent or some douchebag is trying to get onto the train before I have a chance to get off. It's pretty nice, knowing you started out exactly where you're supposed to be. You know?"

Mazursky stuck out his lower jaw and nodded, the universal sign for "I understand what you're saying but I don't really have a response to it."

"It's like, all that time you would have spent looking for where I'm supposed to be, now I get to spend it on figuring out who I am," I continued. "Half the work is already done for me. I guess the point I'm trying to make here, Mazursky, is that if you tell someone you're giving her a ride somewhere and you're actually not, make sure that person hasn't lived here all her life, or she's gonna notice when you miss the turn and keep going."

It seemed like it took him a second for that last bit to catch up with him and then he turned his head to me, his eyes wide. His shoulder twitched as though he was about to reach into his coat. I stuck out the cane, holding the end with the knot directly at the back of his head.

"Mazursky, I have had more than my fill of people trying to kill me this week already," I said, "and if you'd like a shot at the title, be my guest, just know that I am going to knock you the hell out with my big, not-at-all symbolic club before you get a chance to go for your gun. I've been stuck wearing an assless gown, eating food that's shit even by my standards, and experiencing symptoms of alcohol withdrawal all week, and what I don't fuckin' need right now is someone trying to kidnap me who doesn't even respect my intelligence to pretend that's not what he's doing. You're going to pull into the next parking deck we see and tell me what the hell is going on or I'm going to hit you very hard with this, understand?" He nodded. "Tell me you understand."

"I understand."

"Great, no questions?"

"Why a parking deck?"

"Good question. Because you tried to kidnap me and I feel like inconveniencing you."

We had to drive four more blocks before there was a parking deck on our side of the street. I smiled at the attendant and flirted a little, thriving on Mazursky's palpable discomfort.

"Give me your gun," I said, once we had parked and I'd repositioned the shillelagh at the back of his head.

"Okay, hold on . . . ," he said. I whacked him in the face. "Ah! Fuck!" he yelled as I reached into his jacket and took it while he was disoriented. I called the precinct. Once Neville confirmed no one had been sent to pick me up, I gave her our location.

I ended the call and turned back to Mazursky. "Talk. Where were you gonna take me?"

"Hudson Yards."

"What's in Hudson Yards?"

"Judson Crowning owns a warehouse out there. He told me to take you there and kill you."

"Why the hell does Judson Crowning want to kill me?"

"Because of that reporter you're talking to."

"Roane?"

"I don't know his fucking name. Crowning just said he was going to blow up the whole thing and he was probably talking to you about it, and we needed to send him a message."

"Blow up *what* whole thing?"

"The King's Men."

"Mazursky, I don't know what the fuck any of this is, so I think Mr. Crowning may have jumped the gun a little. Who are the King's Men?"

Mazursky explained it to me, and I knew as he did that this was the "*The Shield* shit" Neville had told me about. I had a thought.

"Who killed Donnie Klein, Mazursky?"

"Who?"

"My partner, you piece of shit. Half the NYPD was at his funeral. Who killed him?"

"The fuck do I know?"

"Well, gee, I dunno, I just figured you're apparently the authority on cop-killing here, so—"

"Kinneavy, I didn't kill your fuckin' partner."

I kept both the gun and the cane on him. "Did he?"

"I swear on my mother I don't know."

"Okay, so you don't know. But tell me this: Is he capable of doing what was done to Klein?"

Mazursky turned to face me and there was a strange fear in his face. It wasn't fear of the gun. It wasn't fear of anything he could see. It was a fear of something he couldn't.

"He's capable of so much worse," he said.

I heard sirens drawing nearer and I lowered the gun as two cruisers arrived to take Mazursky off my hands. One of them offered me a ride back to the precinct, but I gave him my home address instead. Something told me this was the wrong time for me to take the psych eval.

ROANE

Kinneavy steadied herself with her weird knotty cane as the German shepherd tugged her lightly across the uneven ground. A passel of cops (do cops come in passels?) followed behind in almost perfect single file, like acolytes behind a priest. I walked at the rear, at sort of an odd adjacent angle, thinking that even if I was getting an exclusive, the classy thing to do was not draw attention to it. Half the cops were looking at me like the kid who's only on the varsity team because his parents made a donation.

It was about seven in the morning. I'd gone to bed too late and the crunching of frost underfoot seemed weirdly abrasive, like a personal taunt. The dog gave another pull—harder this time. Kinneavy held a hand up, and her entourage stopped. She looked over the hard ground, eventually noticing something. She pointed at the ground and spoke to the cop closest to her.

"Here," she said. "Look at the dirt. It's still uneven but it's not natural. Someone dug this up and patted it down."

The cop nodded, and he and two others came forward with shovels. I took a picture of Kinneavy watching as they dug. It was a beauty, if I do say so myself. Kinneavy had a soft profile but it looked commanding in the early morning light. She had on a black scarf over a dark blue peacoat, and she wasn't leaning on the cane so much as holding it for emphasis. She was literally speaking softly and carrying a big stick.

After a few minutes, I heard one of the cops say, "Ah, fuck," and he reached in and gently brought up, only visible from my position for a second, what was unmistakably a human bone. More cops came forth with evidence bags and cameras, and Kinneavy broke from them to come over and talk to me.

"I'm gonna need you to piss off now that we've confirmed this as a crime scene," she said. "Hope you understand."

"Of course," I said. "Thanks again."

She gave me that look that was the closest she ever came to looking friendly with me. "Remember what you owe me."

I nodded and she strode back to the hole, which was expanding quickly enough that it looked like time-lapse photography.

It was a bit of a walk to the closest main road where Rosalind picked me up. I had never commuted into the city from Jersey at that time of the morning, but it made me feel like Kinneavy owed me at least two more favors. I was beginning to worry we'd miss O'Halloran's bagman, but we got to the bar about ten minutes before he came out. We followed him to a boarded-up building in Harlem, where he put an envelope in the mailbox and left, looking over his shoulder.

We watched the box for about twenty minutes, at which point a black woman who looked to be in her midfifties in a brown pleather jacket and black jeans approached the box. She looked from side to side and then withdrew the envelope.

It was a major pain in the ass tailing her in the car without being obvious about it, but she only walked a couple blocks before she reached a walk-up and backed her blue Volvo out of the driveway. We followed her south as she drove out of the city and down I-95. About an hour later, she turned off onto the exit to New Brunswick and onto the Rutgers campus.

"Jesus," Rosalind said. "This place looks like the town from *Gilmore Girls*."

"That was Vermont."

"I feel like it was in New Jersey."

"Nah, nobody was hostile enough."

"The guy from *Heroes* was pretty hostile."

"Wouldn't you be hostile too if you were on *Heroes*?"

"He wasn't on *Heroes* yet, dumbass."

The woman parked in front of the administrations building and walked inside. She was in there for about twenty minutes.

"So here's my question," Rosalind said. "What the fuck business does Frankie O'Halloran have at Rutgers?"

I shrugged. "Sports book?"

"The season's over. Besides, why would she be talking to administrators about that?"

As we talked, I noticed a girl sitting on a bench in front of the building. She was tall and chubby with a pile of red curls, bronze skin, and a dusting of freckles across her nose. She turned in our direction but didn't seem to see us.

A minute later, the woman from Harlem stepped outside, and the girl gave her a running hug.

"What in the shit is going on?" Rosalind said.

"I'll be right back," I said, snapping a picture of their embrace and stepping out of the car.

I jogged over to them. "Excuse me!" I said as they turned. "Hi. My name's Lyle van Dam and I'm an editor for the Rutgers alumni newsletter. I saw the two of you hug just now and I thought it would be a perfect shot for the alumni site, so I took a picture, I hope that's okay."

The girl nodded. "Sure, of course. Can we see it? Don't want my butt looking too big."

"Watch it, girl, that's my butt you're talking about," said the women, presumably her mother, her accent vaguely West Indian. Both of them giggled as I showed her the shot.

"Ohhh yeah, that's a great shot," the girl said. "Will you send it to me too?"

"Sure," I said. "Can I just get both of your names?"

"I'm Letitia Le Grande and this is Nerissa," the woman said.

"Nerissa, I like that," I said. "Shakespeare fans?"

"Everybody's a Shakespeare fan," Nerissa said. "Even if they hate him, they love some other thing that couldn't exist without him."

"I know that's right," I said. "Thank you both so much. I'll email that picture to you as soon as I'm able, okay, Miss Le Grande?"

Nerissa thanked me and they walked off together. I jogged back to the car and explained to Rosalind what I'd done.

She was silent for a second. "This feels . . . gross, somehow. This isn't what we do."

"I owed a friend a favor."

"Yeah, but we're . . . we're exploiting people. People who have nothing to do with all this. I can feel myself becoming more okay with this and I don't like that feeling."

I extended my hand. "Look, how about this, Roz: let's make a pact, this was a one-time thing. This was an off-the-books job. We are reporters and we will never again exploit people like this in support of our reporting."

She pumped my hand so hard I thought it'd fall off.

The first thing I did back in New York was email the picture to Nerissa, and then, to try to assuage my conscience even further, emailed Rutgers's alumni association offering it to them for free. A minute later, I heard the ping of a new email and clicked over to my inbox, figuring it would be a response to one of the two. Instead, it was the familiar encrypted address. I opened it and scrolled down to the main body of the email:

Mr. Roane,

We write to you deprived of one of our hardest-working sisters, Rachel Litvak. While we continue our mission in her absence, it necessitates the moving up of some major agenda items. Today a river will spill its banks on the road to Damascus, and as our long-buried ghosts are unearthed, one from long ago will replace them.

I immediately called Kinneavy and read the email to her. "Do you have any idea what any of that means?" she said. "I do not. Road to Damascus is a Biblical reference, right?" "Yeah, it's where Saul of Tarsus . . . oh shit." "What?" "I know who they're going after next." "What is it, like, a fuckin' riddle?" "They wanted me to see this. I have no idea why, but they knew I'd know. This was meant for me."

She hung up abruptly. I turned around and emailed her the information I'd gotten from Rutgers and then got back to work. I felt terrible about talking to Micky under false pretenses, so I went ahead and actually wrote up that story about the place, getting quotes from other business owners in the immediate vicinity and a couple regulars. Tony loved it.

"Hey, listen, Wendell," he said, after giving me notes, "what do you think about running the King's Men piece in next week's issue?"

"I thought we were waiting for a fairer wind or whatever."

"Yeah, I thought about that for a while, and I decided fuck it, let's make a fairer wind. Let's shine such a big spotlight on this that people are afraid to come at you."

"Ton, are you drunk?"

He shook his head. "I'm leaving, Wendell."

"What? Where?"

"The *Times* wants me. Starting in February. Senior politics editor."

"Goddamn," I said. "That's . . . that's big, Ton. You deserve it."

"You're sweet. I'm gonna level with you, whether I deserve it or not, I feel like I've done all I can do for this old broad. I mean, I've done my best not to be the old-school vet who's terrified of Twitter and email blasts, but this is a young woman's game."

I nodded. "Wait, young woman's?"

"I offered Rosalind my job and she said yes. So I'd advise against pissing her off."

"You'd have advised against that before we had this talk."

"And I'd have been right. Anyway, like I said, I want to run the King's Men story in next week's issue. I'm not gonna go out burying the stories that need telling." He stood up and walked around the desk. "You did an amazing job with this, Wendell, and I'm really proud of you."

"Get the fuck outta here," I said as we leaned in for a hug.

"Oh, by the way," he said as we pulled apart, "Rosalind said to make sure no one takes her desk."

"Even the replacement?"

"Especially the replacement. That whole space is a part of her now. I think she's gonna bite anyone who tries to sit there."

"That's an interesting editorial policy."

"Oh yeah. Before now, it was only okay to bite the interns."

I laughed, and then had to excuse myself. I was happy for him, and I understood what he was saying about his time being through, but I had this overwhelming urge to cry, and I wanted to get back to my desk before it could overtake me.

CATALDO

I t was like looking at a completely different person.

A lot of the bruising on the Russian girl's face was still evident, but something had hardened behind her eyes now. Everything that quivered when I'd found her in that basement was now perfectly still, on top of which her English was better than mine.

"Not to be rude, Miss . . ."

"Oksana," the woman said.

"Yeah, not to be rude, Miss Oksana, but why did you need me here?"

"I wish to thank you, Mr. Cataldo."

"Sorry?"

"I wish to thank you for your kindness. I know your men spoke of killing me to get rid of the evidence and liability."

"I, uh, you're welcome, I guess."

"I also have a warning."

In the time since I'd dropped Oksana off at the church, she'd been very busy. After her escape from the hospital, she'd made contact with some friends from the old country here in the city and gotten some hardware, which she'd used to slowly but surely fill the power vacuum left by the deaths of the

Russians. Remembering what had happened when I didn't pay close enough attention to Degtiarenko, I'd been keeping tabs on her, and I was impressed with what I saw.

"A warning?" I said. "That's where we are now?"

"Where we are now is in this room. You can listen to it or disregard it, but things will happen as a result in either case. My warning is this: anyone in the borough involved in human trafficking gets taken off at the neck. I don't care if it's sex trafficking or domestic workers. This is nonnegotiable."

"Well, I think you've probably heard, Oksana, I don't hold with that shit," I said. "Never have."

"But you didn't care when you heard your subordinate was engaged in it," she said, never so much as blinking. "I'm here today to tell you that's no longer enough. If you sign off implicitly on any human trafficking, first I come for the trafficker and then I come for you."

I smiled in spite of myself. "*Madonn'*. That's gratitude for you. You think because I felt sorry for you, you get to threaten me?"

"Mr. Cataldo, the remains of a bullet are still in my head. I no longer feel the need to conceal what I think and I no longer fear death. The Russians in my neighborhood, they call me *Nocnitsa*, the Night Maiden. You will have the tribute you've earned, but remember what I said, and ask yourself, is this a woman who says things she doesn't mean?"

I shrugged. "I guess not, Miss Oksana. That's fine, then. That's a good rule. No trafficking."

"No one else is here," she said. "If it looks better, you can tell them it's your rule. But it is the rule regardless."

We shook hands and I left the back room of the restaurant. Paulie was waiting by the car.

"How'd it go?" he said.

"Fine. I like that broad."

"Yeah, I'm glad she landed on her feet. America, huh?"

"She's an inspiration to us all."

We drove back to the Lower East Side when I got a call. The number was Soldato's. "Ah, shit." I answered.

"This better not have fuckin' been you, Joe," Soldato said as soon as I answered.

"What the hell are you talking about?"

"I just got the call, goddammit. The Old Man's gonna be arrested."

"What the fuck?" I yelled, making Paulie wince and swerve. "For what?"

"Rico shit. It's bad. It's really fuckin' bad."

"Son of a bitch. Who's acting boss? You?"

"Fuck no."

"Jesus Christ, you just tried to kill me for the job and now you don't want it?"

"This is different. There's shit that needs taking care of now."

That sounded like bullshit, but I didn't have time to scrutinize it. "Paulie, the Old Man got pinched," I said as soon as I'd hung up.

"Shit."

"Yeah. We're going to see O'Halloran."

"You sure about that, Joe?"

"He knows things. Trust me."

We pulled up in front of O'Halloran's chop shop and pounded on the door. The viewing panel slid open and I saw a flash of his Ray-Bans before he opened the door.

"And what can I help you fine gentlemen with today?" he asked, closing the door behind us. Paulie looked like a kid taking a test he hadn't studied for.

"Old Man Dellaponte is going to be indicted," I said. "I need to know the specifics."

O'Halloran sat down at his desk and laughed. "That's an easy one," he said. "You know Mikey Perelli out in Bensonhurst?"

"Sure. Stand-up guy."

"Not so much, as it turns out. He flipped on the boss."

"You're shitting me. How long ago?"

"Oh, just this afternoon. His daughter got arrested."

"For what?"

"That hasn't come in yet, I'm afraid."

We thanked O'Halloran and swung back to Mikey's apartment. He greeted us at the door but followed us down to the car like he knew what was coming. We drove to a garage owned by our construction people and parked. I turned in the driver's seat.

"Mikey, you know what this is about?"

"The, uh, the boss is getting indicted, I heard."

"Mikey, our time is limited, so please don't waste it."

He looked at Paulie as though he was hoping for some support. When he didn't see it he looked back at me.

"Joey, my little girl got caught with those crazy bitches with the knives. The ones who killed Russell."

Paulie and I looked back and forth at each other.

"When did this happen?"

"Only about an hour ago. I got the call from the DA, he said it would take everything I had to get her a deal."

"Mikey," I said, "this is bad. This is really, really fuckin' bad. You just agreed right off? You didn't even talk to us?"

He sounded close to tears. "I didn't have time, Joe! My little girl, she needed me. How the fuck do you think she's gonna do in the can?"

I slammed my fist on the dashboard. "You took a fuckin' oath, Mikey. Same one we all did. No exceptions."

He sighed and buried his face in his hands. "Protect her, huh? I dunno how she ended up with them, but it's a hard world for the girls who hit back."

"She'll be looked out for inside, Mikey."

"Thanks." He leaned back in the seat and crossed himself. "Do what you gotta do."

I grabbed Mikey's wrists and pinned them to his knees as Paulie put a plastic bag over his head. Mikey thrashed harder than I would have expected, until I was practically stretched across the front seat trying to hold him down. His knee caught me in the groin and I screamed, but I maintained my hold until his feet stopped pounding the floor of the car.

Paulie and I both sprawled inside the car, breathing hard for a minute. "I guess we'd better call Soldato," Paulie said eventually.

I nodded. "This . . . this was an eventful day."

KINNEAVY

Some petty part of me was furious with how good-looking Paul Hudson had ended up. Seeing him sitting in his office chair with his wavy hair and green eyes, he radiated all the charisma that made me fall for him in the first place. If he had been a stranger, I would have been preoccupied with how hot he was.

"Is this gonna take long?" he asked. "No offense but I've got a lot of shit to take care of today."

"Mr. Hudson, we need to take you into protective custody," I said, trying to keep my tone as even as possible. "We have intelligence suggesting the terrorist organization called Judith is targeting you."

He squinted at me. "What's your name?"

"My name's Detective Katherine Kinneavy, and you need to come with me, sir," I said.

His eyes widened with recognition. "Oh . . . ohhhhh! Shit! Katie! From Gotham!" I must have looked confused because he then clarified: "Remember, we dated?"

I exhaled through my front teeth. The motherfucker didn't even remember. It had been such an incidental blip in his life that I was just his old college girlfriend. I jerked my head toward the door and turned my back to lead him out, trying to stave off the train roaring toward me again.

> *Gather up the pots and the old tin can,*
> *The mash and the corn and the barley and the bran,*
> *Run like the devil from the excise man,*
> *Keep the smoke from rising, Katie . . .*

"Hello?" he said, and I realized we were in the elevator on the ground floor. "Where are we going?"

"I'll be dropping you off at the precinct, Mr. Hudson."

"That's bullshit. If I'm going to be forced out of my office, where I make your salary, I damn well better get a hotel."

I rolled my eyes. "It's not up to me, Mr. . . ." A black panel van heading down the street in our direction caught my eye. The window was down slightly, and I noticed as it got closer that the window was rolling progressively further down. And then I saw the gun barrel. I tackled Paul to the sidewalk just as fire burst forth from the van. It swerved and made a U-turn at the corner, swinging back around toward us.

"What the fuck?" Paul yelled. "Look what you did to—"

I grabbed him by the shoulder. "Paul. Shut the fuck up!" I said, before turning back to the van. I saw the driver, wearing the now-familiar red hoodie and aviators, lean out the window, gun at the ready. I ran into the middle of the street, aimed a center-mass shot, and fired. The gun clattered to the street as the driver snapped back. The van slammed up against the curb and flipped on its side.

I ran to the van and pulled open the back door, checking the passenger seat. Another woman was struggling to pull a sidearm, with the first woman, alive but breathing raggedly, on top of her. I held my gun on both of them as I radioed for backup. Once I'd given my statement and passed off both Paul and the two women, I made a call.

I was already in a booth at the diner when Judson Crowning entered and sat down across from me. He hung his topcoat on the edge of the bench. "Detective."

"Mr. Crowning."

"I'm curious as to why you wanted to meet. I'm considerably busier than you seem to be."

I leaned forward across the table. "I know you killed my partner, Mr. Crowning."

He smiled a little. "Do you, Detective? I think if you knew that, we'd be having this conversation somewhere else."

"Oh, I'm working on that. But trust me, Mr. Crowning, I'm going to get what I need to burn you for that and I am going to enjoy it." I sipped my coffee. "I met my rapist for the first time in a decade today. Saved his life."

"Why are you telling me this?"

"I'm not sure. Maybe it's because I was a little afraid of you. And now that I've done that, you don't really scare me anymore."

He smiled again, a broad, ugly thing that didn't extend beyond his lips. "I'm glad your personal odyssey is working out for you, Detective. But I assure you, it makes no difference in terms of what I'm capable of."

"Oh, trust me, I know what you're capable of, Mr. Crowning." I leaned back. "You know, when I was a kid, I thought there were actual bad guys in the world? Like the ones on TV. Black capes and spiked armor and shit. Then I got a little older and I figured the bad guys were men in suits with pinkie rings and cigars, ruling little kingdoms of dope and pussy. Now, though, I look at you and I listen to you and I understand what you really are: scared little shits who think if they kill and hurt and rape enough people, they won't feel like the bad guys anymore. You can't even keep your voice from shaking when you threaten me." I laid a tip on the table and stood up. "Next conversation we have? It's going to be the one you talked about."

Night was falling when I got to Frankie O'Halloran's garage. I didn't get out of the car immediately. I sat for a second and thought about what I was about to do, and what it meant for me as a person. Throughout the investigation, I'd been tested but never wondered about the idea of going too far. The email I'd gotten today could change all of that. I pulled the flask out of my glove box and stared at it for a while before putting it back and getting up and heading to the door.

The shop was unlocked. I let myself in. O'Halloran was sitting at the back. He looked up at the sound of the door closing behind me.

"Detective," he said, not getting up. "Nice to see you again. Come, sit."

I sat down across from him. "I guess you already know this, Mr. O'Halloran, but we caught two more members of Judith today."

"I did hear about that, yeah."

"A Violet Kendrick and a Tina Perelli. Her father's connected, apparently."

"Oh, that's a shame."

"Mr. O'Halloran, I know they get their guns from you."

He looked up. "Do you?"

"I do. And you're going to help me get the rest of them unless you want to go to prison for a very long time."

He smiled and stood up. "Detective, do I look like someone who'd have a difficult time in prison?" He sat back down.

"No, I guess not. Which is why I had a contingency plan if you didn't feel like cooperating." I pulled the picture Roane had sent me of the girl at Rutgers out of my coat and slapped it down on the desk. I saw his eyebrows go up very briefly.

"Who's that?" he said.

"Who's that? That's a Haitian redhead who attends Rutgers with no scholarships or financial aid despite the fact that her mother is a receptionist. You know who the fuck that is." I looked at the picture. "Hey, remember back in '95 when Lenny Carcetti tried to go after one of your trucks and his son had an, uh, an accident on the way to prom? Hey, where is Carcetti based? I feel like it's New Brunswick. How do you think he'd react if he knew the man who killed his son had a daughter who lived in the same—"

O'Halloran pounded the table and pulled his sunglasses off. His eyes were dark green and luminous with hate. "You are some nasty cunt," he said.

"I'm a woman with shit to do, Mr. O'Halloran, and I need to know when they're making the next pickup."

O'Halloran pulled a chrome-plated Desert Eagle from under the desk and leveled it at me. "Did you have a contingency plan for this, sweetie?"

"Mr. O'Halloran, I really don't think that's a great idea."

"Maybe I don't give a shit," he said. "Maybe I just really, really want to kill you."

I raised my hands, palms out. "Look, take it easy, okay? Don't do anything you'll regret."

O'Halloran kept the gun trained on me but lowered his arm slightly. I grabbed his wrist with one of my outstretched hands and slammed it down on the desk, pulling my Glock with the other hand and pressing it to his forehead. "I'm Anton Chekhov, motherfucker," I said. "Don't you ever pull on me if you're not gonna shoot me." I pried the gun out of his hand.

We stayed like that for a while, our eyes locked, and I tried not to think about the fact that the cold rage in his eyes looked a lot like what I'd seen in my father's when I told him about Paul Hudson.

"I haven't seen her face," O'Halloran said at last. "She always comes at night, pays me, and loads the shit into a van. You'd have to wait for her the next time she comes."

"And when is that?"

"Take the gun out of my face."

I lowered the barrel, still keeping a firm grip on the gun.

"Tomorrow night," O'Halloran said. "Around eleven o'clock."

I nodded, holstered the gun, and tucked the picture into my pocket. "Thank you for your help, Mr. O'Halloran."

He put his sunglasses back on as he walked to the door to hold it open for me.

"Detective?" he said. I turned. "You understand if anything happens to my daughter, I'm going to kill you."

"Of course I understand that, Mr. O'Halloran. I'll see you very soon. Have a nice evening."

ROANE

Excerpt from the *Septima*, week
of December 13, 2011

THE BLUE MAFIA: HOW A CREW OF CORRUPT NYPD DETECTIVES MOONLIGHTED AS THE MAYOR'S HONOR GUARD FOR 20 YEARS

*BY WENDELL ROANE, ADDITIONAL
REPORTING BY ROSALIND GARWOOD*

*Hugo Martinez (not his real name) was a rising star
in New York politics, and was planning a campaign to
unseat his local councilman, a vulnerable incumbent
and key ally to the mayor.*

*The week before Martinez planned to launch his
campaign, he received a call from a number he didn't
recognize telling him to meet in a local bar. When he
got there, a man was waiting in a booth. He introduced
himself as Al Cavuto and showed Martinez a series of
photographs depicting him kissing a man. If Martinez
launched his bid, Cavuto said, the pictures would be
sent to his devoutly Catholic mother.*

"After that," Cavuto said, "we have more that will be going up online. Worse ones. If you don't have a gun in your mouth by the time they're all out, you're a stronger man than I. But then," he added, "maybe you'd be into that."

Martinez did as the man told him. It wasn't until several months later that he found out he was a detective with the New York Police Department.

Cavuto was one of what members call the "King's Men," a group of NYPD officers who answer directly to the mayor's office and do him personal or political favors, such as ensuring a key ally isn't unseated by a charismatic newcomer. Numerous people, including those in the NYPD, have heard of the group but dismissed it as a legend.

"It's a bunch of horseshit," said one Bronx patrolman. "It's a bunch of Illuminati-type conspiracy-theory crap specifically for people who hate the police."

But documents obtained by the Septima and reproduced here, as well as interviews with those targeted by the group, show a pattern of off-the-books intimidation by NYPD officers, eventually escalating to murder—and it's been going on for years.

The earliest known evidence of the King's Men dates back to the administration of Mayor John Minetti. Minetti swept into office in 1993, painting his predecessor, Daniel Dawkins, as soft on crime and deferential to the black community, but his straight-shooter image took a hit when it was discovered he had a 25-year-old mistress. What was not widely reported was that Minetti had off-duty NYPD officers chauffeur her in unmarked cars, as well as tail her to and from work. The woman, who does not want her name used, said she *didn't know she was being followed until she was flirting with a man at a bar during happy hour and one of them began physically intimidating the man, eventually punching him in the face when he became combative.*

Minetti left office in 2002, by which point the cloud of the initial scandal had largely evaporated due to the optics of his leadership in the wake of the September 11 terrorist attacks. But the King's Men didn't go anywhere. Under the administration of Mayor Vincent Peters, the current roster includes Cavuto, Det. Thomas Mazursky, Det. Carl Dellinger, Det. Jack Dragna, Det. Harry Wexler, and Det. Mark Stamper.

The earliest available evidence of King's Men activity under the Peters administration occurred in May of 2003, when Dragna and Wexler attended a party with several escorts hosted by a Wall Street acquaintance, Ward Feldman. After doing two lines of cocaine, Dragna got into a dispute with one of the escorts, Jill Sinclair, over payment, which escalated to a violent assault on her.

"It was crazy," Feldman said. "He went at her like an animal. And I'm going, 'Shit, this is a problem, guys, this isn't going to go away,' but Harry says, 'That's exactly what it's going to do. Just let us handle this.'"

"I thought I was going to die," said Sinclair, whose medical records indicate she sustained three broken ribs and a broken nose in the assault. "I tried telling him, listen, we're a pretty high-end service, hurting one of us doesn't just go away. He just said, 'Everything goes away, sweetie,' like he knew exactly how to keep this from coming back to him." No charges were ever filed.

In addition to padding members' salaries, membership in the King's Men is a reliable career advance as well. Mazursky, an officer in the burglary squad, for example, "had one of the shittiest clearance rates in the division" when he joined the King's Men, according to Howard Brickman, a homicide detective. "But if you look in NYPD records, he made detective within a month" of joining. (Brickman died in an apparent suicide two days after talking to the Septima for this story.) Mazursky is far from unique. NYPD records indicate that, since beginning their association with the group, every King's Man advanced in the ranks at a far faster rate than higher-performing colleagues, even after controlling for any potential racial or gender bias.

While the King's Men's crimes from their genesis to the last few years were generally limited to bribery, blackmail, or intimidation, evidence indicates that not only have they expanded their repertoire to murder, they have shifted their loyalty as well. In the weeks leading up to reputed Mafia figure Russell Milazzo's murder by the vigilante group Judith, three other men also turned up dead: pimps Drexel Wilson and Marco Clemente and cocaine dealer Yaz Pacheco. All three men were considered business rivals of Milazzo, and all three men were killed with police-issue Glocks. Det. Mazursky filed reports of firing his weapon in unrelated incidents, for which he was cleared, the day of all three killings.

All this could still be coincidence, but in a recording of a call made to Mazursky, available at TheSeptima. com, Mazursky seemingly confirms Wilson's death and discusses his cover story for firing his weapon. But the man on the other end of the call isn't the mayor; it's his chief of staff, Judson Crowning, an essential piece of the *puzzle for anyone seeking to understand why the King's Men have escalated their activities so dramatically.*

Crowning was a frequent patron of foreign sex workers employed by Milazzo, according to Svetlana (not her real name), one such sex worker. Svetlana claims Crowning smothered another shortly before the string of killings of Milazzo's rivals. Crowning neither confirmed nor denied the accusation, but was caught on tape saying, "No matter how many bleeding-heart stories you write, no matter how many campaigns you mount, no matter how many pictures you publish, you will never, ever make the world care about dead whores."

None of the King's Men responded to the Septima's request for comment, but a Freedom of Information Act request (see the pdf on our website) found that, between 2000 and 2011, 28 civilians withdrew complaints of police brutality or misconduct after members of the King's Men undertook unspecified "investigations." Altogether, members closed 78 cases in the same period. The extent to which their involvement in the group compromised the investigations is impossible to tell.

Incredibly, the killings of Pacheco, Clemente, and Wilson do not appear to be the ceiling for Crowning's management of the King's Men. Early this month, Mazursky was arrested after attempting to abduct NYPD homicide detective Katherine Kinneavy after she was discharged from NYU Langone Medical Center, where she convalesced after being injured while arresting a member of Judith. The NYPD's media relations office offered no comment as to whether any indictments would be handed down besides Mazursky, but expressed the belief that the King's Men are an urban legend.

Over the course of just two mayoral administrations, this group has escalated from intimidation to murder, reaching its crescendo by targeting honest police. And yet even as their violence spirals out of control, those in a position to hold them accountable continue to deny they exist.

"In the NYPD, you're one of three things," said Donna Torres, a detective planning to retire at the end of this year. "You either don't believe the King's Men exist, you're involved with them, or you know they exist and want something done. That first group is about 99 percent of the department. So nobody does a thing. No one person really can."

CATALDO

*Q*uiet never really lasts, does it?

It happened at the Old Man's eighty-fifth birthday dinner on the eighteenth. He'd come into the city for the first time in years for the occasion, and we'd rented out the entirety of Rao's. It was the classiest occasion for Our Thing in quite a while. Nobody's suit or dress cost less than a thousand, it looked like, and this was strictly a wives' affair, no goomars in sight. The other family bosses had made it out too, as had Ercole Provenzano from Chicago, Sal Fillone from Pittsburgh, and from Boston, Mona Palladino, a formidable broad in her midthirties known, with her blessing, as *Il Capo Puttana*, the Boss Bitch.

Mona kissed me on the cheek as she came in and took a seat, her dark hair pulled up and back and winged eyeliner on her blue eyes, giving her the distinct aspect of a predatory jungle cat. It was a good look for her.

"How's tricks, Mon'?" I said once she'd smoothed her dress enough that I didn't feel like a pervert for looking at her.

"Not bad, not bad," she said. "Quiet, for once. I dunno why, but the Irish and the Cambodians have both quieted down for, like, the entire year. It's a nice change of pace."

"How's your guy? What was it, Johnny?"

"Jimmy. Kicked his whiny ass to the curb."

"What happened? If you don't mind me asking."

"Oh, insecure man bullshit. Just another one of these guys who expects a pat on the dick for saying he likes 'independent women,' and then when he finds one, he gets upset because he didn't mean independent from *him*."

"He didn't think a woman whose friends call her the Boss Bitch was going to be independent?"

"I think he thought the queen was looking for a king. Which, no, that's not how it works, *dolcezza*, you'd be a prince consort at best."

"What a dumbass."

"How about you? Married to the job?"

"Job's a fuckbuddy at best. Your dress is beautiful, by the way."

She fixed her panther eyes on me and raised an eyebrow. "You're real subtle, Joe."

"What? Oh no, Mon', come on, just a compliment, that's all."

She leaned forward a little bit, and I hoped she didn't notice me noticing her pearls brushing her cleavage. "I didn't say I had a problem with it."

This was interesting, if sudden. Mona was a hell of a woman, and I'd thought for a while that we weren't partnering with Boston to its full potential. Their access to the state legislature meant they had much more influential political contacts than a lot of our other partners, but historically we'd done very little business with them. Whether this was because of a woman running things, the perception of Boston as primarily Irish territory, or the fact that it had historically been treated as Providence's backyard, I wasn't sure. But with the good mood the Old Man had been in the past few weeks, I figured maybe I'd encroach the subject at our next meeting.

Saul Abramowitz, one of the few non-Italians on the guest list, sat down next to us. "Joe," he said, nodding. "Miss Palladino."

"How've you been, Saul?" I said. "Ain't seen you since the cease-fire."

"Ooh, cease-fire, this sounds like a good story," said Mona.

"Another time," I said, jerking my head toward the head of the table as the Old Man sat down, assisted by his much younger girlfriend and Soldato. Everyone applauded his entrance as waiters wheeled in a giant cake and several buckets of champagne.

"*Madonn'*, is all that for me?" Dellaponte said, to a gale of kiss-ass laughter. He got creakily to his feet. "Ladies and gentlemen, a lot happened in eighty-five years. Lot of people tried to make us go away. Thomas Dewey, Crazy Joe, that cocksucker Bobby Kennedy, hizzonner John Minetti. And you know what? None of them could. Eighty-five years and none of those sonsabitches made me go away. I don't know about you, but when people are trying and failing for that long, I start to get comfortable where I am, huh?"

This got thunderous applause. The Old Man reached for a carving knife. "Now who's gonna help me cut this cake?" he asked, just as the door opened and a maître d' rushed over to him.

"Mr. Dellaponte," he said, "I'm so terribly sorry, I tried to turn them away, but they were quite insistent."

"The fuck you talkin' about?" Soldato said. "Who?"

Before the maître d' could answer, about fifteen men in NYPD and FBI windbreakers over Kevlar vests entered the room.

"Okay, folks," said the guy who appeared to be in charge, a city cop of about forty-five with graying black hair. "This party is officially over. You don't have to go home, but you can't stay here. And you five"—he pointed at the boss, Soldato, me, Paulie, and Nicky—"are all under arrest."

"Who the fuck are you?" said the Old Man as another cop cuffed his hands in front of him.

"I'm Lieutenant Mike Ciorra of the New York Police Department, Mr. Dellaponte, and it's a pleasure to meet you."

"An Italian," Dellaponte said, spitting it out like food he'd realized too late had gone bad. "Fuckin' *disgrazia*, you are."

"Yeah, but I'm not going to prison, so that's a nice consolation prize," Ciorra said as the cops cuffed the rest of us.

"Fuck are the charges?" I asked.

"Racketeering, drug trafficking, obstruction, conspiracy, and money laundering," he said. "Oh, and conspiracy to murder Carmine Sandrelli. Busy little bees."

I posted bail within two hours and immediately met with my lawyer, Maury.

"It's not good," was the first thing he said.

"No shit. How not good?"

"Joe, we are in public so I need you not to make a scene when I tell you this, but Soldato is an informant."

I had to grind my teeth to keep from yelling. "How. Long. Has. Soldato. Been. An. Informant?"

"Couple years, it looks like. It would explain the unusual speed with which he made bail too. He's worn a wire on several occasions."

"Occasions where I was present?"

"I haven't confirmed anything, but it looks like he was wired up for at least one meeting at the Old Man's house."

"Jesus Christ. What are my options?"

"Hard to say. This is a massive fucking indictment, but almost all of what they've got is from what Soldato is giving them. They're putting a lot of faith in his credibility."

"Is that good or bad?"

"I mean, it's definitely not bad. The guy's a fuckin' killer. And a felon, more importantly. It's definitely stuff I can work with."

"When you say 'work with,' you mean an acquittal?"

"Ideally."

"Fucking 'ideally,' Maury? Really?"

"Joe, there are a lot of unknown variables until we figure out what he's recorded. If, for example, you're on tape discussing a murder? I can't do much with that. That's why it's going to be essential—*essential*—that you be a hundred percent transparent with me about what you've been a part of through this whole process."

"Wait a second," I said. "The indictment includes conspiracy to murder Carmine Sandrelli, right?"

"That's correct."

"But Soldato killed Carmine. On the boss's orders."

"Okay . . ."

"So why would he give the cops information on that unless . . ." My eyes widened. "Fuck, Maury, is he gonna put that one on me?"

"That, uh, that would make sense, given what you've told me."

"But that must mean he didn't record it, right? I mean, he's there, doing it, so he can't record it without implicating himself."

"Again, that's possible. I'm going to investigate further. I promise, Joe, I'm not going to hang you out to dry on this. Hanging their hat entirely on Soldato was definitely foolhardy."

"Maury," I said, "the past few months have been balls-out insane, and I did not live through them to go down because of a goddamn *delatore*. You understand me?"

"Of course I understand, Joe. This is what I do, okay? I need you not to panic. I need that very much. Can you do that for me?"

"Yeah, Maury, I can do that."

"Fantastic. We will get you through this *mishegoss*, Joe, don't worry. You and Paulie and the boss."

KINNEAVY

Captain Neville hadn't done an interrogation herself in several years. There were a lot of cops in Homicide who figured that meant she was out of practice. By the end of the day, I was firmly not one of those cops.

Mazursky had been charged the same day he tried to kidnap me, but he'd been in protective custody at the station ever since, Neville not wanting him at risk from the other King's Men on the outside or the risks associated with being a cop on the inside—not before he talked, anyway. The downside of this was that he'd had time to lawyer up.

Neville looked through the one-way mirror as she took off her jacket and tie, draping them over a chair. She untied her hair and shook it until it frizzed out in a vaguely leonine way, then took out a bottle of black eyeliner and a compact mirror. Brushing a lock of hair out of her eyes, she applied the eyeliner until her eyes looked like they were popping out of her head.

"Okay," she said, "I think I'm ready."

She stepped into the interrogation room and sat down across from Mazursky and his lawyer, who did a double-take at her hair and eyes but recovered impressively.

"Hey there, Detective Mazursky," she said. "You comfortable?"

"I'm under fucking arrest."

"That is definitely true. I really can't argue with that. So," she said, turning on the recorder, "why did you attempt to kidnap Detective Kinneavy, Detective Mazursky?"

"Why are *you* convicting my client pretrial?" the lawyer asked.

"Oh, I'm the best deal your client's going to get, trust me," Neville said. "Detective, I need very much to know what happened and why, and I need to know it before Judson Crowning decides you can't be trusted anymore. I mean, do you really think it's filling him with hope that you were busted in the first place? Do you think that identifies you as the kind of person he can trust?"

"Are you threatening my client?" the lawyer asked.

"I'm trying to make your client aware of a threat," Neville said. She turned back to Mazursky. "Detective, were you on the force in 1993?"

"Nah," Mazursky said, speaking for only the second time.

"Things were scary back then," Neville said. "I mean, really scary. The bad old days. I was just a lowly detective back then, no offense, and I found myself working this case that brought me into contact with a man named Marcus Pendleton. Now, Marcus was not a fun guy. He was a drug lord and a serial killer."

"A serial killer?"

"Oh yeah. Technical definition of one is anyone who's killed at least three people, on his own, on separate occasions. And that was definitely our man Marcus. He had started a gang war that had, at the point at which my story takes place, killed a total of sixteen people, five of whom were civilians and two of whom were kids. And I don't mean caught in the crossfire either. They were kids Marcus Pendleton killed personally, to send a message. I'd been looking for Marcus for a while, and I was so hot to find him I got stupid, and when we finally met, it was without backup. Well, surprise, surprise, Marcus beat me on the draw. Now he had this massive, terrifying-looking nickel-plated Taurus revolver on me, and he started laughing. He says he can tell just by looking at me that I've never taken a bullet, because there's a look you get after you've been shot and I didn't have it. Well." She leaned across the table. "Do you know what I did then, Detective?"

Mazursky quietly shook his head. Even the lawyer seemed transfixed.

"I grabbed his wrist, shoved the barrel of that gun against my leg, and—bang!" Mazursky and the lawyer both flinched. "I pulled the trigger for him," she said. "And I looked Marcus Pendleton right in the eye and I said, 'How about now? Do I have the look now?'" She leaned back, stood up, and hiked up her left pant leg. I couldn't see what she was showing them, but I could guess. She walked back around the table and sat back down. "So I'm curious, Mazursky: Are you still more afraid of Judson Crowning than you are of me?"

Mazursky slowly exhaled and shook his head.

"So what I want to know, Detective, is exactly how the King's Men operate. I want you to confirm their identities and what you've been told to do, basically anything that wasn't covered in that article."

"Okay."

"Detective?"

"Yeah?"

"Have you committed murder on the orders of Judson Crowning?"

The lawyer was about to speak again, but Mazursky raised his hand. "Yes."

"Will you testify against him, Detective? Or will you stay in here with me?"

"I'll testify."

"Excellent."

The next morning, I drove to city hall with a warrant for Judson Crowning's arrest. There was nobody in the reception area but Krista the intern.

"He's . . . he's in his office," she said, sounding like she was about to cry. "He hasn't been out all morning."

I checked the clip on my gun and tried the doorknob. It was unlocked. I slowly eased the door open.

Crowning was standing at his desk, one hand on top of it and the other not visible.

"Judson Crowning," I said, "you're under arrest for conspiracy to murder Drexel Wilson, Javier Pacheco, and Marco Clemente."

"I assumed as much."

"Mr. Crowning, you need to put both your hands where I can see them."

"Do I?"

"Yes, you do, Mr. Crowning. Because rest assured, I will shoot to maim and you will have more nights than you care to think about to wish you'd finished the job before I got here."

"You seem to have discounted the possibility of me killing you."

"Mr. Crowning, a lot of things might kill me. Fried food, depression, or my own liver. But a scared little man with a gun is never, ever going to kill me."

He stared at me for about a minute, and I felt sweat running down the grips of my gun even though he kept the office barely warmer than outside. Then he slowly lifted a gun upside down by the trigger guard from his desk drawer and heaved it onto the floor between us. I walked around the desk, my gun still on him.

"I used to think I wasn't a bad man, you know," he said. "I don't know that I can pretend that anymore, but I'm not a monster. I'm a human being who's fallen very, very far. But still a human being."

I pulled out my cuffs. "So was my partner. So were those girls. All due respect, Mr. Crowning, I'm here for them, not for you."

I perp-walked him through the reception area and down through the building's main lobby. Neville was waiting for me when I got back to the station.

"I understand you've got a Judith update," she said, closing the door of her office.

I nodded. "O'Halloran's meeting with their leader tonight for another gun buy. Big one this time, since they're down so many people."

"Kinneavy, do you know who Joseph Bell was?"

"He was the inspiration for Sherlock Holmes."

"I hate how smart you are. Anyway, stop me if you've heard this one. Seems he and a group of his friends put their heads together and decided they'd figured out the identity of Jack the Ripper. They wrote down the name and sent it to Scotland Yard."

"Who'd they think it was?"

"No one knows. All we know is that he never killed again after they gave them that name."

"Could be a coincidence."

"Sure. But the end result is still no more bodies. My point, Kinneavy, is that I don't care what you have on O'Halloran, I don't trust him not to fuck us. If this operation's a dud and it's common knowledge, that's a career-ender for me. So here goes: if nobody shows tonight, or if they get away, no one is ever to know. They'll be spooked enough that they likely won't stick their heads back up anyway. That said, if I don't hear from you within fifteen minutes of the meeting time, I send in all the backup I can find. You are not to approach O'Halloran himself under any circumstances. If nobody ever shows up, the plan is to confirm what we suspected up until now, that Rachel Litvak was Judith's organizer and leader. Do you understand all this?"

"Yes, Captain."

"Kinneavy," she said eventually, "you are the toughest god-damn woman I've ever met in this bleak man's world, and it has been a privilege to know you."

"And you, Captain."

"Thanks."

"Captain?"

"Yeah?"

"Was the story you told Mazursky true?"

"Oh, absolutely. But like I said, a story for another day."

I don't remember New York ever being as cold as it was that night. I nearly skidded on black ice multiple times as I drove to O'Halloran's body shop, and I had the heat cranked up so high I worried it would affect my gas mileage.

I got there early and pulled in just out of sight of the street. As I sat, drank my coffee, and checked both my gun and my walkie-talkie, I realized my heart was pounding too hard for me to really feel the cold anymore.

This was it. This was the culmination of the last three months of my life. Of a quest that had killed my partner and opened graves both literal and figurative. I likely never would have seen or spoken to Paul Hudson again without it. All my work as a detective felt like it had led to this case, and yet it felt far too personal to be detective work. This was something more. Whatever this was, I had been hurtling toward it since that night a lifetime ago with Paul Hudson. My entire life had been divided into before Paul and after Paul. Now, I was about to enter the after-Judith stage.

A black van pulled into the shop's parking lot, and a woman dressed all in black stepped out and walked toward the door. I unholstered my gun and followed her soundlessly as she stepped into the alcove leading to the interior door. I stepped behind her and cocked the gun.

"NYPD," I said. "Put both hands where I can see them." I saw her flinch slightly, but then she held both hands in the air and turned her head.

"Well, okay, Katherine," said Jalisa, "but Mr. O'Halloran doesn't like to be kept waiting."

I felt my heart pounding like it was about to burst through my ribcage as Jalisa turned around. In my shock, I'd slackened on the gun and let my hands drop. In that moment, Jalisa pulled a revolver from her boot and pressed it directly against my forehead.

"If we're going to talk about this, K," she said, "you're going to need to take your gun out of my face."

I found my voice. "What the fuck do we have to talk about, Jalisa?" I screamed.

"You don't have any questions?"

"Of course I have questions. I've known you for twenty years, how the fuck could you do this?"

Jalisa lowered her gun and looked me in the eye and I saw the woman who shot Valery Degtiarenko in the face, who cut Martin Vickner's throat and dumped him in Seward Park, the rage I'd seen a thousand times in her legal work and her private life but never recognized as such.

"Because I've known you for twenty years, Katherine," she said. "Because I saw my best friend and the woman I love crying because a man did something unforgiveable that he'd never be punished for. Because when I got into my line of work, I saw the same story a thousand times more, but sometimes the victims didn't keep it together like you did, and sometimes they didn't have someone like your dad."

"This isn't what we do!" I yelled. "You think I never thought about killing him? You don't think I like the idea of getting Old Testament? I see a lot of the same shit as you, Jalisa. I'm a cop, remember?"

"Yeah, exactly. You put the cuffs on them and send them on their way. You don't have to watch them smile and walk away because they tell the court a fourteen-year-old girl led them on, or that a sleeping woman was sending signals."

"Jalisa, you're a fucking terrorist!"

"Exactly," she said. "That's exactly what I am. The world I want? It's a world where the men we fear start fearing us back."

"Hey, Jalisa? Your girlfriends tried to kill me. Remember that?"

"No, they didn't. Trust me, those women don't miss. Rachel was there that night. If they wanted you dead, you'd be dead."

My head was spinning. "Jalisa, I need to sit down. Can we please just . . . can we sit down?"

Jalisa's face softened. "Sure, K."

I eased myself down onto the front stoop, pulling my scarf and peacoat tight around myself. Jalisa sat down next to me and lit a cigarette. "Can I get one of those?" I asked.

She pulled out another and lit it with hers. "Didn't know you partook."

"Special occasion."

We sat and smoked, not looking at each other.

"What now?" Jalisa said after a while.

"J, I have to arrest you."

"Do you, though?"

"What else could I do?"

"Let me go."

"Why would I do that?"

"I don't know if I was serious."

I took a drag on my cigarette. "Did you ever really love me?"

Jalisa turned to me. "Fuck you for asking me that, Katherine."

I sighed and blinked tears out of my eyes. I couldn't do this. I had no right to have judged Donnie, I realized now. I would rather be a good person than a good cop too. I loved her more than I cared about bringing down Judith, and if I chose anything else, I'd never be able to look in the mirror again. This, this was the real culmination, this plunge I had to take. "I'm going to."

"You're going to what?"

"Let you go."

"Are you?"

I stood up. "Yep. Not unconditionally, though."

"Oh?"

"J, no more Judith if I let you go. Your point is made."

"I can agree with that."

"Next, you leave New York."

"And go where?"

"I don't care. Fucking Albuquerque, it's not my problem. But I'll be monitoring crime news in case you try this same kind of thing somewhere else, and if you do, I'll find you. And Jalisa?"

"Hm?"

"You come back to New York to try this shit, I'm going to kill you."

She stood up next to me. "I guess I can work with all that."

"Are there others we haven't caught?"

"Oh yeah. I'm definitely not giving you them. If that's a condition, just arrest me now."

"What if they keep killing?"

"They won't. I can make sure they stay dormant." Jalisa ground out her cigarette. "What'll you do now, if you let me go?"

"Leave the force, I guess."

"K, you've wanted to be a cop since you were a kid."

"It's killing me, J. If I can't make this call, I can't be a cop. Period."

"What, then?"

"Teaching, I think. Plenty of cops in the world. Not enough teachers."

"Not enough of either who give a shit."

I laughed. "That I'm good at."

"I know, Katherine. I've always known." She walked over to the van. "There are things I still have to settle in town."

"I figured as much."

"Is a week okay?"

"Of course."

Jalisa opened the door of the van. "I have to go now, I guess." She turned to look at me. "Yes, K. Yes. I've always loved you, and whatever I burn down to in a year or in a hundred years, that last ember will still love you." She leaned in and wrapped her arms around my shoulders, giving me a deep kiss. I leaned into it and it felt like some precious resource, like we were trapping the only warmth left in this cold gray city between our faces, and if we pulled apart, it would flicker out of the world forever.

We had to eventually, of course. I watched the van pull away down the street and checked my phone. It was 11:29. I radioed the station. "Captain? It's Kinneavy," I said. "Looks like nobody's showing up."

After ending the transmission, I took the picture of O'Halloran's daughter out of my coat, pressed what was left of the cigarette to it, and watched it burn.

CATALDO

Two days after I was arrested, I woke up, walked downstairs, and found a black woman I'd never seen before on my couch.

"I know you?" I asked as I got coffee going.

"My name's Jalisa Thorpe, Mr. Cataldo," she said. "I used to be the assistant district attorney until I put in my two weeks' notice this morning."

"Okay," I said. "Why'd you do that?"

"I'm leaving town," she said. "You see, I'm also the founder of Judith."

I eyed the bread drawer, where I keep a snub-nosed .38. "You here to kill me?"

"Far from it, Mr. Cataldo. I'm here to offer you a proposition."

"What's that?"

"Judson Crowning has to go."

"Crowning? Didn't they arrest him?"

"Yes, they did. But not for any of the women he's hurt. A man needs to burn for what he did."

"And what's this got to do with me?"

"You rescued the sex workers Mr. Milazzo had been trafficking."

"Maybe. And?"

"I know other people have implied as much to you already, Mr. Cataldo, but he killed them. Does that change things?"

I looked up from the counter. "Yeah. Yeah, it does. You want some breakfast?"

I knew Crowning was on the hook for two murders, but it was still a huge pain in the ass posting five hundred thousand dollars' bail. As luck would have it, there was no throng of reporters to avoid when I led him around the corner to the waiting car.

"I don't know how to thank you," Crowning said, although the way he said it made it sound like he literally had no idea how.

"Don't worry about it," I said. "Not gonna lie, Mr. Crowning, I welcome a chance to get you off my ass."

"What's our itinerary?"

"I got a friend who's gonna meet you in Staten Island. He'll drive you to Tampa, where we've chartered a boat to Naples." I started the blue Continental and drove south. "Hey, you mind if I listen to some of my music for a change? I know you like that classical shit, but I can't drive to it."

"I suppose," Crowning said, still seeming vaguely confused.

"Thanks," I said, turning on the Crystals's "Little Boy."

After a little over an hour, we reached Staten Island. I drove off the road until we reached the same spot where I'd taken Will.

"Why are we here?" Crowning asked. "Is this where he wanted to meet?"

"Look," I said, "you're a hot item right now, Mr. C., and that sure as shit ain't my fault. So getting you on the lam is gonna be kind of, whadyacallit, convoluted. Oh look, here they come."

I opened the door of the car and stepped out as a black van and a white Toyota pulled up. Jalisa and Oksana stepped out.

Crowning turned his head as they approached the car, and a look of recognition crossed his face. "Wait . . ." he said, clawing at the door handle. But by then, all three of us were already shooting.

Once we'd emptied our clips into the car, Jalisa wrapped the three guns in a rag and handed them to me. "Take these to the Irishman," she said. She turned to Oksana and shook her hand, then mine. "Pleasure doing business with the both of you."

"Thank you, Miss Thorpe," Oksana said. "For everything."

Jalisa shrugged. "Keep up the good work, Oksana." She got into the van and drove off through the trees.

I looked at Oksana. "So can I get a ride back to the city with you?"

ROANE

I'm the journalist, so I guess it should be me to finish the story.

Long story short, none of us are where we started out.

Short story long, shortly after the King's Men story broke, Rachel Litvak signed a confession indicating she was the founder and leader of Judith. Violet Kendrick, Tina Perelli, and Hermelinda Ramos (Elba Borrero's real name) signed confessions shortly thereafter. Litvak was sentenced to two consecutive life sentences in Bedford Hills Correctional Facility, while the others received life without possibility of parole.

Kinneavy's hero-cop status was reinforced by bringing in almost the entire group, and she was hotly tipped for a promotion, but surprised the NYPD establishment by resigning from the force as soon as she'd completed her teaching certification. She currently teaches English at the Young Women's Leadership School of East Harlem.

Shortly after the case was closed, Kinneavy joined Alcoholics Anonymous and is currently two years sober. This, she later told me over a club soda, meant she couldn't have the drink of bourbon Captain Neville had promised her, but the captain wasn't complaining, since that meant more for her.

Joe Cataldo had all charges against him dropped when the bullet-riddled body of Judson Crowning was found in a Lincoln Continental registered to Giuseppe Soldato, the prosecution's star witness, demolishing his credibility. Soldato protested his innocence and tried to leverage tapes of conversations between Cataldo and Eugene Dellaponte, but this argument proved unconvincing in light of the fact that Dellaponte repeatedly addressed the person he was talking to as "Giuseppe." Soldato was sentenced to thirty years in Attica. Dellaponte was also found guilty but died of a massive heart attack two days before sentencing. After being informally the boss for years, Cataldo made it official, expanding relations with Boston as well as the city's black and Latino organized crime. He's colloquially known as "Reverend Joe" thanks to his "rainbow coalition."

Rosalind and I moved in together in early 2012 and soon after received news that we had been nominated for the Pulitzer Prize for investigative journalism for our work on Judith and the King's Men, as well as a series by Rosalind on a "culture of violence against sex workers" on Wall Street. Paul Hudson resigned from Worldlink after being named in the story and has not been seen in the city since, while Marvin Devaney, who was also named, filed a libel suit against the *Septima*. Truth being an absolute defense, we won the suit, but the court didn't order Devaney to pay our legal fees, which were extensive.

Knowing the alternative was layoffs, I resigned from the *Septima* and found work with an intersectional feminist news site. I miss the newsroom a lot, but being the editor's live-in boyfriend means I'm still always up on the latest.

All the remaining King's Men were indicted within a month of our feature. Shortly after, NYPD Commissioner Liam Clarkson announced his resignation and founded a private security firm the next month. Internal investigations led to the reversal of thirty convictions in cases the King's Men closed.

Meghan Neville, appreciating the prestige of closing the Judith case but well and truly over the Homicide scene, accepted a transfer to Property Crimes. Although the mayor appointed an interim commissioner after Clarkson's resignation, speculation abounds that Neville may be appointed the department's first female commissioner.

Nerissa Le Grande graduated from Rutgers with honors in summer 2014. Both her parents are very proud.

Oksana Zankovetska, the Night Maiden, maintains her hold over New York's Russian-American organized crime with Gabrielle Wilkins at her right hand, and NYPD sources say reports of violence against prostitutes are down seventy-five percent in neighborhoods she controls.

Tony Mendelsohn is enjoying his job at the *Times*, which is free of all our stupid bullshit, although he sounded profoundly sad when he told me that.

JALISA

Cape Cod is a very different place in the winter. Nauset Beach especially.

In the summer, the waves are ice-cold and the sand is three-quarters rocks, but it's all worth it to offset the sun beating down on you.

In the winter, when the air is in on it too, it seems like every part of your surroundings is in on a plan to freeze you and leave you there, undiscovered and unmourned.

We pulled up on the sand at about midnight, a nearly full moon lighting up the waves. I pulled on my gloves and nodded to Oksana, who helped me pull the two bound hooded men out of the back of the van. We put them both on their knees and yanked the hoods off their heads.

Paul Hudson had been planning to head south when I called in a favor with Frankie O'Halloran, who intercepted Hudson and informed him he was going on a road trip instead.

The other man—a man of about thirty-five, blandly handsome, his body the sort of odd barrel shape common to athletes who peak and decline—had been a little harder to find, though we'd had his name for a while. We'd lost track of him briefly after Klein died, and there was no longer any need to give him the name, and it had been a logistical nightmare to find him again. The man had been laying so low once Judith really got going that we'd started to wonder if he was even still in the state before we found him in Far Rockaway.

"What's your name?" I asked Hudson.

"Paul . . . Paul Hudson," he said.

"How 'bout you, Peggy Sue?" I asked the other man.

"The fuck is this, anyway?"

I hit him upside the head with the butt of my revolver. "What's your name?"

"Ah! Shit. Kenneth Stern."

I walked around behind Paul. "Her name was Katherine," I said, and shot him twice in the back of the head.

"Her name was Angela," said Oksana, doing the same thing to Kenneth.

We got back in the van and pulled off the beach, planning a detour in Boston to dump the guns in the Charles.

"So, Miss Jalisa," Oksana said eventually, "where will you go now?"

I smiled. "Still figuring that out, to be honest. I hear Juarez could use some help, though." I turned up "Pirate Jenny" on the CD player.

And the ship, the black freighter
Disappears out to sea,
And on it is me.

ABOUT THE AUTHOR

Zack Budryk is a graduate of Virginia Commonwealth University who reports on health care for a living and quotes *The Simpsons* recreationally. He knows there's an intersection of those two if he just looks hard enough. His writing on autism, feminism, and politics has appeared in the *Guardian*, the *Mary Sue*, and *Style Weekly*, but Judith is his first novel, embarrassingly enough. He lives in the Washington, DC, area with his wife, Raychel, and two cats.

LIST OF PATRONS

T his book was made possible in part by the following grand
patrons who preordered the book on inkshares.com.
Thank you.

Jess Jordan
John McKeown
Kaitlyn Johnson
Kate McDonald
Steven Patz

Quill

Quill is an imprint of Inkshares, a crowdfunded book publisher. We democratize publishing by having readers select the books we publish—we edit, design, print, distribute, and market any book that meets a pre-order threshold.

Interested in making a book idea come to life? Visit inkshares.com to find new book projects or to start your own.

CPSIA information can be obtained
at www.ICGtesting.com
Printed in the USA
BVOW04s1819150517
484195BV00001B/12/P